A Treachery of Swans

A.B. PORANEK

PENGUIN BOOKS

PENGUIN BOOKS

UK | USA | Canada | Ireland | Australia
India | New Zealand | South Africa

Penguin Books is part of the Penguin Random House group of companies whose addresses can be found at global.penguinrandomhouse.com

www.penguin.co.uk   www.puffin.co.uk   www.ladybird.co.uk

First published 2025

001

Text copyright © A. B. Poranek, 2025
Cover illustration copyright © Holly Ovenden, 2025
The moral right of the author and illustrator has been asserted

Penguin Random House values and supports copyright.
Copyright fuels creativity, encourages diverse voices, promotes freedom
of expression and supports a vibrant culture. Thank you for purchasing
an authorized edition of this book and for respecting intellectual property
laws by not reproducing, scanning or distributing any part of it by any
means without permission. You are supporting authors and enabling
Penguin Random House to continue to publish books for everyone.
No part of this book may be used or reproduced in any manner for the
purpose of training artificial intelligence technologies or systems. In accordance
with Article 4(3) of the DSM Directive 2019/790, Penguin Random House
expressly reserves this work from the text and data mining exception.

Set in 11.99/16.95pt Minister Std
Typeset by Jouve (UK), Milton Keynes
Printed and bound in Great Britain by Clays Ltd, Elcograf S.p.A.

The authorized representative in the EEA is Penguin Random House Ireland,
Morrison Chambers, 32 Nassau Street, Dublin D02 YH68

A CIP catalogue record for this book is available from the British Library

HARDBACK ISBN: 978–0–241–62220–9

INTERNATIONAL PAPERBACK ISBN: 978–0–241–62221–6

EXCLUSIVE EDITION HARDBACK ISBN: 978–0–241–77049–8

All correspondence to:
Penguin Books
Penguin Random House Children's
One Embassy Gardens, 8 Viaduct Gardens, London SW11 7BW

Penguin Random House is committed to a sustainable future for our business, our readers and our planet. This book is made from Forest Stewardship Council® certified paper.

For the younger me, who felt like she needed to clip her wings. I'm glad you didn't do it, love – look how far we flew.

Dramatis Personae

Odile Regnault, *actress at the Théâtre du Roi*
Marie d'Odette d'Auvigny, *daughter of the Duke of Auvigny*
Aimé-Victor Augier, *Dauphin of Auréal*
Damien Regnault, *musketeer guardsman*
Regnault, *director of the Théâtre du Roi*
Honoré-Ignace Augier, *King of Auréal*
Anne de Malezieu, *the King's second wife, called the Step-Queen*
Madame d'Auvigny, *wife of the Duke of Auvigny*
The Regent, *brother of King Honoré*
Charlotte Louise, *Princess of Lore*
Pierre, *son of Anne de Malezieu*
Bartrand de Roux, *former advisor to the Spider King*
The Spider King, *grandfather of Aimé*
Morgane, *the youngest of the Bonnes Mères, the spirit of transformation magic*

SCENE I

Théâtre du Roi. Night.

They will tell the story, later, of the white swan and the black, but they will tell it wrong.

It begins as they say: a beautiful girl pale as the moon, at the edge of the lake in the dark of night. And a sorcerer stalking from the shadows, foul-hearted and wicked, with the yellow eyes of an owl and fingertips coated in magic.

The Prince will come later, as will the ball, and the love story doomed by deceit. But for now, there is a theatre house, and there is a play, and there is a villainous girl whose story was never told.

First, allow me to set the stage.

The Théâtre du Roi is a grizzled, devouring edifice, sprawled languidly at the edge of Lac des Cygnes. Tonight, it is a well-fed beast, belly full of roaring noblesse and commoners alike, its candle-lit windows narrowed in satisfaction. It's a Saturday, and on Saturday the Théâtre's resident troupe puts on one of their legendary *tragédies en musique*, affairs of glittering splendour and dizzying dance and operatic, tear-wrenching song.

The play is drawing to a close, and I have been stabbed.

I rush from the stage with a torrent of applause at my heels, the warm slickness of blood sticking my doublet to my skin. The familiar stench of the dressing rooms welcomes me – cheap perfume and old sweat and something suspiciously like strong liquor, though the troupe has yet to locate the culprit of *that* particular smell.

I yank the collapsible dagger from my chest and strip off the outer layer of my costume, a mass of heavy black brocade and pinned-on lace belonging to the play's dramatically murdered Prince. I wipe fat, insincere tears from my eyes. Sweat slips down my spine – my feet ache from the Prince's ostentatious pre-death dance number. Normally, I'd be elated, adrenaline singing through my veins, a satisfied grin on my face. But not tonight. Tonight, I have one more role to play, and it will be the most spectacular of my career.

There's another swell of applause in the distance as the rest of the troupe finish taking their bows. I should be up there with them, but I need a head start to locate the target of my mission. As I pull the now-pierced bladder of hog's blood from beneath my shirt, the other actors and dancers come surging down into the dressing rooms, a blur of gaudy costumes and gaudier faces, wrenching off headdresses and masks and unfastening heeled dance shoes.

There's an uncharacteristic, tense energy to it all, putting a rueful note in the usual backstage banter.

'Mothers be merciful, I nearly tripped over Guillaume's train.'

'Do you think they noticed that I started my aria off-key?'

'Forget the aria, Maurice nearly knocked me off that wooden horse. Then Henri started to giggle, and he's meant to be playing a *corpse*.'

I want to join them, to snicker and commiserate over stage mishaps or forgotten lines, but my stomach is too tight, my mind already on the task ahead. Tonight, the theatre's audience is swollen to twice its usual size, filled with not only the usual attendees – court nobles and wealthy city merchants and any commoner able to scrape together enough to afford the Théâtre's cheaper parterre tickets – but also nobles from across Auréal and beyond, dukes and duchesses and, most importantly, their daughters of marrying age. To them, our performance is only an appetizer, a prelude to tomorrow night's grand ball – a ball celebrating the Dauphin's eighteenth birthday, at which the realm's future ruler is expected to choose a bride.

I pause by the cracked mirror of one of the dressing room's mismatched vanities, wiping away the most garish of my make-up. My true features peer out from beneath – a sharp, boyish face studded with citrine-yellow eyes, nothing trustworthy about either. I leave some paint behind – dark shadows on my eyelids, golden glitter on my cheekbones. I slide my mother's red-and-gold earring back into my right ear. I want to look dangerous – the kind of danger that tempts and seduces, that promises a thrill.

As I work, I catch more snippets of conversation.

'Did you see the young Mademoiselle d'Auvigny?' says one of the men. I recognize the reedy tenor of Henri, the former giggling corpse. 'She was sitting just to our right in the loges. No wonder they say the Dauphin is going to choose her.' One of the other men responds with what I can only describe as an infatuated moan, and I roll my eyes.

'You going to try to seduce her, Henri?' someone teases.

'You think I can't?'

'I think you have the tact of a dazed fruit fly,' replies the former. 'Besides, you remember that ridiculous piece of gossip from years ago, the one the court ladies so loved? I had to listen to Madame Bérengère prattle about it for hours.' He raises his voice to a mocking, feminine squeak. 'They say when the Dauphin first saw Marie d'Odette on the edge of Lac des Cygnes, he thought her an enchanted swan maiden! Sparks flew, flowers bloomed, the Mothers considered returning, and the Dauphin nearly married her on the spot.'

'Please, we all know the Duchesse d'Auvigny spread those rumours,' Henri replies sullenly. 'Laying her claim to the Dauphin, the ornery hag.'

'My point is you have no hope,' his companion replies, still in squeaky falsetto, prompting a smattering of snickers.

Smiling, I slip from the room, snatching a clean black-and-gold doublet from a rickety chair as I go. Marie d'Odette d'Auvigny, only daughter of the family ruling Auvigny province, has certainly made an impression. That has always been a skill of hers, after all. Even I hadn't been immune, when I'd spotted her watching from the loges. The beatific Swan Princess living up to her name – magnanimous and pale, with a gown of silver-blue lapping at her shoulders and lace frothing at her collar, her hair the colour of moonlit sand piled high and studded with pearls.

My chest bubbles with anticipation. If I play my cards right tonight, that gown, those pearls and that hair . . . they will all be *mine*.

I quicken my pace, pulling on the doublet and checking the powder on my wrists, ensuring none of it has rubbed off. The backstage stairwells are dark, stifling things, curling upwards as if through the throat of some great beast. Even here, encased in sombre wood, I can hear the crowd: the chatter of nobles mingling after the performance, the stomp of feet across the parterre as commoners head back into the city.

All of it is broken by the sudden clack of heeled shoes descending the steps, a familiar voice consuming the dark.

'Yes, of course, I will remember. Goodbye, Monseigneur.'

I straighten instinctively as my father swoops into view.

It's like being mobbed by crows – a descent of darkness, a flurry of a black silk cloak, a glimpse of keen eyes and a face wreathed in feathers. Known only by his stage name, never seen without his ornate, owl-faced mask, Regnault has always been mystery incarnate – not a man, but a character, breathed out of the sumptuous stage décor and exuberant melodrama of one of his troupe's grandest plays. Yet tonight there is no mirth, no elaborate jest in his glittering eyes.

'Ah, there you are.' His voice is resonant even at a whisper, filled with a performer's charisma. 'Are you ready?'

'Y-yes.' I wince at the tremble in my voice – somehow, he always makes me feel like I'm five years old again, begging for scraps in an alleyway. I clear my throat. 'Yes, Papa, I'm ready.'

Regnault clasps a talon-like hand on my shoulder. 'Good. Remember, I will be waiting by the lake. Should anything change . . .'

'It will not,' I reassure him, keeping my voice steady. 'I will not fail you.'

My father's thin lips slide up, curling into a too-wide grin that most would find unnerving. I used to try imitating that smile when I was younger, practising in front of any mirror I could find, though I never quite managed to perfect it.

'You know –' he touches his knuckle to my cheek – 'I finally believe that.' His gaze softens briefly, and I can't help but revel in the expression. This is a rare side of my father, a thing to be hoarded and treasured. 'There is a reason I took you in, little owl,' he says. 'Do not make me regret it.'

And there it is, that reminder of doubt. Regnault doesn't yet trust me fully. He is holding back, rightfully so, waiting to see if I accomplish this final mission, the one he raised me for. The task that begins tonight: gain the trust of Marie d'Odette. Take her place. Seduce the Dauphin of Auréal and fool him long enough to steal the Couronne du Roi.

My stomach squeezes. What could *possibly* go wrong?

Regnault's eyes roam over my face. 'I can see you are anxious to begin,' he remarks. 'Go, then. I can hear the others coming.'

He bends to kiss the crown of my head. As he does, a necklace swings from the collar of his doublet. My eyes are drawn to it: it's a thing of fine gold, composed of a brittle chain and a pendant moulded into the face of an owl. At its appearance, the scent of iron and sage fills my nostrils, a prickle of static scattering across my skin.

Sorcery. I grin at the feeling. I still remember the rush of stealing that pendant, three weeks ago.

Regnault had given me the mission after we'd finished a performance of *Le Maître de Malvaine*. There is a custom, at the Théâtre, for the actors to mingle with the noblesse after every performance, the most popular receiving praise or expensive gifts from wealthy patrons in exchange for . . . ah, *favours*. It always pains me to watch as the other actresses simper for attention, allowing themselves to be dragged into shadowed corners by jewellery-dripping noblemen with greedy mouths. I avoid such encounters – unless, of course, Regnault asks it of me.

That night, he'd come up behind me right as I stepped off the stage. He'd bent to murmur in my ear: 'The *Ministre d'État* is wearing a pendant of goddess-gold. I want you to get it for me.'

I am never one to refuse a challenge. After the curtain fell, I had allowed the King's minister to corner me in this very stairwell, his breath stinking of wine, his brocade robes drenched in sweat. I'd endured his wandering hands while I draped my arms around his shoulders, easily slipping the pendant from his neck. Then I'd fled, mumbling some excuse, feigning the shy young girl too flustered by the attention of such a great man.

Regnault's eyes had shone with excitement when I'd placed the pendant in his hand. 'This is it,' he'd exclaimed, holding the pendant to the light. 'With this, I will finally have enough magic for the spell. And when this is over, we will never have to scavenge again. We will have all the magic we desire, and I will teach you all I know.'

Now, Regnault's eyes find mine, and I wonder if he is remembering the same moment I am. After a second, he tucks the pendant back under his collar. 'The tests are over, little owl,' he says quietly. That nickname falls weighted with burden between us. 'Do this, and we will bring magic back.'

With that, he turns away, cloak billowing around him. As soon as he is out of sight, I gulp a deep breath, my pulse pounding.

Do this, and we will bring magic back. A reminder of the true stakes of this mission. The Couronne du Roi, the King's enchanted crown, is the only goddess-gold object with enough magic for Regnault to summon back Morgane. To force the kingdom's once-patron to return and lift her curse from our lands.

A clamour sounds behind me, jerking me from my thoughts. I've tarried too long – the rest of the troupe is coming. I turn and hurry up the remaining steps, squaring my shoulders and putting on my signature devil-may-care grin as I emerge into the gallery.

It's always unsettling, to be above the stage and not upon it, looking out on to the echoing vastness of the auditorium. The galleries spill before me like a bloom of fresh blood, every loge sheltering a row of chairs drenched in crimson velvet. Sconces shaped like hands grip ruby-red candles, and gold shines from the balcony railings. It's a stark contrast to the dark of the parterre below, where the lower class are still filing from the room in a stifling herd.

The noblesse peer down at them from the loges, gossiping shamelessly and sipping from crystalline flutes.

In a way, they are no less garish than the troupe, in their costumes, faces powdered white, heads crowned with perukes and ostrich feathers. Dark fabrics have become popular of late. Deep emeralds and muddy blues and even true blacks dominate, making the crowd appear as if they are gathered for mourning. Mourning what, I couldn't tell you – probably the death of fashion.

There's a flurry of activity behind me as the rest of the troupe catches up, spilling out at my heels. Many nobles rise to greet them with delighted cries, as though spotting their favourite animal at a zoo.

I step to the side and pause, casting my gaze around for my prize. It's not hard to locate Marie d'Odette – she stands out from the crowd in her pale hues, a wash of watercolour against a world of sombre oil paint. Anticipation rises within me, and I plunge into the crowd, skirting actors and dancers and noblesse.

A gaggle of noblegirls, chortling over sloshing drinks, momentarily obscures Marie from my sight. They are close to my age, and I guess they are also candidates for future Queen, all hoping to catch the Dauphin's eye tomorrow night. As I slip by, one of them snorts loudly, her watery eyes landing on me. 'Look, that one's dressed like a boy. I bet it's because she makes such an ugly girl.'

I tilt up my chin and throw her a derisive glare. I long to start a fight, but that would risk my mission. And Regnault's plans are more important than my honour – more important than anything else.

Still, the damage is done. When I look away from the girls, Marie d'Odette has vanished. Muffling a growl of annoyance, I pick up the pace, threading between people until I spot her again: stepping through one of the arched exits connecting the loges to the entrance hall, fastening a ribbon-trimmed cloak around her narrow shoulders.

Marie d'Odette has changed. Gone is the girl I remember from my youth, the troublemaker with a fawn's exuberant gait, who *bounded* more than walked as she pulled me around the Château. Now, she practically glides over the marble, precise and graceful as a dancer. There is no emotion in her face, no wonder in her eyes. It's enough to fool nearly anyone into thinking she's just another noblewoman. Perfectly proper, contemptuously cultured.

But I know better – it's all a mask. And I've seen her take it off.

During the play, when the attention was on the stage and she thought no one was looking, she'd raised her hands, long and dextrous, to the rail of her box, and begun fluttering them to the rhythm of the music. There'd been a frantic sort of longing to it, as though she might leap over the rail and spread a pair of pearly wings, alight among the dancers and join them in a caper.

She may act like she's a forlorn deity, but even goddesses have desires. And I intend to exploit this one.

I pause just behind her and set my feet apart, putting my hands on my hips. 'Leaving already?' I call out, adding a petulant note to my voice.

Marie turns, and I suck in a breath. She was always striking in appearance, but now, she looks *revoltingly* good. Her formerly cherubic face has taken on a celestial regality, her cheekbones high and silver eyes knowing. Her full lips, once always twitching into an eager smile, are now shackled into an expression of demure politeness.

When she sees me – when she *recognizes* me – they part in surprise.

'It's *you!*'

Her voice is surprisingly low, soft in a way I don't remember. I can't help the flash of resentment the sound of it sends through me. For an instant, I am thirteen again, humiliation heating my cheeks as a pair of hands lifts prismatic diamonds from my throat. *Come away. You're going to get your dress dirty.*

I shove the memory back, ignoring the taste of betrayal it leaves behind. With meticulous precision, I curl my smile into one of friendly mischief. 'Is it? I hadn't noticed.' I make a show of inspecting myself. 'Ah, yes, so it is. Unfortunate.'

Marie blinks at my antics, disbelief still in her eyes. '*Odile*,' she says, as though I'm some sort of fairy-tale creature come to life. Then she collects herself, shaking her head minutely, scrubbing any excitement from her face. When she next speaks, it's courteously subdued. 'I . . . I thought I saw you on stage, but then I thought I was imagining it. When did you join the Théâtre?'

'Oh, some time ago,' I say vaguely – a lie, in line with all the others I told her once upon a time. 'But tell me, Mademoiselle d'Auvigny, what are you doing here, all alone and forlorn?'

She frowns. 'I am *not* forlorn.'

I cross my arms. 'It seemed to me you were making a rather swift exit. Some might even call it an *escape*.'

A smile tugs at her lips, but she quickly smothers it. 'I protest. I was making my graceful and very distinguished retirement. Which I should probably resume.' She dips a shallow curtsy and continues towards the entrance hall.

'Wait,' I call after her. 'Can't you postpone said retirement an hour or two? I have an offer for you.'

Marie hesitates, and I hold my breath. To my relief, she glances back at me. 'I . . .' She pauses, eyes flicking up and down the corridor. Ensuring no one is witnessing her continuing to interact with a lowly peasant, I'm certain. But we're on our own, for the most part – the noblesse have either gone into the main hall to gossip, or hidden themselves in the more private loges.

Slowly, Marie allows a glimmer of curiosity to enter her eyes. 'What is the offer?'

'Remember how you always used to wonder what was backstage at the Théâtre? What if I showed you around?'

Immediately, she shakes her head. 'Oh, no. Thank you, but I cannot.'

'Certainly you can.'

'No, I mean . . . things have changed, Odile.' She looks away, lacing her fingers together nervously. 'I cannot simply run off any more.'

I'm losing her. I can't let that happen. 'It's really a once-in-a-lifetime opportunity, you know,' I say impishly. 'Usually we only give tours to our most generous patrons.'

That makes her eyes narrow. 'But I haven't paid you at all, so why are you offering me this?'

I have to hand it to her: she's not as naive as she used to be.

'Out of self-interest,' I say honestly – hide a lie in a truth, Papa always says, and it's harder to find. 'Everyone is whispering that you are most likely to be picked by the Dauphin tomorrow.'

But at the mention of the Dauphin, Marie's expression flickers strangely. 'I suppose so,' she says, looking away.

I don't have time to contemplate her reaction. 'Well, just in case, I'd like to win your favour. Every actress wants a wealthy patron, after all.'

Marie laughs, but even that is strained – as though she might be punished for anything too expressive. 'When did you become so sly?'

'It's a vicious world out here, Mademoiselle d'Auvigny. I'm clever when I have to be, and run away when I can. So –' I hold my arm out to her in a gentleman's fashion – 'what do you say? Can you truly refuse a little bit of freedom?'

That seems to finally do the trick. Marie glances towards the exit, then to me, then towards the boisterous crowd in the distance. A light appears in her eyes, hesitant yet hungry, and I know she's fallen into my trap at last.

'I suppose . . .' Marie places a skittish, silver-pale hand on my arm. 'I suppose I could, if it does not take too long.'

'I will keep it brief, I promise,' I say, holding back a smug, triumphant smile. 'Believe me, Marie, you have *no* idea what's in store for you.'

SCENE II

Théâtre du Roi. Backstage.

The corridors of the Théâtre du Roi always smell like sorcery.

It's a subtle scent, impossible to name by those foreign to magic, a creeping stain of iron and sage that stings the back of the tongue. It precipitates in milky droplets on the aged wood, wriggles down the throat and curdles in the lungs, turning every breath into a heavy, intoxicating thing. It's a smell that gnaws, a smell that hungers.

It's the smell of home.

I take an eager gulp of it as I pull Marie d'Odette d'Auvigny down the stairs and into the dressing rooms. I want to take her through quickly, to bring her to the spot where Regnault is expecting us, but Marie breaks away to marvel at the racks of vibrant clothing, the intricately painted masks arrayed upon tables, and ornate prop swords bristling from a chest along the far wall. As before, she controls her expression carefully, but there is a wondering light in her eyes as she bends to pick up a feathery headdress.

I bite back a groan of annoyance. 'We should hurry,' I prompt, taking the headdress out of her hands. 'Staying too long in the dressing rooms can have ... scandalous connotations.'

'Is that so?' Marie says distractedly, releasing the headdress and turning to dip her finger into a jar of red liquid. When she raises her now-crimson fingertip to the light, a single drop falls on to her pristine dress, and she frowns. 'Good Mothers, is this *blood*?'

'Mulberry syrup,' I say hastily, picking up the jar and setting it out of her reach. 'I thought you wanted to retire soon.'

Marie sticks her finger into her mouth, casting a final, longing glance around the room. 'I suppose I *did* say that,' she admits. 'It's simply been some time since ...' She breaks off.

I frown. 'Since?'

'Since I've been able to breathe,' she murmurs, so quietly that I wonder if I'm meant to hear it at all. I don't pry. Whatever sob story she might have, it's filled with expensive dresses and scurrying servants and goblets of crystal with golden rims. Why should I pity her pain, when she weeps into pillows of the most pristine silk?

After what feels like an eternity, Marie d'Odette strides back over to my side, the *clack* of her heels muffled on the stained carpet. 'Where to now?'

'Right this way,' I say cheerily. I pick up a still-lit candelabra from the vanity as we go, taking the lead as we dive into the darkness.

The backstage hallways of the Théâtre are unwelcoming things, the notched walls hung with ancient, abused paintings in desperate need of dusting. Cobwebs crowd every edge and corner, their stretched shapes flickering in the candlelight.

To my growing frustration, I hear Marie's footsteps pause again. I turn to see her staring at one of the vast landscape paintings.

I know what has caught her attention – it used to catch mine, when I was younger. Beautiful, brightly hued wildflowers scattered over an Aurélian hillside. A lovely little mill in the distance, churning glittering water. A lost hope, a what-once-was. Beauty, when the kingdom still had it, before Morgane took it away.

'These must be from before Bartrand de Roux's betrayal.' Marie speaks with a schoolteacher's condescending air, making me bristle. As though I, of all people, might need to be *educated* on the kingdom's history. She presses her fingertips to the flowers with a sorrowful look. 'That sorcier took so much from us.'

I swallow back a bite of bitter fury. Everyone always blames the sorcier. Bartrand de Roux, the Spider King's advisor. The story goes thus: after decades of serving the Crown, Bartrand grew greedy for power, tired of having to bow at the feet of a red-blooded King. And so one night he staged a coup, using forbidden magic to try to usurp the Crown. Whatever he did, it was so horrifying that it caused the three Bonnes Mères to flee. The youngest, Morgane, cursed the kingdom in retribution; to never witness beauty again, to languish under grey skies and colourless fields. That year, spring saw nothing but wrinkled, wilted blooms, and in the winter the snow fell black as soot.

In the end, only one thread of magic remained. A gift, a gift the King claimed had been given to him by Morgane herself before her disappearance. The Couronne du Roi, a crown of seemingly unlimited power. When few crops grew that year, the King placed the Couronne upon his head and conjured more, crops that could survive under dreary skies. When his palace's famous roses withered away to nothing, he forged new ones, with stalks of iron and petals of solid gold. When his courtiers dared question him, he turned them into gilded statues, left them to stand in the entrance hall of the Château as an eternal warning.

But that was not enough. Nothing was enough. His paranoia was insatiable – it grew and grew, until he dared not look his own son in the eyes, until he saw enemies in every shaded alcove and lightless corner.

He ruled for one hundred fifty years, blessed – or cursed – with an unnaturally long life. And with every day, he plunged further and further into madness, until finally he snapped. Without warning, without reason, he fled, vanishing deep into his palace like a spider into the dark.

Two weeks later, they found him dead, withered away to a husk in a hallway that none knew existed.

That part of the story is never talked about: how no one knows what drove the Spider King mad, just like no one knows what truly happened the night of Bartrand's betrayal, or where the Couronne really comes from. All they care about is that a sorcier is to blame.

And if one sorcier, why not all? That was the Spider King's reasoning when he outlawed any magic but that of the Couronne, declaring it evil. Many sorciers fled the country. Those that remained lived half a life, forced to powder their wrists to hide the shimmering of their veins, to spend the next two hundred years cowering in fear of the hatred of the King and the masses.

Without sorcery, they were – are – powerless.

But if I succeed in this heist, their fates will change at last.

Marie is still lingering in front of the painting, lost in thought. I grit my teeth, rolling my shoulders to try to calm myself. *I ought to have simply knocked her out*, I think glumly.

'Marie,' I say, feigning an alarmed glance over my shoulder, 'I think I hear someone coming. Let us go, before we're caught down here.'

'I thought you said these tours were not all that unusual,' Marie remarks. 'Why the rush?'

I dart a look at her, suddenly nervous I might have said too much. But she holds my gaze steadily, eyes bright and wilful, candlelight slipping through their pearly depths. 'I miss when we used to do this,' she says quietly. 'Before it all went wrong.'

Is she trying to apologize? I nearly scoff. It's too late for that. Five years too late.

'I'll be honest,' I say lightly, ignoring her attempt at amends, 'we usually do not show this part of the theatre to noblesse, but I thought you might enjoy it. They say . . . Well –' I lower my voice – 'did anyone tell you the true story behind Lac des Cygnes?'

She raises an eyebrow, clearly humouring me. 'I *did* hear something about it being haunted.'

'Not only haunted,' I reply. 'They say the ruins beneath

its waters were once a shrine built in the centre of the lake, dedicated to the Good Mothers. That after Bartrand de Roux's betrayal, their wrath is what caused it to collapse. And do you want to know what else?'

'What?'

'They say there were people in the shrine when it collapsed . . . and that the skeletons of those people still rest at the bottom of the lake. When there is a full moon, like tonight, if you close your eyes and still your heartbeat, you can hear their screams carrying across the water.'

I break off as we arrive at the Théâtre's back doors. They are plain and heavy, lacking in decoration – once, they might have been used by a gardener, but in recent years they have been mainly used by actors seeking a place for trysts. That is, until Regnault and I began to carefully spread rumours of ghastly apparitions haunting the overgrown garden beyond. Since then, no one has dared to use these doors, and I can be certain that Marie and I will be alone.

Without hesitation, I push them open and usher Marie through.

'Here we are,' I say with a flourish.

The gardens are not much of a sight, spindly and skeletal and bleached by a wan November moon. Naked trees hold the space hostage, entombed in their own rotting leaves, while ivy chews at cracks in the Théâtre's walls and furious briars grapple the legs of statues. The grass underfoot is bristly and frost-ruined, blades scraping against one another as a cold wind rushes by. The whole is blotted upon a small hill, slipping into the lacquer-smooth waters of Lac des Cygnes.

'It's lovely,' Marie says softly, and she must be lying, because *lovely* is the last word anyone would use to describe the miserable carcass that sprawls before us. Even the lake, in the night, is a slippery black thing, smeared over the landscape like an old bloodstain. Fog writhes over its waters, veiling the distant bank and the Château Front-du-Lac beyond.

But I did not bring Marie here to marvel at its beauty. I brought her here because the gardens are a lonely place, isolating, the perfect hatching ground for an illicit plot.

As if on cue, the candelabra in my hand snuffs out. The doors behind us slam shut as though by an unseen hand, and the wind picks up, tearing at Marie's cloak. She makes a startled sound and turns to me, brushing stray curls out of her eyes. She smiles, barely concealing a nervous unease.

'You know,' she says, 'I'm not usually one to believe in ghosts, but –' She cuts off abruptly. Her eyes widen, fixing on something over my shoulder. 'There's someone else here,' she whispers, just as footsteps rustle upon the grass.

I allow a devilish grin to slide over my features. I know who is approaching behind us – I know him from those feather-light, skulking footsteps, the magic-scent clinging to his clothes, and from the sheer *theatrics* that heralded his appearance.

Regnault never can resist a dramatic entrance.

'My, my, Mademoiselle d'Auvigny, you are even more beautiful than the legends say,' my father murmurs. His voice is quiet, but it washes over the gardens with liquid menace. 'In fact, I believe you are . . . *perfect.*'

He rests his hand briefly on my shoulder before lifting it and pointing at Marie. Golden rings gleam on his fingers, dozens of bracelets jingling from his wrists. Each one is made of goddess-gold, bearing a scrap of magic left over from a faded spell. Each one was stolen by me.

To accumulate this much power has taken me over a decade. A decade of missions, of carefully planned thefts. Here is a fat ring I squirrelled away from a man too drunk to notice. Here is the pendant of a noblewoman I bumped into in the city streets. Here is a simple chain I won at a gambling table. Here it all is, a regalia of stolen magic. And my father wears it proudly.

Marie stares at Regnault, her composure faltering before she schools her features into cautious politeness. 'And . . . and who are you, Monsieur?'

A devious thrill sings through my veins, and I can't help but answer first. 'Mademoiselle d'Auvigny, meet my father, Regnault.'

The scent of magic is suddenly overwhelming.

Marie gags when it hits her, her brow furrowing in confusion as she attempts to find the source of the smell. She is too far away to see it, but I can – a liquid like molten gold, seeping out of every piece of jewellery Regnault wears. It leaks down his arms, his wrists, gathering slick upon his nailbeds before dripping from his fingers.

Only then, when the moonlight strikes Regnault's hands and the liquid glistening upon them, does Marie truly realize what is happening.

'*Sorcier*,' she gasps, her eyes widening in horror. She stumbles back a step, but it's too late – Regnault traces a series of lines in quick succession, leaving spidersilk-like threads of gold hovering in the air before him, forming a web.

The web shoots forward and wraps itself around Marie. Each thread flares with golden light, expanding quickly, sealing Marie's lips before she can scream. It eats away at her cheeks, her collarbones, spreading, spreading. She thrashes once, turning towards me, her agonized gaze filled with deep, drowning betrayal.

Then, Marie d'Odette d'Auvigny's eyes roll back, and she is gone, her body dissolved into globules of faintly shimmering magic. Regnault extends his hands, and the globules drip into his palms, one by one, until he is cupping a pool of molten gold, sticky as honey and oozing between his fingers.

He separates his hands, each holding a glistening puddle of magic. One he raises to the owl-face pendant at his neck – the other he extends before him.

When he touches the necklace, the magic detaches itself from his palms and slips into the pendant, as if it were never there. The other hand, he tips towards the earth, letting the glowing liquid pour on to the soil between his feet. Before it can hit the ground, it expands once more, another blossom of light, until there is a shape curled at my father's feet.

I stifle a gasp. It's a white swan, soft-feathered and moonlit. It rests in Regnault's shadow like a pearl in the maw of an oyster, its body limp, its eyes squeezed shut. He nudges it with the toe of his boot, but the bird doesn't stir. A mocking smile tightens his lips.

I stare, realization hitting me. 'Is that . . .'

'Marie d'Odette,' Regnault confirms.

My heart gives a little shudder. 'She's not dead, is she?'

Regnault rubs his palms together, the shimmering remnants of magic flaking from his fingers. 'This spell would not work if she were,' he replies. 'Death is not our Good Mother's domain. Her magic cannot create or destroy, only transform.' He turns on his heel. 'Come, Mademoiselle d'Auvigny should wake soon enough. We do not want to be here when she does.'

I nod and fall in step behind my father, my pulse pounding with anticipation. I feel devious, eager, a cat on the hunt. This small taste of success has left me salivating for more, for the next victory, for the next step closer to vengeance.

And if there is a tightness in my gut, a discomfort curled somewhere in the depths of me, I don't allow myself to inspect it. Not even when it drives me to glance over my shoulder – back at the unconscious swan we have left lying at the lake's edge, pale as bone against the cold bleak earth.

SCENE III

Regnault's Office.

I duck after my father into his office, the heavy door thudding into place behind us. It's an odd room, squat and tomb-like, one side occupied by discarded theatre props. Old puppets perch crookedly on the stone mantlepiece, staring at a wooden elephant mounted on wheels. A column of cracked plaster guards the shadowed corner, and on it hangs a wolf skin, its mouth drawn in a perpetual sneer.

On the other side of the room is an oak desk laid with unassuming papers, new scripts and finance ledgers and contracts. Nothing about it screams sorcery, yet the magic-scent is strong enough to make my sinuses burn.

Regnault strides behind the desk, tapping his sharp nails on it. 'We are running short on time,' he says, voice low. He unclasps the pendant from his neck and drops it into my outstretched palms. It hums, quietly powerful, against my skin. I know that if I focused hard enough, I could summon up the intricate spell-threads wrapped around it by Regnault, making its magic visible to the naked eye.

'When you put this on,' Regnault says, 'you will look and sound like Marie d'Odette. None will be able to tell the difference, as long as you do not bleed.'

I close my fist around the delicate chain, the words sending a grim lurch through me. A reminder of just how precarious my disguise will be, of the danger I carry in my own blood. Regnault reminds me of it before every mission.

Remember, Odile, they must never see you bleed.

I recall another discussion from long ago. 'What of Damien?' I ask. 'He will be guarding the Dauphin. He's grown up around sorcery – he knows the signs of it almost as well as I.'

Regnault's lip curls, as it always does when I mention my brother. 'You must not involve him. He cannot be trusted.'

'But with his connections . . .' I hesitate. 'Would it not be useful to –'

'It is out of the question,' my father interrupts. 'Damien made his choice. If you cannot avoid him, you must eliminate him. He cannot be allowed to jeopardize everything we've worked for. Yes?'

'Of course,' I say automatically, because my father is always right, because that is what I *should* want.

'Good,' Regnault says, and the gleam of fondness in his eyes is enough to quell the faint twinging of my stomach. 'Now, the dress should have been delivered to Mademoiselle d'Auvigny's quarters earlier today. You will be spectacular, I am certain. And remember, the pendant also transforms clothing. Whatever you are wearing when you put it on, you will be wearing when you take it off. Understood?'

I nod. Regnault straightens, looking down at me with an unreadable expression. He makes even the smallest action look regal, *powerful*, and I'm reminded that his ancestor is Bartrand de Roux himself.

I find myself unwittingly mimicking his posture. I can do this. I *will* do this.

'Find the Couronne du Roi, *ma fille*,' says Regnault. 'Find it, and we will set everything to rights.'

'And you will teach me magic,' I remind him, fastening the owl-face pendant around my neck, feeling it send a pulse of prickling magic along my skin.

Regnault chuckles. 'I will teach you that, and so much more. Now go, and may the Good Mothers guide you.'

It's long past midnight, and the Théâtre du Roi is quiet.

It's not an empty quiet, like that of an abandoned hall or a forgotten street. No, it's tense, watchful – taut as a tongue holding back a curse, coiled like a secret begging to be spilled. It's the quiet of infidelity, of coins passing from nobleman to actress as he buckles his belt and she smooths down her skirts. It's the quiet of gossip, of noblegirls huddled together in a gilt corner, vicious giggles discoloured by the reek of alcohol on their breaths. It's the quiet of longing, of the greasy-haired servant scrubbing the parterre, cursing the superior nobles even as he fantasizes about stealing their places.

This is the quiet that is broken by the heeled footsteps of Mademoiselle Marie d'Odette d'Auvigny. She glides down the staircase like an apparition, the veined marble kissing her skirts, candlelight draped across her pearl jewellery. As always, she is the image of poise, a paragon of control – chin held high, collarbones bared, a liquid smoothness to every motion. Her silver eyes sweep across the room like a rising tide, carrying their usual reticent haughtiness.

She has not changed, of course, since she was last seen in the loges.

Yet she is a lie.

Lying has always been as simple as breathing to me. It's how I first met Regnault, after all – as a snot-nosed five-year-old orphan huddled in the cold and begging for help while my brother attempted to pick a pocket. Damien was a bad thief, but I was a good liar. It kept our bellies full, and it caught Regnault's interest that day. 'Good liars make good actors,' he said to me, as he rubbed off the mud I had smeared on my wrists to hide shimmering veins. 'And I happen to run a theatre house. So why don't you come and work for me? You could be so much more than this.'

And he kept his word – I *did* become more. I became villains and heroes, princes and princesses. I learned to dance and sing and stage fight, to draw attention and avoid it, to feign emotions and toy with them. And after every play, I would wander the galleries and the grand entryway, where a second theatre took place – the social theatre of the noblesse. I would tuck myself into a shadowed alcove or mingle as one of the performers, observing their mannerisms and habits. I learned how they twisted words into subtle betrayals, built scandal from rumours and pried gossip out of one another like digging snail bodies from their shells. Later, I would practise curtsies in the dressing-room mirrors, rehearse different accents until they came to me with perfect ease.

So this is nothing new. Donning a mask, stepping away from my own dull skin and into a flamboyant costume. It's the easy part – it's where I thrive. The only challenge now is keeping back the smug smile that begs to slip on to my lips. Because all these nobles, with their frilly shirts and empty eyes, have no idea I intend to be their ruin.

'Mademoiselle d'Auvigny!' A shrill voice cuts through the space. I don't have to turn to know it belongs to one of the pink-cheeked, swaying girls nursing wine glasses in the middle of the entrance hall, squinting under the light of the crystal-hung chandelier.

I give her a profoundly disinterested smile. I don't have to fake this one.

'Hey! We're talking to you!' The girl growls in frustration, unbridled in her drunken state. The pale-brown mass of her hair makes me think of a disfigured turnip.

'Do you think she can hear me?' Turnip-hair asks her companions.

'Maybe she's too daft to understand,' sneers the one on her left, who has what seems to be a decapitated peacock jutting out of her hat. She starts towards me, nearly sloshing wine across her violently green bodice. 'Hey, Mademoiselle d'Auvigny, where did you go? We were just discussing your *interesting* choice of gown.'

I pause mid-step, a vindictive spark lighting inside me. I may resent Marie, but faced with these vapid socialites, I suddenly want to defend her. Still, if there's anything I know about Marie, it's that she's not easily driven to anger, so I force myself – with torturous effort – to remain calm. 'I was exploring,' I say mildly, and my words come out in Marie's warm, coastal lilt.

'*Exploringggg*,' says Green-dress, rolling her eyes. 'Bet you got lost, silly. Oh, Charlotte, do you think that's the reason her mother locked her up in that tower?' She leans in closer to me, a fat emerald swinging from her neck. I resist the urge to snatch it as she drawls, 'Do you get lost a lot? Is that why?'

Turnip-hair smacks her friend, nearly spilling her drink. 'Quiet. That's all just a rumour.'

A rumour, but it piques my curiosity, and I file the information away for later. Green-dress gives an affected sniffle. 'Oh, you *poor* creature,' she says, with the glee of a wealthy lady throwing breadcrumbs to a beggar. 'No wonder you've been away from court for so long.'

'My mother says *that's* because of some scandal,' Turnip-hair corrects. 'Something about a necklace.'

Just like that, I can feel the weight of diamonds heavy around my throat, the brush of Marie's fingers as she closes the clasp. A delighted laugh. *They suit you.*

No. I shove the memory back furiously. I will not feel remorse.

Turnip-hair is still staring at me, bug-eyed. 'Do you think the Dauphin still remembers you? You had quite the story, once upon a time. The Lonely Prince and the Swan Princess. It was cute, I'll give you that.'

'Ah,' I say, privately fantasizing about setting her vegetable-adjacent updo on fire. 'Thank you.'

She gives a nasal laugh. 'You're shy, aren't you? I like that. You know what, when the Dauphin chooses me, I'll make you my lady's maid.'

The *audacity*. My growing anger turns from a simmer to a boil, and some of it must show on my face, because Turnip-hair gives me a sympathetic look.

'Oh, dear. You must be wondering what I mean. Where

are my manners? I'm Princess Charlotte Louise, second daughter of the King of Lore. But you couldn't tell, could you? I'm told my Auvignian is flawless.' To her friend, she adds, 'I've been practising for darling Aimé.'

As they share a giggling exchange, I bite the inside of my cheek. My confidence is suddenly shaken – I did not expect a princess of Lore to be here. Our north-western neighbour, Lore, was once at war with Auréal, and is notoriously disdainful of any people but its own. Turnip-hair's presence must be an attempt from Lore to bridge that divide – or, more likely, to curl their claws into yet another kingdom. That alliance will likely be a tempting proposition to the Dauphin; perhaps more tempting than finally stabilizing the restless Auvigny, which, with its unique dialect and enduring wealth, has never been quite at home under Auréal's broad wing.

I force my lips back into a gracious smile. This complicates my plans, but it does not change them. The Dauphin is famously rebellious – I will simply have to use that to solidify myself as the perfect candidate. The game isn't over yet.

In fact, it's just beginning.

'Well, it was *delightful* meeting you both,' I say to the noblewomen, curtsying cordially and giving them a cheery smile, hoping they can see the barely veiled threat behind my eyes. 'But I do have to go. It's been such a long night.'

With that, I march for the grand double doors, determination bubbling in my chest.

The city-facing side of the Théâtre du Roi is fronted by a flagstone courtyard, guarded by wrought-iron gates that will be locked once the theatre empties for the night.

There, several carriages and their bleary-eyed coachmen still stand, waiting to collect any straggling noblesse. Behind them, the lights of Verroux cluster together like frightened fireflies.

I get into the foremost coach, lifting Marie's frothy skirts gracefully, ignoring the night's violent chill. The coach's stallions stomp restlessly as I sit down.

'To the Château?' the coachman asks.

I give him a curt nod.

A *snap* of the reins, and the coach is turning sharply away from the city, leaving the Théâtre in the dust and angling towards the forest that surrounds the palace grounds. My chest tightens at the sight – with every stride, the horses pull me further from home, towards a place that too often fills my nightmares.

You see, that's the thing about the Théâtre du Roi: it's nothing but a thin layer of icing slathered over a rotting cake. A commoner walks in, seeing gilt splendour and immaculate grandeur, to watch a play depicting our King as noble and honourable, comparing the Dauphin to the sun, and ending in a victorious, patriotic and horribly sappy fanfare. Once they leave, they believe that the Château across the great expanse of Lac des Cygnes is the same. That beyond the lake lies a resplendent palace ruled by a righteous man, a king worthy of praise and loyalty.

But I have been there, and I know that could not be further from the truth.

SCENE IV

Château. Long past midnight.

It takes no less than fifteen minutes at a brisk trot to make it through the woodland surrounding the lake. It's a raggedy place of jutting bony trunks and unforgiving earth, and it ends as abruptly as it begins, spitting us out on to a narrow foggy path.

And there, old-bone white and impossibly tall, stands Château Front-du-Lac.

If the Théâtre is a gluttonous creature, the Château is a violent one, bleak and lifeless against the pit of night. Its towers are sharp as wolf's teeth, the few lit windows slit like a snake's pupils. There's something vigilant about it, something *prowling* – as though it is grinning, lips pulled back, a predator anticipating a kill.

The coachman stops in the courtyard and helps me down from the carriage before leaving with unsettling urgency. Alone, I find myself breathing shallowly, as if a single sound from my lungs will make jaws snap closed around me. I scan my surroundings, taking in the cracking flagstones, the dead trees ringing a long-dry fountain, and, finally, the wide stair leading to the Château's maw.

'So it begins,' I mutter, and begin my climb.

The air changes as soon as I step into the entrance hall, the Château's heavy doors thudding shut behind me. Ahead yawns a vast, sharply cold room full of flickering light, with black marble flooring and dark wood walls slathered in gold leaf. Golden statues stand at erratic intervals throughout the room, naked and curled in positions of agony. The Spider King's former courtiers, frozen in eternal punishment.

From the epicentre of the room split two grand staircases, each curling up to a dark landing. There's a group of noblesse, mostly boys, gathered at the base of them, but before I can decide if I want to attract their attention, something whistles past my head.

I have only the Mothers to thank for my quick reflexes. I duck aside, narrowly avoiding losing an earlobe as a gold-fletched arrow soars past my head and embeds itself in the chest of a statue behind me.

I whirl furiously, looking for the source of the arrow. The boys near the stairs have burst into laughter, many of them red-faced and hazy-eyed. One of them is cursing vibrantly – he scrambles to his feet, tossing aside an ornate crossbow and pushing off a girl draped over his shoulders.

'Louis, you idiot, you nearly made me shoot – Marie?'

I freeze. Because I recognize the boy. He's the one who I've come to trick, the one I've come to marry – the Dauphin of Auréal, Aimé-Victor Augier.

The Prince stares at me with wide, watery-blue eyes, his brows drawn up in almost comical surprise. I've hardly ever seen him up close – only in paintings, or sitting in the royal family's private box in the Théâtre. He's gangly, in a dainty sort of way, like a colt growing out of its youth. True to his reputation, he's dressed in the most ostentatious rendition of current court fashion – a wine-coloured doublet of gold-embroidered silk, voluminous petticoat breeches, and frankly offensive amounts of lace at his cuffs and collar. The famous golden Augier hair is busy trying to escape its carefully coiffed curls, and a thin layer of face powder hides delicate freckles. Some would call him handsome. I would call him a profligate, questionably dressed pigeon.

The Dauphin teeters as he makes his way towards me. 'Marie!' he cries. He reeks of wine, and I resist the urge to curl my lip. 'Are you all right?'

'I'm fine,' I say graciously, forcing myself to stay still as he snatches my hands, his grip clammy.

'I am *soooo* sorry,' he says, pulling me closer to himself with a stumble. 'The stupid crossbow was my father's gift. He seems to think shooting things will turn me into a less embarrassing son.' He rolls his eyes. 'But Mothers, am I glad to see you. I didn't know if you'd gotten the invitation – I was worried Stepmother would get to it; she's still hung up on that ridiculous fiasco from five years ago. I daresay it –'

'Aimé!' A new voice cuts through the room, shrill and reedy. The Dauphin and his jeering friends fall silent as a woman marches into the hall, heels clacking against the marble. Tall as a thorn and twice as sharp, wrapped in a sapphire gown and a corpse's colourless skin, I recognize Anne de Malezieu, the King's second wife, known derisively as the Step-Queen.

'I believe it is time for you all to retire,' the Step-Queen declares, every word echoing through the hall. 'And . . . what is *she* doing here?'

Her eyes cut to me, twin sapphire shards. They are far too keen, far too *knowing*. I resist the urge to touch the owl-face pendant, to assure myself that my guise is still secure. I look to the Dauphin for help, but he barely glances at me, apparently cowed by his stepmother's wrath.

Fine then. I suppose I must take matters into my own hands. And by that I mean make a prompt and dignified escape.

'It's scandalous, I agree,' I chirp innocently. 'I truly ought to be in bed. After all, tomorrow is a big day, and I do need my beauty sleep.' I wink at the Dauphin, then curtsy to the Step-Queen, ignoring the mounting fury in her expression. 'I suggest you get some as well, Madame, you really could use it. *Bonne nuit!*'

With that, I turn and hurry up the leftmost stairs, leaving the Step-Queen spluttering furiously behind me.

It's only when I reach the landing that I dare look down again. As I do, my attention is caught by one of the guards standing in the shadows.

At first glance, he is unremarkable. He wears a musketeer's cloak, blue embroidered with gold, and from its back snarls the Augier tarasque. His shoulders are broad, his jaw set, and his eyes remain fixed loyally on the Dauphin.

Then there is his hair. It's shaggy, an unruly tumble of black waves, and nearly identical to my own. Nearly identical to our mother's.

Damien.

I clench my fists, swallowing down a wave of betrayed anger, still as potent now as it was five years ago. Before I can do something that I might regret, I force myself to turn into the nearest corridor, leaving the light behind.

Five years ago, at Regnault's behest, I spent two weeks impersonating a maid at the Château. At the time, I did not understand why he asked such a thing of me, but now I am grateful for it. I know exactly where to go, which of the dark, maze-like corridors to turn down in order to find the Château's guest wing. Most of the rooms are already occupied, their doors closed and voices echoing within. One, however, remains empty, the door ajar. A travelling trunk has been left inside, its leather coating tooled with the Odette family crest: a swan flanked by waves. A rectangular package sits on the bed, wrapped in a dark ribbon.

Royal Seamstresses of Verroux, the label reads. *For Marie d'Odette d'Auvigny.*

The door closes behind me with a quiet *snick*. I track my eyes over the room, its dark ebony furnishings and dripping shadows, the faded tapestries on the wall and the single lit candlestick on the vanity. Two narrow windows look upon the fog-cloaked gardens, their iron tracery kinked in hypnotic, menacing shapes.

I cross the room and wrestle the heavy velvet curtains closed, fighting back a shudder. Only once the windows are covered and the doors are locked does the tension finally ease from my limbs.

I've made it. The plan is working.

And somewhere beneath this palace, locked away in a vault and meticulously guarded, is the Couronne du Roi.

It is nearly an impossibility to reach the Couronne. No one knows where exactly it is stored, and it is said to be guarded by horrifying traps created by the Spider King.

I once asked Regnault if we could simply break into the vault and steal the crown from its resting place – his answering *no* was so impassioned I wondered if he had tried it himself and witnessed unspeakable things.

Obviously, that does make everything more complicated. The Couronne is only brought out of the vault in times of dire need, when Morgane's curse once again begins to take its toll on Auréal. To make matters worse, it can only be reached by an Augier king, and despite the pleas of his people, King Honoré has not used the Couronne in over ten years. Which means my only chance at stealing the crown is either at a coronation or a wedding, when it will be brought out so Morgane's magic can bless the new king or queen.

Regnault and I have bided our time for years, waiting for this opportunity. I cannot waste it.

Exhaling sharply, I stare down at myself, at the foreign layers of clothing. My skin has begun to itch; I am suddenly, achingly, aware that I am not in my own body. Unable to bear it any longer, I unclip the owl-face pendant from my neck, feeling my hair shorten to its usual choppy length, my clothing transform back into a black-and-gold costume.

I press my palms to my cheeks, rub the ruby earring pierced through my right lobe. Exhaustion rushes through me. The room's great four-poster bed beckons, weeping heavy curtains the colour of spilled wine.

I give myself a moment longer to breathe, then clip the pendant back on, shuddering as the transformation takes hold. I could call a servant to help me undress, but I don't wish to wait – I simply wrestle the layers of blue gown off myself, looking anywhere but at the linen chemise that is not mine draping over a body that is not my own.

Once done, I seize the candlestick from the vanity and bring it over to the bedside. When I blow it out, the darkness that greets me is a relief.

But my mind refuses to be still. I think of a white swan flying in a dazed panic towards a glossy black lake. I think of spell-threads glowing between my father's fingertips. And I think of a heavy bejewelled crown clutched in my hand.

When sleep claims me, it's like drowning in the dark.

Morning comes, a solemn grey smog that seeps through the cracks in my curtains. I wake slowly, unwillingly, rolling over to press my face deeper into the delightfully soft pillow.

Soft . . . Wait. My makeshift pallet at the Théâtre has never been soft.

It strikes me all at once. Where I am, what I must do.

With a groan, I force myself to sit up in my bed. I might have allowed myself to luxuriate a little longer, but it's a Sunday, which means the noblesse will soon be gathering in the chapel for morning service. I don't care for prayer, but this might be the perfect time to implement my plan – and my revenge – so I can't miss it.

I ring for a maid to help me dress. Normally, a woman of Marie's standing would be expected to travel with at least one lady's maid of her own, if not several. But King Honoré inherited his father's paranoia, and he allows no unfamiliar staff to stay in the palace. Even the Château's own staff is scarce – fewer people in the grounds means fewer people whose intentions he needs to question.

A minute passes before a maid comes into the room. She might be my age, but it's hard to tell – part of the uniform of the Château staff is a golden half-mask, its swirling design bringing to mind a skull. It covers the upper half of her face, from her brow to the bridge of her nose. I want to wince in sympathy. I've worn one of those masks before, and I know they offer limited peripheral vision. It was the Spider King, in his madness, who first mandated them. And his son, in his cowardice, has upheld the tradition.

The girl remains silent as she curls my – Marie's – hair into tight ringlets, secures it in a refined chignon and helps me dress. I choose a gown that is simpler than the previous night's, a shimmering satin in the same silver as Marie's eyes. The skirts are full and pleated, tangling impractically around my ankles. I curse them with every step as I exit the room.

I'd forgotten just how *sinister* the Château Front-du-Lac truly feels. The Spider King's magic lingers in these walls, in these floors. It is old now, decaying, and as it fades from the pieces it once enchanted, they seem all the more unsettling. I pass the statue of a man that bows to me, its movements jerky and startling. I spot a tapestry of a caged bird that still sings, though its song has withered away to a strangled whine. I even walk by a painting of the Spider King – he looks eerily like the Dauphin, in the way a hideous, powder-winged moth might resemble a butterfly – and his enchanted blue eyes track me down the hall.

By the time I arrive at the chapel, several noblewomen are already there, gathered in front of the doors. I recognize Princess Charlotte Turnip-hair of Lore and her friend Green-dress, who today has mercifully opted for a more subdued shade of her favoured colour.

'So bizarre that they would choose this hideous creature,' Charlotte is saying loudly. 'Why not something more noble, like a lion, or a bear?'

I follow their gazes to the source of their discussion: the tarasque engraved upon the iron double doors. The beast's short snout is opened in a snarl, its six feet poised to attack and ruby-inlaid eyes seeming to glow. There are more jewels embedded in its tortoise-like shell, glittering in the faint morning light.

'It's from a legend,' I say, putting on Marie's reserved persona to address them. 'The Little Saint and the Tarasque. The tarasque represents power untamed. Surely you must be familiar with it, considering it's one of Auréal's most famous stories?'

Charlotte flushes. 'I . . . I am. I simply forgot.' She tugs on Green-dress's hand. 'Come, let us go inside. I want to see what these funny little Aurélian chapels look like.'

There is a guard standing by the doors, a musket at his side. He too wears a skull mask, silver instead of gold, and it gleams dully as he pulls the doors open and ushers us inside.

I suck in a breath at the sight that greets us.

Entering the chapel is like stepping into the belly of a pearl. It seems carved entirely from one slab of white marble, floor and columns and vaulted ceiling all blending together like a swan's feathers. The room is lit by two golden braziers shaped like tarasques standing on their hind legs, their too-wide maws holding flames. They have leashes at their throats, golden ropes trailing into the hands of one of three towering statues upon an altar.

There they are. Les Bonnes Mères. The Good Mothers.

They tower all the way to the ceiling, peering down in thunderous judgement, haloes blooming behind their heads. The leftmost, the spirit of life, is made of white marble. She has a human face and holds a swaddled baby, balanced carelessly in one arm. The rightmost, the spirit of death, is chiselled of black stone. Her skull-face is partially obscured by a mourning veil, and one of her hands is raised, brandishing a sickle.

The golden statue standing between them is perhaps the most ghastly of all: half the flesh of her face is peeled back, revealing the bone beneath, and her hands – one human, one skeletal – grip the leashes of the tarasques before her. I give her a minute nod. This is the spirit of transformation, the only one of the Good Mothers to give humanity her name. Morgane, guardian of Auréal and patroness of sorcery.

'But where is my darling Aimé?' Charlotte complains, breaking through any semblance of peace the chapel might have held. 'I heard he's here every morning.'

'Oh, he's up there!' another girl exclaims, pointing overhead. They all crane their necks in unison.

Indeed, the Dauphin leans on the balustrade of the chapel's tribune, weary-eyed, clearly still shaking off the effects of last night's revelry. Behind him, to my dismay, stands Damien in his blue guard's uniform. *He doesn't wear a mask*, I note sullenly. *He must have gone up in the ranks.*

I avert my eyes quickly and follow the other noblewomen to their seats, Charlotte giggling something to her companions. I lean closer, listening. 'He's so handsome, in this light,' she's saying, brushing back a single loose ringlet. 'Looks almost like an angel himself.'

'He's very pious,' I agree quietly, seizing the opportunity to set my plan in motion. 'When we were children, he would pray *all* the time. His favourite colour is white, you know, because it's the colour of devotion. I'm thinking of wearing white to tonight's ball, actually,' I add innocently, like an afterthought. 'Maybe he'll pay more attention to me that way.'

'That's ridiculous,' Charlotte says. 'White is entirely out of fashion.'

I shrug. 'I suppose so. But it's his favourite. I think he would appreciate that, don't you?'

A priestess walks in shortly after, and the service begins, droning prayers begging the Mothers for their return, calling upon Morgane's forgiveness for the crimes of Bartrand de Roux. I don't participate – I know paltry prayers aren't going to bring Morgane back. She must be summoned by a sorcier, and Regnault is the only one left who knows how to do so.

Behind me, the noblegirls have begun to whisper among themselves, debating the importance of dress colours. I smother a smirk behind my hand – I've successfully planted my seed. Now, I have to let it grow.

SCENE V

Château. The Chapel.

Today, the priestess tells the story of the Little Saint and the Tarasque. Perhaps it's for the benefit of foreign visitors, perhaps as a reminder, but I grit my teeth as she tells a bastardized version of the story, where the Little Saint prays to God, and God sends down three angels to assist her. Three Good Mothers.

There is another version of this tale. One that endured in sorcier families for generations, even when the rest of the world wished to forget it. In it, the Little Saint is called the Golden-blooded Girl. And she is the first sorcier.

The legend goes that the original tarasque terrorized Auréal's countryside, slaughtering and devouring peasants as it pleased. Until a young girl, in her desperation, went to an old shrine in the woods and prayed to whatever god might hear her. What answered was not a god, but one of the three spirits of magic that lived there: Morgane, the youngest and most human of the three, who had always been fascinated by the way humans transformed one thing into another – not with magic but by hand, grain to bread or paints to artworks.

Morgane struck a deal with the girl: she would grant the girl magic in exchange for her most precious belonging. The girl brought the spirit a ring of purest gold, given to her by her betrothed. Delighted, the spirit spoke thus: 'As this is your most treasured belonging, you shall be mine, as will all those who come after you.' Morgane returned the ring to the girl, and when the girl touched it, her blood was turned to gold, and she knew she would be able to call upon magic.

The spirit then taught the girl how to wield her new powers, weaving webs of magic to transform one thing to another. How to bind those spells to golden objects, to use later as she wished. 'Remember,' said Morgane then, 'this gift I have given you is limited to my domain of powers: it can only transform, but never create or destroy, for those are magics guarded by my sisters, too dangerous to be shared with mankind.'

And so the Golden-blooded Girl returned to the village to find the tarasque attacking her home, the body of her betrothed lifeless in its jaws. Furious, she took her golden ring and turned it into a collar, then placed it upon the creature's neck. Then the beast was tamed, and it followed her like a calf: so the girl led it to the town square, where it was slaughtered by the townspeople.

I fidget as the priestess drones on. She preaches about the story's morals, about bravery and faith and loyalty. In her version of the story, the Little Saint journeys to the capital, where she kneels before the king, reminding everyone that true power belongs to the Crown.

In the story Regnault always told me, the moral was different.

'The Golden-blooded Girl made one grave mistake,'

he said to me once, when I lay huddled on my thin, cold mattress, Damien snoring softly beside me. 'Do you know what that was, little owl?'

'What?' I whispered back.

'She ought never to have killed the tarasque,' said Regnault. 'She had all that power on a leash, ready to do her bidding, yet she let it go.'

I leave the chapel at a slow pace, eavesdropping again on Charlotte and her friends. My seed has indeed sprouted roots – they're already chattering urgently about how they might procure white gowns before tonight's ball. One of them wonders if she should dress up as a tarasque, shell and all, and I have to stop myself from snorting.

I play my game all day: I join one group of noblewomen for breakfast, then another for a session of embroidery in a blue-walled sitting room. Every time, I'm quiet, listening for the right opportunity to feign guilelessness and talk about the colour I intend to wear that evening. *It's the Dauphin's favourite colour. It'll make him think of a wedding dress. I hear it's the next trend, and you know how the Dauphin loves to keep up with fashion.* I watch their faces go bloodless and panic enter their eyes before they excuse themselves and rush out of the room, presumably to go hunt down a white dress from the nearest city dressmaker.

When the time comes for the royal ball, I retreat smugly to my room. I unwrap the box on the bed, the one my father carefully orchestrated to have delivered last night, and pull off the lid.

Inside sits a simple gown of thick satin, black as ink or as death or as an owl's wings at midnight.

*

I arrive at the palace ballroom theatrically late.

I pause in front of the doors, listening to the tumbling of music and susurration of a mingling crowd within. Instinctually, I touch the owl-face pendant at my neck, then smooth out the full, darkly iridescent skirts of my gown. Floor-length, it fits like a glove – before having it delivered to the palace, Regnault enchanted it to adjust to the wearer's shape, saving me the hassle of hunting down Marie's measurements. It's done in the most recent of fashions, elegantly simple, the front adorned only with a strip of metallic black lace. The neckline is low, exposing my shoulders and collarbones, and the sleeves end at my elbows in lacy pleats. It's a striking design, guaranteed to make an impression.

I raise my chin. I'm eager, not nervous. I don't get nervous before a performance.

One of the footmen by the entrance grunts meaningfully, his eyes glinting with impatience. I give him a curt nod. At my signal, the doors are pushed open, and the footman announces Marie's name in full: 'Mademoiselle Marie d'Odette d'Auvigny!'

The ballroom grows suddenly hushed and still. All eyes turn to me, and my pulse rises in wicked delight. It worked. My plan *worked*.

It is as though the ballroom has been covered in feather-down. There is nothing like the power of a rumour, it seems, because nearly every courtier and foreign noblewoman has somehow managed to procure themselves a gown that is white, or at least as pale as possible. I pity the poor seamstresses that must have scrambled to put them together.

The ballroom itself makes me think of a gaping mouth, the parquet a stretch of crimson and glossy as a wet tongue. Carnelian columns flank arched windows, and crystals drip from the chandeliers like beads of saliva. The red and white roses painted across the vaulted ceiling are enchanted, blooming and wilting and blooming overhead, their thorns a cage of teeth.

The sight dizzies me as I step into the room, my skirts pooling around my feet. I meet the gazes of the noblesse around me, watch their expressions flicker between affront, dismay and fury as they realize they've been tricked. Princess Charlotte, wearing a puffy cream disaster, looks like she is deciding whether to burst into tears or flames.

From the opposite side of the ballroom, the Dauphin is staring at me in utter disbelief. He's wearing the Augier colours of red and gold – at his side is the Step-Queen in her signature sapphire, her raven hair bound up so tightly it looks painful. A little black-haired boy dressed identically to Aimé is clinging to her skirts.

Then I notice the man standing behind them and freeze.

For a moment, King Honoré of Auréal does not notice my arrival, caught in a heated discussion with a nobleman at his side. He may be a monster, but he hides his malice well – he is unremarkable in appearance, with the same shorter stature as his son, but graceless, a golden peruke unspooling over broad shoulders. He shares the Dauphin's freckles, but on him they look like sickly splotches. When his discussion partner breaks off at my arrival, the King follows suit. His gaze, when it lands on me, is twitchy and dark as a blackfly. I wish I could swat it away.

Looking into those cruel black depths, I can almost feel the cold, sticky filth of Verroux's streets squelching under my bare feet, the bony hands of beggars snagging on my skirt. My hand grips Regnault's as he leads me out of the city slums, my brother trailing behind us. *You were not meant to be this*, Regnault tells me quietly. *You have no idea what they took from you.*

What d-do you mean? I'd hardly been able to pronounce the words, my teeth chattering.

He'd clutched my hand tighter, looked down on me kindly. *Magic, little owl. They stole your magic.*

Magic. My father's voice lends me strength as my heels strike the crimson parquet, reminding me who I am, what I am capable of. *Magic.* The noblegirls in their fluttering white dresses part before me like fresh snow meeting a flame. *Magic.* The Dauphin steps towards me as though entranced, shrugging off the Step-Queen's hand as she tries to hold him back, ignoring the King as he growls a low command.

Magic. Aimé claps, killing any lingering murmurs and music. He spreads his hands wide, a benevolent grin splitting his face. 'Beloved guests, I do believe it's time for me to choose my first dance partner of the night.'

He whirls on his heel with a flourish, throws his head like an unruly stallion. When his eyes find mine, they're the eyes of a rebellious child reaching for a rose, wilfully ignoring the thorns poised to draw blood.

'Marie d'Odette, would you do me this honour?'

SCENE VI

Château. The Ballroom.

I could insult a thousand things about Aimé-Victor Augier, Dauphin of Auréal. I could insult his clothing, garishly gaudy and fitted too tight, stuffed with enough lace that I think we might both drown in it. I could insult his perfume, saccharine and cloyingly floral, sharp enough that it gives me a headache. I could even insult his demeanour – the way his confidence is obviously a mask, worn with mutinous stubbornness, fraying around the edges. But there is one thing I could not insult.

The Dauphin of Auréal is a breathtaking dancer.

The musicians play a slow, elegant minuet, and I'm surprised by the fluid way he moves, losing the gangly awkwardness he'd had about himself moments previously. Regrettably, the Dauphin seems all too aware of his talent, because he grins pridefully at me. When I return the smile, he takes it as an invitation to move closer. '*Ma chère* Marie,' he murmurs, 'I must admit you've shocked me.'

His breath is hot, his sugared voice sticking to my skin. I want to lean away, but I cannot – I must play this game until the end. So I mirror the teasing tilt of his head, even as my innards crawl with revulsion. A sorcier flirting with an Augier . . . My ancestors must be rolling in their graves.

'How so?' I enquire of the Dauphin, as we switch sides, taking each other's hands once more.

'I'd heard stories about how you'd become such a polite, well-mannered lady,' he responds. 'One of my stepmother's friends couldn't stop praising how your mother had managed to *tame* you.' The corners of his mouth tilt up, but there is a strange, conflicted edge to that smile. 'That didn't sound anything like the Marie I knew, and I was worried I wouldn't recognize you any more. I'm rather glad to be wrong.'

'And I am glad to prove you wrong,' I reply. I focus for a moment on the dance, and find myself wishing that I did not have to play this charade, that I could simply procure a dagger, press it to the Dauphin's throat and demand he give me the Couronne. Unfortunately, that would probably earn me some sort of creatively horrid execution. Theatrical, but inconvenient.

'And the white dresses?' the Dauphin enquires, interrupting my thoughts. 'Where did that come from, I wonder? I certainly did not mandate it.'

I shrug innocently. 'I think it's meant to make you think of wedding dresses. I'm not sure where the rumour started.'

He makes a face. 'This entire marriage affair is ridiculous. I don't want it at all. But it's tradition, and the kingdom needs an heir, apparently, so here you are and here I am.' He sniffs. 'Might as well enjoy it. Between your controversies and mine, we make quite the scandalous pair.'

Ah yes, the controversies. He must be referring to his reputation: the Dauphin is known to be a foppish, spoiled and incompetent successor to King Honoré. They say he shirks his duties, caring nothing for politics or court social events, preferring to spend his time locked in his room composing music he will play for no one. When he does emerge, it is to spend the kingdom's dwindling resources on wine or clothing. I've heard it whispered more and more frequently at the Théâtre, by commoners and noblesse alike – the kingdom has little trust in Aimé-Victor Augier. And considering how he nearly shot me in his drunken state last night, I can see why.

Marie's controversies, though ... they're more of a mystery to me. I wonder if he's referring to the same thing Charlotte mentioned last night: *Something about a necklace.* In my memory, diamonds wink hypnotically. But she couldn't have been referring to ... no. There is no way *that* caused such a scandal. There must have been a different incident, another necklace. And yet ...

I focus back on the dance, shaking off the nagging feeling. In response to Aimé's words, I give a flirtatious smile. 'A match made in heaven, I daresay.'

To my surprise, the Dauphin's coy demeanour fades momentarily. His eyes flick over my shoulder, and when he turns me and I'm able to see where he had been looking, I recognize my brother standing in the corner of the room, a glum shadow in his guard's uniform. I frown, but before I can say anything, the music ends.

The Dauphin steps away from me, dropping my hand. I curtsy in turn.

'Another, Monseigneur?' I want to continue to pry information from him, but the Dauphin shakes his head.

'I must take another partner, now,' he says. When my

face falls, he leans forward and whispers in my ear: 'You know how it is. I can't show favouritism. I need to pretend to consider *all* the candidates, or Stepmother will have a conniption. Anyway, I think it's time for a drink. I'll certainly need it to survive this night.' He winks at me, bows and whirls away.

As the Dauphin makes a beeline for a servant carrying flutes of wine, I take a breath, forcing the tension from my chest. Now that I'm free, I notice an older nobleman with a face like a prune sliding his eyes over me. Before he can ask me to dance, I turn away and hurry to the edge of the room, where I make a show of eyeing up the ridiculously extravagant pastries. The theme appears to be birds – red cardinals iced on cream-filled choux, macarons shaped like swooping sparrows, fruit cakes topped with little lemon canaries. The result is a lurid, mismatched flock that looks less like an artful arrangement and more like something a house cat might drag in.

I pluck a chocolate parakeet from its basin of ganache just as a hand seizes me from behind.

I turn in panic and come face to face with a broad-chested guardsman, who glares at me down the length of his crooked nose. I remember the day it was broken – he'd been defending me from a particularly aggressive patron after a play.

Damien.

'Monsieur!' I gasp, raising my fist. 'Unhand me at once!'

Damien scoffs. He looks me up and down, then eyes the chocolate parakeet still clutched in my raised fist. 'Are you going to *hit* me with that, Dilou?'

My stomach plunges. He knows. Of course he does.

I place the now-mangled bird back on the table and wipe my hand on the tablecloth before scanning the room anxiously. Thankfully, most of the noblesse are preoccupied either with dancing, flirting or attempting to elbow their way to speak with the King. I turn back to Damien, keeping my expression polite, as though we are strangers. 'How did you know it was me?'

'Marie d'Odette isn't the type to resort to trickery,' he says. 'Also, the owl necklace. Very subtle.'

I scowl, raising my hand to clutch the owl-face pendant protectively. 'What do you want, Damien? Planning to betray me again?'

He glowers at me. I glower back. As usual, Damien breaks first, running a hand over his face. 'I just . . . what are you *doing* here? And what, by the Mothers, did you do with the real Marie d'Odette?'

'I didn't kill her, if that's what you're worried about.'

'I wouldn't put it past you,' Damien replies acridly.

Once upon a time, that might have stung. But I don't care what my brother thinks of me any more. 'Yes, you're right,' I sneer. 'I'm on a rampage, killing noblesse left and right. You should arrest me before I murder *all* the realm's spoiled lordlings, since that would be such a tragedy. But wait –' I give him a pitying look. 'You can't, can you? Because you made a vow to our poor dead Maman.'

Damien, as usual, has no sense of humour. His scowl deepens, but he's smart enough to keep it subtle. 'Dilou,' he says quietly. 'Please. What deranged errand has that man sent you on this time?'

That man. As though Regnault didn't rescue both of us, *raise* both of us, despite Damien being utterly barren of magic.

I would roll my eyes if I didn't have to keep up my charade of dignified Marie. 'What will you do if I tell you?'

'This isn't a game, little sister.'

'Answer my question.'

'I asked first.'

More glowering. Once again, I win. 'You're not even acting like her, you know,' Damien mutters. 'Someone is bound to become suspicious.'

I shrug. 'Let them. Marie d'Odette has not been to Verroux in five years. It's normal for people to change as they get older.'

'And if you are injured?' he growls. 'It's not normal for people to change the colour of their *blood* as they get older.'

I eye him steadily. 'Is that a threat? Because you and I both know you could never bring yourself to hurt me.'

I see the flash of anger cross his face, followed by a wounded petulance. I've won this round as well. Damien's last words to our mother were a promise: to care for me, to protect me at all costs. For someone as foolishly sentimental as my brother, such a vow is not to be broken. Even five years after abandoning me, it seems he hasn't been able to sever that bond, though I'm sure he wishes he could.

Damien opens his mouth to argue again, but before he can, someone breaks into bright, chiming laughter so loud it carries across the ballroom. Damien's whole body tilts towards the noise. When I look over my shoulder and find the source, I nearly burst out laughing.

'Nothing ever changes with you, does it?' I mock, as my brother stares longingly after the Dauphin of Auréal. 'Oh, Damien, you *idiot*.'

I see his fists clench out of the corner of my eye. 'Tell me what he sent you here for, Dilou.'

'I can't,' I say, Regnault's warning still stark in my mind. 'But I'm doing this for us, for our family, so do yourself a favour and *stay out of it*. And if it makes you feel better, I have no intention of harming your precious Dauphin.'

Damien's chest swells in an irritated breath. 'Swear it. Swear you won't hurt him.'

I give my brother my sweetest, most innocent smile, and reach across the table to grab a brioche shaped like a mallard duck. 'You'll just have to trust me,' I sing, and bite off the duck's head before skipping back into the crowd.

After that, the ball does its best imitation of my chocolate parakeet – it melts, abandoning all semblance of propriety, devolving into a mangled caricature that barely resembles its former shape. The musicians play piece after piece, the music becoming frenzied, distorted. The dancing transforms into a blur of silken skirts and tapping feet. Bottles and bottles of various liquors are brought out, first expensive champagnes and then wines of cheaper and cheaper quality, until I swear I'm handed a flute of red-dyed water. The Dauphin reigns over it all, flitting from group to group, patting red-faced swaying lords on the back and winking at their wives before whirling away with their daughters. A cake is brought out, tiered and hideous. Someone knocks it over. Laughter roars.

Swept up in the crowd, I do not stop dancing, even as blisters bloom on my feet. If there's anything I understand, it's this – this pure, exhilarating, *dazzling* chaos. And chaos, I've learned, is the best place to hide secrets.

As I whirl alongside partner after partner, I keep my eye on the Dauphin and the King and Charlotte. Though I keep a sweet smile plastered on my face, I don't like what I see. First, the King is approached by Charlotte and another man – a tall, long-faced lord who must be her chaperone, perhaps an uncle or ambassador. They drift to the edges of the ballroom, deep in heated conversation. Eventually the King and the lord shake hands. Charlotte curtsies to the King, and as she does, her eyes sweep the crowd, searching for someone.

Me. They land on me. She bares her teeth in a triumphant smile.

Not good, I think, but I can do nothing, only take my partner's hand again as the gigue refuses to end. I watch helplessly as, moments later, the King seizes the Dauphin from the crowd, drags him away from a group of young noblemen to whisper in his ear. The Dauphin's face falls, and he opens his mouth to argue, only to be silenced by a dangerous look from his father.

Oh, this is not good at all.

The music ends, mercifully, and I move quickly away from the dancers, heading to the back of the room where the more important-looking noblemen have gathered. The Dauphin. I need to speak with the Dauphin, to find out exactly what bargain the Princess of Lore has struck with the King. My position, so certain merely an hour ago, now seems precarious, shifting under my feet like sand. I cannot fail here. I *cannot*. If I do not secure this proposal, I lose any chance of ever laying eyes on the –

Crack. I throw up my hands in alarm. A bolt of pain sears through my palm, and lukewarm liquid pours down my sleeve. It takes me a moment to realize what has happened – in my urgency, I didn't see the girl headed directly towards me. I jump back in alarm, as does the other girl, shrieking shrilly and dropping her now-shattered glass along with its contents of blood-red wine.

I begin to rebuke her, but she is faster. 'Oh, Mothers, I'm so sorry!' she cries. There are tears in her eyes and flecks of wine on her poorly fitting white bodice.

Some of my anger ebbs. 'It's all right,' I say quickly, wiping my wet, stinging palm on my dress. At least the fabric is dark enough to conceal any stains.

'Mademoiselle, you . . .' The girl's brows furrow in confusion, and she gestures with her wine-dripping fingers to the spot where I just pressed my hand. 'You smudged some of your make-up.'

I look down, and my stomach plummets.

There is a small gold streak spotting the smooth obsidian of my bodice, bright as paint. The same liquid stains my palm, where the shattering wine glass cut my skin open.

Only it isn't paint at all.

It's my blood.

SCENE VII

Château. The Ballroom.

Remember, Odile, they must never see you bleed.

For the first time since my arrival at the palace, I feel true panic. My pulse surges; I clasp my uninjured hand over the wounded one and barely manage to keep my composure.

'Mademoiselle?' the young girl squeaks.

'Excuse me.' I whirl away, cursing the gown's heavy skirts as I nearly trip over them. I force myself to remain calm, dignified, walking at a steady pace even while my every instinct screams at me to run, to hide because they will see, *they will see.*

I manage to keep my composure long enough to leave the ballroom. My skirts rustle behind me – my chest strains against the confines of my tightly laced bodice. The crimson of the ballroom breaks like a tide upon a gallery of black and silver, the polished indigo flooring speckled white as though stars are trapped beneath. Columns flank the room, and I duck behind one to catch my breath.

I inspect my hand, assessing the damage. The cut is blessedly small; I suck on it, and am relieved to see that the bleeding has already slowed. I exhale and begin rubbing off the stain on my bodice, when footsteps come echoing through the room.

'. . . high time for change,' a voice is saying. When I peer around the column, I see it belongs to a short, balding man, the buttons of his doublet straining to contain his stomach.

Beside him walks a nobleman of middling age, thin brows lording over a thinner face, a scar carved across his nose. 'Yes, yes, so you've said,' he drawls, as the pair approach my hiding spot. I tuck myself tighter against the column as they pass. 'At least my brother still inspires enough respect in this court to keep it from falling apart entirely. But that brat of his . . . you've seen it first hand. Never in the history of Auréal has there been an heir more unfit for the throne.'

'At least his incompetence has an advantage,' says his companion.

'And what is that?' asks Scar-nose, adjusting his auburn peruke. The guards flanking the ballroom doors pull them open, sending golden light gushing through the dark gallery.

The balding man snorts. 'The little pest is easy to get rid of.'

Their laughter trails behind them as the doors fall shut again.

I frown, turning their words over in my mind as I rub any remaining blood off my palm. My shoulders ache with tension, and I roll them before heading back towards the ballroom.

Before I can reach the doors, they go flying open. For a second time that night, a figure crashes into me.

'Marie!'

It's the Dauphin. He reels back in surprise, his cheeks red and eyes even redder. His golden hair has come undone around his face, any confidence he'd worn previously shed in favour of genuine despair.

He sways for a moment, staring at me piteously. Then, 'Marie, I'm so sorry,' he wails, and throws his arms around my neck.

It takes all my willpower not to punch the Dauphin of Auréal. 'You're sorry?' I echo, trying to peel him off me. His perfume has turned sickly, spoiled by sweat and alcohol. 'What are you talking about?'

'The bargain. I couldn't do anything, he's already arranged it, it's all ruined –'

This time, I do succeed in shoving him off. 'What bargain?'

'The one we made as children! I knew, after the scandal, that it might be difficult to keep, but now Charlotte wants an alliance – though we all know this is just about *power*, when has Lore ever done anything without ulterior motives? – but my father somehow thinks that's a better idea than strengthening Auréal, or perhaps Anne talked him into it – she can be so *cruel* sometimes – or . . . or –'

'You will not choose me, then.' A wave of furious disappointment rises up inside me.

His shoulders sag. 'I cannot. The King has sworn to the ambassador of Lore that I will marry Charlotte. And I cannot disobey him.'

Coward, I want to say. Instead, I smile gently, gathering what little scraps of kindness I can dredge up from my withered excuse for a heart. I take Aimé's hand and pull him away from the doors, through the gallery, and into the glittering entrance hall beyond. 'Monseigneur, correct me if I am wrong, but I believe your father is already married.'

He frowns, brushing tears from his eyes. 'Y-yes . . .'

'So he cannot possibly be choosing a bride.'

'Yes, but –'

'Then, this is your choice to make.'

The Dauphin shakes his head violently. 'I can't go against him, not again. When I tried to do it at the last Conseil meeting, he – Regardless. He knows better than I.'

'Perhaps he does. But this is your happiness in the balance. And mine,' I admit. That much is not a lie.

The Dauphin bites his lip. 'If I undermine him in front of the whole court –'

'He can do nothing.'

'You underestimate him.'

'Your choice is made publicly,' I say. 'I doubt he will force you to change it after the fact. That would be a sign of discord, of instability within the court.'

He smiles wanly. 'I missed you. And your ridiculous problem-solving.'

It appears Marie d'Odette and I have something in common after all. I put a hand on my hip, trying to mimic her stern manner. 'You don't really want to marry Princess Charlotte Turnip-hair, do you?'

'Marie!' A surprised laugh bursts from him.

'What? Do you disagree?'

He sniffs. 'Personally, I think it looks more like a beet.'

'A discoloured beet, perhaps,' I muse, then grow sober again, eyeing him carefully. It's time to finish this game.

And for that I must draw on a resource I rarely use: honesty.

'Monseigneur, listen to me now.' I take the Dauphin's hand in mine, hold his gaze with fierce conviction. 'Aimé-Victor Augier, I swear this upon the Mothers. I do not want to be queen, truly I don't. What I want . . . what I want is to restore this kingdom to what it was always meant to be. To bring about a new era. But without you, without *this*, I can't do it.'

His eyes have gone wide and hopeful, in a way that almost makes me pity him. Almost. 'Do you think so?'

Before I can reply, a shadow falls over us. 'There you are.'

We both turn to see Damien, his expression an excellent imitation of a thundercloud. He blatantly ignores me and walks up to the Dauphin, his eyes gentling a fraction as he bows to the wayward prince. 'It's time for you to make your announcement, Monseigneur.'

The Dauphin scowls. 'Mothers, I hate it when you call me that.'

Damien looks weary. 'You know I cannot –'

'I know. You do so love reminding me.' The Dauphin rubs his eyes. 'Must I do this?'

Damien puts a hand on his shoulder and draws him away from my side. 'The King is waiting,' he says, with a tenderness to his voice I have seldom heard. 'This ball must end eventually. You cannot draw it out forever.'

'You're right, I suppose. Though I do resent it.' The Prince turns back and bows to me, his eyes dark and thoughtful. 'Mademoiselle d'Auvigny.'

I curtsy in return. 'Remember my promise,' I say, and ignore the deadly look Damien shoots me. Watching my brother usher the Dauphin away, Regnault's words ring in my head: *If you cannot avoid him, you must eliminate him.*

Well, Damien hasn't told anyone of my identity yet. He's a variable I'll have to worry about later; for now, I can only wait and pray my words to the Dauphin have been enough to change my fate.

'*Mesdames et Messieurs*, may I claim your attention for one last time tonight? After some . . . deliberation, the Dauphin has made his choice.'

I'm glad of Marie's height as I peer over shoulders, weaving between the press of bodies to attempt to get to the front of the crowd. King Honoré stands in the centre of the ballroom, the Dauphin fidgeting beside him. One of the King's meaty hands grips his son's arm, and even from a distance the gesture does not look amicable.

'Well?' The silk of the Dauphin's sleeve creases under the King's tightening fingers.

'I have made my choice!' the Dauphin says, forcing a smile as he addresses the crowd. 'Thank you all for coming tonight and placing your offers of alliance before me. I make this decision with difficulty, but also with reassurance, for I have found someone who I believe I can trust, with my heart and with the kingdom. Someone who, someday, will make an excellent queen.'

My chest feels tight. I watch with dread as the Dauphin's eyes land on Charlotte, who is tapping her foot impatiently. The Dauphin opens his mouth again, hesitates.

The King shakes him by the shoulder, as though to break him from the silence.

I push past the man standing in front of me to emerge from the crowd. The movement is enough to bring the Dauphin's eyes back to me – his gaze pools with the panic of a much younger boy, caught in a riptide and struggling not to be pulled under. Despite myself, I feel a reluctant stab of kinship. Aimé-Victor Augier's brand of chaos is different from mine, but it comes from the same place. We are both birds trapped in cages. Only, while he is batting brokenly at the bars, I'm determined to pick the lock.

That is what I try to convey as I hold his attention. Understanding. A final play on his pity, in case my vow earlier was not enough.

The Dauphin looks away. Straightens. And steps away from his father, forcing the man to release his grip.

'My beloved guests, I present to you the future Queen of Auréal, Mademoiselle Marie d'Odette, daughter of Auvigny!'

The world becomes a blur. The musicians play a jarring, rushed fanfare, and the Dauphin rushes forward to grip my hands and press a tense kiss to my cheek. I dart a look at the King – though his face is without expression, he watches his son with cold, vicious rage. The Dauphin, wisely, avoids his father's eyes as he pulls me towards the gathered court.

The crowd bursts into applause, though it sounds malicious somehow, threatening. As I walk by them, their faces blur together, artificial as theatre masks, lifeless eyes and painted lips and too-sharp teeth glinting as they seethe their congratulations. They think I will be an easy meal, I realize, the Swan Princess of Auvigny, pearlescent and pure-hearted and ripe for their devouring.

But they're wrong. I'm not the delicate, white-feathered bird they believe me to be. I'm the darkness of cold gutters and merciless nights, the bruised shadows beneath a thief's desperate eyes. I'm nothing but a lie, a twisted reflection, a black swan.

And my teeth are just as sharp as theirs.

The Dauphin does not release my hand until he has pulled me out of the ballroom, through the gallery and into the empty entrance hall. Only then does he let me go, his hands shaking minutely, urgency replacing his previous dignified façade. He beckons forth one of his musketeers, a short, square-jawed man.

'Armand will take you to the Dauphine's apartments – they were prepared this morning in anticipation of my new betrothed.' He cringes as he says the word. 'Go with him, now, before my father is no longer occupied by formalities. I will have to calm his ire.'

Am I wrong, or is there fear in his voice? 'How badly have we upset him?'

I wonder just how many enemies I've made myself today, how many people will try to get between me and the Couronne.

He shrugs. 'It hardly matters – he's always upset. It only gets worse as the years pass, really, even without the . . . Never mind.' He shakes his head, sending dishevelled locks bouncing around his face. 'Regardless, thank you, for giving me courage. It felt good to finally make a decision he could not reject. I –'

'Where is that *idiot* boy?' The King's growl reaches us from the gallery. Over the Dauphin's shoulder, I can see King Honoré storming towards us. Behind him, music continues to thrum through the ballroom, the celebrations unceasing even now.

'Go,' Aimé mouths, and I don't need to be told twice. I turn and follow the guard up the left staircase, in a direction I remember leads to the royal chambers. I hold up my skirts as we go up the stairs, then wait as the guard pulls a sconce from the wall to light the way.

Even from this distance, I can hear the fury in the King's hushed voice. 'Aimé, what is the meaning of this?'

I can hardly make out Aimé's trembling response. 'I thought – I –'

'Speak up, boy,' his father snarls. 'Explain this ridiculous prank.'

'It's not a . . . I only – I thought a Lorish queen, now, would be the equivalent of letting in a spy. If they learned just how precarious –'

The sound of a slap echoes through the hall. Beside me, the guard flinches. 'We should go,' he murmurs.

I can't move. The King's voice shakes with anger. '*Precarious*. What do you know about any of this? About Lore? About *Auréal*?' He scoffs when the Dauphin doesn't reply. 'That's right. Nothing. Yet somehow you are arrogant enough to interfere with my plans. You will go back in there, and you will tell them all you've changed your mind.'

'If it weren't for Lore,' Aimé argues, 'you would have been perfectly content with my choice. I know how long you've wanted to strengthen our bond with Auvigny –'

'Oh, you know what I want, do you?' the King cuts in. 'Then why aren't you *doing as I say?*'

'He cannot.' Another voice joins the fray – I recognize the stern tone of Anne de Malezieu, the Step-Queen. Her heels echo as she approaches the men. 'My King, you know he cannot. As unwise as this decision may be, to rescind it would only make us seem irresolute.'

The Dauphin speaks up again, bolstered by the Step-Queen's defence. 'Besides, this ensures Auvigny's support, and with the rumours –'

'Quiet, Aimé.' This time, it's the Step-Queen who silences him.

But his words have already added fuel to the King's fire. 'Do not pretend you did this for any other reason than childish fancy,' he growls. 'You're still infatuated with that girl.'

'I'm not infatuated with any girl!'

There's a beat of silence, and I realize I'm bracing myself for the sound of another strike. It doesn't come. Instead, the King makes a sound more animal than human. 'Out of my sight, both of you. And pray to the Mothers that I can soothe the King of Lore before he declares war on us for this slight.'

The guard's hand brushes my shoulder, breaking my concentration. 'Mademoiselle,' he urges, 'come.'

This time, I follow.

The Dauphine's apartments are a gaudy, bloated place. The furniture shines greasily in the low light; the bed is swollen with pillows, and the lace laid over the table and vanity looks more like trimmings of animal fat. The lancet windows show a glimpse of the gardens and lake, wreathed in bulky emerald curtains with a pattern that is probably flower bouquets, but looks more like heads of broccoli.

I stare at them as a maid peels away heavy layers of

ballgown and prises apart coils of pale hair. Once she is gone, I sit on – or rather sink *into* – the overstuffed bed. 'I win,' I tell the ugly chandelier. '*I win*,' I repeat, then rub my eyes in frustration.

I can't find satisfaction in my victory, not when my mind reverberates with sounds: the slap of the King's palm striking the Dauphin, the crack of the shattering wine glass, my brother's pleading voice. I'm not used to feeling uncertain, and it unsettles me. I've spent my life under Regnault's guidance, every move dictated by his plans, every choice made in search of his approval. Even now, I want to run back to the Théâtre and tell him everything, then ask him how to untangle the threads of intrigue that seem to be drawing tighter and tighter around me.

But I can't, not yet. Not until I have the Couronne in my hands.

When this is over, we will never have to scavenge again. We will have all the magic we desire, and I will teach you all I know.

My father's promise rings in my ears, bringing me a spark of much needed hope. When I crawl into bed, I'm bone-tired but keen for the morning, for the next step of my plot, the next step closer to *magic*.

I fall asleep clutching the owl-face pendant. In my dreams, it burns against my palm, and a floor of black-and-white tiles stretches like a chessboard in front of me, golden blood streaked down the middle.

Something is coming, daughter of the blood, says a voice that rattles like a drowning man's lungs. *Something is coming.*

I wake to the sound of sobbing.

For an instant, I'm afraid I'm still dreaming – buried by something heavy and stifling, my back slick with sweat.

I scrabble around, panicking, until I finally manage to untangle myself from the lavish bedding of the Dauphine's apartments and gulp night-chilled air.

The crying, however, does not stop. It comes from a distance, crawling through the hallways, reaching my chambers only as a quiet echo. Slowly, the sound multiplies, until I can make out more raised voices, more hysterical sobs.

I climb from my bed and check the owl-face pendant before pulling a silk jacket from the chest to throw over my chemise. A red-wine dawn spills through the chamber windows, bathing me in violent shades as I rush towards the door. Foreboding fills my gut as I grip the handle and pull.

I do not get the chance to step out before Armand the guard is bearing down upon me, his mask jagged in the eerie light. 'Mademoiselle, you can't leave your chambers,' he says gruffly.

My heart leaps into my throat. Has my ruse been discovered? 'Why?' I demand, gathering as much queenly authority as I can muster while likely resembling a bedraggled, sleep-deprived rat.

'We are still assessing the situation. You will be told when it's deemed safe.'

'Monsieur, please, I must –' I cut myself off as another wail echoes down the corridor. It seems to be coming from the entrance hall. I pause to listen, attempting to distinguish one panicked voice from another. A command is barked. A woman's voice argues back. Then, a third wail carries into the hallway.

'No! Bring him back!'

The Dauphin.

I step closer to the guard, nose to nose and glad once again of Marie's superior height. '*What* is going on down there? Why is my betrothed weeping?'

I can't see the man's expression, and the frustration of it makes me want to dig my nails under his mask and peel it from his face. He seems to deliberate. I force myself to be still, even as I feel as though sparks are trapped in my chest.

Finally, he says, 'The King is dead.'

The King is dead.

My chest lurches. I'm not sure whether to laugh or cry. How is this possible? It was mere hours ago that I saw him alive, bearing furiously down upon the Dauphin.

'How did it happen?' My voice comes out too matter-of-fact, too callous for tactful Marie. I force a handful of fat tears into my eyes so I don't look *too* conspicuous.

The guard sounds haunted. 'They found his body by the lakeside,' he says. 'Halfway to the theatre house.'

I frown. 'What was he doing out there?'

'They say he went for a ride to clear his head. They found his guards dead, too. All bloody.'

Now *that* gets my interest. 'Bloody?'

The guard shifts uncomfortably, realizing he has said too much. 'This is a sensitive matter, Mademoiselle, too violent for the ears of a lady. I'm sure the Dauphin would better decide what details you should know.'

I force a demure smile to my lips and let a few more tears fall. 'Please, Monsieur,' I say piteously. 'I must know what is causing the Dauphin such distress.'

'It is . . . unspeakable.'

An ominous feeling slips along my bones. 'Monsieur, you must tell me. You *must*. I'm your future queen.'

Beneath the ridges of the guard's mask, his eyes squeeze shut. He weighs his options in harrowed, irritated silence. Finally, he begins to speak again. 'He was murdered by his own guard.' His voice turns rough and halting, as though it's snagging on his teeth. 'One of the best musketeers in the regiment, too, a favourite of the Dauphin's. Prince Aimé took him off the streets, treated him like an equal. And this is how he repays him, the ungrateful bastard.'

My heart plunges. That sounds *far* too familiar. 'Monsieur, what . . . what is his name?'

'I do not think you would know him, Mademoiselle.'

'Still, I should like to hear it. Please.'

The guard regards me through narrowed eyes, as though my insistence is an annoyance. 'If you must know, his name is Damien.'

SCENE VIII

The Dauphine's Apartments. Dawn breaks.

The world blurs at the edges, unreal, mocking. I take a step back, my hands falling uselessly to my sides. The guard's masked face is a slash of silver against the dawn-soaked surroundings.

'Mademoiselle,' he says gruffly, 'do you know him?'

I shake my head. 'No.' *Yes*, I want to scream. *Yes, by the Mothers, that's my brother.*

But he's not, I remind myself. *He betrayed you, remember?*

I take a breath, gathering myself. 'Let me through,' I say.

'I already told you –'

My temper shatters in its entirety. I pretend to see something terrifying over his shoulder, and clap my hands over my mouth. 'Good Mothers, he's *here*,' I say dramatically.

The guard starts in alarm and turns on his heel. I use the distraction to shove past him and out into the corridor.

'Mademoiselle!' He reaches for me, but even in Marie's body, I'm still nimble. I duck under his outstretched arm and take off towards the stairs, my footfalls echoing behind me, my pulse pounding in my ears.

By the time I reach the entrance hall, I'm breathless. I have to pause halfway down the stairs, leaning on the balustrade and taking in the chaos of the dark hall.

The space vibrates with anxious voices. A group of stately noblemen stand in a small cluster in the middle, clad in nightclothes and hastily thrown-over cloaks. Half the candles in the enormous chandelier have gone out, and darkness reaches eagerly to fill the hollows of their cheeks and the bags beneath their eyes. In the centre of it all is the Step-Queen, wearing a silk robe of deep blue. Pressed against her is the Dauphin, violent sobs wracking his body. The same words bubble from his lips, over and over again.

'No, no, no, it can't be, he would *never*, no, *please*.'

I watch, surprised, as the Dauphin attempts to jerk out of the Step-Queen's arms. She pulls him to herself, shushes him, but there is no tenderness in her eyes. Her mouth is tight, cold.

'Please,' the boy repeats, and struggles once more. This time, he breaks free from the Step-Queen's grasp and turns towards the gathered courtiers. 'Please, you must listen to me. It doesn't make sense, he – he would not do this, he's the most loyal of my men, he –'

I frown. He's not talking about the King – he's talking about Damien.

One of the lords runs his hand exasperatedly over his face. I recognize him from the ball – it's the man with the scarred nose. In the faint light, his skin looks paper-thin, his eyes glittering shrewdly. 'I understand that is what you think, nephew, but you are blinded by your affection for the man.'

'But it doesn't make sense!' the Dauphin argues feebly. 'What reason could he possibly have . . .' He trails off, tries to gather himself. 'Please. Listen to me. I'm the King now.'

'You are not King until you are crowned,' says the scar-nosed man. 'Until then, *I* am regent, and I will take care of this matter.'

I wonder if I should interfere, but something in me thinks it's better simply to watch this unfold. There's a jagged tension in the air, every word a blade grown rusted by resentment. I would prefer not to get impaled.

'At least let me see him,' the Dauphin pleads. 'Let me hear him out.'

'I do not think it is a good idea for you to be speaking with a murderer, Aimé,' says the scar-nosed man – the Regent. 'Not in this state.'

The Dauphin's eyes hold the same wild, watery desperation as those of a trapped animal. 'Uncle, please,' he begs. When the Regent doesn't reply, he turns to the Step-Queen, clutching her robe. 'Stepmother?' The Step-Queen shakes her head, and he sobs. 'Please, this isn't *fair*.'

The Regent lays a hand on his shoulder with cruel gentleness. 'All these tears. Do you see? This is precisely why you cannot be trusted with decisions right now.'

I take a step back, my mind buzzing from all I've heard. I realize there's nothing I can do here, no way I can twist this to my advantage. There are too many people present – too many *variables*, as Regnault would say, for me to attempt to manipulate the situation.

The Regent turns his attention to the Step-Queen. 'I think the Dauphin should be returned to his bedchambers.

He clearly needs time to grieve. Laujon, please escort him.' He addresses the last words to one of the tallest guards in the hall, a bear-like man with an ugly, stretched face. The guard stomps towards the Step-Queen and the Dauphin, and the Dauphin flinches further into his stepmother's arms.

I watch as the Step-Queen guides the Dauphin away, even as he continues to whisper small, pathetic pleas under his breath. Frustration surges through me at the sight. This is the future King, the man who will one day rule Auréal, and here he is manipulated like a rag doll by his own uncle. He is making the same mistake the Golden-blooded Girl made – all this power within his grasp, and he is letting it be torn away from him.

I shake my head sharply and begin to turn away. As I do, my neck begins to prickle. I pause and turn, slowly, to catch the pale eyes of the Regent, the scar across his nose seeming to stretch and warp. My chest tightens in sudden, painful warning. *Look away, look away*, it screams. For a moment, I can't, as though all my willpower has been stripped from me, my gaze sucked into the mire that is the Regent's attention. Then, at last, I manage to tear away. Heart thudding, I touch the owl-face pendant and hurry back the way I came.

I know from the crawling, greasy feeling on my skin that the Regent watches me until I'm out of sight.

Any formalities I might have been expected to handle as the soon-to-be Dauphine are forgotten as the Château reels from news of the murder. I have breakfast in my chambers – after all, I'm meant to be *mourning* – and restlessly pick at a plate of syrupy viennoiseries.

My mind churns. According to the maid who brought me my breakfast – who heard it from the cook, who heard it from a footman, who overheard it from a guard – Damien has been taken to the dungeon. 'Apparently,' the maid tells me in a gleeful whisper, 'he was covered in blood when the guards found him leaning over the King's body. He had a knife in his hand.'

I squeeze my eyes tight, rubbing my temples. What a fine mess my brother has gotten himself into. I might resent him, but Damien has always firmly believed in justice. He's not a killer. And if he *were* to kill someone, it would be in a fair duel, not with a knife in the dark.

Then again, a voice in my mind whispers, *you haven't seen him in five years. People change.*

Frustrated, I shove my chair back and stand. There's too much I don't know – I cannot decide on my next course of action until I learn more about what happened last night.

'I believe I will go for a walk in the gardens,' I declare to the maid who has been waiting on me. The girl nods and fetches my jacket, helping me into it. 'Shall I summon some of the court ladies for company?'

I wave my hand. 'No, I'm going alone. I must clear my head.' Before she can protest, I rush out the door. To my relief, Armand is not there to stop me – it seems most guards have been summoned away to deal with post-murder chaos.

It did not take long for tidings of the King's death to spread across the Château. You might as well have announced an epidemic – ever since the news broke, the palace has emptied out like an overturned bucket, spilling nobles from its bowels and into glittering carriages.

Some are still awaiting their turn to escape, milling about restlessly in the entrance hall and shuffling into the main courtyard. I avoid them and head for the gardens instead.

I draw in a breath when I step outside, frost-sharp air pricking my lungs. Ahead stretch the Château grounds, occupied by a hedge-maze of jagged rosebushes nearly as tall as my head, obscuring most of Lac des Cygnes from sight. The hedges, though lifelike, are made entirely of iron, peppered with large, shining roses of solid gold.

The rosebushes are a brutal reminder of all the kingdom has lost. Once, Morgane had blessed Auréal, ensuring it was fertile and plentiful. Hers was the domain of transformation: winter becoming spring, seeds turning to crops, butterflies bursting from chrysalises. But after her curse, flowers refused to bloom. Crops failed. Foals and calves were born sickly. When all his beloved roses withered, the Spider King, in a fit of fury, placed the Couronne du Roi upon his head for the first time. With its magic, he grew new roses of metal, deathless imitations of former beauty. Then he travelled the kingdom and used the crown's powers to force the failing crops to grow, to rekindle some little life within his dying kingdom.

Picking up my skirts, I step between the hedges, relishing the silence, a welcome change from the noisiness of the Château. The gardens' treasures peek over the tangles of metal, offering glimpses of dilapidated secrets – the forehead of a crumbling statue, the tip of a trellis, the occasional stunted fruit tree.

I made my way through this maze more than once as a maid, so I know where to go. I reach my goal soon enough – Lac des Cygnes, a sleepy, rippling entity, the

Théâtre du Roi a fog-veiled speck on the opposite bank, a scattering of swans drifting nearby. I wonder which one of them is Marie – I wonder if I would even be able to tell.

I pull my jacket tighter around myself and begin my slow trek around the lake.

It doesn't take me long to find the place where the King died. It's obvious even from a distance: dried blood darkens the earth between forest and lake, the bank littered with crushed leaves and footprints. The bodies are gone, but I can see indents in the soil where they had lain, still stained the colour of rust.

Before drawing closer, I check my surroundings carefully. Once I'm certain that I'm alone, I take off the owl-face pendant and turn back into myself. It would be rather odd if Marie d'Odette returned to the Château with her skirts stained with blood. I'm not entirely sure how I would explain that one. *Oh dear, I went for a stroll and stumbled upon the scene of a grisly murder. Silly me!*

My chest loosens now that I'm no longer in disguise. I walk slowly up to the imprints in the earth before crouching by the one nearest to me. I can make out the silhouette of splayed legs, grooves carved by clawing hands. The grass around them is sticky with gore, bits of flesh tucked between bristly blades. Whatever happened here, it was violent.

And Damien is not a violent man. So what was he doing near the corpses?

I chew on my thumb, considering. Damien is Aimé's closest confidant, his valiant protector. Without him, Aimé would be exposed, left almost entirely alone. First the King, then the Dauphin's closest guard? This seems too convenient.

Could Damien have been framed? And does this mean the Dauphin might be in danger?

'This will not do,' I mutter to the trees rustling overhead. 'No one is allowed to kill the Dauphin until after the wedding. I need that crown.'

As if in response to my words, splashing erupts from the lake ahead. I look up, startled, then realize that it's just one of the swans, beating its wings against the water as it draws closer.

I begin to relax ... until I meet the creature's eyes, and its gaze brightens with furious, frighteningly human recognition. It stretches its neck forward and hisses, slamming its wings against the water in threat. I leap to my feet, scrambling back from the bank.

'M-Marie?' I stammer.

The swan seems to puff itself up in righteous anger, wings spread wide and menacing.

Then it charges.

SCENE IX

The Lake. A dreary day.

Let me tell you, there is nothing more terrifying than being attacked by the scorned equivalent of a glorified goose.

I nearly trip as I stumble backwards, away from the lake's edge and out of reach of the furious swan's wings. Swan-Marie is not discouraged – she advances on me frantically, water erupting around her as she beats the surface again and again. I begin to turn on my heel, ready to abandon my fledged opponent and flee back to the palace, but the look in her eyes makes me falter. In those piercing black depths is something desperate and urgent. Something *haunted*. My breath hitches in realization.

'Marie.' I take one more step back, just in case I misread her intentions. My foot sinks into the blood-soaked soil. 'Have you been by the lake all night?'

Swan-Marie pauses in her attack, her wings still flared in threat. I don't speak Swan, but something about her posture makes me think I'm right. Hope swells in my chest.

'Did you see what happened?' I ask quietly. 'Did you see what killed the King?'

The swan makes a low, keening sound. Then, she tucks her wings tightly against her body and dips her head in confirmation. Water ripples delicately around her.

'Who was it?' I can't help my eagerness. I approach the lakeside and crouch, murky water lapping at the toes of my boots. 'Who killed him? Was it a boy with black hair? He . . . he would have been a little older than me. Dressed like a royal guard. Did . . . did he stab the King?'

Swan-Marie stares at me. There's an edge of annoyance to her glower as she opens her beak, then snaps it shut again.

'Oh.' I bare my teeth. 'Right. You can't speak. My apologies. Can you tell me at least if he matched that description?'

The swan shakes her head decisively, and I'm surprised by the surge of relief I feel. Not Damien, then. Of *course* it wasn't Damien.

'Did you see him? Was he there when the King was killed? Or . . . or after?'

Swan-Marie contemplates my question carefully. Her eyes are pained. After a moment, she dips her head in a sinuous nod.

'He was?' I exclaim. 'How? Why? What was he doing there? He's the Dauphin's guard. Why would he be with the King?'

Marie spears me with a derisive look and shrugs her wings exaggeratedly. The meaning is clear: *How am I supposed to tell you?*

I rub my face, dragging down the cold skin under my eyes. So close and yet so far from answers. And my only source of information is stuck in the body of a swan.

Unless . . . I drum my fingers on my knees. Unless I can convince Papa to turn Marie back into a human, even for a moment. Long enough for her to tell us what she knows.

'Marie,' I begin, pressing my fingertips together and leaning my chin on them, 'I don't suppose you can momentarily set aside any grievances you might harbour towards me for, ah . . . identity theft, and help me find who did this?'

The swan hisses.

'Noted,' I say dryly. 'What if I told you the Dauphin might be in danger?'

This seems to get her interest. She stills, her head tilting ever so slightly.

'There's a chance that whoever did this might be targeting him.' I explain. Quickly, I tell her what I realized about Damien's involvement. 'So you see why this changes things.'

Her eyes are intent on me, no longer furious but still mistrustful.

'Naturally, I'll have to turn you back into a human.' *Temporarily*, I add in my thoughts. 'You help me, I help you, see?'

The scepticism in her expression does not lessen. I sigh.

'The man accused is my brother,' I admit. 'I don't like him very much, but I can't let him rot in prison.' There. Honesty. Mothers, I *hate* honesty. It feels like losing blood, like too much will leave me weak and defenceless.

Thankfully, it seems to work. Swan-Marie inclines her head, though the motion still looks reluctant. She drifts forward, then climbs on to the bank in front of me. Even as a swan, she has an untouchable, archaic sort of beauty –

powerful and refined, scraps of sunlight slipping off her feathers, water dripping from her underbelly.

Slowly, she extends a wing towards me.

I arch an eyebrow at her. 'Really?'

She huffs in annoyance.

'Fine. Very well.'

And so, on a dreary Aurélian midday in the grounds of Château Front-du-Lac, I, Odile Regnault, shake hands with a bird.

As I leave Marie behind and head towards the Théâtre, some of the jittery energy finally eases from my limbs.

Now that I'm moving, now that I'm *acting*, I can finally think straight. Even as a child, I could never sit still for very long – if I was not given a task by my father, I became destructive, prising apart theatre props, sticking my fingers into the jars of face paint and smearing colours over myself, the walls, the carpets. I loved being on stage, but I hated rehearsals – hated watching the older actors fumble through their lines, miss their cues, make foolish mistakes and giggle about them carelessly.

I would always correct them with annoyance, but that only ever seemed to amuse them: to be scolded by the little raven-haired girl with her sharp tongue who seemed to haunt the Théâtre. They would coo, pinch my cheeks, and I would gnash my teeth at their fingers in retaliation, hating that they would not take me seriously. Their affection meant nothing to me – all that mattered was Regnault's praise. It frustrated me that they could not see it, that they did not take their roles as seriously as I did. Did they not understand that they would face Regnault's ire if they failed? Did they not fear the thunderous rebuke of his eyes when they displeased him?

I was eleven years old when I first disappointed Regnault. He'd tasked me with picking the pockets of a nobleman who had been particularly cruel to one of the dancers the previous week, and I'd done so, tracking him through the streets of upper Verroux. He'd caught me midway through cutting his purse, seized my wrist and thrown me to the hard ground. My knees had split brutally, spilling gold all over the city cobbles. *Sorcière!* he'd cried after me, as I scurried away in a panic, carrying off a handful of his coins.

I received no proud smile, no kind words from my father that day. Instead, he looked down at me without expression, his gaze so dark and heavy I felt it like a physical blow. 'What did I tell you about bleeding?' he demanded. 'Now there will be rumours of a sorcier child running about the city. This could come back to you. To *us*.'

I stared at my feet, trying to keep my bottom lip from wobbling.

'Perhaps I was wrong, and you are not destined to free magic after all,' Regnault said softly, musingly, but with such venom that I could nearly see it oozing between his teeth. 'Perhaps I ought to take you back to the gutter where I found you.'

'No,' I gasped, tears in my eyes. 'No, Papa, please! Don't take me back.'

I grabbed the hem of his cloak, sobbing, begging. He seized my collar and hauled me off him emotionlessly. 'Enough of your weeping,' he said. 'I will give you one more chance, but I do not want to see such tears again. Show your pain, and it will be exploited.'

That was when Damien came running in.

Damien was only thirteen at the time, but he was tall and broad for his age. He'd never been much of an actor, but he handled much of the heavy stage décor and ropes used to change backdrops. 'Put her down,' he snarled at Regnault. 'Put her down right now.'

Regnault loosened his hold on me, enough that I could inhale a sharp breath. 'Ah,' said my father, 'and here is the other street rat. Aren't you both ungrateful? It is I who gave you shelter, who feeds you and provides a roof over your heads. Who promised you *greatness*.'

'We don't need you, or any of that!' my brother seethed. 'We can survive on our own, and we'll be better for it. Come on, Dilou. He's a monster.'

My heart sank. I looked between my brother and my father, my ribcage mercilessly tight.

'Odile,' Damien urged. 'Come *on*.'

Regnault chuckled. He lowered himself to one knee, sliding a knuckle under my chin so I had to look into the pitiless depths of his eyes. 'You can go,' he said, terrifyingly calm. 'If you think I'm a monster, as your brother says, then you may go. But remember that you and I share the same golden blood. *His* blood runs red. If I'm a monster, then what does that make you?'

The Théâtre's doors give a baritone hum as I push them open. During the day, the backstage hallways have a satiated sort of laziness, shadows sprawled languidly in corners and spiders ambling across the windowless walls. Laughter blossoms from inside a practice room as I pass, the troupe rehearsing rowdily, seemingly unaffected by last night's tragedy.

A surge of fondness fills me at the sound of their banter. I consider stepping in to greet them, but think better of it. I've never truly allowed myself to grow close to the troupe. Once I'd outgrown my childhood skittishness, I became friendly with them, but never too close, too familiar. Regnault always reminded me they could not be trusted. They might seem kind, but one look at the colour of my blood and they would turn on me as the doctors had on my mother, as the mob of villagers had on Regnault's family.

I keep walking until I reach Regnault's office. Somehow, the sight of the familiar door makes an inexplicable dread bubble up inside me. I pause momentarily to rehearse my words, turning each phrase over and carefully wiping any doubts from my expression. I clench and unclench my fists once. Then, I knock. 'Papa?'

The door opens with a *snap*, and it takes all my willpower not to flinch. Regnault is staring at me through the feathered slits of his owl mask, his brows slashed down in a surprised scowl.

'Odile? What are you doing here?' He looks me up and down, eyes narrowing. 'Why are you not in disguise?'

'Nothing has gone wrong!' I burst out immediately, scared he'll come to the wrong conclusion. 'Well, *something* has, but it has nothing to do with the plan.' I twine my hands together, pressing my thumbs against my knuckles to steady myself. 'May I come in?'

Regnault ushers me in quickly and closes the door behind me. 'Does this have to do with the King's death?' he asks. 'I already know. It's irrelevant to our goals, regardless.'

'So you've heard about Damien's arrest, then?' I say quickly. 'I think he's been framed.'

'Odile,' Regnault says flatly. 'What did I tell you about that traitor?'

'Yes, I know. But I think the Dauphin might be next, or at least someone is trying to isolate him, and . . .' I hesitate.

'And?' Regnault prompts, looking impatient.

'And Marie saw,' I say. 'Marie, as a swan – she saw the whole thing.'

His eyes darken. 'You've spoken to her?'

I give him a look. 'She's a bird.' That, at least, draws a spark of amusement from him. I forge onward. 'Which is inconvenient. If you could turn her back, only for a moment, or if you had some way for her to speak –'

I break off as Regnault chuckles in amusement. 'Odile, what are you saying?'

'I –'

He holds up his hand. 'I've heard enough. The answer is no. You are not to jeopardize the plan.'

'This is for the good of the plan,' I argue. 'Because if the Dauphin is killed . . .'

'Then protect the Dauphin. But do not lose sight of your goal, and do not *risk* it by getting involved in something that could cast suspicion on to you.'

Something inside me wilts. 'But Damien . . .'

'Odile,' my father says with slow exasperation, as though I am a particularly foolish child. 'You're not being sentimental, are you? After *everything*?'

I stare at my feet. I can't stand to face his disappointment. 'It's not like that.'

Regnault hums under his breath. His cool fingers brush along my cheek, and I wince when the sharp points of his nails dig into my skin. 'You know better than this.'

'Yes, Papa,' I say quietly, but it's more in surrender than agreement. Regnault nods, giving me a pitying smile, and lets go of my face.

I stare at him as he walks back to his desk, frustration sizzling inside me. I should never have mentioned Damien. Regnault never liked my brother – he only tolerated his presence because he could see how much Damien meant to me. Because we'd been inseparable.

I'm reminded again of the time I disappointed Regnault, of when Damien ran in to try to defend me. After, I'd been furious with my brother, humiliated by his interference. I'd fled from the room and climbed all the way to my favourite hiding spot: a round chamber tucked under the cupola of the Théâtre's auditorium, where the chandelier was sometimes hauled up to be dusted.

Damien found me promptly – he somehow always knew where I would go. As a peace offering, he brought me my favourite blanket, and a slightly stale brioche bun he'd bought that morning at the Verroux market. Once I was no longer hungry and somewhat less furious, he pulled me close. 'I'm sorry, Dilou. I only wanted to protect you.'

I nodded. At the time, I thought I would always forgive him.

'Will you stay?' I whispered.

He was quiet for a too-long, frightening moment. Then he sighed. 'For you. I'll stay for you.'

And that, perhaps, is why I can't simply forget about Damien, like Regnault demands. Why my conscience will not let me rest. Yes, Regnault is right. *This* Damien abandoned me, and I could easily let him rot, but I cannot forget the past. Because my brother was once all I had. Because our reunion reminded me how much I missed *that* Damien, the one before betrayals and mistakes. The one that knew my favourite snacks and hiding places and made me promises I thought he would keep.

The one I was convinced would never hurt me.

'Odile.' Regnault's voice jerks me from my thoughts. He pulls open a drawer. 'Come here. I have something for you.'

I venture forward cautiously, my cheek still smarting where his nails had pressed in. But whatever disappointment my father seems to have felt has thankfully abated, because he smiles at me and lifts something from the drawer. It's a golden button, shining and unassuming. He presses it into my fingers as I stare at him in confusion.

'Turn it over three times,' he says. 'Keep your fingers loose.'

I flip the button in my palm tensely. One, two, three. On the final turn, it *melts* – transforming briefly into liquid magic before lengthening to a flintlock pistol of pure, gleaming gold.

'A pistol?'

'Indeed. And every time it transforms, it becomes loaded, so you have no need to carry ammunition. You just need to turn it back into a button, then back again.'

'It's beautiful,' I whisper.

He smiles. 'There was some magic left from the goddess-gold, just enough for me to enchant this for you.' He taps it three times, and the pistol shrinks back into a button.

'I would like you to have something in case ... Well, I hope that this can be done without spilling blood. But if anything goes awry, you can do what needs to be done.'

'Thank you,' I say hoarsely. My father has never given me a gift before. It's a small thing, but it warms me, especially after his reprimand. Looking at the button gives me a sudden idea, and I focus my sorcery on it until the threads weaving the enchantment on it become visible. 'Does each one of these do something else?' I ask, eyeing the tangle of magic. This one is far simpler than the one on the pendant, each individual thread perfectly visible. My hand itches to touch them.

Regnault crosses his arms. 'Now is not the time for this.'

It's the same answer he always gives when I ask about magic. Before gifting me the pendant, Regnault had never allowed me to touch his enchanted items, much less understand how they were created. His office door was always firmly closed to me when he worked. The little I know, he taught me so I could identify goddess-gold. I used to become frustrated by his refusals to teach me, my desperation driving me to tears. It never worked before, so now I try a different strategy.

I pout playfully, sticking out my bottom lip. 'But you promised that if I succeeded, you would teach me all you know.'

'Once you have the Couronne, yes.'

I slump my shoulders, doing my best impression of a kicked puppy, as I used to do with him when I was a girl and was begging him to buy me pastries. 'Well, I sort of succeeded. Partially.'

That manages to break through his severe demeanour.

'Very well,' he says, chuckling, and a tiny part of me dances at the victory. 'Yes. Every thread is like a . . . a word. And together they form sentences.'

'Is that why you told me not to touch them?' I ask, thinking of when he handed me the pendant for the first time.

He inclines his head. 'When you touch a thread, your will becomes tied to it. Even a stray thought can change its meaning, or render it incoherent. Modify the wrong spell-thread, and the whole enchantment will unravel.' He takes the button out of my hand again, causing the threads to vanish. 'Best-case scenario, it transforms into something you did not intend. Worst-case scenario, the spell implodes. That could kill you, or leave you disfigured, or Morgane knows what else.'

'Oh,' I say faintly.

He hands the button back to me and squeezes my shoulder. 'Be patient, little owl. Once we have true magic back, I will show you how to weave spells like this yourself. Until then, no more questions. Yes?'

'Of course,' I say, though my thoughts are already churning with what I have learned. I can't do what he asks, not while Damien is involved.

If Regnault isn't going to give me the answers I seek, I'll simply have to find them another way.

SCENE X

Château.

I am accosted by the Dauphin the moment I step back into the Château.

'Marie!' His voice echoes through the high-ceilinged hall. I stare at him, part of me forgetting I am back in Marie's body after my brief time without the owl-face pendant. I realize I'm still holding the enchanted button from Regnault – I've elected to call the weapon Buttons – and quickly slip it into the pocket of my skirts.

Thankfully, the Dauphin doesn't seem to notice. He sprints up to me and snatches my hands, pulling me to a stop in front of one of the windows. He's wearing a damask jacket in mourning black, and it does no favours to his complexion. His breaths come short and urgent, and the beam of wan light cast by the window highlights the bags under his eyes.

'Where have you been?' he gasps. 'I have been looking for you everywhere.'

'I was in the gardens,' I say, feigning confusion.

He frowns. 'I looked in the gardens, but you weren't there.'

My heart gives a twitchy little thud. It seems I need to be more careful about any future detours. 'You must have missed me. It isn't hard, you know, in that maze.'

'You must bring guards with you next time,' the Dauphin says, looking harrowed. I open my mouth to protest; his clammy grip on me tightens. 'You cannot be alone out there, not after everything. It's too dangerous.'

I blink innocently. 'But why? They caught the killer, did they not?'

The Dauphin releases my hands to rub his arms, as though to dispel a chill. 'Y-yes,' he says, and the lie is so painfully obvious I nearly laugh.

'You don't sound very convinced, Monseigneur.'

'Aimé,' he says. 'Please, call me Aimé.'

'Aimé,' I prompt. 'Was he caught?'

'That's what everyone seems to think,' the Dauphin admits unsteadily, running his hands through his hair. 'But I'm not sure. The man they arrested . . . he's my personal guard. The one you met yesterday. I don't think he would . . . but what does it matter? No one will tell me anything. No one will even *listen* to me.'

He takes a shuddering breath, runs his hand through his hair again, and I can see him draw on a mask with the movement, collecting every distraught, misplaced piece of himself and slotting it back into place. When he meets my eyes again, he smiles crookedly.

'We ought to have been celebrating,' he says, then extends an arm. 'Walk with me, my darling intended?'

I smile genially and oblige, placing my hand on his arm with a flourish. The marble floor is polished to mirror smoothness, and our reflections accompany us as we stroll – wavering, distorted silhouettes. Against the Château's seemingly unconquerable shadows, we both look like phantoms.

'Are you doing all right?' the Dauphin asks suddenly. 'After last night. I dragged you into a horror. If I had known how bad it would be . . . and for my father to . . . and now he's dead.'

His voice shakes. I glance sideways at him, and realize I can make out the red mark of a handprint on his cheek, buried under the fine layer of powder coating his face. I don't understand it. How can he grieve a monster?

'I don't regret our engagement, if that's what you're asking,' I say. 'I'm exactly where I need to be.' I know I should follow up with something along the lines of *And how are you doing, the day after your father's murder?* because that is the exact sort of ridiculously sentimental thing Marie would know to say. But before I can muster up a convincing amount of concern, we are interrupted by the appearance of a maid at the end of the hallway. At the sight of her, the Dauphin's face brightens. He pats my hand. 'Do excuse me,' he says and walks briskly to meet her.

At his approach, the maid drops into a startled curtsy, talking with rapid excitement. She must be past my father's age, her black hair streaked with grey, what little I can see of her face etched with lines of exhaustion. I frown as she grips the Prince's hands tenderly, gazing at him with shining eyes. She seems far too old to be a lover, but truly, I wouldn't put any level of poor taste past the Dauphin of Auréal.

Finally, Prince and maid finish their hushed exchange, and the maid hurries off.

I give the Dauphin a questioning look as he returns to my side. He shakes his head, lips pressed together. 'Never mind that,' he says, strangely sheepish.

I don't comment – I have bigger fish to fry than the Prince's torrid affairs. I'm growing weary of trying to be delicate, tiptoeing around the subjects I truly want to discuss.

'Aimé, I've had a thought,' I say.

He glances at me, eyes nearly colourless in the rheumy light.

I lower my voice further, carefully keeping out of earshot of nearby guards. 'Has D– The man they arrested for murder, has he been questioned yet?'

The Dauphin looks away, swallows tightly. 'He – Yes. I tried to stop them, but my uncle said it was . . . necessary. No one would tell me how the . . . interrogation went. So I'm in the dark. Unsurprisingly.'

Oh, Mothers. 'Have you tried to speak to him yourself?'

He shakes his head. 'My uncle has forbidden it.'

'Are you not the King? Why would that stop you?'

His hands turn red where he wrings them. 'I disobeyed my father, and now he's dead. I'm afraid to . . . to do something like that again. It's probably better to let my uncle make the decisions.'

I feel the same frustration I did last night, when he let himself be dismissed from the entrance hall. How can he let his power be stripped from him so easily? 'The King was murdered, Aimé,' I say firmly. 'We hardly know how.

Or why. Do you really think it's wise to let yourself be kept in the dark?'

'What else am I supposed to do?'

'Start by speaking to the prisoner,' I say. 'I imagine he is more likely to talk to you than to anyone else. And think about who might stand to gain from King Honoré's death. And why.'

He gives me a strange look. 'You really have changed,' he says, and I suppress a wince.

'Is that . . . a good thing?'

He laughs. 'It's neither good nor bad. I simply miss when we were children, playing by the lake. Everything was so simple back then.' He taps his chin, then exhales heavily. 'I do not like this, Marie. I fear he will not want to speak to me.'

'I will go with you, if it helps.'

To my relief, he nods. 'With you . . . perhaps I can try. But I don't think it will go well. I don't think it will go well at all.'

Damien, the Dauphin tells me, is being kept in one of the cells beneath the guards' garrison for the duration of his interrogation. As we walk, thunder snarls in the distance, the sound muffled by a wadding of ragged clouds. Behind us trail two guardsmen in musketeer blues, silent and stoic, their sharp gazes sending discomfort crawling up and down my spine. I try to ignore them, focusing on the mission at hand, a task made difficult by the Dauphin's nervous silence.

The holding cells are located beneath the garrison building, in an unforgiving pit not unlike a cellar. The space is vengefully cold, the sharpness of it crawling into the roots of my teeth and making them chatter. It reminds me, horribly, of the weeks Damien and I spent in the Verroux slums.

There are only two cells, both hollow, echoing lockups strewn with filthy straw and caged by crooked bars. One of the guards lights a torch and holds it out, the flame highlighting old streaks of filth along the floor. There are splatters on the wall that look dreadfully like blood. The Dauphin flinches when he sees them.

'I shouldn't have brought you here,' he whispers.

'Nonsense,' I say. 'I want to be involved.'

He opens his mouth to respond, but in the same moment, the torchlight falls on the figure curled up on the floor of one of the cells. Despite everything, my heart seizes. I know that mess of hair, that broad back.

'Damien?' the Dauphin calls gently.

My brother is on his feet in an instant, eyes searching and wild, straw flying off the tattered remnants of his clothes. Bruises mottle his cheekbones and dried blood cakes the lobe of one ear, no doubt the result of the guards' *interrogations*. When his attention lands on the Dauphin, his shoulders slump.

'You should not be here.' His eyes dart from the Dauphin, to me, to the guards behind us. Aimé seems to understand his meaning, because he turns.

'Could . . . could you leave us?' he asks them.

They both hesitate. 'Monseigneur,' says the one on the right, a man with a curling black moustache, 'I do not think it's wise to leave you with this . . . this . . .' He seems to struggle for words, pointedly avoiding Damien's eyes.

I can guess why: one day ago, they were still comrades, brothers in arms. Now one of them has been accused of the worst sort of treason.

'You don't truly believe that, do you?' the Dauphin says softly. 'Please, just for a few minutes. He will not hurt me.'

The men do not move.

'Your future King has given you an *order*,' I say sharply, losing my patience. 'Why are you ignoring it?'

The men flinch. The one with the moustache gives us all a pained look, before turning and heading back up to the entrance, his companion at his heels. They leave the torch in a sconce by the stairwell, too far away to provide much illumination, but close enough to make everything look sharp-edged and unsettling.

'Good men, those two,' Damien says as soon as the guards are gone, looking to Aimé with flinty eyes. 'Loyal. Keep them close. Do not trust any of the others. Especially not the ones from noble families.'

The Dauphin frowns. 'What do you mean?'

'The Regent has at least half the garrison in his pocket,' Damien says. 'The nobles show more loyalty to the one who wears the crown and controls the coffers. It doesn't help that the Regent told them all you've been using the garrison budget to buy exotic wines.'

The Dauphin's eyes widen. 'But I never –'

'I know this,' Damien says, his voice feverish and unusually cruel. 'The more reasonable of the men do, too. But rumour is powerful, and you must admit you have never fought this reputation the courtiers put on you.'

'You know I couldn't.'

'Couldn't you?' Damien growls hoarsely, and I realize I'm witnessing the continuation of some long-standing argument.

The Dauphin sways delicately. In the torchlight, his eyes shine with tears. 'Let me help you,' he whispers, stepping up to the bars, reaching for my brother even as the other recoils. 'Please, Damien. Tell me what happened last night.'

'I will not let you get involved in this,' Damien says. 'I am a lost cause. Forget me, Aimé. Focus on keeping yourself – and the Crown – safe.'

'The C-Crown?' the Dauphin stammers. 'Surely you don't think my uncle is somehow responsible for this?'

'I don't know what to think!' Damien snaps. His gaze flashes to me like a sword strike, pinning me even as I back away, into the shadows. 'I don't know what to think,' he repeats, the words aimed in my direction this time.

There is a beat of silence, broken by a distant crash of thunder. I try not to look too closely at the bloodstains on my brother's shirt. Try to ignore the way my chest twists in pain, seeing him like this. Try to tell myself there's nothing more I can do for him right now without arousing suspicion. I know I have to try to free him. But for some reason, I can't bring myself to tell him that. Perhaps it's because a cruel part of me wants to watch him squirm, in revenge for abandoning me five years ago. Or perhaps it's because, even now, I refuse to let Damien win – to give him proof that I'm not as heartless as I want to be. As I *should* be.

Show your pain, and it will be exploited.

In the end, in my frustration, all I can manage is a cold sneer.

Damien looks away, jaw clenching in fury. To the Dauphin, he says, with pointed force, 'Aimé, listen. Whatever was done to King Honoré . . . it was *monstrous*. Something no ordinary human would be capable of.'

'But they said he . . . he was stabbed,' the Dauphin stammers. 'That *you* stabbed him.'

'Stabbed him?' A grating laugh shakes Damien's frame, a sound immediately followed by a groan. He doubles over, clutching his ribs, and shakes his head ruefully. 'I didn't see what happened. I didn't even know it was the King I was following – just mysterious shadows in the grounds. By the time I found him and his company . . . everyone was dead. Why they were out there, so late at night, I do not know. Yes, there was a knife thrown on the ground nearby, and I picked it up, foolishly. That was the weapon they found me with. But it was not the weapon that did the killing. You only had to look at the body to know that –'

He breaks off as a clamour reaches us from the stairs. A moment later, a sapphire-clad figure descends into the prison like a storm cloud, trailed by Aimé's guards.

'What are you doing down here?' Anne de Malezieu screeches. The Step-Queen's face is white with fury, one hand clenched, the other lifting her silk skirts high off the ground in disgust. With surprising force, she snatches the Dauphin's wrists and drags him away from the cell, stepping between him and Damien.

'Why are you speaking to this . . . this *monster*? Was this *her* idea?' She jerks her head in my direction. Before Aimé can open his mouth to respond, she begins to usher him towards the stairs. 'Out,' she demands. 'Out!'

I look over my shoulder, trying to catch a final glimpse

of my brother, but he has retreated into the depths of his cell. Sighing, I gather up my skirts and follow the Dauphin up into the rainy daylight.

The Step-Queen escorts the Dauphin all the way back to the palace. It has begun to rain in earnest, a slate-grey torrent that soaks us all in an instant, turning the ground slick and treacherous. We trail it into the Château hall, dripping rainwater on to the marble flooring. Only then does the Step-Queen release Aimé's wrist, wringing water from her soggy raven ringlets.

'What were you thinking?' she demands. 'Going down to see a murderer? It is fortunate one of the garrison guards had the sense to alert me. *Your* guards I will have to see about demoting, Aimé. They should have stopped you . . .'

The Dauphin opens his mouth to protest, but cannot seem to make a sound.

'And you!' The Step-Queen turns on me, pointing. 'Those doe eyes might be fooling the rest of the palace, but they do not fool me. I warned the late King you were nothing but trouble! He always said I was exaggerating, but here you are, and dragging my *son* into this, no less.'

'Stepmother, please!' The Dauphin takes her hand. '*I* wanted to do this. *I* dragged *Marie* into it.'

'I don't believe that. You're not capable of such scheming.'

'Maman,' Aimé says again, pleading.

She looks at him at last, and some of the tension leaves her body. 'Oh, my foolish son,' she says quietly, lifting her hand to touch his cheek. 'I only want to protect you. Especially now that your father is gone.'

'I know,' he says.

'Then do no more of this.'

'But . . .' The Dauphin stares at his feet like a chastened child. 'No one is telling me anything.'

The Step-Queen sighs softly. 'I will tell you what you need to know, I promise. But you must stay within my sights, understood? Only I can keep you safe. No one else. Not your uncle, not the guards, and certainly not this *girl*.'

At her last words, the Dauphin looks up sharply, a defensive stubbornness to his jaw. 'Marie and I are betrothed now. Please, I beg you, let this grudge go.'

The Step-Queen's response to the Dauphin's plea is a rueful laugh. 'For you, Aimé, for now, I will,' she says. 'But in time, I know you will come to admit I was right.' She pulls the Prince into her arms, stroking his hair, but she is looking at me, red-painted lips curling into something cunningly cruel.

A chill creeps down my spine. I look away, reaching for Buttons, seeking reassurance in the enchanted weapon's weight against my palm. I can feel that strange web of intrigue tightening around me, as though I am a fly caught in some great spider's creation. Regent, Step-Queen, Dauphin, Damien, a dead King and his crown – too many threads, too many variables, every one a danger to my mission. Speaking to my brother has only left me feeling hopelessly tangled, questions and questions and *questions* wrapping mercilessly around me.

And there is only one person I can think of who would be able to answer them.

But to speak to her, I have to defy my father.

SCENE XI

The Dauphine's Apartments. Midnight.

I wait until the Château is well and truly asleep before sneaking out of the palace.

It's surprisingly easy – the Dauphine's apartments have a balcony overlooking the lake, close enough to the ground that, with a bit of manoeuvring and a considerable amount of luck, I'm able to lower myself off it and fall soundlessly to the earth. My landing is cushioned by damp leaves, ivy clinging along the Château wall brushing against my back. I've taken off the owl-face pendant – right now, I need my own body, my own muscle memory.

Once again, I find myself grateful for my childhood at the Théâtre. Being nimble – and eagerly reckless – meant I had little to constrain me from performing dangerous leaps and tricks on stage; and when I was not performing, I was clambering the backstage scaffolding with Damien. Now, that sure-footedness serves me well as I move quietly through the clutches of night.

Adrenaline hums through me, a pleasant prickling in my veins. The gravel walkway splashes mutedly beneath my feet, the air still stained with the scents of the earlier thunderstorm – brisk rain and sodden leaves, rotting things soaked to the bone. The Château looms over me, water resting on its walls like sweat on a soldier's skin, and around me the gardens have begun to fill with fog.

I make my way through the maze of iron thorns, ducking down when I spot the silhouettes of patrolling guards. Once they are out of sight, I make my slow way around the lake.

I find the swans slumbering near an old dock. Well, *dock* is a generous word – it's more a slab of mouldering wood jutting crookedly over the water, pierced by bulrushes and strangled by duckweed. I cross it carefully, the wood bobbing beneath my feet, sending hypnotic ripples slipping across the water. A few of the swans raise their heads at my approach, eyeing me in confusion before moving slowly away.

'Good evening, swans,' I say, putting my hands on my hips. 'Which one of you is Marie d'Odette?'

For a moment, there is no response, only the murmur of cold wind over colder waters. Then, one of the furthest swans raises its head, tilting it towards me. The expression in its eyes is somewhere between haughty, suspicious and vaguely murderous.

'There you are,' I say. 'I've come to keep my side of the bargain.'

Swan-Marie approaches me with hesitance, gliding smoothly through the water. I sit at the end of the dock and cross my legs, pulling the owl-face pendant from my pocket.

'All right,' I say to it. 'Here goes nothing.'

Staring at the glinting pendant in my hand, my stomach begins to churn nervously. Not only am I breaking my promise to my father, but I'm going against his teachings, ignoring his warnings about the consequences of undoing spells. This could go very, *very* wrong.

And yet ... hasn't Regnault also told me magic is my birthright? Hasn't he taught me to be clever and resourceful? Surely I can figure this out.

All I need to do is find the right thread.

There's a muted splash, pulling me from my thoughts. I look up to see Swan-Marie staring at me intently, her breast nearly touching the dock. To say she looks sceptical would be an understatement.

I quickly wipe any uncertainty from my face. 'I know what I'm doing.'

She makes a noise that sounds almost like a snort.

Slowly, I focus on the goddess-gold, finding the little ball of magic stored within and tugging it to the surface. The spell appears around the pendant in a tangle of a thousand threads, golden and shimmering like spidersilk at sunset.

Something inside me quivers at the sight. This spell is nothing like the one on Buttons – that one was far less intimidating, every thread clear and legible. This is more of a cobweb, an unforgiving knot of criss-crossing lines.

'See this spell?' I say to Swan-Marie, because talking distracts me from the unnerved somersaults of my stomach. 'My father wove it. Each thread means something else. By pulling the right one, I can undo the curse he placed upon you. So remember whose mercy you're at,' I add, because I can't help myself. 'If I'm feeling cross, my fingers might slip. Instead of a human, you might wind up turned into something horrible, like a toad.'

Steeling myself, I hover my fingers over one of the furthermost threads. It glows brighter, and the taste of magic coats my tongue. My mind fills with a thought: not quite an image, not quite a word, but a loose suggestion, a concept. *Borrowing*. Like a coin passing from one hand to another, meant to be repaid. I pull away, reach for another. *Replacement*. A guardsman takes the place of his comrade as he finishes his shift. *Fledged*. Feathers sprouting over delicate skin. The rush of air over wings. It intersects with a thread that rings of *noblewoman*, makes me feel the weight of invisible skirts around my legs.

Confusion swamps me, my heart beating frantically. Could it be one of these? But what if I'm wrong? *When you touch a thread, your will becomes tied to it*, Regnault had said. *Even a stray thought can change its meaning, or render it incoherent.*

So how do I make sure that doesn't happen? How do I ensure I don't *accidentally* turn Marie into a toad . . . or worse?

I rub my temples, trying to keep any frustration I feel off my face. Then I go over the threads again. And again. And once more, my impatience growing, my composure fraying. I should have found it by now. Why can't I find it? The right thread is here somewhere, yet none of them *feel* right, and there are so *many* –

A flash of white in my periphery alerts me to Swan-Marie, stretching her wings to get my attention. There's an enquiring look in her eyes. She inclines her head towards the threads and the pendant in my hand. I'm hit with a sudden memory, of a much younger Marie sitting cross-legged on the bank of the lake, trying to teach me how to solve her wooden puzzle toy.

'No,' I snap. 'This is sorcery, not some paltry riddle.'

She sighs.

'I know what I'm doing,' I repeat.

She shuffles her wings in irritation.

And, because the sunrise is drawing closer, because I am already tired of sitting here staring at magic strings, I give in. 'Fine. But if anything goes wrong, you'll only have yourself to blame.'

I pass my hand over the threads again, describing each one. I know it's dangerous to make Marie aware of the magic binding her, but it's not as though she can change the spell on her own. And I need the information she possesses. For the Couronne's sake, and my brother's.

'This *has* to be it,' I say at last, pointing to *noblewoman*. But when I reach for it, Marie extends her neck and bites me.

I yelp, dropping my hand. 'What was that for?'

She glowers, then eyes another thread, one passing just beneath the intersection of *noblewoman* and *songbird*. I hadn't paid it any heed before: it's the shortest of the threads, so fine it's nearly invisible. My attention had skipped over it previously, but now, I reach for it. This one is perhaps the most abstract of the spell-threads so far: the passage of day into night, the cracking of a butterfly's chrysalis after a long slumber.

Metamorphosis. This is the one – there's a rightness to it I hadn't felt with any of the others. I should be relieved, but instead, my cheeks grow hot with anger. Somehow,

Marie saw what I could not. How is it that a red-blooded, pampered princess – trapped in the body of a swan, no less! – found what I was looking for, while I did not even notice it?

But of course. Of *course*. Is this not just typical Marie d'Odette? Even now, she must remind me how perfect she is, how terribly inferior I am. I might as well be thirteen again, cowering in a dusty stable as Marie abandons me to my fate, the feeling of her hands on my throat still lingering like a burn.

Well, there is one thing I can do that she can't.

Morgane, I think, *wherever you are, do me a favour and don't let this end in disaster.*

I focus on the thread once more. This time, I hold the images it forms in my thoughts, let them wash over me. Then, I imagine them unravelling. Dawn returns to night, butterfly to chrysalis, swan to girl. A reversal, an undoing.

My fingers tingle, my body hums. I squeeze my eyes tighter, focusing fiercely. A trickle of warmth pulses from the thread into my body. Then another. Then a third, this time more painful. I gasp – it feels almost as if my very blood is aflame. It is painful, yes, but also pleasant somehow. Like the burn of a long-unused muscle.

I open my eyes to see the thread shimmering in the moonlight, flickering like a distant star. For that brief instant, excitement surges through me. Is it working? Could it truly be this simple?

Then the flickering stops. The thread returns to its usual steady glow. Before me, Marie remains unchanged, still watching me through the dark eyes of a swan.

My stomach drops. It didn't work I'm doing something wrong. But what?

I close my eyes again, this time trying to think of one thing and one thing only: Marie as she was before her transformation, with pearls in her hair and her sea-blue gown. She leans over the railing of a balcony, eyes moon-pale and bright with wonder. Enthralled. Ethereal. As though she were standing on a precipice, longing to take flight.

The spell-thread flares bright as sunlight, sending a pulse of pain through my arm.

Then it explodes.

SCENE XII

The Lake. Minutes from dawn.

When I wake, there's a ghost wrapping cold fingers around my throat.

I gasp, my vision fogged, and attempt to push the creature off, only to feel its firm, slender fingers tighten around my trachea in warning. The ground bobs up and down beneath my back. The world smells of rot, of old wood and older waters.

'Easy, sorcière,' says the ghost. Its voice is warm and husky, shaking almost imperceptibly. My palm is burning at my side, sending pangs of pain through my body. I flex my hand and memories come suddenly flooding back to me.

The pendant. The swan. The spell.

And above me, Marie d'Odette d'Auvigny, not a ghost at all but a girl once more. She watches me carefully, eyes glinting like fish scales. In the darkness, the planes of her face are angular, almost aquiline, but her eyes remain soft, their heavy lashes dipped in moonlight. One of her hands rests on my throat, squeezing, but her grip is hesitant. I bare my teeth at her, and she flinches.

'Don't move.'

I laugh. 'Are you really trying to threaten me? I've been in far worse predicaments than this.'

I try to raise my head, and Marie allows me enough motion for me to realize that she is straddling me, her lithe knees pressed into the jut of my hips, left hand on my throat. The close proximity makes my heart give a funny little flutter, my nerve endings sparking where our bodies make contact. 'In fact,' I say, shimmying a little just to taunt her, 'this is rather pleasant.'

She flushes. 'Enough.'

'Oh dear, did I make the princess uncomfortable?' I clench my hands, preparing to shove her off, and freeze.

The owl-face pendant is no longer in my grip. It's *gone*.

I try to keep the panic from my features and fail.

Marie, unfortunately, notices. 'Looking for something?' She holds her hand out of my reach, and I recognize the shine of the owl-face pendant's chain. My heart skips a beat, but I force myself to remain still.

'Give it back.'

Marie hides the pendant behind her back. 'First, I need you to tell me why you cursed me. And . . . and what you were doing in the palace.'

'Give me a single good reason I should do that,' I reply sweetly.

'If you don't, I'll destroy it,' Marie says. 'And I'll return to the Château and tell everyone what you've done. You'll be arrested. Hanged for treason.'

'Attempted grand larceny, actually.' As I talk, I slowly inch my hand towards my pocket. Towards Buttons. 'And I don't think you'll do that.' It's in the uncertainty of her words, the careful way she holds me down, as though she is worried she might hurt me. It's in the uneven way her chest swells with every breath, straining against her bodice, too quick and stuttering with adrenaline. It's in the fact that she's still here, when she could have run while I was unconscious. 'If I may, Princess, I'd venture a guess that you're enjoying this.'

'I'm not,' she snaps. 'And stop calling me that.'

I roll my eyes. 'Whatever you say, *Princess*.'

I palm Buttons from my pocket and turn it over. Marie notices the metallic flash just as I swing the butt of the pistol at her head. Her reflexes are surprisingly fast for a spoiled noble. She dodges easily, but the movement forces her to ease her grip on my throat, and it's all I need to kick her off and reach for the pendant.

My hand closes around her fist as she recoils. With unexpected strength, she wrenches me back and we grapple for a moment, equally matched.

'Give it to me,' I seethe, trying to pull her fingers open. 'That pendant lets me turn into you. Which means that even if you're not a swan, part of you is still bound to the spell inside it. I'm not certain what destroying it would do to you, but I doubt it would be pleasant. You must give it back.'

'I can't do that,' she pants, wispy curls falling in front of her eyes, the silk of her skirts brushing against my legs. 'I can't let you hurt anyone.'

'Who said I'm going to hurt anyone?'

'In case you have already forgotten, you had me turned into a *swan!*' She pulls her hand from my grip and leaps back, stumbling to her feet as if to run. But I'm faster – I bring Buttons up, pointing the pistol at her and cocking it.

She freezes.

'If you don't return it to me, I'll shoot.'

'You wouldn't do that,' she says reasonably. 'If you were going to kill me, you would have done it by the Théâtre.'

'You're right. I won't *kill* you,' I say. 'But no one said anything about maiming.'

Her eyes roam over me with careful intensity. I grin wider. It's not a lie – if I have to hurt her to get what I want, I won't hesitate. She must see it in my eyes, because she sighs and tosses the pendant back to me. I catch it, tucking it away swiftly. Fog churns around us restively, the bulrushes clattering and hissing. I must have been unconscious longer than I thought, because the air has taken on the taut, unsettled quality of dawn about to break.

'You know,' Marie says, cutting through the silence, 'I always knew there was something off about you. Different, even when we were girls. It was why I wanted to be friends with you, despite everything. I thought you were like me.'

'You and I are *nothing* alike,' I sneer.

She blinks, looking genuinely hurt. 'I trusted you.'

'Your first mistake.'

I expect her to grow more furious, but she only looks sorrowful, her hands flexing at her sides. She glances over her shoulder, towards the Château, and I wonder if she's considering running back to the palace anyway.

'If you try to flee, I'll turn you back into a swan,' I say.

'Are you certain you know how to do that?' She says it matter-of-factly, without spite, yet the pricking of shame inside me intensifies, reminding me that I couldn't have done any of this if Marie hadn't noticed the spell-thread.

I run a cold hand over my face, pushing back my bangs. 'Listen, Prin– Marie. Whatever you may think, I *did* keep my side of the bargain. So at least hear me out.'

She grips her elbows with opposite hands, considering with an innocent sort of steadiness. Hers are the eyes of a doe encountered in the woods, grappling between intrepid curiosity and the instinct to flee.

I press my tongue against my teeth and reluctantly lower Buttons, shrinking the pistol back into its original form and tucking it into my pocket. Only once it is gone do Marie's shoulders relax, her body falling out of its defensive tightness.

I beam. 'Excellent. Now that we've gotten past all –' I wave my hand vaguely – '*that*, I need to know what you saw last night.'

Her eyes darken suspiciously. 'And what . . . what will you do with that information?'

'It's like I told you yesterday. I'm trying to protect the Dauphin.'

'Because he's useful to whatever this plan of yours is.'

'Yes,' I say. 'And because as far as anyone in Verroux is concerned, you, Marie d'Odette, are currently betrothed to him.'

She starts. 'What?'

'See?' I grin. 'Isn't that what you wanted? I promise I'm not going to ruin your life. Or your reputation. So you can relax, Princess. Enjoy your time by the lake. Meanwhile, I'll deal with the horrid noblesse and this whole regicide business. And, ideally, free my brother from prison. So please. Tell me what you saw.'

'I don't suppose I have a choice, do I?' Marie says, inclining her head to where I hid the pendant. 'You control my fate.'

'I promise, this is all mutually beneficial.'

She smiles sadly. 'Oh, Odile. I don't think you quite understand what it is you are getting yourself into.'

The quiet words, smothered in dread, fall heavily over me. It takes all my willpower to keep my expression even and unaffected. How is it that despite my obvious advantage, I somehow always feel like she has the upper hand?

'Then did you see who did it?' I demand. 'Enough of the suspense.'

She is quiet for a moment. Then, heavily, she says, 'What happened to King Honoré, it is . . . beyond horrifying. I hesitate even to remember it at all.'

'Who was it?'

She shakes her head. 'You're asking the wrong questions, sorcière.'

Frustration turns my words into a growl. 'What do you mean?'

'Not *who*,' says Marie d'Odette, eyes dark. 'But *what*.'

A shiver runs up my spine. I draw back, assessing Marie's expression, looking for the flicker of a lie or jest in those earnest silver irises. I find none. 'What . . . what did you see?'

Behind Marie, the sky lightens, the first glow of day cowering behind the trees, as though even the sun is frightened by her revelation. 'Some sort of . . . creature.' She presses her lips together, her eyes far away. 'I hardly saw it, it was so fast. It was so late into the night, and dark, horribly dark. But I know it was a ghoulish thing.

Tall as a horse, with grey skin that looked nearly like stone. Mothers, it's all a blur. And all I could do was *watch*.' She shudders. 'One moment I was watching the King and his guards, riding through the night, the next they were lying on the ground, blood gushing from their bodies, and that . . . that *creature* ripping into them.'

I suck in a breath, my mind spinning as it conjures images of bloodied teeth and screaming men, a lakeside slick with blood and offal.

'Is that all?' I prompt.

Marie shakes her head. 'No. I remember . . .' She frowns. 'The guards were dead in an instant. But the King . . . he fought. And he managed to wound it. But . . . but its blood – it wasn't red.' She meets my eyes with fierce intensity. 'It was gold.'

My breath hitches. Marie watches me knowingly, her expression grave. I open my mouth, formulating my next question, hoping to prompt her to dig through her memories. Did she see the creature's eyes? Where was the King going? When did Damien arrive?

But in the same moment, the first ray of dawn stumbles through the trees, ripping itself apart on the needles of pines. It falls on Marie first, a scrap of rusty light, bleeding bronze over her silvered curls.

Suddenly, her face twists. Her eyes go wide, her mouth parting in a gasp of surprise. Before I can react, she leaps to her feet. It happens in the blink of an eye, so fast it is almost beautiful, in the way of a comet streaking across the sky.

Glowing white feathers erupt across her body. They burst from her cheeks and brow, spread down her limbs, spring from her hands and lengthen and lengthen until she spreads magnificent wings. The light flares until it is blinding, forcing me to put up a hand over my eyes.

I hear her voice once more, shaky and resigned. 'You lied to me.'

And then I am standing before a swan, with a pale beak and paler feathers, a look of betrayal in her pitch-black eyes.

I stare at Swan-Marie, barely concealing my shock. *This certainly wasn't supposed to happen. I must not have picked the right thread after all – or perhaps my jumble of thoughts affected the spell when I was modifying it. But I can't let Marie know that, can't let her see that I'm just as confused as she is.*

So, instead, I simply give the Swan Princess a smirk. 'Of course I did.'

SCENE XIII

The Dauphine's Apartments. Dawn breaks.

Climbing back up to a window is certainly less simple than jumping out of it, and by the time I crawl back to my chambers I'm breathless, my fingertips scraped where I clung to the rough stone of the Château walls. Dawn spills in after me in a wash of crimson light, turning my chambers the red of a ruby's bowels.

Exhausted, I put the owl-face pendant back on and ring for breakfast, collapsing face down on the bed.

Golden blood. The King was killed by a monster, and it has golden blood. Which means that there must be a sorcier involved in all of this. Either they conjured the beast, or they *are* the beast – I don't know enough about magic to tell, and not for the first time, I find myself frustrated by my father's secrecy, his adamant refusal to teach me anything about my powers.

Still, the fact remains: if there is a sorcier involved, then they could still be in the Château. And if Damien could see through my disguise, then a sorcier will be able to do so easily.

My mission could be in danger.

I want to sleep, but there's no time for rest. I need to know more, to move faster. What I have done isn't enough. It won't be enough until I know the truth.

Which is why my next act, after scarfing down my breakfast, is marching all the way to the Dauphin's apartments and barging in unceremoniously.

'Aimé, we need to ta– Oh.'

I freeze, startled by the sight before me. The Dauphin's chambers, much like the Prince himself, seem to be rebelling against the sombre gravitas of the rest of the Château. Here, bright tapestries cover dark walls, gilt chairs upholstered in pastel-blue silks stand amid plush floral carpets. A painting of two turtle doves hangs over the mantlepiece, the dainty birds ruffling their feathers against a cerulean sky.

In the middle of the room stands the Dauphin, wearing a black-and-gold damask jacket, teacup in hand.

And he is not alone.

The Step-Queen looks up, her lips parting in a surprised, viciously red O. She doesn't move from where she stands, midway through pouring a thin stream of sickly-looking yellow liquid into the Dauphin's teacup. 'My, it seems someone has forgotten all their manners,' she drawls.

'Apologies,' I say sweetly. 'I was so consumed by lust for my betrothed that I forgot to knock.'

The Step-Queen scowls and rights the vial, corking it and tucking it into the mourning-black folds of her gown. She watches me as she does so, as if daring me to say anything, to challenge her, but I only glower back. A smouldering quiet spreads between us.

The Dauphin groans. 'Enough of this,' he says. 'There is truly no reason for such animosity.' He downs the tea in one gulp, grimaces, then sets the empty cup aside. 'What is it, Marie?'

'Might we speak alone?' I meet his eyes meaningfully.

To my relief, he nods, then looks to the Step-Queen. 'Stepmother, if you don't mind.'

The Step-Queen shakes her head. 'Aimé, I do not think that is wise, in your current condition. Especially not after yesterday's . . . escapade.' She crosses her thin arms, inclining her head at me. 'Speak, girl. What you say to the Dauphin you should be able to say to me as well.'

The Dauphin opens his mouth, closes it again. A flash of frustration passes over his face. 'Stepmother, please,' he says. 'Were you not just saying you need to attend to Pierre?' I recognize the name of the Step-Queen's young son. 'Besides, Marie and I need to discuss the wedding, and the duties she will soon have as Queen.' He takes her hand, widening his eyes until they are almost comically pleading. 'Please. Uncle is bad enough, treating me like I need to be confined to my room lest I do something foolish. I beg you, at least, to trust me.'

To my shock, his piteous, puppyish expression seems to have its desired effect. The Step-Queen's face softens – a feat I thought impossible – and she steps away. 'You are too trusting, my son,' she says heavily. 'Be cautious of her words. And come see me when you are done.'

With that, she strides from the room.

As soon as she is gone, the Dauphin sheds his pleading expression and groans. 'My apologies. She can be overbearing sometimes.' He eyes the empty teacup with distaste. 'Mothers, but she makes me feel like a half-witted child.'

'You seem to play the role quite well,' I say before I can stop myself.

The Dauphin makes a choking noise. 'Marie!'

I throw up my hands. 'I meant it as a compliment! You were very convincing.'

He pounds his chest, laughing. 'You really *have* changed.'

'I was rather dull, wasn't I?' I can imagine the real Marie's unimpressed stare in my mind's eye. 'But you've changed, too. You've become so . . .' I reach for a polite word.

'Useless? Pathetic?' He smiles wryly. 'It's what everyone thinks.'

I don't admit those are the precise words I was thinking of. 'Well . . .'

'Trust me, I know. That little act of mine unfortunately works only on my stepmother. Everyone else thinks I'm too sentimental, too emotional, to do what must be done. My father made no secret of how disappointed he was in me. My uncle apparently thinks I'm unfit for the throne.' He sets the teacup aside and sprawls out on the bed, putting his arm over his eyes. 'And now my best friend, my *only* friend, is in prison, while I can do nothing but *wither* away.'

For the first time since entering the room, I notice the empty wine bottle on his nightstand, the crossbow he was gifted the eve of the ball shoved into one corner. There's a crack running its length, as though it was thrown in anger. I almost feel a stab of pity, almost, until Regnault's voice rasps through my mind: *He is your enemy. His grandfather is the reason there are hardly any sorciers left. Do not lose sight of why you are here.*

He's right, of course – I force my thoughts back to the task at hand. 'Speaking of Damien,' I say, 'I keep thinking about what he told us yesterday.'

As soon as I utter my brother's name, Aimé sits up again. 'I do too. None of it makes sense.'

'It doesn't,' I agree. 'How could one man kill not only the King, but the two guards riding with him?'

'Precisely!' the Dauphin exclaims. 'I tried to say that, but no one is listening to me!'

'Have you thought about why that may be?'

'Of course,' he says sullenly. 'They're hiding something from me.'

'I think so too.' I tap my fingers on the table, carefully formulating my next words. 'And I have a suspicion it has to do with the cause of death. The *real* cause of death, not the stabbing Damien was blamed for.'

'My uncle has proclaimed to all that he was present when the royal surgeon inspected my father's body,' the Dauphin says. 'He insists the wounds were clearly from a knife.'

Suspicion prickles at me. First Damien's warning about the Regent's corrupt guards, and now this?

'I'm assuming you have not seen the body yourself.'

'No,' the Dauphin admits tightly. 'It is well guarded, and frankly I . . . I have not dared.'

Well, that will not do. If what Marie told me is true, the King's body is likely covered in scratches from the monster. But I can't simply reveal that to the Dauphin without raising suspicion. He needs to see it himself – only then will he have proof that Damien is innocent, proof he can confront the Regent with. In the meantime, I can search the body for any clues as to the beast's sorcerous origins.

'Where is the body being kept?' I ask.

'In the chapel. No one is allowed in but the priestesses – they are preparing it for the funeral.'

I move for the door. 'Then we must go see it now.'

'No, we can't!' He grabs my wrist, his eyes imploring. 'You saw how my stepmother reacted yesterday. I cannot go against her again. And Mothers forbid my uncle finds out, he might simply have me locked in my room for good. No, it is not worth it.'

'So you would rather sit in your rooms and let yourself be *lied* to?' I burst, unable to hold myself back any longer. 'Your father is dead and your favourite guard is imprisoned. Your uncle is leeching power from you. And you're really going to content yourself with this – this *withering*?'

The Dauphin laughs hollowly. 'The universe seldom leaves me any choice,' he says, uncorking the near-empty bottle of wine and pouring the remaining few drops on to his tongue. He lowers the bottle and gives me a dispassionate look. 'You do not understand, Marie. Every time I have *ever* tried to take a matter into my own hands, it has been torn from me ruthlessly.'

'Then perhaps you weren't holding on tight enough,' I say.

He smiles wanly. 'You sound like Damien.'

Now *that* is an insult I will not tolerate. 'Would Damien tell you to break into a chapel to look at a corpse? I think not. Now stop moping and get up.'

*

Unfortunately, it does not take long for the Dauphin's suspicions to be confirmed, as we are stopped at the chapel doors by two guards.

'No one is permitted to enter at this time,' says the guard on the left, an auburn-haired man built like a mountain.

The Dauphin's shoulders slump in immediate resignation. 'I told you this would happen.'

'This is nonsense,' I declare, whirling on the guards. 'On whose orders?'

'The Regent's. He believes the Prince is too fragile to see the King's body. He fears it may turn the Dauphin hysterical.'

'I am *not* hysterical,' the Dauphin mumbles.

I huff and pull him aside. 'You need to command them. They can't refuse a direct order.'

'What's the point?' he says. 'My uncle is probably right about me.'

I cross my arms. 'Power is claimed, not given, Aimé. You did not take it, so your uncle did. Now you must wrest it back.'

'But how . . .' Aimé's brows draw together. 'How do I get anyone to listen to me?'

I shrug. 'Well, when diplomacy doesn't work, you can't go wrong with some good old-fashioned threatening.'

'Threatening?'

'Try it. Thank me later.'

The Dauphin sighs in resignation. Then he takes a shaky breath and squares his shoulders, lifting his chin. 'This feels ridiculous,' he mutters, then approaches the guards once more.

'Stand aside. I would like to see my father's body.'

The guards look at each other. 'By the Regent's orders –' the one on the left begins, but the Dauphin interrupts him with a surprising amount of passion.

'I am the *Dauphin*,' he proclaims. 'Heir to the throne, soon-to-be-crowned King of Auréal. You will let me pass.'

'Or be punished for insubordination,' I whisper.

'Or be punished for insubordination,' he echoes unconvincingly.

'It will be painful,' I add.

The Dauphin gives me a flat look.

Unfortunately, the threats fall on deaf ears. The guard sets his jaw. 'I'm sorry, Monseigneur,' he says to the Dauphin. 'But you are not yet King. The Regent was very firm in his orders.'

The Dauphin wilts visibly. He looks away, tugging at his lace cuffs, then sighs. 'Very well,' he says. 'I will not force discomfort on you. You are both only trying to follow orders.'

I glance at him, startled by the change in demeanour.

He turns away, then seems to remember something. 'Your name is Thomas, is it not?' he says to the larger guard. 'Your father was the old Captain of the Guard. Recently retired.'

The man's brows shoot up. 'How did you know?'

'You look alike,' the Dauphin says. 'He taught me to shoot, you know, your father – I miss that man dearly. I would trust him with my life.' He offers the man a smile and begins to walk away.

The guard's eyes flicker with sudden conflict. Then he steps forward. 'Wait.'

The Dauphin pauses, hope lighting his eyes.

Thomas and his companion exchange looks, then Thomas sighs. 'I can give you five minutes,' he says. 'But that is all.'

Thomas opens one of the chapel's double doors for us, ushering us through. Inside, the white of the chapel is overcast, nearly grey. It has begun to rain outside, threadbare raindrops casting themselves upon the narrow windows.

Once the door is closed, I turn to the Dauphin with a grin. 'Impressive. I did not think you had that in you.'

He looks perplexed. 'Had what in me?'

'Manipulation,' I say, wiggling my fingers. 'How did you know that bringing up his father would make him feel guilty?'

'Oh.' The Dauphin's brows dip. 'That was not my intention. I simply wanted to know if I was right about Thomas's identity. I try to remember the names of all the men of the guard. The Château staff, too.' He chuckles ruefully. 'Sometimes, they're the only people that will really listen to me. I try to pay the favour back when I can.'

Ugh. I could shudder at the *nobility* of it. No wonder he gets on with my brother so well.

I make a noncommittal sound in the back of my throat and turn my attention to the chapel. As the rain intensifies, the shadows within begin to twitch and writhe across the white flooring, making the looming Mothers seem to grimace. Someone has left a section of the arched windows cracked open, and water leaks along the wall, dripping monotonously into a slick pool. The high-ceilinged chamber still smells of incense, but the scent is joined by the heavy grimness of decaying flesh.

Suddenly, the Dauphin sucks in a breath. I follow his gaze as a chill crawls over me.

On the altar, covered by a sheet of pristine white silk, lies a body.

The Dauphin wrings his hands. 'Oh, Mothers,' he whispers. 'He's really dead, isn't he?'

The wavering in his voice makes my chest clench in discomfort. Mothers, I hope he doesn't *cry*. 'Took you a while to notice,' I say, trying to keep levity in my voice. Then, impatient, I waltz up to the altar and seize the corner of the sheet. It rustles in the rain-heavy breeze. 'Come on,' I urge. 'Let's do this before we are seen.' Without waiting for his response, I tug it away from the figure.

What I see beneath makes bile rise in my throat.

The King of Auréal looks smaller in death. His skin puddles around him, white and bloodless – his face is slack, his mouth is frozen in a perpetual, almost comical scowl. He lies naked, vulnerable, the thick hairs on his legs standing like the bristles of some wild hog. And . . .

The silk sheet slips free from my hands, falling at my feet.

Most of the King's chest is missing.

Violent, deep grooves have all but ravaged his torso, his sternum reduced to a nub, splinters of his ribs scattered over the spongy surface of his exposed lungs. Part of his heart can be seen, slick as ripe fruit, framed by flaps of jagged flesh. As I track my eyes over the damage, I notice there are deep teeth marks in his right arm and shoulder, as though he had raised it in defence.

For a moment, I'm entranced by the image, filled with a mixture of revulsion and grim fascination.

Then I hear the quiet sobbing behind me.

I turn to glance at the Dauphin. The Prince's face is buried in his hands, his shoulders shaking as he tries desperately to keep his cries quiet.

'Aimé?' I ask, uncertain.

The Dauphin drags his sleeve over his eyes. 'Forgive me,' he says hoarsely. 'He was only ever disappointed in me. I don't know why I am upset at all.'

His words strike a strange chord inside me. I know this, understand it somehow: why the Dauphin mourns a cruel man. It's what might have been. The missed chances to prove himself, the pride he will never see in his father's eyes. The scarce memories of softer moments, when his father might touch his shoulder, or listen to his worries, or even smile from a distance. Small kindnesses, ones that would make it all worth it.

I shake my head sharply and turn back to the King's body, unwilling to acknowledge the sympathetic pain blooming in my chest. The Dauphin is a fool to show this weakness in front of me. He's a fool for letting himself fall apart at all.

'I was right,' I say instead, my voice ringing discomfortingly loud in the vast chamber. 'There's no way a human did this.'

The Dauphin sniffs wetly behind me. 'What . . . what do you mean?' A second later, he steps up beside me, his face glistening with tears, his lips still pinched as though holding back another sob. 'Mothers,' he whispers, pressing the back of his hand to his mouth. 'Mothers, how did this . . . What . . .'

'Exactly,' I say, eager to move on to a more practical topic. 'I doubt this was a wolf or bear, either. These lacerations are too large.'

He shakes his head. 'We don't have such creatures in the Château forest, anyway. Perhaps a few foxes, but –'

He cuts off as the sound of a door opening comes from the back of the chapel, followed by muted footsteps down one of the column-flanked aisles. 'Who's there?' the soft voice of a priestess calls.

'Time's up,' I say, and snatch the Dauphin's hand before he can protest, yanking him out of the chapel and back into the hallway. I don't let go until we've reached one of the high-ceilinged corridors feeding into the entrance hall. Only there do I pull us both into an alcove and say, breathless, 'Whatever left those marks was unnatural, and your uncle knows it. Perhaps that's why he lied – to keep panic from spreading. Or perhaps . . .'

'You don't think he might be responsible, do you?' Aimé asks.

'I'm not sure,' I say honestly. 'I think if we figure out what did this, and how, we'll find the one behind it all. Who had a reason to want to kill King Honoré? And where would they have gotten such a creature from?'

Aimé utters a small gasp. 'Could it have been a sorcier?' Immediately he shakes his head. 'But no. That's impossible. There are no sorciers here. They left Auréal after Bartrand de Roux's betrayal.'

'They didn't *leave*,' I snap. 'They fled, or were chased out by angry mobs. And the Spider King did nothing to protect them.'

He stares at me, lips parted in surprise. 'Oh,' he says. 'That is not what my father told me.'

'King Honoré did not know everything,' I say.

Aimé looks down at his hands, and I notice they're

trembling slightly. 'This is all wrong,' he says, voice tight. 'I have to tell my stepmother. And my uncle. Damien is innocent, I must get them to let him go, and put the guard on alert for this creature, I –'

He moves to step past me, and I grab his arm. 'Wait. What if someone among them is responsible for this? Knowing that you know about their ruse could put you in more danger. It could give them a chance to cover up their tracks.' I shake my head. 'Besides, this is not enough proof – in fact, it's no proof at all, when the surgeon has already declared it a stabbing. We need more evidence, evidence even the Regent cannot refute. Our best bet is to find who did it, and force them to confess.'

'Marie, you and I both know I'm not clever enough for this.'

He says the words with a mocking smile, but there's a troubled edge beneath it. Perhaps I would have agreed with him, two days ago. But now I can't, not after witnessing the way he coaxes the world into motion around him – from calming the Step-Queen this morning to convincing Thomas to let us pass, all without a single lie or pretence. I was always taught that earnestness is a weakness, yet Aimé manages, unwittingly, to turn it into a strength.

'You must stop thinking so little of yourself,' I tell him, and I'm surprised to find I mean it. 'Besides, we're in this together, and *I'm* clever enough for two.'

He laughs. 'That you are, *ma chérie*,' he says, but I catch the glimmer of gratitude in his eyes.

A thought strikes me then: *Letting Aimé get involved in this was a mistake.* He's too yielding, too naive. Yet I let my guard down, let myself indulge in this ridiculous camaraderie, and now here he is, the grandchild of the Spider King entwined in my plot. It's too late to drive him away. And, though it irks me to admit, I don't want to. I'm not an idiot – I don't *trust* Aimé-Victor Augier. But for the first time since Damien left, I am not entirely alone. I will betray the Prince eventually, of course. But for now, it's reassuring to have someone watching my back.

I glance down the oily length of hallway, fixing the sleeves of Marie's gown. 'We need to figure out what this creature is. Does the Château have an archive, perhaps? Somewhere we can find old stories, myths, or even records of animal attacks?'

Aimé shifts. 'Well, there is the library. My father kept an old vault of documents from before my grandfather's time. He never went in there, but I did. I remember there being journals and such, though I have not seen them in years. It could be worth looking into?'

'Perfect,' I say, eager to get moving. With the funeral being tomorrow, I doubt I will have much time for sleuthing. 'Then that's where we start.'

SCENE XIV

Château. The Library.

The Château's library is a dusty jewel of a room, an elegant contrast between gilt shelves and dark fraying spines. Plush emerald carpets muffle our footsteps, and the domed ceiling depicts a wild forest and a young, golden-haired girl kneeling before a crumbling shrine – the Little Saint summoning the Mothers. Some of the Spider King's magic lingers in the fresco, as a few paper-thin leaves peel off the ceiling and fall to the ground, vanishing before they can land.

The main room is clearly intended for the public, set with velvet chaise longues and writing desks splattered with candlewax. It smells warmly of old paper and leather and ink, tickling my nose. Aimé leads me through the room and past rows of bookshelves until we reach a small gallery displaying mismatched vases. I inspect them as Aimé approaches a small door, but my focus is quickly broken when something flashes in my periphery. I turn in alarm to see Aimé brandish a thin dagger and prick the pad of his thumb.

'What are you –' I start, but he only throws me a grin and holds up his hand, a crimson rivulet slipping down on to his palm.

'The doors demand a sacrifice,' he says cryptically, and presses his thumb to the door. It swings open with a muted creak, and he beckons me inside. 'One of my lovely grandfather's creations. It will only open for fresh royal blood. Apparently, the same spell is on the door to the Couronne's vault.'

I startle at his nonchalant mention of the Couronne. 'Have you ever been in the vault?' I ask.

He shakes his head. 'Never. My father never allowed me to accompany him. But they say it's a maze. A maze only the Augier King can navigate. If anyone else attempts to enter, they will be killed by the Spider King's traps. I do not look forward to my first visit there.' He shudders in emphasis and holds the door wider for me. 'After you, my dear fiancée.'

Three hours later, I find myself squirrelled away in a small room with walls panelled in dark wood and filled to the brim with archaic books – rows upon rows of stained spines squeezed into sagging shelves, tucked into crevices and stacked on tables. My sleeves are grey with dust – I keep fighting back a sneeze. My leg has begun to bounce under the table.

'Nothing.' I toss aside another useless book. 'Mothers, does anyone in this world even enjoy reading this stuff?'

'I do,' Aimé admits sheepishly. He looks out of place here, a polished coin against a dirt path, his golden head glinting over a stack of discarded books. All have proven to be mundane, illegible journals or ledgers detailing imports and exports. 'Well, *did*, when I was younger. This was my . . . sanctuary, I suppose. I'd hide away here with my favourite books when my father –' He cuts himself off, shakes his head. 'When I needed to get away. The fairy tales were my favourites.'

'Fairy tales?' I repeat, baffled.

'What? Is it truly so startling to think I engage in a bit of escapist whimsy?'

'Startling for the Dauphin.'

He snorts. 'My darling father would have agreed with you. *Fairy tales are for children and wastrels and idiots who think they're fairies,*' he quotes, doing a frighteningly good imitation of King Honoré's baritone. 'He said that to me once, before all his courtiers. I was sneered at for a week after.' He chuckles, as though the story is meant to amuse me. 'Never set foot in here again after that, but it did no good. My reputation was already on the path to destruction.'

'If gossip is to be believed, you shirk all your duties,' I tell him mildly.

'I do now,' he admits. 'But there was a time I tried to be taken seriously. Attended every Conseil meeting. But I didn't have what it takes. I wasn't . . . strong enough. Once, there was a riot in Verroux, over the rising poverty in the city. It was brought forth to the Conseil, and the noblesse were so . . . callous about it. Saying it was a necessity that taxes be raised, because of the toll Morgane's Curse was taking. As if it was the responsibility of the common people to shoulder the burdens of their rulers. I tried to speak up, but my voice started to shake, and that was enough. I was dismissed for merely showing emotion. I can't say I blame them, really.' Aimé sniffs. 'When I stood beside my father, who was confident and severe and perfectly composed . . .

it did make a ridiculous contrast. *He* never read fairy tales.' He sighs. 'Didn't stop one from killing him.'

I push the journal aside and pick up another, but find only some old noblewoman's diary filled with gossip on long-dead noblesse. 'Sorciers aren't fairy tales.'

He looks at his hands. 'I thought they were all gone. My father always said they simply fled, because the kingdom had nothing left for them any more. He called them traitors. It didn't quite make sense to me. Now I see why. I . . . I did not know the people had turned on them.'

'It's what happens when you decide to blame the sins of one man on a whole people,' I say, and I can't keep the bitterness from my voice. 'Many of them lived off their sorcery. They were considered artisans, and sorcery an art.'

I feel a pang of longing as I say it. There is nothing I want more than to be able to wield sorcery the way it was intended: to bring beauty, life. I still remember the stories my mother would tell me – stories that had come from her grandmother, from a time before Morgane's disappearance. Of my great-great-grandmother hunched over a workbench, imbuing jewellery with spells that could alter the wearer's face or body, change the colour of their eyes or turn weariness into energy. Shoes with a golden clasp could grow, changing sizes with the wearer. A golden coin placed in a bucket could clear the murkiest of waters.

'When magic vanished,' I say, 'the sorciers were left with orders they could not complete, facing angry customers, many of them wealthy noblesse. They lost their income and were called liars for it. The Spider King did nothing to help them.'

Aimé stares at me, wide-eyed. 'I have never been told any of this. How could I not know, and yet you heard of it, all the way in Auvigny?'

I've let myself get carried away, let my bitterness show. But I can't help it. I want him to know. To see the truth. To *care*, like his predecessors did not. 'I met a sorcier man, once,' I say honestly. 'He told me stories.'

'Oh,' Aimé whispers. 'And you trusted him?'

'I did.' That's all I say – I need to change the subject before he asks too much, gets too close. I stand, stretching my arms. 'Speaking of sorciers, have you found anything?'

'There's something here. It's a journal from a noblewoman who seems to be obsessed with eternal beauty. She mentions her favourite sorcier was able to keep himself almost ageless, but wasn't able to do the same for anyone but himself. She calls him a fraud, along with several other colourful words.'

'Pleasant,' I say, then frown. Regnault has never told me anything about sorciers and ageing. 'Does it say *how* he managed to do so?'

'Unfortunately not.' He pushes the book away, looking drained. 'That's all she says about him.'

I sigh and turn, surveying the room, the shadows swamping its corners, the sticky cobwebs clinging to several old, thick manuscripts. I inhale sharply, then freeze as I notice a familiar scent tucked between the smell of aged wood and binding glue: magic-scent. Sage and iron, barely there but unmistakable. I walk across the room, and it grows stronger. After a moment's searching, I spot the source beneath a stack of books: a small brown chest with a tarnished keyhole. My breath catches in excitement – I have to hold myself still. Whatever is in there is enchanted, and I would rather not reveal too much to Aimé until I know what I'm dealing with.

In the same moment, Aimé groans and drops his forehead to the table with a defeated *thunk*. 'Mothers, perhaps I ought to send my guards to prick the fingers of every courtier, to ensure none has golden blood.'

Horror spears through me at the thought. 'Surely that wouldn't go over well with the noblesse,' I say, keeping my voice steady. 'And it would alert too many people to something being amiss.'

To my relief, he nods. 'I suppose you're right.' He pushes up from the table. 'I think I am going to speak to the guards, have them keep an eye out for any strange animals. In case whatever did this is still out there somewhere.'

'Be careful not to –' I begin, but he puts up a hand.

'I know, I know, I won't tell them too much, I promise. Mothers, Marie, do you trust *anyone*?'

'Trust is for fools,' I say flatly. 'Just look at the tarasque. After it was tamed, it trusted the Little Saint with its life. And she led it to slaughter.' I wave a hand at him. 'Go. I'm going to stay longer. I will see you at dinner.'

The Dauphin gives me an exaggerated salute before exiting. As soon as he is gone, I am back by the little chest, running my fingers over the worn wood. I wrench it from under its mound of old books, then blow a cloud of dust and debris away. The dry corpse of a spider goes flying off the lid, and I shudder.

The box is locked, but that's rarely a problem for me. One of the first things my father ever taught me was to pick locks. I take two pins from my hair and shove them into the keyhole, fiddling with the mechanism. It takes me some time – even for someone experienced, the lock is tricky – but eventually it capitulates to me. The lid comes free with a muted *click*.

The scent of magic strikes me first. It has an unfamiliar edge to it – the earthen scent of decay. I bring a candelabra closer and peer inside.

Within lies a journal, bound in red leather, its pages seeming uneven, loose, either from poor binding or frequent use. The whole is encased in a cage-like contraption of golden filigree.

My pulse surges. I reach for the little book eagerly, too excited to be cautious. Some of the crisp pages bend under my fingers, but I don't pay any attention as I lay the book out in front of me. I trace the golden casing, and feel a faint, barely-there hum – it's old magic, but not so old that it's reverted back into its raw form. A tug on the spell within reveals old, faded spell-threads in an incoherent cobweb. I drift a hand over them quickly, and find a tangle of *hide*, and *conceal* and *lock* and *turn* and more and more and more until I pull away again, blinking. I don't dare try to undo this spell, not here. Not after how disastrously it went with Marie.

I press on the cage with my thumb, and realize that the pattern moves – it's broken into thousands of tiny pieces, each one capable of rotating. When I turn one, it makes a strange *click*, and another piece on the opposite side of the journal turns beneath my fingers.

'Ah, *merde*,' I groan. 'Morgane, you must hate me.'

The journal's cage is a puzzle.

I shove the journal into the pockets of my dress – it fits, just – and I'm able to squirrel it back to my rooms. I spend the rest of the day wrestling with the strange cage, flicking pieces left and right until I want to throw it out of the window in irritation. When the time for dinner comes, I excuse myself, claiming a headache, and have food brought to my room. I remain in my chambers to curse and fidget with the journal.

By nightfall, I have accomplished nothing.

I throw the journal on to my bed. 'Fine, then,' I say to it. 'If you're going to be so stubborn, then I'm taking you to my father.'

Vibrating with frustration, I throw on my cloak and head for the balcony, clambering quickly down to the ground.

Following the day's discoveries, the Château gardens have taken on an eerie, funereal quality. The usual restless mist lies over the grounds, turning the rose hedges into no more than snarled, crawling silhouettes. Something creaks in the distance. A light swings over to my left, and I jump, only to see the shape of a masked servant heading into the palace. He vanishes into the fog like a spectre.

I exhale through the pounding of my heart, and pick up the pace determinedly.

I take off the owl-face pendant once I am in the shelter of the trees, trying not to jump every time a feathery pine frond scrapes against my skirts. I wish I had brought a lantern – the moon is not bright enough tonight to light the way.

And anything could be in these trees. I shudder at the thought.

Wind whistles. I curse, nearly tripping over a log. I am not far from the little dock where I last met Marie, and I stop to catch my breath, surprised to feel a pang of longing. The noblegirl might be infuriating, but there's something about her restrained energy, her calculating eyes, that sends a thrill through me even when I think of her. She's a challenge – I want to tear her walls down, one brick at a time, and expose all the little secrets cowering behind them.

It's that curiosity that has me gravitating back towards the lakeside. I wonder if she is here tonight, as a swan. I wonder what she will do if she sees me.

I step through the trees and pause in shock.

There is a girl sitting on the end of the dock, a wraith-like figure against a midnight lake, her pale skirts pooling around slender ankles and her cloak discarded beside her. She has taken off her shoes. Her toes are dipped in the water, eddying the surface.

'Marie?' I can't help my exclamation at seeing her human again.

She doesn't even startle. She cants her face up towards me, and for reasons I hate to examine, the sight of her steals the breath from my throat.

'Sorcière,' she greets me, with mild distaste. 'I wondered if I would see you again. It appears you kept half your bargain, at least. Did you mean for this to happen? For me to become human again when the sun set?'

'Of course I did,' I say, too fast, and wince internally. 'It's all part of my nefarious plot. I've trapped you to become human only when it is convenient to me.'

But I can tell that there's no fooling her. 'I see.' There's an edge of amusement to it. 'How very conniving of you.'

Mothers, she's *annoying*. 'You make a better swan,' I growl, unable to think of a better retort. 'Perhaps I'll turn you back into one.'

'Will you now? Magic seemed to go *swimmingly* for you last night, if I recall.'

Her eyes are twinkling, and it sends a hot spike of anger through me.

'What are you doing?'

'Taunting you,' she says innocently. 'It's easier than I expected.'

Oh, I could *strangle* her. I open my mouth, close it again, then hiss in frustration. Half of me wants to stomp my feet like a little child throwing a tantrum.

Smiling faintly, Marie tilts her head back, silken hair falling around her shoulders. The fog presses affectionately against the curve of her spine, and I grit my teeth, hating the way the movement fascinates me. She looks like a fairy tale, in this strange light, a mystery given flesh, spun from tall tales told by moonlight.

'It is a good thing I stayed by the lake,' she remarks. 'If I had been flying when the change happened, especially over somewhere populated like Verroux, I fear I would have caused quite the stir. A maiden unexpectedly falling from the sky.'

I raise an eyebrow. 'You've been here all day?'

'I'd rather assumed I was forever condemned to be a swan.'

'You don't seem terribly distressed by the idea.'

A flicker of conflict passes over Marie's face. 'I like having wings,' she says at last, softly.

She doesn't say anything more, but the silence stretches out before me like an open hand, inviting. For reasons I can't explain, I find myself walking towards her, plopping down beside her on the dock. 'The Dauphin and I went to see the King's body today.'

'Oh?'

And suddenly, I'm telling her everything. From visiting the chapel to the search in the library and my discovery of the locked journal. She makes small sounds of affirmation, makes the occasional off-hand comment. Finally, I realize what she is doing – leaving spaces for me to fill, drawing information out of me. Her mere presence is a siren song, and I've let myself get caught in its thrall.

I cut off abruptly. 'You're clever, aren't you?'

She looks at me with confusion I almost believe is genuine. 'What do you mean?'

'Listening like this. Waiting until I give you information you can use against me.'

She blinks. 'Is that what you think I'm doing?'

'Well, it's not like you're actually going to help me,' I say acidly.

She considers me, her bottom lip jutting in the smallest pout. I wonder what it would feel like to catch it between my teeth. Or . . . *no*. I stop myself quickly, unsure where the thought has come from, annoyed by its potency. In the same moment, Marie flutters a dainty, long-fingered hand towards me.

'Let me see the journal.'

I draw away from her, barking a laugh. 'Please, do you think I'm an idiot?'

'Odile.' She says it like a scolding parent. 'You said it's a puzzle.'

'It is.'

'Exactly.' She stretches her arm out further. 'That's my speciality.'

Desperation wins me over. I withdraw the journal from

under my cloak and hand it to her, watching tensely for any sign of betrayal to leap forward and snatch it back.

To my relief, Marie places the journal gingerly on her lap, drawing her feet up out of the water and curling them under her, fog eddying gently around her form. She frowns at the journal, tracing an index finger over the strange filigree casing. She tests one side, then the other, observing the rotations of the pieces.

Then she gets to work.

It is like watching a master artist conjure a perfect portrait. She sets her brows low and pokes her tongue out from between her teeth, abandoning her perfect posture to hunch over the journal like a crone. There's genuine delight in her movements, her face opening up in a way I haven't seen since we were girls. When I try to interrupt, she waves me off like I'm a pesky gnat. I can't help the surprised chuckle it draws out of me, the bloom of warmth at our old familiarity. There was a time when I had liked her. When I had nearly, *nearly* trusted her.

Then she ruined it all.

When I was twelve, nearly thirteen years old, my father gave me the most challenging of my missions.

'I have a new task for you,' Regnault hummed in my ear, cold fingers brushing down the back of my neck. I was doing my make-up for the night's performance – my face stared back at me from the mirror, caked in powder and paint.

'It's about time.' I grinned at him, tracing dark paint over my eyelids. 'I was starting to think you'd forgotten about me. What is it?'

'I want you to infiltrate the Château Front-du-Lac as a servant, and observe the noblesse. Learn as much as you can, how they speak and act, their likes and dislikes. You will be there for one month, and during that time I want you to steal something precious from one of them, and to bring it back to me.'

My stomach twisted nervously. This was my most difficult task yet. But I had never refused Regnault, and I was not about to start now. I set down my paintbrush and put my hands behind my head, tipping back in my chair to look at my father upside down. 'How shiny do you want this "something precious" to be?'

He ruffled my hair, chuckling. 'I leave that to your expertise.'

That night, I made my way down to the Château's servants' wing. There, I identified one of the maids, and waited until she was asleep to slip a foul concoction into the cup of water at her bedside. The next morning, when she did not show, I benefitted from the confusion to introduce myself as a new hire from the city, and was immediately put to work in her place.

I befriended the other young serving girls – I took platters of fancy foods to the noblesse, listened to them gossip as they downed enough pastries to feed one of the serving girls' families for a week. I memorized the way they talked, their speech eloquent and distinguished until it became slurred by wine. I dodged their clumsy punches and greedy hands once it was.

Then, one day, she arrived. The only daughter of the Auvignian duke, come to be introduced to the Dauphin, her mother's hand clasped around her wrist like a pale fetter. I knew magic, I knew sorcery, yet could not understand how this girl captivated me, enthralled me as she did.

Part of it was her peculiar, dawning beauty – she'd been in the spring of it, gangly yet sharply elegant, a rose before bloom. But it had been more than that – it had been the way she held herself apart from the other noble children, as though she were straining at the end of a tether. The way she never quite seemed to listen to their idle chatter, the way she stood, fidgeting, while her mother boasted about her like she was a prize-winning calf. Here, I thought, was someone like me. Someone caged by fate, wings clipped, longing for open skies.

The first time I spoke to Marie d'Odette, she'd been escaping. I'd run into her in the servants' wing, sneaking out towards the stables. She'd startled and yelped, then covered her mouth.

'I thought you were a shadow!' she gasped. She was wearing beautiful pearl earrings, and I remembered my mission from Regnault.

'Maybe I am,' I replied, with the whimsical mischief only a child can have. 'Where are you going?'

'Away,' she said, grinning. 'Do you want to come?'

And so we escaped. I did not have duty until evening dinner, so I showed her to the stables and we called the stacks of hay bales our fortress, leaping up and down them. After, I carefully picked stray stalks from her silken hair before she returned to the Château.

The next day, the cook sent me to report to the mistress of the lady's maids, who gave me a new, more ornate gown. I was to be a companion to young Marie d'Odette d'Auvigny for the duration of her stay. I was thrilled – it was the perfect opportunity to complete my mission.

I became Marie's servant and playmate. Marie had a

love of mysteries, and there was no greater mystery than the Château itself, with all its strange enchantments. We would run about the palace, sometimes unaccompanied, sometimes with other court children, exploring every nook and cranny, our hair wild and clothes smelling of old magic. It was exhilarating – I was still naive enough to let myself forget, temporarily, about my mission, to believe I could trust someone that wasn't my father or brother.

Then came the time of the Dauphin's banquet. The day Marie was given a beautiful diamond necklace.

Watching her now, I wonder where that lively, adventurous girl I'd met in my youth has gone. When did she bury her exuberance and replace it with dignified silence, with this aching, timid melancholy? Something about it feels unnatural – a mask that has slipped just a little as she works away at the puzzle, that old, youthful Marie winking through like stars behind a velvet drape of clouds.

'Aha!' There's a final *click*, then a louder *snap* of something breaking in two. I jolt upright, blinking bleary eyes to stare at the journal in Marie's lap. The golden cage has now twisted together to form the outline of an intricate rose, and on the other side, when she turns the journal over, is a bird's silhouette.

'How –' I stare at her, a strange, heated admiration spreading through me. 'I tried everything.'

'Hm. Well, there was a pattern to the chaos. I realized I could make out elements of the final images – the tip of a wing, the edge of a petal.'

'Images? I didn't see any images. It was just a jumble.'

She arches an eyebrow. 'Did you take the time to look?'

Here she goes again. Perfect, clever Marie, reminding me of my inferiority. *So what* if I hadn't noticed the pattern she had. I'd fiddled with the thing for hours, hoping to stumble upon the right combination. And she solved it without breaking a sweat.

I look away sulkily.

Marie's muted laugh swirls into the night. 'It was an educated guess, really. Once I had an idea of what the puzzle was *supposed* to look like, it was easier for me to tell which direction to move the pieces in. You just have to be patient. Here –' She tosses the book to me. 'Open it.'

I snatch the journal out of the air without looking at her, still moody. I waste no time opening the loose pages, letting them crack beneath my fingers.

In the same moment, a stray gust of wind rips through the trees, snatching up half the pages from the small book and carrying them out on to the lake.

SCENE XV

The Lake. A foggy midnight.

'No!' I scramble for the edge of the dock, ready to jump into the water after them, but Marie grips me quickly, her hands warm and firm on my waist. 'Odile. Odile!'

I shove at her, despair screeching through me. What if one of those pages had the answers I need? Worse, what if it could help me get the Couronne? I pull myself out of Marie's grip. 'No, let me go, I need them!'

'There's nothing you can do!' It's the first time I have heard her raise her voice, and it is such a stark contrast to her usual sultry warmth that it stuns me into stillness. I turn to stare at her, tears of disappointment pricking my eyes.

'They were barely wet. I could still have saved them!'

She steps away from me, sweeping loose curls out of her face. 'I doubt it. And it isn't worth risking a horrid cold.'

'A cold.' My laughter comes out of me in a bitter wheeze. 'You think I care about a *cold*? That journal had magic all over it! There's no telling the knowledge I just lost.'

'Odile –' She reaches out as if to soothe me.

It's petulant, but I don't care. I slap her hands away. 'No. No, I should have known better then to ever involve you. You're just a spoiled princess, gifted with the perfect clothes and the perfect life. You could never understand. You're worried about a cold? My brother is imprisoned and there's a monster in the palace and the Mothers are gone and *I have no magic.*'

I stumble back, clutching what's left of the journal to my chest. Part of me knows that I'm being unfair towards her. But if I let go of my anger, nothing waits behind it but tears, and I refuse, utterly *refuse* to cry.

I look up at Marie once more, and that is a mistake. She's staring at me, brows tilted up in regret, and there's a soft, apologetic light to her eyes that I hate, hate more than anything. Because it taunts me to say *I'm sorry*, to say *I know it's not your fault*. I whirl on my heel and storm off towards the Château, teeth clenched and eyes stinging, the remnants of brittle paper clutched tight in my fingers.

Only once I am stowed away in the Dauphine's apartments do I dare to open the journal once more. I sit by the vanity, my own reflection hovering, pale and windswept, in my periphery. I light a candelabra with shaking hands, the three candleflames winking like dying fireflies. Beneath their hesitant light, I inspect what remains of the paper.

What I find is a scrawled mess, great loops of writing that I can barely decipher. Between them – my heart leaps – drawings of spiderwebbing spells, the lines labelled with letters so small I cannot make them out. Sorcery. These are notes – no, *musings* – on sorcery. And thanks to my own foolishness, my own impatience, I might have lost precious information to the lake's greedy waters.

My eyes droop. Two sleepless nights have begun to weigh on me, pressing heavily on my eyelids. And yet I can't seem to stop. I find a drawing of a spell that seems relatively legible, and my heart speeds up with excitement. *A simpler way to transform a whole into pieces*, the author begins. A smaller scrawl in the margin's notes: *May be useful.*

Beneath, the spell-threads intersect in a hexagon, a small paragraph beside each thread instructing how to form each one. *Envision the material*, says one; *envision an object of said material in pieces*, says another. The line in between instructs the sorcier to carefully imagine their object of choice shattering.

I look up at the mirror before me, stretching out my hands. I envision golden, raw magic pooling in my palms. In my imagination, I use no goddess-gold – only true magic, summoned from Morgane, just as the youngest Mother taught the Golden-blooded Girl to do. I draw each spell-thread in the air, focusing my thoughts. *Mirror*, I think, imagining the looking-glass before me silvery and whole. Then, *shards*, a razor-sharp sliver pricking my thumb. Finally, *break*, a pane of slick glass splintering outwards.

A childish part of me hopes to hear the musical peal of shattering glass. But the mirror does not break. Nothing happens at all. There are no sticky spell-threads hovering before me, no sage and iron acrid against my tongue. There is no magic for me to call on at all, because Morgane is gone.

I clench my hands into fists. My words to Marie at the lake, though embittered, were true. I'm tired of creeping around in shadows, of being starved of magic, of sustaining myself on Regnault's promises. I want *this*. What's in this journal, in my blood.

If I'd had magic when Damien left me, I would not have cared about his betrayal. If I'd had magic when my mother died, I would not have mourned so deeply. If I'd had magic when Regnault threatened to cast me out, I would have left him with my head held high.

I could have called on Morgane and let her fill my every crevice, gorged myself on power.

With magic as my timeless companion, I would never be alone.

Stomach tight, I swipe my hand across my eyes and flip idly to the end of the journal. There, the very last words remain, unstained, written in a bold hand, every arch and dot pregnant with determination.

We long for freedom. Should all go as planned, we will gain the power we have always deserved yet never been given. We will have endless power, endless potential. No more limits. No more fear.

Something inside me lurches at the words. There's an odd, disfigured familiarity to them, like the wavering face of a stranger seen only in a dream. With frantic motions, I flip back to the front cover, searching all the places an author might sign their name.

And then, I find it:

Property of Bartrand de Roux.

It is scrawled, crookedly unassuming, on the inside of the front cover.

For a moment, I forget to breathe. My pulse surges in my ears. This isn't just the journal of some court sorcier – it's the journal of the man who attempted to assassinate the King. The man whose actions cursed his own kin, saw their livelihoods ruined, forced them to hide their veins filled with golden blood. My father's ancestor.

And yet, when I touch the faded ink, I feel reverent.

After all, no one truly knows what happened that night. Had Bartrand de Roux attempted to stop the King from going mad? Had he seen something no one else saw? The creeping of insanity, already at the edges of the King's words, his movements, his actions?

I close the cover, wedging my quill between the pages to prevent the little book from locking. I do not want to have to seek Marie's help again.

As I slip the journal beneath the mattress, my thoughts turn, unwillingly, to Marie d'Odette. To a girl trapped on the edge of the lake, cursed to become a swan by day and a maiden by night. Soon, the sun will be up, and feathers will once again swallow her. And I will be walking around in her skin, no more than her caricature, an owl wearing a swan's mask.

I turn the owl-face pendant over in my hand, and for some reason, I can't bring myself to put it on.

I don't sleep long before a maid is knocking on my door, reminding me that morning has come, and, with it, the King's funeral.

I clip the owl-face pendant back on reluctantly before unlocking the door to my chambers and allowing her inside. I sit numbly as she tuts and fusses about with pale-honey curls, stare at my feet as she cinches me into a dull, unforgiving gown the colour of a crow's corpse. My thoughts feel scattered, as though blown apart by a stray wind.

The maid suddenly clears her throat, the soft sound cutting through the room. 'Take care of the young Dauphin,' she bids me gently. 'Today will be trying for him.'

I frown, then realize I have seen her before. This is the woman Aimé conferred secretly with in the hallway, the day after King Honoré's murder. I must look sceptical, because she shakes her head at me. Her greying hair frizzes around her mask.

'They tell lies about that boy,' she says. 'Sent the royal family's doctor to my home, he did, when my little son broke his foot and no city healer could set it right. When he learned Cook's husband had died and left her with debt, it was suddenly paid off. He told no one, of course, but we knew. There are other stories, too, of kindnesses done quietly. The court may speak ill of him, but you will not find a servant who will, not even the youngest scullion. He is not as grand as his father, perhaps. But when you are grand – well, you don't see the little things.' She taps my arm. 'Come. I will take you to him.'

The morning passes in a flood of black – black clothes, black casket, black silk stretched over the chapel's pearl-white pews, and burnt-black clouds smudged over an anaemic sky. The King's body is wrapped in golden damask and borne from the chapel, to be displayed in the sprawl of the Verroux cathedral. I sit in a gilt carriage with Aimé as the procession of casket and horses and loudly weeping courtiers rattles through the narrow streets. The Dauphin's hand flexes where it rests on my arm, his thigh pressed rigidly against mine. I don't look at him, distracted by my abrupt return to the stink and noise of the city I once called home.

Jaw tense, I watch the crowd clotting around the main street, watch how colour seems to melt away from it as we leave the upper sectors of the city – vibrant gowns of wealthy merchant ladies morphing into dirt-stained workers' clothes and the filthy rags of pickpockets.

As the colour vanishes, so do sorrow and mourning. They are replaced by hunger and bared teeth, and a palpable tension in the air. It all feels strangely foreign to me, more vicious than I remember, more desperate even than when Damien and I haunted these streets. Two hundred years of a dying, cursed land is taking its toll.

I wonder if the mysterious beast is not the only monster Aimé should fear. Verroux is starving, and if things do not change soon, it might begin to devour everything. First itself, then the noblesse, until finally, bloodstained and bristle-haired, it will bury its fangs into its would-be King and bleed him dry.

SCENE XVI

Château. The Royal Dining Room.

'There is unrest at the Château.'

The Dauphin's voice rings like a bell through the room. Before me, a long, regal dining table seems to stretch into infinity, laden with a gargantuan display of foods – slabs of veal slick with grease, a pheasant with its feathers splayed out, vegetables carved into odd, abstract shapes, and frosted goblets of exotic wine. We are in the royal dining room, a low-ceilinged chamber with walls of dark wood and an odd, earthy scent to it, as though we are trapped in a great coffin. Overhead, arcs of silver lightning flash quietly over a ceiling painted with a roiling storm. As with most of the Château's enchantments, this magic is fading – the bolts, instead of streaking majestically across the vista, merely meander through it at a leisurely pace.

One such lightning bolt crawls over the Regent's head as he leans forward, giving his scarred nose an unflattering highlight.

'From whom?' he enquires, his reedy voice seeming to send the wine glasses shaking. 'Who dares utter dissent within these walls?'

The post-funeral banquet has turned into an unofficial meeting for the Conseil du Roi. The Step-Queen is present, as are all the most important secretaries of state, and the whole affair is going about as amicably as one might expect.

'Why does it matter who it was?' the Dauphin says faintly, leaning away from his uncle, though a table separates them. 'They are not wrong to worry.'

'Gossip about the Crown is *treason*,' the Regent replies sharply. 'Any who spread it must be arrested.'

Like you arrested my brother? I want to say, but keep myself demurely silent, biding my time. I think of the funeral, the grey ocean of commoners with dull, desolate eyes. Apparently the cracks in Auréal's foundations reach all the way to Château Front-du-Lac.

Confronted by the Regent, Aimé seems to waver. He opens his mouth, closes it again. The Regent sits back, seeming to expect the Dauphin to agree and confess. For a moment, it seems that is what Aimé will do, his breath shaky and audible. But then, to my utter shock –

'They're worried, uncle. And if my own courtiers are expressing concern over the stability of my reign – over the effects of Morgane's Curse – then I can't imagine what is being said of me in the city below.'

Grimaces and dirtied faces, clothes hanging off thinning frames.

'Anyway, I thought we could –' But the Regent cuts Aimé off:

'Dear nephew.' The man smiles kindly, but his eyes glitter with unashamed derision. 'Should you not be resting? The last few days must have taken a toll on you – your father, my beloved brother, has only just been buried. Why not allow me to perform my duty as Regent, while you focus your attention on your future Queen?' His gaze plasters on to me, slimy and stubborn as a leech. I resist the urge to scrub at my skin. The other Conseil members chuckle, while the Step-Queen presses her lips together.

Aimé's cheeks have gone red. When he says nothing, the Regent's smile curls into something jagged and gloating. 'So I thought. You agree, then, that it is best that I handle this my way. I understand you want to take charge now, before your coronation, but you are still grieving, and we all know of your . . . ah, *nerves*.' He crosses his arms, an image of thin, looming authority, like a lengthened shadow at sunset. 'You have stayed out of royal business for so long, dear nephew. It may be best if you wait a little longer.'

Beside me, Aimé's shoulders drop in defeat. He pulls his hands under the tablecloth, and before he can fully hide them, I see they're shaking minutely.

I gnaw on my thumb, shoving down a wave of frustration. The Regent has turned to the courtier to his left, and they're discussing the unrest within the kingdom. I hear the word *militia* muttered, and beside me, Aimé tenses. I remember what the Regent's friend said about the Dauphin the night of the ball. *The little pest is easy to get rid of.* I can't help but wonder: what if there were unspoken words then, between them? What if he had wanted to say, *The King will be harder.* Kill the King, control the Prince. But the beast had golden blood – sorcery was involved in its creation, and the Regent is no sorcier. Which means he must be working with one.

I wish, once more, for my father. He has always held a wealth of knowledge about magic. He might know a way of tracking down another sorcier, if there is one present.

If only I could bring my father here . . .

A sudden idea springs to my mind, and I'm leaping to my feet before I can think it through. 'What if we moved up the wedding?'

The Regent's head snaps towards me.

'What did she say?' says the sallow-faced courtier at his side.

'Nothing of importance,' says the Regent immediately, turning back to him. 'You know how women are.'

I grind my teeth together, understanding, suddenly, why the Step-Queen remains silent. I want to push over my wine glass, shatter a plate, whatever it takes to gain their attention. But – *You are Marie d'Odette*, I remind myself. *Be diplomatic.*

'My apologies.' I address both the Regent and the elderly courtier. 'I see I should speak louder to accommodate those of more . . . mature hearing.' I suppress a smile as the Regent purples. 'I was thinking we could move the wedding up. Say, by two weeks.'

Beside me, Aimé nearly chokes on his wine. 'What?'

'You say the people doubt Aimé's strength?' I say. 'What better way to show them that the Crown is as united as ever than by a grand celebration? Perhaps you could even put some magic into the event, bring out the Couronne for –'

'No.' The Step-Queen's voice breaks through my words like a well-aimed arrow. 'That is not how the Couronne works. It should only be used in dire need, not for frivolous party tricks. The late King understood that.'

'Yes, so he let the kingdom languish instead,' Aimé mutters.

'And thus avoided becoming a second Spider King,' the Step-Queen points out.

Aimé's eyes blaze suddenly. 'I would gladly go mad if it meant keeping my people from starving!'

There is a snap of silence, and the old courtier sidles into it awkwardly. 'This is a good idea,' he says, wiping his lips with a napkin. 'The wedding, I mean. It would be an excellent way to take the court's mind off the recent tragedy.'

'But the magnitude of planning such an event –' Aimé's hands still clenched together under the table – 'of organizing the food and décor and sending out invitations at such short notice . . . it would be impossible.'

'Not impossible,' I say. I have to manoeuvre this discussion carefully now, to make sure the outcome is as I want it. Overhead, a bolt of lightning flashes across the ceiling, and for a heartbeat every noble at the table is turned into a brightly lit ghoul. 'Surely there must be someone at the palace who is adept at managing such events. Someone with knowledge of decoration, of coordinating people. Someone who can make an impression.'

Silence falls as all present seem to try to think of such a person. I sit back, worrying my bottom lip, wondering if I should have been more pointed with my words.

To my relief, Aimé gives a soft 'Oh!' of realization. 'Uncle, Stepmother, what about the theatre director?'

It takes all my self-control not to smirk with satisfaction.

'Monsieur Regnault always puts on the grandest spectacles. Even Papa used to praise him, and we know how he hated frivolity. Surely we have all had our breath taken away many times by Monsieur Regnault's plays. And what is a wedding, really, if not a grand performance?' He adds the last with a touch of irony.

Another courtier speaks up. 'I think the girl has a point,' he says. 'It would be a good way to reassure the noblesse that the King's death was a regrettable anomaly, and that there is nothing to fear at the Château. All myths are just that: myths.'

'Very well,' the Regent says, rubbing his temples. There is an edge of vitriol to his words, the sound of a man who may have admitted defeat, but is already plotting revenge. 'We will send for this theatre master, and let him manage the preparations.'

'We can hire staff from the city, too,' Aimé pipes up. 'And some more guards, as well. We need to be prepared. And perhaps we can keep the new servants on, afterwards. Bring some life back to this place.'

And so it is settled. Dinner ends, the company dispersing to attend to their individual duties, and I am left filled with conflicting emotions, thick as the storm clouds painted overhead. I am eager to see Regnault again. Once he is here, everything will be easier. Once he is here, we can plan the rest of this heist together.

I stand, smoothing out Marie's skirts, and make to leave the room. But a sudden suspicion has me pausing at the threshold, tucking myself behind the wall to eavesdrop.

At the end of the table, Aimé is approaching the Step-Queen, a teacup in hand. They exchange quiet words, and she once again reaches into her pocket, procuring the strange yellow vial. Just as on the previous day, she pours it into Aimé's drink, watching intently as the golden-haired Prince raises the cup to his lips. Her gaze does not leave him until he swallows every last drop.

If anyone nearby is surprised by the sight, they make no indication. Nor does the Step-Queen try to hide her actions. And yet, a sense of wrongness overcomes me. There's something too intense, too urgent, in the Step-Queen's eyes. *Just what*, I wonder, *is in that vial?*

I detach myself from the wall and head back down the gloomy corridor, my mind churning. Ridiculously, a part of me wishes for Marie, for her steadying attentiveness. I wish I had not burned that bridge. I wish I could sit beside her again, tell her of my discoveries in a way I could not even tell my father, because he would tell me to focus on the Couronne, and only the Couronne.

I want to speak to Aimé about the mysterious vial, but he's already been ushered away to another meeting. I am left in the corridor, utterly alone.

The Château walls seem to lean in towards me, a jeering mass of dark wood. I scowl at them.

'I will solve your secrets,' I declare. 'I will take everything back. My brother, the crown, magic . . . I will reclaim it all, and I will win this ridiculous game.'

Later, a maid tells me the Dauphin has finally retired to his rooms. As I climb the stairs to his apartments, the shrill scream of a violin comes tearing down the stairwell in a violent crescendo. The melody is haunting and fierce, tugging at my skin, wanting to strip it from my bones. Beneath my feet, the stairs seem to pulse to the rhythm, and in a nearby alcove an enchanted statue twitches furiously, drawing on the last dregs of its magic to claw at its ears.

I finish climbing the stairs, the music growing louder. I don't knock – I simply shove the door open and step inside.

I am greeted by a flare of light, the candles on every surface of the room lit and brightly burning. They chase away shadows, reflecting in gilt accents, making the room swirl with dizzying streaks of fire. In the midst of this strange, flaming miasma, Aimé is an image of languorous glamour, wearing only a loose white shirt and breeches, his fingers dancing across the strings of the violin, its body the colour of a midday sky.

He breaks off when he sees me enter, his smile that of an entertainer, all pomp and teeth.

'Marie! Perfect timing, as usual.' He lowers the violin and takes a sip from a nearby wine bottle. 'I've just had a visit from my wonderful Secretary of Finance. Apparently, our coffers can barely support the wedding. I certainly hope that theatre director can work miracles on a pitiful budget.'

'Are you drunk?' I question, squinting at him.

'I'm wallowing.' He holds out the bottle. I take it and sniff, cautiously. I don't have a refined taste for wines – I've never liked how drinking dulls my reflexes – but the scent is sweetly luxurious, and I have nothing better to be doing. I take a swig and return the bottle to Aimé.

'You know,' I say, the wine's sour tang on my tongue, 'you might gain more respect from your courtiers if you weren't constantly trying to send your liver into an existential crisis.'

He sighs, staring mournfully at the bottle. 'You're probably right.' He sets it aside, then looks down at the violin in his hand. 'Oh, how far I've fallen.'

He's quiet for a moment, his eyes dark. Feeling irreverent, I cross the room and flop down on his bed. He glances at me, surprised, and a part of me is suddenly terrified I've made a horrible mistake. I've just lain on the bed of my intended – I might have indicated I want something that I certainly do not. Then again, I've seen the way he looks at my brother. I wonder if his interests – and his heart – lie entirely elsewhere.

My suspicions are furthered when Aimé merely smiles at me fondly. 'Make yourself at home, I suppose.'

'Thank you.' I turn over on my side, propping up my head on my hand. 'It's beautiful, by the way. The music. I mean, it's absolutely horrifying, but that only makes me like it more.'

'My, how very gracious of you,' he says wryly, putting aside the violin.

'Did you compose it yourself?'

'Indeed.' He sketches a dramatic bow. 'I call it "Help, Who Decided It Was A Good Idea To Make Me King? In E Minor".'

'You're not King yet,' I remind him, though his antics bring a laugh out of me. It feels strange, a sorcier laughing with an Augier. Forget rolling, my ancestors must be performing whole acrobatic routines in their graves.

You are here for a reason, I remind myself. I sit up on the bed, crossing my legs beneath Marie's overabundant skirts. 'Aimé,' I say carefully, 'can I ask you something?'

'Whatever you wish, *ma chérie*.' He clambers on to the bed beside me, limber as a cat. To my absolute shock, he rests his head on my knee, staring up at me through heavy lashes, as though we are long-time friends. And to him, we are. I imagine this is how he might have looked at Marie when they were both young and careless, trading gossip in the Château gardens.

But we're not young royals beneath a kind blue sky. I have a mission to complete and a brother to rescue. I can't let myself forget that.

'That drink your stepmother gives you,' I ask the Dauphin. 'What is it?'

His smile dissipates. He turns over on to his side, his head still on my knee. 'I suppose I ought to tell you,' he says morosely. 'Since we are to be *married*.'

I take a page from Marie d'Odette's book and remain quiet, allowing him to fill the silence.

'It's . . . it's medicine,' Aimé says at last, wearily. 'For my nerves.'

'Your *nerves*?'

He nods, his hair rustling against the silk of my dress. 'I . . . I'm not very good with . . . busy places. Pressure. I get . . . My hands begin to shake. Sometimes it gets hard to breathe. The medicine helps. Most of the time, it's enough. It keeps me from truly panicking.' He closes his eyes tightly. 'It's the real reason I stopped . . . trying. At court. I've dealt with it since I was a boy, but every meeting, every humiliation, would make it worse. Stepmother has had to increase the dose.'

I narrow my eyes at that, but say nothing.

'I should have told you earlier,' he says, sighing. 'That I'm mad. Hysterical. Melancholic. Call it what you want.'

'Is that what your father called it?'

He says nothing, but the shine in his eyes is the confirmation I need. 'King Honoré was the lesser shadow of a madman,' I tell him. 'He will be remembered for doing nothing, *changing* nothing. He kept the kingdom afloat, but did no more than that.'

'Don't say that,' Aimé says, swallowing. 'He sacrificed much for Auréal. As much as he thought he could, at least.'

I frown. 'What do you mean?'

The Dauphin shakes his head. 'I'll show you tomorrow. Not . . . right now.'

'All right,' I say. 'But listen, Aimé. What I meant to say was . . . you're nothing like those men. You have the potential to change things. To make them better.'

He snorts. 'You don't believe that.'

'I do,' I say, and I wish it were a lie, because it would make things so much easier. Because then I wouldn't have this kindling of a friendship, this newborn warmth of it, to make me feel conflicted, *guilty*, about my true mission.

Aimé's gaze drifts towards the far wall, to the painting of the turtle doves, the downy brushstrokes of their feathers and gleaming, candid eyes. 'My mother painted that, you know. For me, before I was born. She hoped I would be soft, kind. My father said she cursed me with it – that because of it, he was left with a weak and witless son.'

'What happened to her?'

'She died right after I was born. They say it was a sudden illness – one night, and she was gone. The violin was hers –

Stepmother taught me to play it, so I could honour her. I wish you could know Madame de Malezieu as I do, Marie. She can be very kind.'

'Yes, well, she can also hold a ghastly grudge.'

He laughs. 'That she can. But she risked my father's ire for it, you know. Teaching me to play. He hated all art, be it music or painting. *Pastimes for a bored noblewoman*, he would say. He only kept the theatre houses running because he knew how powerful theatre could be in forming the public's opinion of the court.'

I think of the many grand performances my father has put on, each one glorifying the history of Auréal, painting the Spider King as a hero – not a madman but a genius, putting the kingdom back together after the Mothers abandoned us, wielding the Couronne, a relic gifted by the Mothers themselves. Lies, all of them.

Aimé raises an arm to rub his eyes. 'You know, it's funny. I don't actually miss my father at all. I'm almost . . . relieved. That he's gone. What's wrong with me, that I think that way?'

He stares at me as though I might have the answer to his question. There is wetness gathering in his eyes. I shift awkwardly.

He sits up, blinking tears away furiously. '*Mothers*,' he curses. 'That was insensitive. I shouldn't say such things, what with your father . . . well. I apologize if I've made you uncomfortable.'

Marie's father? I knew he was dead, but nothing more than that. I file the information away for later.

'It's all right,' I reassure the Dauphin. 'I'm not . . . I don't know what to do when people cry, is all. It seems . . .'

Weak, I almost say, but that wouldn't be very diplomatic. 'Vulnerable.'

'Yes,' he says, sniffing. 'I suppose it is. But I trust you.'

The words strike me in an odd place, sending aftershocks long after they're uttered. *Don't be a fool*, says a voice in my thoughts, my father's voice. *He doesn't trust you. He trusts Marie d'Odette. And when you reveal your true identity to him, he will call you what you truly are: thief, liar, villain.*

Another bloom of guilt spreads through me, more potent this time, and I turn away from Aimé, unable to face the defencelessness of his expression. Past the room's ornate windows, night spreads, a ribbon of black satin drawn over the sky like a mask, the stars white pearls sewn into the fabric. Despite myself, I wonder what Marie is doing. If our assumption is correct and I did accidentally curse her to become a swan by day, then she must have returned to her human shape by now.

'I need to go,' I say tightly to Aimé. 'I hate to leave, but I'm weary. Any longer and I might fall asleep in this bed, and I presume that would be misconstrued as something scandalous.'

'Mothers.' Aimé rubs his eyes with a groan. 'Don't remind me. Sometimes I forget that our marriage will involve . . . marital *duties*.'

'Let's live in ignorant bliss,' I declare, getting to my feet. 'I don't want to think about it either.'

I don't tell him that it'll never come to that. That moving the marriage up by two weeks has merely sped up the deadline for my heist, and that the moment the Couronne is brought out from the vaults, it will be gone, and I along with it. I don't tell him that I've come to understand why my brother thinks he's worth protecting. I don't tell him that I wish we could truly be friends.

I merely rush from the room, perhaps faster than I should have, because I don't want to picture the heartbreak on Aimé-Victor Augier's face when the time comes for me to betray him.

By the time I make my escape into the gardens, the Château looks drowsy, its golden windows flickering in the dark like shuttering eyes. The cold is more bearable today – autumn caught in its final, desperate throes before winter's jaws close upon it.

I stare at the vast lake ahead, that ever-present shroud of mist spread across it like a layer of stiff icing. *Marie.* I shouldn't want to see her, not after last night's argument. Yet there's a tugging in my chest, incessant, urging me to find her again. *It's for the mission*, I tell myself. *I need to make sure she hasn't changed her mind and done something to betray me.* Yes. That's all this is. I'm being practical.

Squaring my shoulders, I make my way through the maze of iron roses, the Château turrets growing smaller behind me.

Just before I reach the lakeside, an ice-cold hand clamps down on my mouth.

SCENE XVII

Château Gardens. Night.

Immediately, Buttons is in my hand, pointing towards my assailant's throat.

'This again?' A warm, familiar voice brushes against my ear, sending shivers across my skin.

I freeze. 'Marie?'

Indeed, I turn to find Marie d'Odette standing behind me, hands held up in surrender, a mildly surprised look on her face and Buttons's muzzle inches from the elegant curve of her jaw. 'Tell me,' she says, 'do you always greet people by threatening to shoot them?'

I lower Buttons, rolling my eyes, then look around to ensure that we are well concealed from the Château. Thankfully, we are far from the palace, hidden by high hedges and the obscuring fingers of darkness. Neither of us carries a light, and I can hardly make out Marie's features by the waning moon. Still, I squat, pulling her down with me in case a guard walks by.

Only then do I relax slightly. Marie's skirts billow around her as she crouches, and I notice something is different about her clothing. She's no longer wearing the oceanic gown from the first night, but a dress and cloak of rougher make, a plain skirt and bodice in shades of washed-out blue.

'What happened to your clothes?' I hiss.

'Took a trip into Verroux last night after you left,' she answers in a whisper. 'Ran into a young seamstress opening her shop and traded them for something less . . . assuming, and a bit of coin. She was rather excited about it. It was a very expensive dress,' she adds, sniffing.

'What were you doing in the city?' I try to keep the anxiety out of my voice. Has she told anyone what happened at the lake?

'Exploring,' she says, and her eyes are bright enough that I can almost mistake her for the girl I knew in my youth. 'It was rather wonderful. To walk around in a city in the dark, where no one cared who I was or how I looked or how I was dressed.'

'I'm glad you're living out all your peasant dreams,' I say tartly. 'I'm sure you'll have a *wonderful* time indeed once you get robbed, or worse.'

'I'm not *that* incautious,' she assures me. 'I know to be careful.' She hesitates, her eyes dragging over me unhappily. 'Do you think you could . . . ah, change? This is getting rather odd.'

I realize with a start that I am still wearing the owl-face pendant. Marie hasn't been seeing Odile – she's been speaking to a dark mirror of herself, dressed in obsidian instead of sophisticated silver.

'You're taking this rather well, all things considered,' I remark. 'Close your eyes and I'll change back to myself.' I don't want to give her the opportunity to snatch the pendant.

'Very well,' she says, and squeezes her eyes shut.

I unclip the necklace and slip it into the pocket of my jacket. 'There. You can open your eyes, Mademoiselle d'Auvigny.'

She looks me over, taking in my true appearance with a strange, appreciative heat. 'Much better.' Then she sighs heavily, her mood sobering. 'Odile, we need to talk.'

'Why?'

'Because after what you told me yesterday, I decided to do some investigating of my own.' She clasps her hands in front of her, long fingers twining elegantly. 'I flew over the palace this morning, and spent the afternoon in the basin of one of the fountains. As the sun was setting, I saw a cloaked figure walking across the grounds. I thought it might be a maid, but when I looked again I realized it was Anne de Malezieu.'

I lean closer, intrigued.

'Naturally, I followed her, flying overhead. She walked across the gardens to the rightmost boundary wall, the one that runs along the forest. I lost sight of her once she was under the trees. She reappeared sometime later, holding a little bundle to her chest. She went back into the castle through the servants' entrance.'

My heart is already thumping with excitement. 'Can you show me the place where she disappeared?'

'That's why I came,' she says. 'I think I can retrace the way on foot well enough.'

Our journey across the grounds is slow, cautious, careful of patrolling guards. By the time we reach the Château's boundary, the night has plunged into its darkest hours, and we can barely make out the jagged woodland ahead.

I withdraw a little candle from my pocket and light it, carefully shielding it with my hand. It spreads tingling heat down my fingers.

'This is the place,' Marie says, her tone hushed and tight with anticipation.

The wall along the boundary must date back to Auréal's Middle Ages, made of ancient, crumbling stone and coated with moss. As I hold my candle up towards it, I notice it is broken by a small archway, a thick, wild tangle of blackberries blocking what appears to be a rotting wooden door stained by lichen and crooked on its hinges.

'It looks like there's a narrow path back here,' Marie says, peering behind the briars, her back pressed to the wall. She gathers her skirts against herself and shoves her way through the thorns, towards the old door. I follow behind her, shielding the candle, the rough stone scraping against my shoulders. Marie pushes open the door, and I'm about to reach her, when –

'Ow!' I jerk back at the sudden pain. I'd been so focused on keeping my candle away from the briars that I did not notice the giant thorn until it was stabbing into my skin. I stare down at my arm, at the deep gash already welling with shimmering blood. A mangled flap of my skin hangs off the thorn, shivering in the wind.

'Are you all right?' Marie asks worriedly, midway through wrestling the old door open.

I grit my teeth against the sting. 'Fine,' I say. 'It's just a scratch.'

It doesn't *feel* like a scratch, but I'm not about to admit that. I finish my struggle past the thorns and slip through the door as Marie holds it open, ignoring the wet stickiness of the blood on my arm.

The forest engulfs me immediately. It is dark and damp, the smell ancient, like old bones rotting by a riverside. The trees seem to fidget restlessly, rubbing against one another, boughs clattering and trunks creaking. Ahead, a small path snakes between the trees, bare branches and evergreen fronds forming a latticework overhead, the soil underfoot crackling with pine needles. Strange, spindly plants cluster on either side, their shadows crooked and lengthened by candlelight.

'They're *blooming*,' Marie says in surprise. She crouches by a patch of the plants, carding her hands gently through their leaves. Like any flowers that survived Morgane's Curse, these are wrinkled, unsightly things, their edges curling like burnt paper.

But Marie coos at them, gathering a few blossoms carefully in her palm. 'Oh, how long it has been since I've seen real flowers,' she murmurs. 'Look, Odile.'

I wipe the stream of blood off my arm on to my shirt, ignoring the aggressive throb of pain, and walk over to her side, eyeing the little blooms in her cupped hands. In the faint light of my candle, Marie's skin looks just as soft as their petals, and I have a sudden urge to touch her palms.

Obviously, I resist it. Instead, I pluck one of the flowers and hold it between my fingers. I squint at it, and notice with a start the colour of its petals – a familiar, sickly yellow.

Medicine, Aimé had said. *For my nerves.*

'This is what she comes here for,' I say. Marie looks at me questioningly, and I tell her about the drinks I've seen the Step-Queen give Aimé.

'I never saw him drink anything like that when we were children,' she says, her brows drawing together. 'It seems odd.'

'Odder still,' I add, 'why come here disguised? Surely, if it's only a mundane medicine, there would be no need to keep the location of these flowers so secret.'

Marie's eyes widen. 'Do you think it could be poison?'

I nod, chewing on my bottom lip.

Marie huffs. 'I never did like that woman.'

'She seems to have a particular hatred for you,' I agree. 'Care to explain?'

Marie glances at me in surprise, curling her fingers around the flowers. 'You . . . you really don't know why?'

I have my suspicions, most of them revolving around a diamond necklace, but I don't tell her that.

'If you don't know, then I'm glad,' she says, and that's all. Her tone makes it clear that she doesn't wish to continue the topic, and I don't pry, focusing back on the flowers.

'The Step-Queen has a motive,' I reason. 'If she were to kill Aimé, her son would be next in line. That would only give her more power.'

'Yes,' Marie agrees. 'It does, though –' Her attention abruptly drops to my arm. 'By the Mothers, Odile!'

Her sudden exclamation makes me jump. Disconcerted, I follow her gaze from the flowers to my arm, and the breath whistles out of me. I was so distracted by our discovery that I had forgotten about the pain in my arm. Now, I see, my entire forearm is marbled in streaks of gilded blood, and I have left a trail of shimmering drops behind me on the narrow path.

Marie reaches for my arm, but I pull away instinctively.

All I can think of is Regnault's thunderous gaze the first time he saw me injured, his scolding words. Since then, I've never let anyone see my wounds. Not even Damien.

'No,' I say, too sharply. My voice rings in the silence. Marie's lips part in surprise, and I force myself to take a shuddering breath. Quieter, I grit out, 'I'm fine. I can deal with it myself.'

I pass her the candle and pull a fraying handkerchief from my pocket, pressing it against the gash. I wince as it soaks through almost instantly, the contact sending waves of pain up my arm. Mothers, how badly did I cut myself? I raise the handkerchief to check, and realize the bleeding isn't slowing at all. For some absurd reason, panic begins to fill me. What if it doesn't stop? What if it needs *stitches*? I don't know how to stitch a wound, and I can't ask anyone for help without revealing my identity as a sorcier. Am I doomed simply to bleed out here, all over the forest floor?

'Odile.' Soft hands close around mine, pressing the handkerchief back to my arm, and I realize I've begun to shake. Shame floods me, and I jerk away.

'Odile, it's all right.' Marie's tone has grown cautious, muted, as though I'm a skittish bird on the verge of taking flight. 'Here, let me see.'

She kneels in front of me, taking my forearm gently and pulling it towards herself, laying it in her lap. Shaken and still somewhat woozy, I can't find the willpower to resist this time.

'*Mothers*, that is *deep*,' she says, turning my arm over. 'What did this, a thorn? Can you stand? We need to wash it off somewhere.'

'It'll be fine,' I argue feebly.

'Not if it gets *infected*,' she counters, her jaw set. 'Hold that there – no, don't lift it. You need to apply pressure.'

'I know that,' I growl, furious at myself for getting into this situation. I really thought I would go out in a blaze of glory, but here I am, utterly undone by a shrub.

Marie tugs on my elbow. 'Come on, we're not far from the servants' wing. We can use the well water there. Hopefully everyone will be asleep by now.'

I wobble when I stand, feeling oddly light-headed, and something presses into the small of my back. I nearly jump out of my skin, until I realize it is Marie's hand, attempting to steady me. I give her a sideways look. I want to tell her that I can walk on my own, that I don't need to be *coddled*. And yet, I can't bring myself to shake off her touch.

As we walk away, Marie swipes her foot over the earth, carefully wiping away the stains my blood has left on the wet loam. I blow out my candle, and we navigate again by moonlight. By the time we reach the servants' wing – an aged, morose part of the Château, smudged stone walls imprisoned in a cage of leafless grapevines – my black handkerchief has turned entirely gold, and blood has begun to drip from my arm again. I lean sullenly against the old stone well, watching for guards as Marie hauls up a bucket of water with surprising ease. In the distance I can make out the stables – the ground is littered with stray bits of straw, and a cold breeze carries the smell of horse, sweet and musty.

Marie sets down the bucket. A moment later, there comes the sound of fabric tearing, and I turn in surprise to see Marie with her outer skirt pulled up, tearing her cotton petticoat into strips. My eyes are drawn to her exposed calves, their lovely, slender curve, and something flutters in my lower stomach. I wrench my eyes away, annoyed at myself, at her, at the *world*.

After a time, Marie approaches me, gesturing to my arm. I let her take it, trying not to think of how long it has been since anyone has touched me like this – with gentle steadiness, fingers leaving tingling traces, skin gliding against skin. She begins to pour crystalline water carefully over the wound, and though I wince, I'm grateful for the momentary relief. Then she begins wiping my arm with a scrap of fabric, and I wonder if I will simply burst into flames.

'Why are you helping me?' I exclaim frustratedly, unable to bear the tension any longer. 'I don't understand it. I've been nothing but cruel to you.'

Marie hums, not looking up from her work. 'What makes you think I'm not doing this out of self-interest? Perhaps I merely want to make sure you're not dripping conspicuous golden liquid in the Château while wearing *my* face.' She draws my arm closer to her body and begins binding it carefully in white cotton.

'That's just it,' I say. 'You're being so casual about all of this. You've been cursed – twice, if you count my failed attempt at undoing the first curse – and I've been walking around pretending to be you. Yet you've hardly put up a fight since that first night.'

She is suspiciously silent at that.

'Ah, so I am on to something,' I say slyly, feeling like I've finally gained the upper hand. 'You don't want to go back to court at all, do you?'

Marie continues to avoid my eyes. Her expression is

unreadable – the only sign that my words have affected her is the slight tremble of her touch against my skin. Finally, she ties off the makeshift bandage and sighs, bowing her head slightly. Her brows cast her eyes in shadow.

'You're right,' she says, and there's an edge of shame to her voice. 'I do not wish to go back. The last time I was here, as a girl, I nearly ruined my family's reputation. I've dreaded coming back ever since.'

'You? Ruin someone's reputation?' I raise my eyebrows. 'But you're so . . . proper.'

The statement seems to make her wither. She lets me go, seeming not to notice the golden smears of my blood left on her palms. 'I am,' she says quietly. 'Because when I was not, I made mistakes. Terrible mistakes.'

Foreboding creeps through me. Surely, surely, this cannot be about –

'Do you remember that diamond necklace?' Marie says. 'The one the Step-Queen lent me?'

My chest seizes up. Mothers, I was right. I didn't want to be. I thought I'd fixed it; I thought I'd undone that mistake.

'I do,' I reply hoarsely.

She presses the heels of her palms to her eyes. When she pulls them away, flakes of my blood glint on her cheeks. 'I lost it,' she says. 'Soon after I took it back from you, it vanished. That's how it all started.'

She tells me about it, but I remember a different story. It tears from me like a scab from a still-healing wound, old pain becoming new again, crimson regret welling to the surface.

*

The Dauphin was having a birthday banquet, and Marie d'Odette d'Auvigny did not want to go.

'Why not?' I said, tightening the back of her bodice, the velvet-soft ribbons sliding between my fingers and the warmth of her back against my hands. 'There must be so much food.'

'And so much *formality*,' she said drearily. 'Maman will not let me breathe. If I so much as slouch she will jab me in the back with her finger. If I speak too loud she will glare, or pinch me until I fall quiet. Sometimes I'm sure she wants a doll, not a daughter. If it weren't for Papa, she probably wouldn't even let me outside. Just put me up on a shelf to ripen like an apple until I'm nice and sweet for the Dauphin.'

'Sounds like an easy life,' I said, feeling a pang of resentment. It felt unfair that Marie should have a doting mother, when I hardly remembered mine – only plague sores on skin and desperate eyes on Damien and the words *take your sister and go*.

'She sold my horse,' Marie said quietly. 'Before we came. I fell off him and got all muddy, so she decided I was too old to go riding. According to her I shouldn't be doing things so reckless – only sitting indoors doing embroidery, or whatever it is real ladies do.'

'That is terrible.' I tried to sound sympathetic. Her life still seemed idyllic to me. Banquets and wealth and parents and safety. She didn't have to work for anything – it was all handed to her on a golden platter.

'I wonder if we could steal one of the Dauphin's horses,' Marie mused impishly. 'He has beautiful ones, and he never rides them. Says he's worried he'll hurt one, though I don't see how he would – he's shorter than I am and built like a feather. Oh –' She reached for something on the dresser. 'Can you help me put this on?'

My breath caught. It was a necklace, a dazzling necklace of diamonds. Its faceted jewels swallowed light, turning it over in their bellies before spitting it out in prismatic beams. Between them were little roses of gold, their small petals impossibly thin and frail.

'It's beautiful,' I breathed, and my fingers itched to tuck the necklace away. But then Marie said –

'Aimé's stepmother gifted it to me to wear tonight. *If you wear a lady's jewels*, she said, *then you'll remember to act like one.*' She made a face. 'I can't tell if she likes me.'

'Sounds patronizing,' I grumbled as she swept her glossy ringlets off her shoulders, baring her neck to me. Something about the sight of it, the sun-kissed column arching gracefully into sharp shoulders, made me flush. I didn't understand it, and I didn't want to.

Hastily, I clipped the diamonds around her neck and stepped back. 'It's like the Step-Queen thinks you need taming,' I said.

Marie wrinkled her nose. 'It does look like a collar, doesn't it? *Mothers*, I don't want to be tamed. I don't want to be like *them*. I want to see the world, not be trapped in a stupid marriage. Aimé doesn't want this, either.' She sniffed, then smiled faintly. 'We have some time before the banquet. We should go to the stables – I hear the King's got a new stallion. Imported from Lore, my father said. I've never seen a horse from Lore.'

'Won't your parents be looking for you?' I asked. I'd been taking my duties as her companion rather seriously – I couldn't afford to get in trouble and ruin my cover.

She shrugged. 'Eventually. So we should hurry.'

And so we did. We escaped to the stables, and stole hay from the loft and fed it in great chunks to the sleek bay beast that would be King Honoré's mount. When we grew bored, Marie pulled me aside and spun me in a circle and said, 'I wish I could bring you with me to the banquet.'

My eyes found the diamonds on her neck again, and I felt a rare shock of guilt. She thought I was truly her friend, and I wished I could be. It had crossed my mind to steal her necklace for my father, but I decided then I couldn't do it. I couldn't hurt her. She was too kind to me.

'I wish I could go,' I said with mischief. 'I would gorge myself on as many pastries as possible. Then I would stand on the table and sing a loud bawdy song and scandalize the whole court. I would go down in history.' I made a dramatic bow. 'Alas, I have not the dress. Nor jewels.'

'I could give you these.' Marie reached for the clasp of the diamonds. 'Come here. I want to see how you look in them.'

I obeyed her, because I always did what she said. She had a warmth, a light, that drew me into her orbit – I was a moth and she a flame, I the tide and she the moon. Whatever we were, she was always, always the light, and I the thing skulking in the dark.

I had longer hair back then, a tousle of jet black that just passed my shoulders. She tucked it behind my ears meticulously, her fingertips hot against my skin. 'Lift up your hair.'

I did as bidden. Tide to moon, moth to flame.

The diamonds settled their weight carefully into my skin.

Marie sucked in an excited breath. 'Oh, Odile. I do wish you could see yourself.'

I was certain I looked ghoulish, a filthy peasant in noblesse gold. Still, I put my fists on my hips and struck a pose. 'How do I look?'

She smiled delightedly. 'Beautiful.' She began to fiddle with her earrings. 'Here, let's –'

'Marie.'

We both froze.

Madame d'Auvigny stood at the mouth of the stables, a silhouette like a giant's against a whitewashed sky. 'What do you think you're doing?' Her voice was not like the Step-Queen's. Instead of being needle-sharp, it was a blunt weapon, every syllable a hammer strike. And with every one, Marie flinched as if struck.

'Get away from that girl. I told your father giving you a peasant playmate was a terrible idea, and here is the evidence.' She turned her eyes on me, two boulder-grey weights that seemed to press in on my skull. 'Shame on you, leading my daughter into such boorish activities. Evidently you've been corrupting her, and you will be punished accordingly.'

Fear speared through me. Serving girls weren't treated kindly. I'd seen vicious slaps and pitiless whippings in my short time masquerading as one, and it had made me hate the Augier King all the more.

I opened my mouth, but I couldn't speak. My heart was pounding – I wanted to shout that it wasn't fair, that this had been Marie's idea. I'd never been easily cowed, but something about Madame d'Auvigny's looming silhouette, the sharp points of her shoulders, the precision of her stare – it made me think too much of Regnault, and I couldn't force a single word through my throat.

I turned desperate eyes to Marie. *Help me*, I wanted to cry. *Tell her the truth. Tell her I don't deserve punishment. Do something. Anything.*

But Marie was looking at her feet.

'Marie, come away,' Madame d'Auvigny said with vicious calm. 'You're going to get your dress dirty. And get that necklace off that girl's neck. If that cow from Malezieu saw how you'd sullied it . . . well. She has the King's ear, and we need his favour, and I will not have you ruining this for me with your foolishness.'

Marie didn't look me in the eye. With cold, jerky movements, so unlike the warmth of minutes before, she pulled the diamonds from my neck. My cheeks burned with humiliation as their weight left me. The fragile trust we'd built over weeks fissured more with every movement. And when she walked away, leaving me there alone, it shattered with a *snap*.

Fortune, for once, was on my side. In the chaos of the banquet, my punishment was forgotten, and I was assigned to serve the noblesse. One red-clad masked face among many, I went unnoticed. And I profited from the chaos and press of the crowd to bump into Marie d'Odette, lingering tired-eyed and inattentive near the wall, to knock her to the floor and pretend to help her up while slipping the chain of shimmering diamonds from her neck.

'I don't know when I lost it. I'm not sure if it was during the banquet, or after.' A breeze has picked up, ruffling the short downy hairs that frame Marie's face. She rubs her arms, and I nearly offer her my jacket. Five years may have passed, but some part of me is still drawn to her, still seeking her out in the dark, even though I once vowed to hate her.

'The Step-Queen was furious. The diamonds were an heirloom, worth as much as an estate. She called me frivolous and careless. She went so far as to ask if I had stolen it. So you can imagine how she reacted when she ordered my rooms to be searched and found the necklace under my pillow.'

Something inside me wilts. So *that's* what happened. I had thought myself careful, clever even. Subtly plucking at a knot that I myself had tied, unravelling it without anyone noticing. But it seems I was wrong.

'She was most angry at my mother. For raising a thief and a liar as a daughter. Told my mother she never wanted to see my face at court again. That she would ensure the Dauphin would never marry me. So you see. Reputation, ruined.'

And I'm the one who ruined it, I should say, but I can't bring myself to admit the truth. And why should I? That would only make her resent me, and she's much too useful. I need her on my side if I'm going to complete this mission.

Instead, I press my hand to my throbbing arm. An owl hoots in the distance. The night bears down, coldly watchful, and I find I can't look Marie in the face. 'You're worried about your reputation, yet you're helping *me*,' I point out. 'Despite the fact that I've stolen your identity. Why?'

She chews on her bottom lip, troubled. 'You managed to convince Aimé to ask for your hand in marriage, which I do not know if I could have done. You've avoided suspicion thus far. I imagine you will continue to do so – if you were to do something truly ridiculous, then you wouldn't have gone about it this way, because everyone will realize something is wrong if Marie d'Auvigny begins to act bizarrely.' I stare at her in surprise. She has read me like a book, and the realization leaves me simultaneously awestruck and deeply uneasy.

She continues, 'Besides, I do not think you intend to continue this charade forever. If I were to guess, you plan to eventually reveal your true identity. You'll want to gloat, show the court how you fooled them. Once they know you were never truly me, I will be absolved of any blame.'

I snort. 'You really think you know everything, don't you?'

'I know you,' she says quietly.

No, you don't, I want to scream. *Because if you did, you would not be standing here.*

Marie's eyes are soft, and I clench my teeth, suddenly hating her, hating what she does to me. 'I care little for the court,' she says finally. 'It is a vile, unwelcoming place. Aimé is all that is good about it, and you're protecting him. This arrangement of ours is bizarre, I will admit, but . . . my winged form is proving useful. And . . . you're not as wicked as you pretend to be, Odile. I think, when the time comes for you to make a decision on this quest of yours, you will make the right one.'

Ah. That's what this is about. She thinks she can *change* me.

'You're wrong,' I say sharply, pushing up off the well, ignoring the throb of my wounded arm. 'I know what you're thinking: that deep down, I have a good heart. That

I will turn back to the light. You have no idea what I'm capable of. You have no idea what's at stake.'

'I do,' she says quietly. 'You told me yesterday. *Magic*. And if you would simply tell me the truth, the whole truth, about what you're trying to do here, I could be your ally. I miss the flowers dearly, Odile. I want to see real white snow, not the soot-black curse that smothers us every winter. And I wish, more than anything, for a world where you don't have to be afraid every time you spill blood.'

I hate her. I *hate* her. Because for a moment, I am tempted. For a moment, I want to tell her everything. She's under my skin, tugging at my most soft-bellied desires, making me hesitate, making me *weak*. But I'm not thirteen any more. I won't fall for that again.

'You enjoy this, don't you?' I seethe, gripping my injured arm. 'Toying with my emotions. Dissecting me, piece by piece.'

'I told you, sorcière,' says Marie – infuriating, ethereal, unbreakable Marie, Marie who betrayed me, and who I betrayed in turn. 'I'm good at puzzles.'

SCENE XVIII

Château. Early morning.

I storm back to the palace, fuming, just as dawn breaks over the lake, a golden flare like leaping embers. My fingers are shaking with such force that I nearly drop the owl-face pendant. I keep a careful eye out for guards, and when I see one near my balcony, I double back and end up forcing open a window on the lower floor, slinking into a dark hallway I know to be near the dining room. The injury on my arm sends routine throbs through my body, and my eyes are sticky with exhaustion. Still, even as I sneak my way back to the Dauphine's apartments, my blood continues to boil.

Marie d'Odette. The arrogance of her, the *audacity*. To presume she could possibly trick me into telling her of my plans. To think all it would take from her would be a soft smile and a gentle touch and my defences would crumble.

If only she knew I was the villain in her story.

After stealing Marie's necklace, I escaped the Château and waltzed back to the Théâtre to present it proudly to my father.

'Very good,' Regnault said, running the necklace through his hands. I waited eagerly for more praise, but he only tutted and handed the necklace back to me. 'But it's not goddess-gold.'

My heart sank. 'You didn't say it needed to be.'

'No, I didn't,' he agreed. 'You may keep it, then, as your reward.' He dismissed me without another word.

When my brother came to see me, that night, I was sitting in our usual secret spot, under the cupola, fighting back tears and aching from it all: Marie's betrayal, Regnault's disappointment, my own foolishness. I told Damien everything, expecting him to take my side. But when he heard of what I'd done, his brows furrowed in anger. 'You must return it,' he said sharply. 'Aimé told me the Duchesse of Auvigny's daughter has gotten into a considerable amount of trouble for losing that thing.'

'Aimé?' I repeated. 'So you're still meeting in secret with the swoony-swoony Dauphin?' I wiggled my eyebrows at him, but it failed to elicit the usual smile.

'Dilou, this is serious. The Step-Queen has been talking to everyone about how the Auvignian heiress was so frivolous she lost her favourite diamonds. It's quite the scandal. If you don't return the necklace, it's going to ruin Marie's prospects of marrying Aimé.' He said the last with barely hidden distaste, and I cackled.

'I've done you a favour, then. One less competitor.'

'Odile.'

I threw my hands in the air. 'She deserves it, Damien! She made me her playmate – no, play*thing* – and then cast me aside when it was convenient!'

Damien's jaw tensed. 'That was cruel of her,' he agreed

steadily. 'But, Odile, what you've done to her is just as cruel, if not more so. I don't think you're quite aware of what you've condemned her to.'

'Please,' I snapped. 'How bad can it be? She's rich and pretty and has people fawning over her. She'll marry the Dauphin and give him little blonde babies and live happily ever after.'

'That's not fair, Odile, and you know it.'

'What do you know about fairness? You haven't seen the things I have!'

'And what do you see, beyond Regnault's ridiculous missions? They're all you care about!'

'Ridic–' I spluttered, affronted. 'How can you say that? I'm doing this for *us*. For you and me and Papa. So we can have magic back as we were supposed to.'

'And what comes after? What will you do once you have magic?'

'The Kingdom will be saved, and I'll be able to learn sorcery.'

'It's not that simple!' Damien said, the usual I-know-better-than-you-because-I'm-two-years-older note creeping into his voice. 'Do you think Regnault will stop there? That he'll sit back and retire after bringing magic back? He hates the noblesse, and you know it. He wants them all dead!'

'Good,' I growled, irritated at being talked down to again. 'It's only right, after what they did to the sorciers.'

'Hurting a whole group of people for the actions of one man would make you no better than the Spider King.'

I curled my lip. 'So? You're just worried about your precious prince.'

'So what if I am?' It was rare for Damien to shout, and the echo of his voice made me flinch. 'I'm protecting you, too! Or do you really think you can look at someone – maybe someone your age, like Aimé or that girl Marie – and drive a knife into their heart?'

I crossed my arms. 'I could if I had to.'

'And what if it were me?' my brother asked suddenly, quieting.

I stared at him in confusion. 'What do you ... Why would it be you?'

'The Dauphin, he ...' Damien rubbed the back of his neck, staring at the dome overhead. 'He offered me a place in his guard.'

My heart stopped, then. *Thud*, and then silence, as if I were dying, as if I were already dead.

No, this couldn't be happening. Not again.

I wish I had been strong – wish I had taken the news with dignity. But I curled my knees up to my chin, cold fright washing over me, and whispered a pathetic, 'You're leaving me?'

'I don't want to,' Damien said. 'I don't, Dilou, I swear. But I can't stay here any longer if I have to keep watching as that man turns you into his little minion –'

My panic veered sharply into disbelief. 'That man?' I echoed. 'You mean our *father*?'

'That's not what he is,' my brother said passionately, and I could see this was something that had been eating at him for a long time. 'He calls himself that to make you feel like you owe him loyalty. But he's not what a father should be like.'

I snorted. 'He's much better than our real father.'

I met his eyes, and I knew that we were remembering the same thing: our mother's shaking hand; her voice, faint and rasping, rotting away like the rest of her. *You must go, now. Take your sister and go.*

'I'm trying to keep my promise to her, Dilou,' Damien said quietly. 'But I can't do that when you keep choosing Regnault over me. You're becoming like him. Vindictive. Cruel.'

'I'm not cruel,' I said furiously. 'I'm merely seeking justice.'

He looked up at me, soft brown eyes – so much like our mother's – filled with earnest, rippling sorrow. I realized with a pang that I had sounded exactly like Regnault.

'Damien . . .' I said shakily.

'Give back the necklace,' Damien said. 'Prove me wrong.'

It was something about the way he looked when he said it. The upright posture, the patronizing tilt of his chin. As though he were chastising me, as though I were a small child he was punishing for a temper tantrum.

'Why can't you take *my* side for once?' I shoved the necklace into my pocket, jabbed a finger at his chest. 'All this talk about leaving me, but you've already left me, haven't you? You've chosen that idiot prince over me. I guess it makes sense. You don't have magic – you'll never really understand.' My anguish was a tidal wave, giving my fury momentum. 'I think you're right. I think you should go.'

Damien looked stricken. 'What?'

'I said you should go!' I couldn't look him in the eyes, because I knew I'd see betrayed hurt pooling within them. He never had been good at hiding his emotions. 'Go back to the Château, to your precious little Aimé, so you can protect him instead. I'm sure he's just *perfect*, not all vindictive and cruel like me.'

Damien drew in a sharp breath. The sound reverberated through the air like the crack of a whip. His hand, I noticed, was clamped around his opposite wrist, as though feeling the red blood pumping beneath his skin, separating us as surely as a wall.

I couldn't stop myself any more. I hurt, I hurt all over – my chest ached, my heart felt as though a fist had closed around it. Damien was going to leave me, just as our birth father had. Just like our mother had. And in that infinitesimal moment, I wanted to hurt him just as he was hurting me.

And so I spat, *'Traitor.'*

Regnault found me later sobbing in the dressing rooms, my face buried in a pair of feathered black wings I had been using as a pillow. I told him everything, and when I was done, he drew me into his arms. 'Oh, Odile, do you see now?' His voice was achingly tender. 'I am the only one who will never leave you.'

By the next day, the guilt had set in. It battered at my walls no matter how much I tried to harden myself against it, no matter how often I reminded myself that Regnault wouldn't care, so neither should I. Every time I closed my eyes, I saw the words *vindictive, cruel*. I pictured Marie's luminous silver eyes filling with tears as she was ridiculed by the court. The diamond necklace weighed heavy in my pocket.

Unable to look at the thing any longer, I went back to Château Front-du-Lac. I donned my servant's reds for the last time. And when I was sent up to the guests' rooms to clean, I slipped the diamond necklace from my pocket and left it under Marie d'Odette's pillow.

Now, I take out the small yellow flower from my pocket. I hold it between my fingers, tight enough that its petals creak beneath my touch. Any more pressure, and I would crush it. I wish I could hold my guilt the same way, squeeze it until it capitulated and crumbled. So what if I hurt Marie? She's only a means to an end. It matters not how much I crave her touch, how cleverly she tempts me with her sweet, generous trust. How much I regret my role in her ruination.

I can long for her, and still hate her.

After all, does a moth not hate a flame, when it learns that the very thing that attracts it is the thing that will see it burn?

'At least all my suffering wasn't for nothing,' I murmur, pressing the yellow flower between the pages of Bartrand de Roux's journal and closing the book carefully. Tomorrow, I will decide on what to do with it, and I will think of Marie no longer.

I sleep until it is nearly noon, until the slam of rain on my window and the knock of a maid forces me, groaning, back to my feet. The stiffness of bandages on my arm draws me up short. The previous night comes rushing back to me – the thorn, the well, *Marie*.

'A moment!' I call to the maid.

I peel the bandages off and toss them angrily into the room's chest, ignoring the way my stomach lurches at the memory of torn cloth and burning touch. I'm relieved to see the wound beneath has closed itself smoothly. I cover it with face powder and dab more on to my wrists, then wrap the wound in lace and ribbon, hoping it will look like a quirky choice of accessory.

Only then do I let the maid in. Once I am dressed, I pull both journal and yellow flower from beneath my mattress and slip them into the pockets tied beneath my skirts. I think of showing Aimé the yellow flower, telling him my concerns. Then I pause. What if I'm wrong? What if the Step-Queen is truly helping Aimé, as he claims, and all I do is cast suspicion on myself for following her around the Château grounds?

I consider my options as I head down the stairs, unsure yet whether I should angle myself towards the library or the Dauphin's chambers.

Before I can make a decision, I notice a familiar silhouette in the entrance hall, and freeze in my tracks.

Regnault stands in the middle of the chamber, black cloak brushing the marble, his auburn hair slicked back and raven-feather mask shining in the daylight. He is speaking with the Regent, and based on the servant hurrying away with a small trunk of his belongings, I assume he has just arrived.

For no reason I can explain, my heart begins to pound uneasily. I have not seen my father since before I tried to unravel his spell on Marie. What if he felt something was amiss? What if he's displeased by the way I have handled our plans? Worse, what if he realizes I have been … *fraternizing* with not only the Dauphin but Mademoiselle d'Odette, who, as far as Regnault is concerned, should still be spending all of her time as a bird?

The men are deep in conversation – I consider ducking into the shadows and skirting around them, or doubling back and going a different way. But I don't get the chance to move before my father's eyes land on me.

It's like being pinned by an arrow. His gaze glitters, sly and unyielding. My heart begins to pound harder, my knees feeling strangely weak. The wound on my arm throbs urgently. I try to calm myself. I wanted this. I orchestrated this so we could work together. Regnault is the only person who truly understands me, after all.

So why do I feel afraid?

My father opens his arms. 'This must be the Dauphine-to-be!' His voice booms, animated and charismatic. There is not a trace of familiarity in his actions. He greets me with a bow and a flourish, in character as the peculiar theatre master. 'You have been the talk of the court, Mademoiselle.'

The Regent notices me, and his lip curls. 'Yes,' he says, hardly trying to hide his disdain. 'This is she. She is, ah . . . *eccentric*.'

'I must introduce myself, then,' my father says, giving the Regent another, shorter, bow. 'Excuse me while I speak to the Dauphine about her wishes for the upcoming wedding. Monseigneur, do send for me if you have any further questions.' He rubs his hands together, striding towards me.

I realize with a start that I have reached the bottom of the stairs. I did not even notice I was moving – it is as though a force has pulled me, against my will, towards Regnault. My father takes my hand and kisses the back, the image of a gentleman, but when he looks up his eyes flicker with wicked intensity, landing on the owl-face pendant.

'P-pleasure to meet you,' I stammer, barely remembering to play along. My father beams gallantly and lays a hand on the small of my back.

'Why don't you show me around the palace?' he says. 'I must become familiar with the space if I am to organize this grand event.'

I know there is no refusing. I let Regnault escort me from the room, trying to hold my composure with all my strength.

Regnault's smile drops as soon as we are out of sight. His hand retracts from my back, and he scowls down at me. 'I did not think we would see each other again so soon. And *without the Couronne.*' The last words are razor-sharp, and I feel them like the skim of a knife against my skin.

I look at my feet, hidden beneath heavy bronze skirts. 'I'm sorry,' I say. 'I –' But how to explain this? That instead of finding out where the Couronne lies, I have been busy attempting to solve a murder and prove my brother's innocence? 'The King's death complicated things,' I say at last, forcing myself to look my father in the face. 'But I managed to convince the Dauphin to move the wedding up.'

My father crosses his arms. 'So this was your doing?'

'I told him it would take the people's minds off the tragedy,' I say, allowing a tentative grin. 'And of course, I planted the seed for the Dauphin to hire you. He thinks it was all his idea.'

Regnault's lips quirk up briefly, but his gaze doesn't change, cold and scrutinizing and finely honed. I fidget, increasingly nervous.

'D-did I do well?' I realize, too late, how pathetic that sounds. How desperate.

Regnault considers my question. 'Is that all you have managed to accomplish since I sent you here?'

'I –' My pulse quickens again. My hands drift to my pockets, to the flower and journal. 'There's, um, there's this.' I slip out the yellow-petalled flower and present it to him. 'I found the Step-Queen gathering them. In the garden. I think they . . . they might be important somehow.' I don't show him the journal – I don't want to risk him taking it away.

Regnault's face betrays no emotion. He doesn't take the flower from me, hardly giving it more than a glance. 'Is this all?'

I make the biggest mistake possible – I hesitate. Regnault's eyes narrow immediately, a predator spotting its prey. 'Odile?' It's both question and warning. 'Is there anything else you want to show me?'

'I am working on something. I will tell you . . . later.'

'Odile, what is it?' he demands. 'What are you hiding?'

'Nothing! I swear it!' I try to step away, unable to bear his looming presence any longer. 'I must go, I need to –'

Before I can move any further, Regnault reaches out and snatches my arm – my injured arm – his fingers digging in.

The bolt of pain is so sudden I cry out, tearing my arm away.

Regnault's eyes widen in realization. 'Are you *injured*?'

'N-no,' I stammer. 'No, I was just surprised –'

'Marie!' A familiar, chipper voice reaches us, cutting off whatever my father was going to say. It takes all my willpower not to collapse in relief as Aimé-Victor Augier appears at the end of the hallway, petticoat breeches rustling as he approaches. I hurry away from Regnault to loop my arm through Aimé's, plastering a pleasant, demure smile on my face.

'Ah, *mon amour*,' I greet the Dauphin sweetly, my heart still rattling. 'I was just talking with Monsieur Regnault about the upcoming wedding. He has some truly *excellent* ideas for dessert.'

Regnault's eyes flicker as he quickly reins in his fury at me, concealing it from the Dauphin. Part of me can't help gloating at having weaselled my way out of answering his questions. I press closer to Aimé's side, and he gives me a surprised look. I realize there's a concerned shine to his eyes – he must have heard my shout when Regnault grabbed me.

'Are you all right?' he asks.

I nod with as much conviction as possible. 'Just tripped on my dress. Monsieur Regnault is such a gentleman – he helped me back to my feet. Why don't I leave you two to speak?' I gesture between the two of them, eager to make my escape. 'I'm meant to meet some of the court ladies for tea.'

'That's a wonderful idea,' Aimé says tactfully. 'And, Marie?'

I pause mid-step. 'Hm?'

'Meet me in the Queen's Tower at three. There's something I want to show you.'

I try to catch Aimé's eyes, trying to discern what this *something* could be, but he is already looking towards Regnault, giving me an opening to leave. I take it, picking up my skirts as I go. I do not, in fact, have tea with the court ladies. Instead, I hide in the empty library, trying to calm myself after my encounter with my father. I scavenge for books and manuscripts detailing Aurélian flora, searching for anything that might resemble the odd, wrinkled flower. I find no answers – but I do find myself staring at pictures of beautiful, colourful blooms that have not been seen in Auréal for two hundred years.

I trace my fingers over a dainty painting of a rose the colour of ripe peaches, and for no reason I can explain, I imagine how lovely it would look tucked into Marie's hair, pink against silver.

And if you would simply tell me the truth, the whole truth, about what you're trying to do here, I could be your ally.

I groan and shut the book, rubbing my eyes. Marie, Marie, Marie. Why can't I stop thinking about her?

Because you want her, whispers a treacherous little voice in my mind.

No, I tell it. *I want to hate her.*

Then I get to my feet.

I search until the brass clock on the far wall strikes three. Then I replace my books, abandon the dusty room and ask a guard for directions to the Queen's Tower.

The Queen's Tower is one of the few places in the Château I did not go as a servant – no one did, as it was unused, said to be haunted by the Queen's ghost since her death. Though I don't believe the stories, I approach the first stair cautiously, growing bolder only when I hear humming carrying faintly down. I recognize Aimé's boyish lilt, and the high-pitched notes of the piece of music he played last night.

Curious, I begin my climb. The Augier tarasque is painted in vivid colours on the tower walls, its long tail coiling downwards, the wrinkled length of its neck extending overhead. At the very top of the turret is a room, the tarasque's head snarling from the keystone. The door is cracked open, letting out a waterfall of pale light. Beyond, I glimpse a grand room, perfectly circular, white tarps settled over the furniture and a massive, canopied bed.

On the bed sits Aimé-Victor Augier, a book open on his lap as he waits, staring out of the window. This is one of the few rooms that looks not over the lake, but across the brown, bare woodland that strangles the front of the Château. There, humps of distant mountains peer over a clot of bleak, leafless trees and a winding carriage path. A few dried leaves have become trapped on the windowsill, and they rasp wetly against the panes.

'Good afternoon,' I greet him, keeping my voice hushed. Something about the room makes me think of a mausoleum, as though a word spoken too loud might indeed awaken a restless ghost.

The Dauphin starts. When his gaze snaps to mine, his eyes are haunted, murky instead of crystalline. He hastily wipes at tears on his cheeks, his expression growing sheepish. 'Apologies,' he says. 'I didn't hear your approach.'

'I walk quietly,' I say. 'You look troubled. What is it?'

Aimé sighs. I realize, suddenly, just how weary he looks – how the bruises under his eyes seem only to have darkened, how his cheeks grow more gaunt by the day. I think of the yellow flower, of the potions, and wonder: is it just exhaustion? Or is there something more to all this?

'It's Damien,' Aimé says finally. 'He's been transferred to the city prison.'

The mention of my brother makes my chest clench. 'What . . .' I swallow. 'What does that mean?'

'They're going to try him.' The Dauphin's throat bobs. 'I do not doubt he will be found guilty, because my uncle needs a scapegoat. And he will be executed before the wedding.'

'Before the –' My breath catches in my throat. By moving up the wedding, did I inadvertently condemn Damien? 'Why? Why now? Why not wait until –'

'Because a wedding needs guests,' Aimé says quietly. 'And most nobles are too frightened to return, after my father's death. They need to know they are safe. And what better way to do that than to show them the murderer has been caught and hanged?' Aimé wrings his hands, and I resist the urge to grab him by the lapels and shake him with all my might.

'Can you not do anything?' I demand. 'You're the Mothers-damned Dauphin!'

'I tried!' he shouts, and the sound is so fierce that I back away, stung by the strength of his feeling. 'I tried. But my uncle is right, Marie. The people *are* afraid. They need someone to blame. The only way I can save Damien is by finding the true killer before the wedding.'

'All right,' I say, trying to project assurance into my voice, though it rings false and grating in my ears. 'With that, at least, I think I can help.'

'What do you mean?'

'I think I found something, in the gardens. But you're not going to like it.'

'There are few things I like these days, it seems,' Aimé says, forcing a laugh. It comes out strangled. 'What is it, then?'

I take a breath. 'The medicine Madame de Malezieu gives you. I don't think . . . I don't think you should drink it any more.'

Aimé blinks. 'What?'

'I think it might be poison.'

He laughs in confusion, an edge of panic to the sound. 'Why would you say that?'

I steel myself, softening my voice as much as I can before delivering the suspicion that has been haunting me since Marie and I found the flower.

'Because I believe Anne de Malezieu is trying to kill you.'

SCENE XIX

Château. The Queen's Tower.

'No. No, you're wrong.' Aimé stares at me, white-faced, his shoulders heaving as though he has run miles. 'You're *wrong*.'

Carefully, I walk over to the bed and sit down in front of him, opening my hands in supplication. 'Think about it, Aimé. She has many connections at court, yet goes mostly unnoticed. She had your father's trust, has your trust –'

'My father was killed by a beast,' Aimé interrupts, desperately.

'A beast of impossible size. Most likely created by a sorcier.'

'My stepmother has red blood,' Aimé says adamantly. 'I saw her prick her finger, once, on an embroidery needle. She's no sorcier.'

'But she could have contact with one,' I argue. 'She could have let the sorcier know where the King would be, and the sorcier sent the beast after him.' The more I explain it, the more the picture begins to come together. There's something terribly satisfying about it, like the easy *click* of puzzle pieces.

'But this doesn't explain what my father was doing out in the grounds mere hours before dawn.'

'Perhaps Anne asked him to meet her there. Orchestrated some sort of meeting or another ruse. And ensured Damien would arrive just on time to find the bodies.' I lean forward. 'It makes sense.'

'No, it doesn't.' Aimé's jaw is set now. 'Let's . . . let's say that you're right. She did kill my father. Why not kill me the same way?'

'Because if another similar death occurred while Damien was in prison, he would be absolved. So she's relying on the potions to kill you slowly. What if the reason your nerves have gotten worse isn't despite the medicine, but *because* of it?'

'These are all assumptions. Theories.' Aimé gets to his feet, slamming shut the book in his lap and beginning to pace. 'I know you are trying to help, Marie, but I cannot believe this. This strange rivalry between you and my stepmother is skewing your perception of things. Anne would never hurt me. She . . . she doesn't have a reason to.'

'She does,' I argue, feeling a sear of frustration at his dismissal. 'If you were to die, who would inherit the throne?'

He pulls up short. I see the realization dawn on his face. 'Pierre. But he's just a little boy.'

I raise my eyebrows. 'Easy to control.'

'Stop this.' He covers his face with one hand. 'Anne isn't like that.'

But I can't stop. Not with my brother at stake. The timeline has been shortened, and I can feel desperation gnawing on my bones. 'Do you know what's in the medicine, Aimé?'

He shakes his head minutely.

'I do.' As he turns towards me, I pull the flower from my pocket and hold it out to him. 'I found this near the border of the palace grounds. I heard a rumour that Anne frequents a certain spot there, so I went to look. Found a patch of these. I tried to identify them, but in all the Château's botanical books, I could not find a single mention of anything similar.'

A flicker of doubt ghosts over Aimé's face. Then he huffs sharply. 'No. I can't believe this, Marie, I'm sorry. So Anne uses strange flowers to make my medicine. That doesn't make it any less effective. I've been taking it since I was a boy – it is the only thing that helps me.' He shakes his head, dislodging a few golden ringlets to fall around his face. 'All this is merely an assumption. Without proof, it is meaningless. And it won't save Damien.'

Disappointment and urgency whirl through me in a storm. He's right. I don't have proof, and for all my excitement about my theory, it is really just that: a theory. I need evidence. I need to identify that flower. But how?

I try to put myself in the shoes of a poisoner. Where would I hide my secrets? Not in my bedroom, surely, a place that would see a constant flow of servants. But nowhere too strange, either, nowhere that would raise eyebrows if I went there too often. The Step-Queen has a study, I remember, somewhere in the Château's north wing. It is her private space for letter-writing, and not even the King was allowed to enter. I never went there, as a servant – there was only one maid permitted to clean the space, a shy girl who spoke little and kept her head down. I thought little of it at the time, but . . . it's possible Anne de Malezieu has been doing more in there than simply writing letters.

Now that I am no longer pressing him, Aimé stops his pacing. He puts down the massive tome on a fabric-swathed table, sending up a puff of dust. I realize it is some sort of ledger – or perhaps a journal, judging by the wear and tear to the spine.

'What's that?' I ask.

'It's what I wanted to show you,' he says, staring at it in reproach. 'Technically, it's a ledger of finance. My father kept it up here with all his other . . . *memories*. Except this one wasn't my mother's, but my grandfather's. My father showed it to me once when I was a boy. As . . . a warning.'

I come closer. 'A warning?'

'Yes. You'll find it's rather . . . *maddening*.' He laughs quietly at his own joke, one I don't understand. I frown and open the tome. The first pages are written in a neat, precise script, sums and charts detailing imports and exports, debts and budgets. Looking at the numbers, my head immediately starts to throb, and I continue flicking through the pages. Halfway through the journal, however . . .

'See the writing here? See how orderly it is?' Aimé turns a few more pages and stops. 'Look at the date.' He points to the top of the yellowed paper, and I suck in a breath. October 25th.

'The day of Bartrand de Roux's betrayal,' I say.

'Exactly.' Aimé flips the page again. 'Now watch.'

As he gets further into the journal, the Spider King's writing begins to grow more and more lopsided, going from perfectly shaped letters and numbers to a maddened, frenzied scrawl. Eventually, the writing breaks off entirely, devolving into three words, ink-spotted and panicked and never-ending.

> *HE IS COMING HE IS COMING HE IS COMING HE IS COMING*

The longer I look at the words, the more my skin crawls. Aimé glances at me, his eyes sheepish. 'This is what it does, you see? The Couronne. This is the big secret. It's not just a magical artefact – whatever is inside it drove my grandfather to the brink of insanity. The more he used it, the worse it got. According to my father, he would simply stare for hours at the thing, like it had him in some sort of thrall. Sometimes he would talk to things that weren't there. Towards the end, he didn't even recognize my father, his own son.'

Dread slips through me, cold and biting. Regnault always told me that the Couronne was impossibly powerful, full of enough magic to summon back Morgane. Could it be that very magic which drove the Spider King mad?

'This is why my father was always so reluctant to use it,' Aimé says, closing the book, brushing his sleeve over the leather cover. 'Do you remember the drought, three years ago? It would have decimated southern Auréal, had my father not travelled there with the Couronne to encourage crops to grow.' He toys idly with the edge of the pages, eyes distant. 'He was never the same, after. Sometimes he would mumble under his breath, or stare at nothing with his eyes glazed. His anger got worse. Much worse. So he swore never to use the crown again, no matter what befell us. I think he believed that . . . that Auréal could survive without it. But with every year, the crops bear smaller yields, the trees less fruit. The courtiers go hunting and complain that they find no quarry, only old carcasses. This kingdom is *decaying*, Marie. I'm certain even Auvigny has felt it. The only way to keep it from rotting entirely is to use the Couronne's magic. Once I am crowned, that duty will fall to me.' He sighs, then laughs. 'Thankfully, I'm already going mad. No one will be able to tell the difference.'

'Aimé,' I say tightly, and that's all I can manage. For a brief, baffling moment, I consider telling him everything. About the Couronne, about my father's plan. About how I could save him from madness, how I plan to bring magic back.

But at the end of all this, I want the power Regnault promised me. I don't want to bow like the Golden-blooded Girl before a king. And though a foolish part of me – the part that let Marie place diamonds around my neck, the part that thought my brother would stay by my side – wants to trust Aimé, I still bear the scars from old burns.

So I tell him nothing. I sit beside him and let him rest his head on my shoulder, while somewhere in the distance a mourning dove cries out. But while my body is still, my mind can't seem to quiet. I am already deciding on my next move.

The Step-Queen's secrets prove difficult to unravel.

That day, and the next, I attempt to locate her study, to no avail. Many of the Château servants are new, it seems, and unaware of its existence – she spends most of the day surrounded by her court ladies, they say, moving between sitting rooms and tea rooms, seemingly no different than the rest of the noblesse. It is only the evenings that she spends alone. I bide my time, hiding in the shadows near the north wing. Near sunset, she arrives, walking with purpose, a whirl of mourning black and blazing sapphire. I try to follow, but I am too slow – she's already been swallowed up by the crooked maze of hallways.

By the next day, the first wedding guests begin to arrive. The Dauphin rises early to arrange a welcoming feast for them, the Step-Queen hovering by his side. 'Your medicine,' I overhear her whispering to him. 'I've brought it for you.'

Perfect. I ensure I sit beside the Step-Queen, and when she is distracted, slip the vial from her skirt pocket. Midway through the meal, she realizes it's missing, and excuses herself promptly, whispering something to Aimé before she leaves. I wait a moment before following. I see the hem of her skirts disappearing around the corner, and rush after her, only to be blocked by two of the newly arrived guests. One of them – a young man who seems to have *antlers* protruding from his skull – mutters something in irritated Orlican.

I ignore him and shove past, picking up my skirts and following my quarry. The Step-Queen passes the chapel. She turns down one dark hallway, then another. Past a group of murmuring servants, an empty drawing room full of glass-eyed hunting trophies. Finally, her footsteps slow. I hear the *click* of an opening door, then silence. I peer carefully around the corner to see a black door of unassuming ebony, and –

A shadow seizes me. I'm shoved against the wall, cold fingers closing around my throat, the metal press of rings jutting into my windpipe.

'I always knew there was something strange about you,' the Step-Queen snarls. Her flat teeth gleam yellow in the muted light, the sharpness of her perfume needling into my sinuses. 'And finally I catch you, red-handed. Now, tell me what you're plotting.'

'Plotting?' I school my expression into one of angelic innocence, despite the panicked thundering of my pulse. 'Madame, I'm not plotting anything, I swear it.'

Her fingers tighten, making me wheeze. 'Do you take me for a fool? I know you've been following me.'

'I was, but –' I press my back further into the wall, trying to loosen her hold. I'm acutely aware that if she manages to draw blood, she will uncover my ruse. 'I only wanted to . . . to return this to you.' I shift enough to slide my hand into my pocket and palm the vial of potion. 'Here.'

Upon seeing the vial, she pulls back somewhat, her eyes narrowing. I know what she's thinking: if I'm truly plotting something, why admit to having the potion in my possession?

'I found it on the ground,' I say, holding it out to her. 'I know it's the Dauphin's medicine, but I thought it best to return it to you, since you're the one that gives it to him.'

The Step-Queen scowls. For a moment, I fear she will not take the bait. But after a furious pause, she releases me, snatching the vial from my outstretched palm. Immediately, I scramble away from her, but she steps in front of me, blocking my escape.

'Once a thief, always a thief,' she says, pointing a bony finger at me. 'Know this – I see through this façade of yours. You're still trying to sink your claws into something that does not belong to you.'

Her words might as well be a confession. She's after the Crown, just as I thought, and she secs me as a rival.

'I truly don't know of what you speak,' I say, with as much honesty as I can muster. 'I was merely trying to help.'

'Save your lies for my foolish son,' the Step-Queen growls. 'And remember this: I am watching you. One step out of line, Marie d'Odette, and I will ensure you're sent back to Auvigny in shame.'

By that evening, the Step-Queen has made good on her promise. I catch guards shadowing my every step, trailing me around the Château like phantoms. I curse my incaution. I should be better than this – Regnault would be disappointed in me.

But I refuse to be outsmarted.

I hatch a new plan. A plan which, to my great disappointment, will need the assistance of the one girl I cannot seem to stay away from.

SCENE XX

The Lake. A starry night.

Three days have passed since my last, turbulent parting from Marie d'Odette. Seething with irritation, I decide that it is perhaps best to offer her an olive branch, so I filch a few pastries from the kitchens and take a cloak along with me. It's a surprisingly pleasant night, clear and bright, and the lake is perfectly still, dusted with the reflections of stars. I find Marie in her usual spot, watching the lake's swans as they slumber nearby.

I expect her to meet me with some level of aloofness – or perhaps even anger, considering how I stormed off on her last time. But when she sees me again, she merely tilts her head to the side, eyes bright. 'I knew you couldn't stay away for long.'

My heart gives an excited skip at the sound of her voice. I scowl. 'Don't be so pleased, Princess. I need you for something.'

'Of course you do,' she says serenely. 'How's your arm?'

'Still attached.'

She laughs, and it sounds like spring rain, pure and sweet. I want to gather it up in my palms, feel it trickle between my fingers. I want to forget I ever heard it.

Mothers, I *hate* her.

'Odile –' Marie begins, her voice growing serious.

She's going to say something about our argument, and it's not something I want to talk about. 'Forget it,' I say. 'I cursed you. It's your right to irritate me to the ends of the earth.'

She shakes her head. 'I just wanted to tell you that I don't . . . you're not just a puzzle. That's not how I think of you.'

For some reason, her words make my cheeks prickle with heat. 'I said forget it!' I snap, hard enough that one of the swans twitches awake.

Marie flinches back, startled. 'My apologies.'

'No, it's . . .' I run my hand over my face, then remember the pastries I've wrapped up in paper and tucked beneath my cloak. 'I brought you something. An olive branch.' I set the pastries down beside her, utterly refusing to make eye contact.

I hear the rustle as Marie unfolds the paper, then her delighted gasp. 'Oh, Odile, do you know how long it's been since I've eaten a pastry?'

'I thought it was a staple of the noblesse diet,' I say resentfully. 'It's all I've been eating. I'm surprised my blood hasn't turned to powdered sugar yet.'

That elicits another laugh from her, and the effect it has on my body is so physical I can imagine it being found if I am ever dissected, protruding from my innards. She picks up a small, somewhat crushed cream puff, takes a careful bite and swallows.

'You know, when I'm a swan, there are some instincts I can't resist,' she says.

I cock my head. 'What do you mean?'

'Well, I've been living off pondweed.'

'You're joking.'

The mournful look she gives me reveals she is, decidedly, not joking. 'My human brain tells me it's disgusting. My bird brain tells me it's delicious.'

I snort at that, then quickly cover my mouth. 'Sorry. It's not funny. I . . . ah, did this to you.'

She glances at me sideways, her smile small and fond.

'What?' I demand.

'I haven't heard you laugh like that since we were girls.'

I don't know how to respond. I pick up a macaron and stuff it petulantly into my mouth.

I sit quietly for a moment, the sugary confection melting on my tongue. Then, abruptly, Marie says, 'Did you find out anything more about those strange flowers?'

I shake my head. 'I tried, but it seems I found only more mysteries.' Quickly, I recount to her the events of the past few days, from my father's arrival to my confrontation with the Step-Queen. When I'm done, Marie worries her lower lip contemplatively, then suddenly gets to her feet.

'Come on,' she says. 'Let's go to the city.'

'The city?' I echo.

'We could look for an apothecary's shop. Where better to ask about mysterious herbs?'

'Will any be open at this hour?' Though I came to see Marie as soon as I could escape without notice, it's still rather late – eight or nine, at least.

'Surely at least one must be.' Her eyes glitter eagerly, and I huff.

'You want to explore the city.'

'Perhaps,' she says, flicking her hair over her shoulder.

I stare, unable to restrain a fond smile of my own at seeing her old, adventurous authority shine through her usual veil of propriety. I should refuse. Verroux is dangerous – Verroux at night doubly so. But she is right. Perhaps the city will hold answers the Château does not.

'Very well, then,' I say. 'But we won't go beyond Upper Verroux, and we avoid trouble at all costs.'

Marie's lips curl up. 'Between the two of us, that's rather a tall order, wouldn't you say?'

I have little love for Verroux. It's a spiderweb of a city, unravelling in thin, slick threads from the cathedral at its heart, clinging to the Théâtre on one side and the fat, snaking Verroux river on the other. Upper Verroux is for the wealthy, for lesser nobles and merchants – expensive shops, the buildings neat and clean and fronted by arches and columns. Marie and I weave through them cautiously, seeking any promising establishments.

The upper sector appears to have only one apothecary. It is, to my dismay, closed, forcing us to leave the secure embrace of orderly streets to continue our search. As the city deepens, its façade of finesse peels away like apple skin, revealing a mouldering brown core. Filth lines the flagstone roads, livestock bray in muddy pens, beggars slump in alleys. We stick to the main street – the evening is cold, but the street is lively, music erupting from nearby taverns and drunken men swaying under eaves.

Eventually, the street spits us out into the lower town square, meant for markets and gatherings. In the centre is a neglected fountain depicting the Good Mothers, their hands outspread. Once, I imagine, water burst from their palms. Now, they are still, a fine layer of frost spread over the basin's green water. A fiddler plays nearby, and a young urchin entertains a small crowd with a gambling game.

Marie draws her cloak tighter around her shoulders. She starts forward eagerly, ravenously taking in the chaos of the square.

'Wait.' I tug her back, feeling strangely protective. The wonder in her eyes is that of someone unaware of the world's darkness – and though this area of Verroux is safe enough, I've learned that *safe enough* is the siren song of danger. 'We have to be careful,' I whisper. 'Two young women out unescorted are certain to draw attention.'

Sure enough, one of the gamblers turns to stare at us, beady eyes glistening. I try to pull Marie even closer, but her eyes have already caught on a small shop across the square, candlelight still flickering inside and jars of what looks like herbs in the windows.

'That looks promising,' she says. 'Come on, it might still be open.' To my shock, she seizes my hand in her own, her elegant fingers wrapping around my calloused ones. It's like being struck by lightning. I nearly stumble when she tugs me along, my heart pounding ridiculously.

We don't get far before we both splash into a large puddle, which we failed to notice in the dim lamplight. Marie gasps at the cold kiss of water, and I can't help my chuckle.

'Scared of a little mud, Princess?'

She kicks some of the water at me in response, and I barely manage to jump out of the way. She giggles. 'It appears you are, too.'

'Why, you –' But before I can think of adequate revenge, a roar goes up from the group of gamblers in the corner of the square. We both turn to see one of the men rear back, gripping the skinny wrist of the little urchin.

'You cheater! Where are you putting it?!'

'I'm not putting it anywhere!' The urchin tries to tug his hand free to no avail. 'I swear, look under the cups! It's there!'

One of the other men shoves him aside, the scar over his eye giving him a vicious appearance as he storms across to the little overturned crate with the three cups stacked on top. The boy had been shuffling them around. The burly man turns over the first cup – nothing. The second – also nothing. The third reveals a golden coin. Another roar goes up.

'It wasn't there a moment ago,' says the man holding the boy. He's built like an ox, with a thick red beard.

'It was, Monsieur!' the boy cries. 'I haven't been cheating, I swear!'

Red-beard tightens his grip, spittle flying from his lips. 'If you weren't cheating, then how come none of us have won?'

The boy tugs his hand free and leaps back. 'Maybe you're just bad at the game!'

Red-beard growls. He lunges for the urchin, who ducks aside only to be grabbed by the man with the scar over his eye. 'I've another explanation,' Scar-face snarls. Something glints in his free hand. 'Little whelp could be one of them sorcers. Usin' magic to cheat.'

'*Sorciers*, you idiot,' the red-bearded man corrects, grinning hungrily. 'They're called *sorciers*. And I think you might be on to something.'

I freeze, horror spearing through me. I know where this is going – I've seen it happen before. My pulse thuds against my ears. 'I can't be here.' The words slip out of me inadvertently. I reach out shakily, seize Marie's sleeve. 'Come on.'

But she doesn't move. 'We cannot simply leave him!'

'There's nothing we can do!' I hiss back.

In front of us, Scar-face snaps his teeth near the boy's ear, making the child cry out in fear. 'Only one way to find out, isn't there?' He raises the object in his hand – a knife, gleaming viciously in the darkness. He presses it to the boy's cheek. 'What colour do you bleed, little rat?'

My vision narrows to one thing. The boy's wrists are covered in mud – too precise to be unintentional. These men are simple, fattened on paranoia and folktales of evil golden-blooded traitors. They're too dumb to understand that magic is gone from Auréal. That even if the boy *was* cheating, he wasn't doing it through sorcery.

It doesn't matter to them. If the boy bleeds gold, they will kill him.

Run, something inside me screams, trembling and feral. *Run!*

The man presses the knife deeper.

'Stop!' Marie shouts suddenly. The Swan Princess brushes past me, striding towards the group of men. 'Unhand him, right now! That's my brother!'

Four pairs of beady eyes turn to her, four cruel mouths curling into wicked grins. My heart slams into my throat, beating too fast. *Runrunrunrunrun*.

Marie ignores the danger. She shakes out her beautiful coils of pale-gold hair and lifts her chin high. 'What do any of you think you're doing, anyway, threatening a little boy?'

Scar-face sneers, lowering his knife a fraction. 'This *little boy* was cheatin' us of coin.'

'Playing games, as little boys do.' Marie may wear simple clothing, but the nobility in her bearing, in her voice, is undeniable. She drifts across the square like a deity, like she has been woven from dreams and supplications. 'Now release him. Unless you want to answer to my brother, the Duke of Auvigny.'

'The Duke of –' Red-beard's eyes widen. 'Wait. You're the Prince's betrothed?'

Scar-face hesitates. 'If that's the Prince's betrothed, why is she dressed like a peasant?'

There's a beat of silence, every figure in the square unmoving.

Then the little boy gives a shrill cry and kicks Scar-face between the legs. He snatches a small bag off the stones and takes off down an alleyway, vanishing into the gloom.

Marie freezes, suddenly aware she is too close to the press of furious, drunkenly irrational men. Feeling danger, I begin to move, just as Scar-face blinks dumbly.

'The bastard took our coins,' he says.

It all happens very quickly after that. Red-beard gives a bellow and turns on Marie. I dart forward and catch her by the wrist, pulling her away just as Red-beard's knife arcs towards her.

'You lying bitch!' Red-beard shouts.

'Run!' I manage, and we take off back the way we came, away from the apothecary's shop and its promise of answers.

'Odile!' Marie shouts, but I shake my head, pulling her along behind me. A carriage comes rattling towards us, and we narrowly avoid its wheels. Marie trips with a yelp, and I seize her by the waist, pushing her on to her feet.

'Keep moving,' I pant, hearing the roars of the men behind us. 'Come on!'

We gallop down the street, window lights and streetlamps blurring around us. The voices of the men begin to fade, but I don't let her go, don't stop running.

'Odile!' Marie calls again, but I ignore her, adrenaline screaming through me.

Runrunrunrunrun.

'Odile, they're gone!'

They're gone, but we're not safe, we're never safe, we need to run –

Suddenly, the Théâtre du Roi is rearing up in front of us, its maw yawning open eagerly, columns flashing white as teeth. The statues of famous playwrights lining the roof seem to jeer down at us.

I pull Marie through the gate, across the courtyard and around the Théâtre, until we're back at the lake's edge, the overgrown garden engulfing us.

Only then do I release Marie's hand, turning on her. 'Mothers, what were you thinking?' I say between wheezing breaths. 'You could have gotten us killed!'

'He needed help!' She wipes sweat from her eyes. 'I . . . I couldn't just stand there and let him get hurt!' *Like you would have* – she doesn't say the words, she's too tactful for that, but the accusation is sharp in her eyes.

I grit my teeth. 'You think you're so much better than everyone else, don't you? You think all you have to do is say *please* and *thank you* and the world will bow to your wishes. The Swan Princess,' I sneer. 'You'll learn, eventually, as I did. You can't save everyone.'

Marie recoils, hurt flashing across her face, as surprised by my outburst as I am. But I can't stop. Frustration, fear, panic – it all continues to pour out of me: 'And that boy? He would have been fine on his own, I promise you that. He would have figured out how to get away.'

She shakes her head. 'You can't possibly know that.'

'I do!'

'How?'

'Because I used to be just like him!'

Marie stares at me, her brows curled up in concern. 'What?'

'That's what becomes of us!' I'm still shouting, still fuelled by remnants of panic. 'Of sorcier children. If you're lucky, you're born to a sorcier parent who *understands*, who knows how to protect you, but sometimes magic skips a generation. Sometimes both your parents have red blood, and your older brother has red blood, but then you're born golden-blooded and your father makes your mother choose: get rid of you and stay with him, or leave along with her newborn sorcier child.' I break off in a gasp – I can't seem to catch my breath. 'And sometimes you're lucky and your mother chooses you, but the world is hard for a woman alone, and she works as a maid and barely scrapes together enough to keep a roof over your heads until she catches the pox and suddenly she's *dying*.'

I know I'm being irrational, I'm ranting, but all I can see is the knife pressed against the boy's cheek, all I can think of is the nobleman throwing me on to the cobblestones and my knees cracking open, all I can hear is my father reminding me that *they must never see you bleed*.

'Sometimes,' I pant, 'the doctor comes to treat your mother but he realizes one of her children is golden-blooded, so he refuses to help, because he's afraid, and the next thing you know there's a rumour and the city wants to drive you out, so your mother tells your brother to *take your sister and go*.'

'Odile –' Marie tries, but I grip my elbows, unable to look at her.

'So you escape, and you wander the streets for a year, nearly freezing in the winter, nearly starving every moment. Then luck smiles on you: you're found by the director of the Théâtre du Roi, who has blood just like yours, who names you his daughter. And he tells you that none of this would have happened if the Mothers hadn't left, if you still had magic. He tells you there's a way to bring it back, to become so powerful no one can ever hurt you again. All you need to do is steal the Couronne du Roi.'

I hear Marie's sharp intake of breath. 'That's what this is about,' she says.

I slump down on the grass, burying my head in my hands. There's a lump in my throat, but I refuse to cry. 'That's what this is about,' I grit out.

And suddenly, I'm telling her everything. About Regnault's training, about the first time I failed him, about Damien leaving, about how I ended up working at the palace. I even tell her about the journal. I tell her, though I should hate her. I tell her, though she was meant to be a means to an end. I bleed myself dry in front of her, rivulets of my history pooling between us, knowing that I am weakening myself with every word, giving her a weapon to turn against me.

And yet, somehow, it feels good. It feels like *relief*.

The only thing I omit – because I can't bring myself to shatter this fragile, hoarfrost thing that has barely begun to gather between us – is the truth about the diamond necklace. That, I leave buried in the depths of me, because I need her trust, I need *her*.

I break off at last, the sweat soaking through my clothes growing cold, the night's frost pulling billowing clouds from my lips with every breath.

Marie turns to look at me, her expression open, contemplative.

Then she puts her arm around my shoulders and eases me against herself.

It draws a sound of surprise out of me. 'What are you doing?' I demand, but don't pull away, because there's something regrettably comforting about the weight of her arm over my shoulders, no matter how strange it all feels.

'It's called *affection*,' Marie says with faint amusement. 'It's meant to make you feel better.'

'Hm,' is all I can say to that. Because she's right – it does. I let my head fall on to her shoulder, loose coils of her hair tickling my cheek. She smells warm, yet wild, like honey and spices and young summer midnights.

'I'm sorry,' I mutter. 'What I said earlier. It was unfair of me.'

She hums in acknowledgement. 'I understand it, now. I understand more than you know. Our lives have not been similar, but I know what it's like to feel alone.'

'I wasn't really alone,' I say defensively. 'I had Regnault.'

Marie makes a sound in her throat, not quite agreement. 'And yet, you have been fighting on your own for so long. You don't have to, any more. Tell Aimé all you've told me. Let us *help* you.'

It's tempting. Oh, it's tempting. But then the doubt begins needling into me, as it always does.

'No,' I say, shaking my head. 'I can't trust an Augier, Marie, I can't.'

'You trusted me.'

'A lapse of judgement,' I say woefully. 'Besides, it's too much of a risk. If I reveal myself to be a sorcier now, Aimé could think *I'm* the one who killed his father and lock me up in Damién's stead. I need to find the true killer first. The Step-Queen seems the most likely suspect, but now I've made her suspicious of me. She had guards tracking me all evening. Which –' I pull away at last, shifting further back and ignoring the sharp stab of longing I feel at the loss of Marie's touch – 'brings me to the true reason I came to see you tonight.'

Marie arches an eyebrow. 'Oh? It wasn't because you simply missed me?'

'I would never admit to such a thing,' I say, feigning offence. Then I take a steadying breath, reality sinking its talons into me again. 'Marie . . . look. I have a plan, to find out the Step-Queen's true intentions. But it could be dangerous. And I'm going to need your help.'

SCENE XXI

Château.

I wake late the next morning, groggy and sticky-eyed and taut with nerves. The events of last night are still stark in my mind, as is the knowledge that Damien is running out of time. But I cannot set my plan in motion until nightfall, and for it to work, there is one more person I must recruit: my father.

I wind through the Château halls in search of him. More guests seem to have arrived today, clad in the latest lacy fashions, dripping with jewels and self-importance. Before them, the Château has put on its own luxurious mask, every candle lit and banister polished, plush carpets rolled out over cold marble and a sudden gush of crimson-clad servants flooding the halls to attend every guest. It's all a veneer, a thin varnish. The guests seem to sense it – there is ever an edge of paranoia in their eyes, ever a pause in their step as they turn a corner, as though there is a monster waiting unseen on the other side. They eye the Château like vultures might a corpse – skittish and mistrustful, yet eager to pluck every last morsel of gossip from between its rotting bones.

I find Regnault in a drawing room speaking to several courtiers, gesturing grandly as he entertains them with some story or jest. The gathered noblemen stare at him, transfixed, and when he finishes the tale, they all burst into raucous laughter. My father, I note, has successfully seized control of the court's ravenous chaos. Even as theatre director, he was always careful to maintain the good regard of the noblesse. Now he has been rewarded with new authority, new importance, for the time of the wedding, and he is using that to ingratiate himself with them. He is able to endure their patronizing amusement in a way that I never could, presenting himself as an attraction, a jester. It's a clever sleight of hand – the more they enjoy his presence, the more they seek him out, the more power he gains.

I curtsy as I walk up to him, all too aware that we are both playing parts, and I must maintain my guise of Marie. 'A word, Monsieur?'

Regnault dips his head and leads me to a quiet corner. There, I tell him a lie: I need him to organize an event tonight, a distraction, so I can investigate a clue that might help us steal the Couronne sooner.

It's a small lie, a half-lie, really, but when Regnault nods and agrees, something inside me shrivels in shame. I have never before told so many lies to my father, hidden so many truths from him. I can only hope that, in the end, it is all worth it.

That evening, after nightfall, the court and the guests and anyone of importance are called to attend an elaborate, many-course dinner.

Minutes before twilight, I open my window to an ashen, windswept November sky, dark clouds reflecting the dwindling sunset like cinnabar flame. Against them, a single figure appears: a white swan approaching from over the lake, graceful wings flapping with smooth, steady strokes. As she approaches, she halts mid-air, and for a moment she is motionless, the last ray of light against a gathering dark, every feather dyed by dusk. Then she folds her wings and dives through the window.

Before her feet can touch the ground, a burst of golden light swallows her body. Moments later, Marie d'Odette drops daintily to her feet, flexing her shoulders as if to fold invisible wings. Her eyes open slowly, grey as a storm-tossed sea

'Good evening, sorcière,' she greets softly. There's an uncharacteristic, nervous edge to her voice.

I throw her a grin. 'Evening, Princess. Welcome home.'

She smiles wanly, but doesn't reply. Her gaze skips across the dark room as though she expects it to tighten around her like a snare. I've never seen her so skittish, so reluctant, but I don't remark on it. I don't have Marie's talent for comforting words nor, as she put it last night, *affection*.

'Are you ready?' I ask instead, gesturing to the pile of silver satin laid out on the bed.

She nods, a strained motion.

Marie carefully removes her peasant's clothing until she's in nothing but a lacy chemise, a cold tongue of wind slipping through the window to lap at the hem. I help her into the gown. It should be a simple act, familiar – I did this many times when we were girls. Yet now, I am all too aware of it, of *her*; the thin layers of silky fabric between us, the tantalizing slope of her collarbones over the low-cut neckline. The pale divot between them where I could press my lips.

I wonder what it would feel like to ruin her, tangle my legs with hers and stain her pristine, pallid perfection with my darkness.

I clear my throat, ushering the thoughts away with haste. 'The plan is as I told you last night,' I say, to distract myself from the proximity of her skin as I tug on the ribbon lacing of her bodice. 'All you have to do is keep Anne de Malezieu's attention, and make sure she stays in the dining room for as long as possible. I will do my best to be swift, but no matter what I find, I will return here in two hours.'

'What if Anne leaves before then?' Marie asks.

'She shouldn't. She's the Dauphin's stepmother, after all – she's expected to be present and entertain guests. But if she does decide to leave, you must stop her. Ask her about her earrings. Spill wine on her dress. Challenge her to a duel. Anything, just keep her in place.'

Marie shoots me a sceptical look. 'Challenge her to a duel?'

'Be creative!' I say cheerily, tucking the ribbons away and stepping back. 'Oh, and try to avoid my father. I doubt he will be present at the table – he'll likely be busy coordinating the staff. But if he *is* there, and he asks you what you're doing, tell him the plan has changed. Tell him you have everything under control, and that you will explain tomorrow.'

Marie nods, understanding. 'He thinks I'm you.'

'Yes. And everyone else thinks you're you.'

'Of course.' She takes a steadying breath, breasts swelling against the firm constraints of the bodice. One of the blue ribbon closures along the front has come undone, and I resist the urge to reach for it, to get close to her one last time. Marie ties it herself, then squares her shoulders.

'Very well,' she says, heading for the door. She reaches for the handle, then pauses, looking back at me. 'What happens after tonight, Odile? What happens to . . . to this?' She gestures between us.

This. Memories of the previous night, of the soft brush of her hair against my cheek. Mothers, how did I let myself become so distracted? '*If* I can find evidence of the Step-Queen's plot,' I say matter-of-factly, 'we tell the Dauphin the truth.'

Marie raises her eyebrows. 'All of it?'

I nod, reluctant, but, for once in my life, honest. 'All of it. Now go.' I shove her shoulder, so I don't have to witness the proud, pleased edge to her smile. 'Go pretend to be me pretending to be you, my silver-eyed muse.'

'You're absurd,' she tells me.

'I'm an actress, Mademoiselle.' I bow dramatically. 'It's a mandatory affliction.'

Her only response is a laugh, birdsong-soft, as she slips out the door.

I wait until I can no longer hear voices or footsteps echoing down the halls before I slip from the room. I put the owl-face pendant back on as I walk – it will be easier to explain myself if I'm caught, as long as someone hasn't just witnessed the real Marie d'Odette in the dining room. With the attention of the whole court on the dinner, the remainder of the palace has grown tight and sinister, as though I am walking not on marble but on thin, creaking ice. My stomach twists with anticipation.

I follow the path the Step-Queen took the previous day until I reach the obsidian door where she cornered me. I survey it carefully: there's a keyhole in the very middle, tarnished bronze, and little other decoration to speak of.

I kneel in front of the keyhole, pulling out my trusty pins and slipping them inside. After some fiddling, it clicks open easily. The metal around it seems to shimmer, but I blink, and all looks normal. A trick of the light, I decide, and push open the door.

Magic-scent hits the back of my throat with such force that I barely manage to mute a cough against my knuckles. Beyond the door lies a threadbare room, smaller than I expected for a queen, furniture scattered about it haphazardly, all of it archaic and worn and splashed with strange substances. The air seems strangely foggy, and the scent around me changes, taking on a sour, fermented edge.

On a distant bookshelf, I notice row upon row of vials and bottles, all containing liquids of different colours. I approach them carefully, my breath quickening. One of the jars has been left on the edge, set aside as though it has been recently opened. Within are the strange flowers from the forest, all crushed together, their soggy corpses piled against the walls of the jar. Around them, a watery liquid has turned a sickly, eerie yellow.

Nearby is a writing desk set under a narrow window with crimson curtains drawn tight. Upon it lie stacks of papers – notes, I realize – and I gather them up with jittery excitement. There are dates written on the tops of pages, and I find the more recent ones, scanning them quickly. Fragments of words catch my eye – *subject is beginning to show signs of toxicosis . . . lower dosage ineffective, led to disastrous results . . . improved with reduced psychological symptoms . . . completely undetectable . . .*

Poison. The Step-Queen has been experimenting with poison.

I set the papers aside and reach for a heavy book bound in red leather lying just beneath. My heart skips when I read the title: *Medicinal Applications of Sorcerous Elixirs*. Something inside me vibrates urgently – this is it, I know this is it. I open the book and begin to flip through it. I go through pages of recipes, of pictures of herbs and flowers and mushrooms I have never seen. *Witherwort, for prolonging the effects of a potion. Wolf-lily, to enhance a sorcier's power. Bluefang, a universal antidote.* And then . . .

There it is. The yellow flower from the forest, though the illustration clearly comes from times before Bartrand de Roux's betrayal, because it is not small and wrinkled but gloriously blooming, leaves outspread like a sun's rays.

This is it. This is the proof I need.

But before I can read a single word, an unpleasant, reedy voice rings through the room: 'I think that's rather enough, don't you?'

SCENE XXII

The Secret Laboratory.

The Step-Queen struts towards me, sapphire gown swishing around her ankles, eyes flashing red with anger. I shove the book behind myself, as though it isn't obvious what I've been doing, as though I haven't made a mess of her carefully arranged notes. A worried voice slips through my thoughts: *How did she know I was here? Why didn't Marie stop her?*

'W-wait,' I stammer. 'It's not what you think.'

'I doubt that,' she says, coming closer. I have nowhere to run – my tailbone slams into the edge of the desk. 'Now tell me, who is that impostor downstairs?'

My brain scrambles to concoct a worthy lie, coming up with an impressive, resounding *nothing*. Instead, I try for a distraction. 'There was a spell on that door, wasn't there?' I only now realize the shimmering I had seen was spell-threads, so faint I hadn't noticed them in my excitement. 'You cast it. You're a sorcier.'

'Aren't you clever,' the Step-Queen purrs. Step by step, she comes closer, a prowling wildcat. Her eyes gleam in the low light.

'But you . . . you don't smell like one,' I stammer. Keep her talking, until I can think of a way out.

'My potions do their work well,' she says. 'Hidden in plain sight, as my husband wanted me to be.'

'Your husband?' I echo. 'The King knew what you were?'

She smirks. 'He married me *because* of it, you fool.'

My fingers tighten on the book. 'And now you're trying to kill his son.'

'I'm – Ha! Is that what you think?' She shakes her head in disappointment. 'You poor, *stupid* little creature. You know, I never understood what my boy saw in you. Never understood why he took your word over the word of his own stepmother. But you made him happy, so I allowed your dalliance, decided to bide my time to see if you had changed. But I see now I should have gotten rid of you the moment you stepped foot in this court.' With a *snick*, she draws something from behind her back. A black dagger, a single sapphire glinting in the pommel. 'I suppose it is time to rectify that error.'

My blood goes cold.

'Before I kill you,' the Step-Queen hisses, 'know this. Once I am done here, I will ensure the impostor downstairs is captured and questioned. I will know the truth behind your actions.'

Fear, true fear, shoots through me. 'I won't let you touch her,' I growl, squaring my shoulders, my muscles tensing in preparation. 'And you're wrong. The girl downstairs is not the impostor.'

The Step-Queen hesitates. 'What?'

'*I* am,' I sneer. Then I hurl *Medicinal Applications of Sorcerous Elixirs* at her head.

The Step-Queen rears back in surprise, and I claim the moment to make my escape. I don't get far before she closes the distance again, moving almost unnaturally fast, her skirts a flurry of shadow around her. I try to slip past her, but my foot catches on the leg of an armchair and I'm sent crashing to my knees just as the Step-Queen closes in on me. I reach for Buttons, but before I can even turn him over, the Step-Queen's dagger slashes down towards me. I try to twist away, but I'm too slow. Pain explodes through my side. I gasp and stumble away, clutching my side where the dagger passed over my ribs. Buttons slips out of my hand, clatters to the floor and rolls away into the darkness.

A strange, tingling sensation spreads from the wound, travelling across my body like flame devouring firewood. The feeling is so intense I crumple to my knees, gritting my teeth as my muscles twitch involuntarily.

The Step-Queen stands back, a victorious smile slicing across her angular features, distorting them into a ghoulish rictus.

'What –' I lean back, grimacing, against the wall. 'What did you do to me?'

Before she can answer, the door clicks open. We both turn to see Aimé in the doorway, breathing heavily.

'Maman, I'm here, what did you . . .' He trails off as his eyes notice me lying injured on the floor. I press my palm harder against my side, but I know it's too late – I can feel the golden blood leaking between my fingers.

'Marie? But –' His eyes widen.

That's when it happens. The tingling reaches a crescendo – I don't know how to describe the sensation other than *melting*, as though a layer of me is peeling away and pouring off my skin in a cold wave. The hair that has fallen in front of my face shortens from Marie's shining coils to my own black hair. When I move my legs, I realize I'm wearing breeches again, from the black-and-gold costume I'd worn at the Théâtre.

My disguise is gone. Aimé is seeing a golden-eyed stranger.

'Aimé,' the Step-Queen says, voice low, 'go get the guards.'

'Aimé, don't listen to her,' I plead. But when Aimé's eyes meet mine, they're filled with bleak, frightened betrayal. He shakes his head mutely and turns on his heel, bolting out of the door.

'Aimé!' I shout after him, despair shooting through me. The Step-Queen sneers, crouching down in front of me and skimming the point of her dagger along my throat.

'Surrender,' she says sweetly. 'Your ruse is ov–'

Then we hear it. Aimé's scream. The sound is cut off abruptly, interrupted by another bone-chilling noise: a growl like a thunderclap, so powerful the walls seem to shake with it.

A look of potent, understanding terror passes over the Step-Queen's face. *'No!'* She leaps to her feet, and I make to follow, but the pain in my side is too great and my hands slip on my own blood.

The Step-Queen runs for the door, dagger raised. 'Aimé!' she shouts, and all I see is the hem of her sapphire skirts, the heels of her boots as she rushes towards whatever horror is approaching down the corridor. There's another growl. The sound of her feet against the ground is joined by the rapid clicking of claws as the beast gallops towards her.

'Stop!' the Step-Queen shouts at the unseen monstrosity. 'Stop, you must stop, I'm your – *Aargh!*' She is cut off by the horrid sound of claws meeting flesh. A spray of blood flies past the doorway. Something heavy thuds against the ground. There is a beat of utter, deafening silence.

Then comes the worst sound of all: the smacking of lips, the wet tearing of skin from bone. My blood freezes in my veins as I realize what I'm hearing.

The beast is *eating* her.

If I'm going to get out, it has to be now, while it's distracted. The thought is chilling, but I force myself to move, hands scrabbling against the wall behind me as I haul myself up on shaking legs.

I peer around the corner, and the sight that greets me makes bile rise to my throat.

A few metres away, a hideous, unspeakable monstrosity is bent over the crimson-slathered remains of Anne de Malezieu. It looks part-wolf, part-boar, every bit of it ill-shaped and wrong. Its skin is grey and leathery, cracked in places like ancient stone. Beneath its massive, bear-like paws, I see shreds of sapphire gown twisted around a ribbon of slick, dripping muscle.

I can't see a second body – no glints of Aimé's golden hair or scraps of flamboyant lace. Relief shoots through me. *Please, Mothers*, I pray, *let him have gotten away safely.*

I keep my eyes on the creature and move slowly, silently, despite every inch of my body begging me to flee. I back up step by step, one hand desperately staunching my wound and the other reaching for Buttons, only to remember I dropped the weapon earlier. Thankfully, the beast does not notice, too focused on nosing over the Step-Queen's corpse.

I continue. Step by step. My pulse throbs in my skull – nausea stirs behind my breastbone. Something glints near my feet, and I look down to see Anne's dagger. I stoop to pick it up, shove it into my belt, and keep moving. I'm almost at the end of the corridor now. This wing of the Château is isolated, but it connects to the entrance hall – if I can make it there, there will surely be guards present that might be able to kill the beast . . .

Suddenly, a drop of my blood slips through my fingers and plops on to the floor. It's quiet, quiet enough that the sound is almost, *almost* muffled by the sound of the monster's smacking jaws. For a moment, I dare hope my presence has gone unnoticed.

Then the beast's nostrils flare.

Its head snaps up.

Our eyes meet, and my heart stops. The beast's bullish jaws are slathered in gore, its eyes black pools of hatred. Boar-like tusks jut out from behind wide, dribbling nostrils, and I nearly gag when I realize one of them still has a scrap of sapphire fabric caught on its tip.

'*Merde*,' I mutter.

The monster grunts. A rivulet of saliva slips from its jowls.

Then it charges.

I turn on my heel and run.

My wound screams in protest, my heart thuds so hard against my ribs I nearly expect it to break through its cage. I can hear the monster getting closer, the scraping of its claws rapid and desperate. It snarls in frustration, and the sound is like a jagged knife dragged down my spine.

Cursing, I force my aching legs to move faster, blinking past tears. Part of me is glad that my disguise is gone, that I am wearing trousers and flat-soled boots. Ahead, the vast double doors of the chapel appear, the twin tarasques upon them menacing with their glinting shells. Behind me, the monster roars, the sound horribly close. Panic cuts me to the quick: I'm not going to make it to the entrance hall.

There is one way I might be able to escape, but it's a desperate, fool's hope. I turn on my heel towards the chapel doors, shove at their heavy weight until there's a mere crack for me to slip through. The doors fall shut behind me. A moment later I hear the monster slam against them. They're not going to hold for long, I know.

I don't stop running. The chapel's pews are long, the exit on the opposite side beckoning. But if I go that way, the beast will see me, and it will catch me. I need to shake it before my stamina runs out. So instead, I bolt up the stairs that lead to the tribune. As I run, I hear the monster break through the doors, sniff the air with a rasping inhalation. As I reach the top, it growls, and I hear the scrape of its shoulders against stone as it crams itself into the narrow stairwell.

I pause to catch my breath, looking around the blindingly white room. The Mothers stare at me blankly, utterly unhelpful. The monster roars again.

In front of me is a window, narrow and tall, one of many that line the walls. I'm one storey up – if I could break through the thick pane, I could probably survive the jump.

But how?

I clutch the owl-face pendant, and jolt in realization.

The pendant feels *wrong*. No longer can I feel the intricate humming of spell-threads within. Instead, the magic is . . . raw. Unravelled. Returned back to its natural, molten form.

Whatever the Step-Queen did to me when she stabbed me, it destroyed my father's spell. Years worth of stolen goddess-gold, of scavenged magic, gone.

My stomach sinks – Marie, what does this mean for Marie?

Behind me, there is an eager, blood-curdling snarl. The monster reaches the top of the stairs, drags itself through the narrow opening. Its head whips around, searching for me.

No time to think. I press myself into the shadows and tear the pendant from my neck, wincing at the quiet *snap*. I pull at the magic within, feeling it pool in my palm, wet and sticky. With that same hand – now dripping gold – I weave the spell I remember from Bartrand's journal, one shimmering thread at a time: *mirror, shards, break*, and then, finally, *window*.

Then I slam my palm against the glittering glass.

The spell bursts around my hand, a single spiderwebbing flare of light. The window shatters in a diamond display, thousands of twinkling shards raining down around me. The sudden sound alerts the beast to my location – I hear the bellow of its fury, the screech of its claws as it barrels towards me.

I leap through the opening without hesitation, curling my hands over my face. A line of agony sears down my side as the beast reaches after me, its claws snagging on my doublet in one final, failed attempt to seize me in its grasp.

Then I am falling, falling, *falling*, the night opening up to swallow me in jaws of starless obscurity.

I do not remember hitting the ground. The next time awareness returns to me, I am lying, gasping, on the cold earth, scrambling to hold on to consciousness even as it slips from me. My skin feels tacky, lathered in stale blood. I can only pray my father finds me before the guards do.

The last thing I hear is my name, sobbed desperately through familiar, tear-stained lips.

Soft fingers brush my cheeks, and I swear I see glorious white wings unfurl above me.

Then, I slip into darkness.

SCENE XXIII

Théâtre du Roi. The Loges.

Reality slinks back to me like a kicked dog, trembling and blearily hesitant. Everything aches – I feel ancient, as though my joints are wrought of iron and being chewed on by rust. When I shift, I half expect to hear arthritic creaking. An undignified moan escapes me, and distantly, I think I hear a gentle 'Shhh,' as though I'm a child waking from a nightmare. I realize there are fingers carding through my hair, light as feather-down, and the feeling acts as a momentary distraction from the dull pain in my body.

'You're all right.' Marie's voice wraps around me like a cloak, and, Mothers, I have never been so happy to hear a voice in my life. I realize it is her touch brushing against my scalp, and despite my disorientation, my stomach curls pleasantly. *Safe*, a small, primal part of me hums, the part of me that is normally dedicated to keeping up my walls in desperate self-preservation. I contemplate feigning unconsciousness a little longer, if only to enjoy the unfamiliar attention.

Then Marie whispers, 'You're all right,' again, and I realize her voice is shaking. As though she doesn't quite believe her own words.

Reluctantly, I force my eyes to open. I'm greeted by an unexpectedly familiar sight: the cradle of gold and crimson of the Théâtre's loges wraps around me, the dark of the auditorium visible over the balustrade to my right. Judging by the opulent furnishings, this is the box reserved for the Augiers. I'm lying on a satin-cushioned chaise longue, and beside me, Marie d'Odette d'Auvigny sits in a puddle of silver skirts.

I want to say something dignified, ideally witty. Instead, all I manage through my dry throat is a crackling 'Marie.'

Her eyes meet mine, their silver depths brightening in relief.

'Oh, thank the Mothers,' she breathes.

Everything feels unreal somehow, impossible, a flicker of candleflame and a blur of crimson velvet. There's a bruise blooming across Marie's cheekbone, and I can't peel my eyes away from it.

I reach up hazily to brush my thumb along the mark, half expecting her to be a mirage, for my fingers to pass through. But my touch finds warm, smooth skin, and Marie stiffens in confusion.

'You're hurt,' I say.

Her lips uncurl from their worried frown into something almost sheepish. 'I fought a guard. Well, tried to.'

'I see.' I knit my brow in a frown as I try to force my memories free of the hazy void of my mind. They come swaying back drunkenly: the Step-Queen's chambers, the potions and notes and books. Golden blood seeping between my fingers, crimson blood pooling beneath a stone-skinned monster's claws. A scrap of sapphire fabric caught on its tusks. A shattering window.

And . . . 'Marie,' I whisper. 'I did it. I used magic. Real magic. Like my father does.' I clench my hand, remembering the feeling of magic leaking between my knuckles, the way it transformed into long, thin spell-threads as I traced my fingers through the air. 'The pendant is gone,' I say, realizing. 'But you're still alive. I didn't know if you would be, after the Step-Queen stabbed me. I thought . . . the spell . . .' I try to sit up, and pain lances down my side, hard enough to make me gasp.

'Odile, slow down,' Marie pleads. 'You need rest.'

I fall back on to the chaise longue obediently. 'And you saved me.'

She gnaws on her bottom lip. 'I'm not certain I would call it *saving*. The injury in your side was shallow enough; thankfully, it had already stopped bleeding when I found you. Did . . . Were you *stabbed*?'

I nod through clenched teeth. 'Regrettably. The Step-Queen caught me in her rooms.' I glance at her. 'You were supposed to keep her distracted.'

I don't mean for the words to sound accusatory, but as soon as I utter them, guilt roils across Marie's face. 'I tried, Odile, I swear it. But when I tried to intervene, she only shoved me aside. "Do you take me for a fool?" she said. "I can sense your plot unfurling. Who did you send?"'

'I said I didn't know, feigned ignorance. She took off. I tried to follow, but she commanded one of the guards to grab me, saying I was drunk and needed to be escorted to my rooms. He began to lead me away, but I fought him. That's when he elbowed me.' She points to the mark on her cheek. 'I think he was frightened to realize he had injured his future Queen because he released me right after, apologizing profusely. I ran after Anne, but by the time I arrived, it was too –' She stammers somewhat over the word, her voice growing hoarse and haunted. 'Too late.'

I squeeze my eyes shut. 'What did you . . . what did you see?'

'B-blood.' Marie shudders, an action I feel more than see. 'Everywhere. Anne de Malezieu's body. And I could h-hear . . . I could hear the beast. Hear it running down the hallways, chasing . . . chasing something. Chasing *you*. I thought it had gone outside, to the gardens, so I ran out into the night, and –' She cuts off, her breath hitching strangely, as though she has caught herself just before telling a lie.

I furrow my brow, suspicion digging into me. 'What is it?'

'I saw you jump.' The words are strained, tainted somehow. 'From the chapel window. You fell. And I –' Again, her breath catches oddly. 'You were just lying there, covered in glass, bleeding from your side. Mothers, there was blood *everywhere*.'

'Did you . . . did you see the beast?'

'No. It was gone by the time I got there – I think it gave up chasing you after you jumped. We were both covered in your blood, so I picked you up and hid us in the shadows until I was certain we were alone, and then –'

'Hold on,' I interrupt. 'You *picked me up*?'

Marie sweeps her hair over her shoulder. 'I'm stronger than I look.'

Which certainly doesn't help the image my mind has conjured of Marie cradling my limp form in her arms like a knight carrying off his bride. My cheeks heat. 'I see,' is the only respectable response I can think of. 'And then?'

'And then I brought you here.' She presses her palms to her eyes, and it's the first time I've seen her truly weary. She sits back on her heels then, and I notice a low table behind her, a candlestick set upon it for light. Beside it lies a pile of items: my blood-smeared doublet, the Step-Queen's dagger, and –

'Buttons!' I exclaim.

Marie looks around in confusion, then follows my gaze to the enchanted button. 'Oh, yes. I found it in the Step-Queen's study when I was looking for you. I recognized it from – well, from the time you threatened me. Several times.' She huffs a laugh, reaching over and passing it to me. 'I did have to . . . ah, remove your jacket.' I could swear she blushes, then. 'To bandage your wound.'

I take the items from her then lift up my shirt curiously, to find a layer of red silk wrapped around my abdomen. It looks to be a scarf – a familiar scarf, no less. 'Did you get this from the dressing rooms?'

She pouts. 'I only have so many petticoats, you know. And they *are* expensive.'

I shake my head at her, and slip Buttons into the pocket of my breeches before picking up the Step-Queen's dagger. The sapphire glints at me slyly from the pommel.

I scowl at it. 'After Anne stabbed me with this, my disguise vanished.' I tell her quickly what happened in the study, how Aimé had run in to see me transform. 'There must have been a spell on it.'

Marie squints at the dagger. 'Can I see it?'

I hand it to her, and she holds it up to the light, turning it over in her hands. She scrapes her nail along the flat of the blade, then knocks the sapphire pommel against the side of the chaise.

'Hey!' I exclaim. 'Be gentle with that!' I had been intending to add the weapon to my arsenal.

Marie doesn't acknowledge me. She gets to her feet, still frowning at the knife. She taps her fingertips on the sharp edge, sniffs them. Then she moves to the nearby candelabra and sticks the dagger into its flame.

I make a strangled sound of alarm.

'What?' Marie demands, not shifting her focus from the weapon.

'I said be gentle with it!'

She gives me a flat look. 'I am.'

'You're setting it on fire!'

'I'm setting it on fire *gently*.' She pulls out the dagger once more, redness fading from the heated blade. The edge of it sizzles strangely and a moment later, a scent reaches me – faintly, unpleasantly sweet, like a rose stem rotting in the stale water of a vase. A few spots along the dagger have blackened.

'Poison,' I realize. 'Of course.'

'Most of it was gone,' Marie says. 'I imagine it rubbed off when she . . .'

'When she stabbed me. Pleasant.'

'Well,' Marie says, 'that would explain why you looked on the verge of death when I found you, though your wound was not very deep. And why you wouldn't wake up. Your body must have been fighting the poison.' The recollection leaves her looking troubled. 'Do you think the beast was her doing?'

'It must be. She was using sorcery – or at least, she was able to create potions that allowed her to use sorcery. I've never even seen my father do that.' I don't admit that there is much my father has withheld from me when it comes to magic. 'Regardless, she certainly knew the beast. She tried to reason with it before it killed her. It seemed like she lost control of it.'

'So the mystery is solved,' Marie says. 'We can only hope the guards managed to capture that monster and killed it. I'll . . . I'll have to go back to the Château soon and gauge the situation.' She seems to dread the prospect.

'Aimé will be a problem,' I point out. 'He saw me bleed gold right before the beast appeared. He will think it was my doing.' I rub my temples, trying not to remember the Dauphin's scream of terror. I didn't see his body after the beast's attack – I need to believe he's still alive.

'If that is the case,' Marie says tightly, 'then we will find a way to prove your innocence. To convince Aimé to take our side.'

My chest swells with sudden gratitude. I have tried to push Marie away so many times, yet she keeps helping me, keeps *saving* me. I do not know what I've done to deserve it, and I'm certain it will not last, but I want to clutch on to it, white-knuckled, for as long as I can.

I slip my hand into hers, rub my thumb against her palm. Her fingers are cold, and they lie limp in mine, unresponsive.

'I'm sorry, sorcière,' she says after a moment, staring at our interlaced hands. 'This was my fault, all of it. I didn't manage to distract the Step-Queen, and everything fell apart because of me.'

I stare at her. I'm so taken aback by the fact that she is *apologizing* to *me* for my own *horrible plan* that I bark a disbelieving laugh. 'Don't apologize to the villain, Marie. I had it coming.'

I know immediately I have said the wrong thing. Marie draws in a wet-sounding breath, and her bottom lip trembles before she presses her mouth into a tight white line.

'I wish you wouldn't call yourself such things.'

'Why not?' I demand. 'It's the truth – I *am* a villain.'

'I don't believe that.'

I snort. 'Of course *you* don't. You're kind and honourable and pure – it's your nature to see light in everyone. And it's my nature to be forever in the dark. I came here with the intent to steal a crown and destroy the Augier dynasty. None of it was selfless, none of it was kind. Everything I do, I do for my father's cause. For power.'

She looks away. 'Yet I wish I could be like you.'

'Why . . . why *ever* would you wish that? You're *perfect*.'

Her eyes are murky, tempestuous waters churning in a storm. 'Perfect? I'm a *coward*, Odile.'

I blink, surprised by her outburst. 'What?'

Marie pulls her hand out of mine, gets to her feet. 'It matters not. I'm going to . . . to take some air.'

'Marie, wait!'

But she's already gone.

SCENE XXIV

Théâtre du Roi. The first rays of dawn.

I find Marie d'Odette in one of the Théâtre's galleries, staring out of a tall, narrow window. Beyond, the sky has begun to blush with the first pink of sunrise. As I watch, a gush of warm light blooms over the trees, flaring behind Marie in a halo. She stands against it, motionless and luminous, a breeze tousling her pale curls.

I hold my breath, waiting for golden magic to envelop her body, for white feathers to erupt from her shoulders. But nothing happens.

'I was right,' I whisper. 'The curse is broken.'

For a moment, she doesn't reply. Gooseflesh stands stark against her skin, and I notice she is cradling a lit candle in her hands. Wax drips on to her fingers, but she seems not to feel it.

'I . . . I suppose so,' she says, and she doesn't sound glad at all. She casts me a furtive glance. 'Go back and rest, Odile. I'm fine.' There are tears in her eyes, glittering like diamonds. She looks anything but fine.

She looks like she wants to fly away.

I limp closer, trying not to wince at the throbbing in my side. 'This is a good thing, isn't it?' I say. 'You can return to the palace and explain everything to Aimé, convince him to help us, help *me*, in restoring magic. Then you'll marry him and be Queen and –'

'Do you think I *want* any of that?' Marie's voice trembles abruptly.

I pause, taken aback. 'Why wouldn't you? You'll have everything. Wealth, power, safety . . .'

'Except one thing,' she says. 'Freedom.'

I venture closer to her side. 'What do you mean?'

'I told you, it matters not.'

'It matters to *me*,' I say, pressing. And it does. I don't know why, but it does.

Another droplet of wax falls on to her fingers, making her flinch. 'I have a brother,' she begins. 'He's a year older than me – we were raised together. I was taught to ride and hunt and wrestle, just as he was. We used to gallop down to the nearby villages, spend time with the fishermen like we were local children. We'd listen to the sailors tell tales, dream of stowing away on a ship and seeing different shores. My mother abhorred it, but my father would always calm her. "Let her be a child," he'd say.' She shakes her head, and the candleflame wavers in tandem.

'Oh, my mother tried to put restrictions on me. But I was always restless – I wanted to travel, wanted *adventure*. I devoured books on history, on other countries, but paid no attention to those on etiquette. Eventually, my mother grew frustrated. She decided to take me away from our home, to stay in Verroux and learn manners from the court. She had this plan that I would befriend the Dauphin and make him fall in love with me. And . . . well. I suppose you know how that went.' She laughs bitterly.

There's a knot of dread growing in my chest, and I can't bring myself to speak around it.

'After Madame de Malezieu found the necklace,' Marie continues, 'she sent my family away in a fit of rage. My mother blamed me, but she also blamed my father, for allowing me to become such an unruly girl. Their arguments grew, and it was a mere few months later that my father's heart gave out.' She exhales heavily. 'It was my fault. If I hadn't caused him such stress –'

'Then he might have still died,' I interrupt, pained.

'You cannot know that!' she exclaims. 'Maman said that if I continued to misbehave, tragedy would surely strike again. And I was so afraid that . . . I was so *afraid*. So I surrendered myself to my mother. I let her lock me in the tower of our castle so that . . . so that I couldn't cause any more trouble. I was allowed only as far as the gardens, and visited only by tutors to teach me manners and propriety. Maman said I could atone by becoming the perfect lady, by marrying well and undoing all the damage I had done.

'At first, my brother tried to talk me out of it. But he had to turn his attention to managing the estate after my father's death. And I forced myself to accept it. All of it. I stopped longing for my horse and my bow, for hikes with the hounds and the smell of the forest. I became . . . perfect, as you put it. I learned to walk like a lady, to flutter my eyelashes and make small talk. I learned to tolerate the suitors my mother sent my way, even though they . . . even though I . . . I *hated* it. All of it.'

For a moment, her composure wavers, her voice shaking. When she collects herself, it's like watching an artisan fit pieces of stained glass together. 'So you see, I am a coward. Ever since my father died, I've done nothing but my mother's bidding. She's the one who sent me here. She found me a suitor, at home, an old and wealthy lord who will take me if I don't succeed in marrying Aimé. It's a cruel penance, I suppose, that I am destined to be imprisoned. If not by my mother then by . . . by my status, or by marriage. To think I used to dream of travelling the world.'

She stares off into the light, the sunrise turning her eyes to burnished bronze, illuminating the sorrow within. I want to comfort her. I don't know how. Don't know if I should, considering that I still haven't told her the whole truth.

Marie shakes her head abruptly. 'If I had been brave, I would have taken fate into my own hands. But the idea of hurting my family again . . . it frightened me. So I chose to endure. To do the safe thing, by becoming what my mother was, and what her mother was. Noblewomen to be sold off to the highest bidder. Raised and trained to be small and obedient and polite.' She gives me a crooked smile. 'It's why I envy you. You don't let anything stop you. If you want change, you fight for it.'

'Fighting can be exhausting,' I tell her.

'So can standing still,' Marie says, then chuckles softly. 'You know, the day your father cursed me might have been the best day I've had in five years. When I woke up with wings and realized I could go where I pleased, do what I wanted. I could be wild, the way I was as a girl. I was almost disappointed when you showed up at the lake and offered me a way out. Part of me wishes I could have stayed a swan forever.'

'*I* think the swan thing was getting old,' I blurt. 'You're prettier this way.'

I flush as soon as the words leave my mouth. I'd meant for them to sound teasing, but they came out all yearning and flustered instead. Marie stares at me, and I consider making a prompt *exit, stage left*, out of the window.

Then she giggles, and it's the sweetest and most tender sound, until suddenly the laugh fractures and turns into an abrupt sob. She makes a move as though to hide her face in her hands, but realizes she is holding the candle, and tucks her chin against her chest instead. I stare stupidly. It feels wrong, to see her without that calm, unflappable demeanour that so often irritates me. I feel as though I am intruding on something deeply private.

No, I realize, she's letting me see this. She's letting me *in*. This diamond-skinned girl, cursed with caring too much, who let herself be caged by her mother's cruelty and blame. My heart clenches. I walk up to her hesitantly.

'Hey,' I murmur, prising the candle gently from her fingers and blowing it out. I set it aside and pull her away from the windowsill, into my arms.

For a moment, Marie goes rigid, and I'm worried I've done something horribly wrong. Then she melts against me, burying her face in my shoulder.

I hold her gingerly against my body. The sky lightens further, from pink to pale lavender. The candle's smoke wraps around us. After a time, Marie tries to take a steadying breath, which only devolves into another dramatic sob, one loud enough to drag breathy laughs out of us both.

'Am I doing *affection* right?' I wonder into her hair.

She nods, her cheek wet against the crook of my neck. Finally, she sniffs and pulls away, wiping her eyes. The dawn light paints her in downy, angelic hues, and *Mothers* she truly is beautiful. In another world, a softer world, I know I could have loved her.

My heart clenches, and suddenly I can't keep it in any longer. 'Marie, there's something I have to tell you.'

'What is it?' she says, ever genial, ever gentle.

I open my mouth, preparing to tell her everything. But before I can, a familiar voice rings through the playhouse.

'Dilou, are you here?'

SCENE XXV

Théâtre du Roi.

My breath stutters at the sound of my brother's voice carrying in from the entryway. Marie looks at me questioningly.

'That's Damien,' I say, bewildered, turning on my heel to stare down the hall. 'Damien?'

'Odile?' His voice sounds oddly strangled. 'Odile, thank the Mothers. I'm here.'

It's as though an invisible string is pulling me towards him. I'm moving before I can think twice, rushing back down the corridor, my hurried footsteps echoing through the empty Théâtre.

'Odile, wait!' Marie calls behind me, but I hardly register it. Damien is here – Damien is *free*. Emotions toss and turn within me, each more conflicting than the last. The last time I saw my brother, he was glaring at me with potent fury from a prison cell. I doubt that anger has faded.

But I have a different perspective now. Marie has helped me see that perhaps there is value in telling the truth. Once I reveal my plot to Aimé, I'm certain he will do whatever it takes to save Auréal, even if it means giving me the Couronne. Perhaps I can accomplish Regnault's mission without lies, without deceit. And once my father realizes the Dauphin and Marie have helped us, surely he will no longer be so resentful of the noblesse. It's an impossible, honourable plan. A plan Damien would approve of.

Perhaps once he hears it, he will forgive me.

I could have my brother *back*.

But when I turn the corner and see Damien, I realize how much of a fool I am.

Because my brother is not alone.

Behind him stand the Regent, the Dauphin and two guardsmen, their muskets pointing straight at me.

'That's her,' Aimé says as soon as he sees me, gripping Damien's shoulder with white knuckles. His eyes are no longer the soft blue of open skies – they're the brittle, frosty hue of ice shards. 'That's the sorcier I saw in my stepmother's rooms.'

The Regent steps forward, the guards flanking him. My pulse surges in my ears as I realize what is about to happen. Before I can turn and warn Marie, the Regent commands:

'Seize her!'

The guards rush towards me. In the same moment, Marie arrives in the foyer and pauses, wide-eyed, as she takes in the scene. I try to shout at her to run, but one of the guards covers my mouth with a meaty hand, the other wrenching my hands behind my back. I struggle futilely, bile rising in my throat as the Regent seizes Marie's arm.

But to my surprise, he only pulls her to his side. Aimé rushes up to her, taking her hands and steering her away from the Regent. 'Are you hurt, Marie?'

Marie stares at him. 'Not at all. What's this about?'

'How long has she held you hostage, Madame?' the Regent asks.

'Who?' Marie demands.

'She must be confused by some spell.' It's Damien who speaks up. His jaw is visibly tense, his head turned pointedly away from me. Of course. Too much of a coward to even meet my eyes. 'This girl here –' my brother points at me – 'she kidnapped you and took your place at the palace.'

Marie begins to shake her head, and I realize – not without shock – she intends to *defend* me. But I know that would be futile – if she admits to being involved with me, whatever I'm being accused of will fall on her, too. Panic surges through my limbs, and I clamp my teeth down on the guard's hand, wrenching my head free. 'That's right,' I say breathlessly, before Marie can speak. 'I kidnapped her. She's been locked up in the Théâtre all along while I have been sowing chaos in the palace in her place.'

Damien scoffs. '"Sowing chaos",' he says in that low, patronizing tone. 'Is that what you call trying to kill the whole royal family?'

Oh. Of course that's how this must look from Damien's perspective. His vengeful sister shows up at the Château with mysterious plans, and soon after, the King is murdered. No wonder he looked so furious when I visited him in the dungeon. After all, didn't I once tell him that I would kill if I had to?

Marie makes a sound of indignation at Damien's words, clenching her fists. 'You're wrong. That's not at all what happened. If you would only listen –'

'She's under my spell,' I say desperately, willing to do *anything* to stop Marie from becoming implicated in this. 'She's only defending me because I'm making her do it.'

Marie gives me a sad smile, and I know she can tell what I'm trying to do. 'I'm not under any spell,' she says steadily. She looks from Regent to Prince to guards with a ferocity to rival any warrior. 'I'm defending her because I want to. Because Odile is better than any of you deserve, because she didn't –'

'*Marie, it was me!*' I shout. When she turns back to me, I hold her gaze with savage focus. 'It was me. I stole the necklace, the night of the banquet. I left it in your rooms the next day. I'm the one who ruined your life.'

For a moment, Marie's brows furrow in confusion. Then realization spreads over her features. She takes a step back, hands rising to her chest as she takes a shaky breath, then another.

I can't watch this, can't witness the moment she realizes she should hate me. I seize the opportunity instead to whirl on my brother. 'What did he promise you?' I demand, jerking my head at the Regent. 'Did he vow to free you from the dungeons if you sold me out?'

'I didn't promise him anything,' the Regent interjects, tapping his fingers along the pommel of his rapier. 'Aimé simply made a compelling case for his innocence. After all, Damien here was locked in the city prison when Madame de Malezieu was killed. Quite a straightforward alibi, I must admit.'

Damien looks away. His time in the city prison was not kind to him – there is a fresh cut across his lip and scrapes shine on his knuckles. He looks like a martyr, self-righteous suffering and all. He looks haunted. But I refuse to pity him.

'Why?' I ask him hopelessly. 'Why do this?'

At last, at long last, he meets my eyes. 'Because I should have done it long ago.'

Something inside me crumples. I take a step back, my knees going weak, and the only thing holding me up for a moment is the guard clutching my wrists. I look to Marie almost instinctively, seeking out some little comfort. But when she sees me watching, her face shutters. She looks away. Regret squeezes my chest. I'd expected this – I'd *wanted* this – but it still aches to know that, moments ago, I'd held her in my arms, her cheek against mine and her delicate hands curled around my shoulders. Now I've lost her.

Like Aimé, like my brother.

If Regnault were here, I know what he'd say. *You should have known better, little owl.*

'That's enough melodrama, I think.' The Regent's harsh voice cuts through the brief, heavy silence. 'Take the sorcier girl away. *Discreetly.*'

The guard holding me adjusts his grip. I hear the clink of something metal being procured. Behind us, the Regent says, 'I believe the wedding can now proceed as planned?'

At the same time, the cold kiss of iron presses against my wrists, and I freeze, an animal panic seizing me. I try to push through the feeling, focusing instead on Aimé's response.

'I . . . I don't know if that's appropriate,' the Dauphin says shakily.

Snick. A shackle closes cruelly around my left wrist, making my pulse jump. I force a breath through clenched teeth as the Regent responds to Aimé. 'Don't be a fool. We have guests from across the kingdom and beyond come to witness the event. The wedding *must* go on.'

'But what about everything Marie has been through?' Aimé argues. Out of the corner of my eye, I see him reach for her, but she hardly reacts.

Then – *snick*. The second shackle closes.

'I think Mademoiselle d'Auvigny must agree with me.' There is a vicious sneer in the Regent's voice. 'After all, I doubt her family would survive another scandal.'

Oh, the *snake*. Unable to help myself, I jerk against my new restraints, wishing I could launch myself at the horrid man. Unfortunately, all my attempt earns me is the bite of cold metal against my wrists and a warning growl from the guard gripping me.

He begins to lead me away, but not fast enough.

Because I still hear Marie d'Odette speak up, her voice faint and devastated. 'I agree with the Regent. The wedding must go on.'

I am thrown into the dungeons.

The cell is tight and chilling, the stone ground flecked with straw. It is bleak and punishing, cruelly mocking – the perfect reflection of my own internal thoughts. I crash to my knees on cold stone as the guard locks the bars behind me. I struggle to my feet and rush up to him.

'Wait!'

He scowls at me from beneath his mask, tucking the keys away. 'What do you want?'

'I'm innocent. Please, you must believe me.' It's humiliating, to beg like this, but I have no other choice. 'Get the Dauphin, please, tell him I can explain everything – or Marie, at least let me speak to Marie –'

'The Dauphin and his betrothed will be busy preparing for tomorrow's wedding. After, they may deign to grace you with their presence. If not, perhaps one of them will attend your execution, sorcière.'

The word sounds wrong, coming from the mouth of a guard, all splintering and twisted like a badly broken bone.

'Please.' I grip the bars so tight the rough metal pricks my skin. 'It was Anne de Malezieu. She was a sorcier, too. *She* conjured the beast that killed the King.'

The guard laughs harshly. 'You may have convinced the Dauphin there was a beast, but no one else believes it. A beast, in the Château? We would have seen it.'

My stomach lurches. 'What do you mean?'

'I mean, I'm no idiot. You sliced up the King, and then you sliced up the Queen, and we're fortunate you didn't manage to get to the Dauphin before you were stopped. No beast was seen, and so, there was no beast.' He bangs his knuckles on the bars and strolls away, whistling to himself.

I sink back on my heels, burying my head in my hands. No one saw the beast. How is that possible? Worse, does this mean the creature is still freely roaming near the Château? Could it return to wreak more havoc, even without the Step-Queen commanding it?

I crawl into the corner, shivering. The guards stripped me of my cloak, jacket and boots, leaving me in nothing but a loose shirt and breeches. Some primal part of me had taken over, and I had tried to fight them, landing myself with several impressive bruises from steel-toed boots. The wound in my side has started to ooze blood again, staining my shirt.

Night crawls in, dragging its cloak of ragged shadows as it scrapes fingers of rime across the floor. I blow into my hands, trying to keep them warm. A few more hours and Marie will be walking across a colourless chapel in a dress of purest white, to a marriage that will clip what remains of her wings. What will she do now? Will she try to clear my name with Aimé, as we planned? Or have I lost her entirely after admitting my betrayal?

And what has happened to Regnault? Has Damien betrayed him, too? Will he still try to steal the Couronne without me?

The uncertainty of it all is unbearable. I need to get out of this cell, and fast.

Think, Odile, think. I shove my knuckles between my teeth and bite down until I feel the flesh give way with a *pop*, until my lips stain with gold and I taste nothing but its metallic bitterness. The pain helps release some of the frustrated, furious tension in my chest. *Think.* I wipe my bleeding knuckles on my breeches and force myself to breathe. I scan the floor, the ceiling. I test the iron bars, the thick lock upon them. I find nothing. Despair sinks into me. I feel as though the walls are closing in, pressing tighter and tighter, mocking me cruelly. Trapped. Is this how Marie felt for all those years in her tower?

Eventually, the cold defeats me. I slump down against the wall, draw my knees up to my chest. Shivers wrack my body. Finally, my eyes drift closed.

What follows is not a dream.

I stand upon a floor of black-and-white tiles expanding before me like an infinite chessboard. My surroundings are dark, churning as though made of black fog. From within, something watches me, though I see little of it but a brief flash of chipped teeth.

When I open my mouth to call out to the entity, lake water floods across my tongue. I cough, splutter, but what I spit up isn't lake water at all: it's blood. Golden blood.

That is when the creature speaks.

'It is almost time, Daughter of the Blood. Claim your power.'

I jerk awake, disorientated and panicking. My mouth still tastes of the not-dream, rancid lake water, and the iron tang of my own blood. The damp of the prison has seeped through my shirt, sticking it to the icy stone wall. And . . .

There are footsteps approaching my cell.

'Well, well, well.' A faint light appears at the end of the hallway, cutting through the filth and silence of the dungeons. 'I think we have learned a lesson, haven't we?'

'Papa,' I gasp, and I know I sound desperate, like a child finding its parents after being separated in a crowd. I swipe quickly at my eyes as a familiar silhouette appears, spindle-thin, holding a lantern aloft.

Regnault's eyes glitter in the gloom, his lips thinning as he takes in my dishevelled state. The feathers of his raven-feather mask seem to shiver as he approaches. 'Whatever have you done to yourself, little owl?'

I scramble to my feet. 'I'm so sorry, Papa. I swear I was going to tell you everything –'

He puts up a hand. 'I care not for your excuses. Trying to

befriend *noblesse*, after all they have done to us. Mothers, what put such an asinine idea into your head?'

'I only . . .' I look away, unable to handle his mocking eyes pressing into me. 'I thought that we could work with them to free magic. Aimé, he . . . he seemed like he would understand, he . . .' I trail off, realizing how naive I sound.

My father clicks his tongue. 'Oh, Odile, you foolish girl. All it took was one word, one baseless accusation, from your traitorous brother, for the Dauphin to turn on you. You think a half-drunken fop prone to flights of fancy will ever listen to reason? He only ever cared for you because he thought you were his pretty fiancée. He would never listen to you like *this*.' He gestures to me, and my skin prickles self-consciously.

'He m-might,' I say, shrinking back. 'If Marie –'

'Oh, Marie.' He chuckles, a sound so serrated it raises the hair on the back of my neck. 'Yes, then there is Marie d'Odette, who should still be a swan. I must commend your audacity, *ma fille*, in going against my word. But for all your efforts to help her, the sweet Princess seems to have no intentions to return the favour. In fact, she's been proclaiming to any who will listen that she was misled by you, *corrupted* by you, into helping with your plans.'

'You're lying.' The words come out strangled.

'She's betrayed you before, hasn't she? What made you think she wouldn't do it again?'

I think of the dim stable, of Marie's downcast eyes as she walked back to her mother's side. It's mortifying how quickly I'd forgotten that old resentment when faced with the Swan Princess's doe eyes, her careful touches and easy reassurances.

'I thought . . . I thought she . . .' I can't manage to say it. Can't manage to *admit* it.

My father's eyes hold nothing but disappointment. 'Oh, my poor little owl,' he says. 'Did you actually think she *loved* you?'

The words are like a punch to the gut. My stomach seizes, the air rushing out of me, and when I open my mouth to deny it, my tongue sits leaden in my mouth. I can do nothing but grit my teeth, shame curdling inside me.

'You see now,' Regnault continues pityingly, 'no one else could ever understand you, not like I do. All it takes is one mistake, one misstep, and they will abandon you. But not I. I will always be here, even when you lie to me and betray me as you have done. Even after all your misdeeds, I'm ready to forgive you. That is why I came: to offer you a chance at redemption.'

I can't help the surge of relief his words send through me. I'm not alone, not entirely. I have Regnault – it is something I never should have taken for granted. Something I never should have questioned.

The light from my father's lantern is the only warmth keeping away the midnight frost. I step closer, letting the heat of the small flame wash over me, and meet his eyes determinedly.

'What do you need me to do?'

SCENE XXVI

Château. The Dungeons.

'Your mission,' Regnault begins, setting the lantern on the ground between us, 'will be to disguise yourself as a maid and bring something into the Dauphin's rooms.'

I nod, crouching before the lantern and warming my hands. Regnault remains standing over me, his features lit from below as he awaits my response. This is familiar – him giving me a mission, me executing it. I have done this since I was a girl. After days of suffering the consequences of my own poor decisions, putting my faith in my father's plan is a welcome reprieve.

'What is it?' I ask.

'In a moment.' He takes a bundle from his cloak and passes it to me through the bars. It is light, mainly fabric. Clothing of some sort.

'Servant's uniform,' Regnault explains. 'For the wedding tomorrow. You will be one of the servants attending the royal lovebirds.'

I clutch the bundle to my chest in surprise. 'How did you get this?'

'Connections,' he says, inspecting his nails. 'The Regent

is a terribly simple man to manipulate. His greed rules him. And greed –'

'Is the easiest vice to exploit,' I finish. It's one of his favourite phrases.

He ruffles my hair, a rare proud gleam in his eyes. 'Precisely. I have his ear, and his favour. He called away the prison's guards so I could give you these. You will, however, have to escape on your own. I can't risk you being seen walking out of the prison. But it appears that, conveniently, a window has been left open near the guardroom. And there are no guards on duty.' He winks at me.

I nod, grinning back, desperately reassured knowing I have a way out. 'But what about Damien?' I ask, remembering my earlier worry. 'Has he not told Aimé about your relation to me?'

'I am certain he has tried.' Regnault bends to pick up the lantern again, clearly signalling our time is running out. 'But the Regent holds far more power than the Prince, and as long as our interests align, I am safe.' He raises the lantern higher, gesturing to the clothes. 'You will find a bundle of dried herbs in there. Take the Dauphin's morning tea to him, and sprinkle them into his cup. Make sure he drinks it.'

'What is it?' I ask, frowning.

'It . . .' Regnault runs his tongue over his teeth, wording his answer carefully. 'It won't harm him, if that's what you're worried about. I would gain nothing by killing him before the marriage.' He turns to leave, then gives me a conspiratorial look over his shoulder. 'Don't fret, my owl.

When the time comes, we will get rid of anyone who has ever stood in our way. Starting with that useless Prince.'

Once my father is gone, I quickly change into the clothing I have been given – male servant's clothes, and a golden mask. My discarded clothing I stuff with straw and arrange in a foetal position. Hopefully, to a bored guard inspecting the cells, it will look like I am still here, asleep.

Inside the pocket of the trousers, my father has left me a folded handkerchief containing a sprinkling of blue-hued petals, along with a candle, lockpicks and, to my absolute delight, Buttons. I make quick work of the cell lock – it is of an old make, and rusty to boot – and sneak out of the window of the garrison.

By the time I reach the Château, I am breathing hard, more from fear of being caught than exertion. My timing couldn't be better – the servants' wing is already bustling with activity. Smoke rises from the chimneys, the scent of baking bread and cooking meats drifting through the grounds. The palace must be in uproar preparing for what I'm sure is to be an extravagant wedding feast.

Chaos is a weapon to those who know how to wield it. It is the perfect disguise, the ideal co-conspirator. Beneath its wing, I slip into the palace, making my way to the roaring, smoke-filled kitchens. I make myself useful, joining a nervous little boy in peeling what appears to be two centuries' worth of potatoes, biding my time until the bell is rung for the Dauphin's morning tea. I watch another maid prepare it, then I snatch the tray and scurry off before anyone can stop me.

The servants' wing is a plain hallway, narrow as a snake's belly, and it spits me out into the glittering entrance hall. I keep my eyes low and head bent, carefully avoiding the eyes of anyone I pass, be they servant or noblesse. When I am finally alone, I set the tray down and quickly pull the strange petals from their square of cloth, sprinkling them into the tea.

By the time I make it to Aimé's apartments, sweat is dripping down my ribs. I tug at my collar and knock.

'What is it?'

I deepen my voice. 'Your tea, Monseigneur.'

'Bring it in!' The Dauphin's voice holds its usual chipper, boyish quality. It makes my blood simmer – he sounds utterly unaffected by recent events. I wonder if he feels any remorse at all for locking me away without even speaking to me.

I step inside and freeze.

Aimé is not alone – Marie is sitting across from him, her posture perfectly poised, her hands curled delicately in her lap. My heart begins to pound. I look around for a place to leave the tea, and realize from their positions that they're expecting me to place it between them.

I thank the Spider King for his mad idea of having all the servants wear masks. I pause at the doorway, considering my options. I settle on simply acting like a serving boy in a hurry to get back down to my next task. Then I falter. It occurs to me that I am alone in a room with two people I might have almost, *almost* considered friends – or perhaps it was something more, with Marie, but I don't have time to consider *that* right now – and all it would take is for me to unmask myself and reveal my identity. I could explain myself.

'Are you *certain* you want to go through with this wedding?' Aimé is saying carefully. 'We haven't seen each other in five years. At least . . . not truly.'

Marie nods, her eyes mirroring the same awkward hesitance I can see in the Prince's expression. They lean away from each other, as if to make space for all the lies I piled between them. 'As long as our bargain still stands.'

'It does.' Aimé offers her a shy smile. 'If neither of us can have true love, we can have friendship instead.'

'If I must marry, I am glad it is you,' Marie says. Am I wrong, or do I hear a note of regret in her voice?

I drift forward hesitantly with my tray. All I need to do is say their names. All I need to do is say *I'm sorry*, say *I'm not the person my brother thinks I am. I'm no longer the girl who stole the diamond necklace.*

But then Aimé sighs, dragging one of the tasselled pillows on to his lap. 'I really thought I could trust her, Marie,' he says, fidgeting with the tassels. 'I was so desperate for companionship, for someone to tell me I wasn't the worthless idiot the whole court believes me to be. If I'd known what she was . . . I would never have trusted a word out of her mouth.'

Marie smooths her palms over her knees, the satin rustling. Her voice is soft. 'She did hold affection for you, Aimé.'

Aimé scoffs, snatching both teapot and cup off the tray before I even manage to set it down. 'Thank you,' he says, hardly sparing me a glance before pouring himself a cup and turning back to Marie. 'A snake holds some affection for its prey, I believe, as it sinks its fangs in slowly and waits for the venom to spread.' He stares down at the steaming cup. 'That doesn't make it any less vile.'

The words are a well-aimed arrow, piercing through bone and muscle to strike my very core. My grip tightens around the tray as I back away, and I can't help but glance desperately at Marie. *Say something,* I beg in my thoughts. *Tell him he's wrong, tell him it's not true. Give me a reason, any reason, to stay.*

But Marie d'Odette d'Auvigny says nothing, and I do not stop walking.

I keep my eyes on the floor as I rush down the Château hallways, tapestries and paintings flashing by in a blur. Aimé's words turn over mer有cilessly in my thoughts, seeming louder and crueller the more I dwell on them. *That doesn't make it any less vile.*

Something cracks inside me. A small fissure, but growing, expanding with every step I take. Damien betrayed me to the Regent. Aimé condemned me as soon as he discovered my true identity. And Marie, well . . . I did that myself. I cannot blame her for realizing my true nature, not when that is exactly what I intended. But if what my father says is true, if she really has been telling the noblesse I corrupted her . . . it awakens an old ache within me. Especially after witnessing the cold look in her eyes when Aimé called me a snake. I've seen that look before – she wore it five years ago when she took diamonds from my neck.

Very well, then, I think, *so be it.* I am back where I started – alone, with a single mission: steal the Couronne du Roi for my father.

I pause mid-step, struck by a sudden idea. Marie is currently with Aimé. Which means her chambers are empty. And unless someone has performed intense renovations in the last two days, Bartrand de Roux's journal should still be where I hid it. I change course and head to the Dauphine's apartments.

As expected, the rooms are entirely empty. When I walk inside, the window is cracked open, heaving gasps of chilly air. The curtains and bed canopy sway in the breeze. I search beneath the mattress and come away victorious, the precious journal and yellow flower clutched in my hands. I shove them in my pocket and sneak once again out into the hall.

By the time I manage to find my father, the palace is writhing with activity, noblesse crowding together in the hallways, slowly filing down to the chapel where the wedding is to take place. I find my father in the grand ballroom, directing sweat-soaked servants in arranging crystalline bowls and glassware and shouting for last-minute changes. I blend in with the other servants – he doesn't notice me until his eyes snag against mine, black catching gold.

'Is it done?' he asks simply as I approach, nodding approval to a servant showing him a bottle of wine.

'Yes,' I reply, keeping my voice hushed. 'Though I am not certain if he drank it. His betrothed was present – I had to leave promptly.'

His brows furrow with displeasure. 'Very well. I will find out later, and adjust the plan as necessary. Your tasks are complete until the ceremony – find a way to be in the chapel, and wait for my signal.'

I incline my head and turn to leave, then pause. 'What will happen if Marie drinks it?' I ask worriedly.

'Nothing,' Regnault replies. 'Now go.'

I give him a small grin before bowing and leaving. The hallways are swamped with guests, the air thick with anticipation. Normally, this sort of chaos would inject energy into me. Instead, I only feel twitchy. I have to trust that Regnault told me the truth about the blue petals – that whatever the herb is, it will not harm Aimé. But if it isn't harmful, then what *is* its purpose?

I reach the chapel and slip inside, blinking at the blinding whiteness of its innards. The room is still mostly empty – a few guests murmur in the shadows of a column, and before the altar, a lone maid is busy arranging flowers of glittering diamond and ruby and gilt iron. Her movements are listless, her eyes bruised and weary. I wonder when she last slept.

I move silently along the far wall until I reach the stairwell to the tribune. Even the sight of it sends my heart rattling – the last time I was here, I was running from a monster. If I look closely, I can still make out the faint grooves where its claws struck the marble, and the window I shattered seems to have been hastily replaced.

Forcing my eyes away, I make my way up the stairs to a discreet spot behind a column, one unlikely to be seen from the nave, though I can easily think of an excuse if I am noticed.

Slowly guests begin to be ushered in – Aurélians and foreigners alike, a mass of gold and burgundy and obsidian, bunching together in the pews. Their whispers swell and clash like waves against the shore, filling the cavernous space. Musicians file in and begin tuning their instruments. Finally, three priestesses enter from behind the altar, the one in the centre wearing a glittering chasuble of pure white, the two flanking her dressed in red and carrying incense. Smoke fills the chapel, sickeningly sweet.

Music begins to play. The murmuring crescendos, then drops entirely to a hush as Aimé makes his entrance. His doublet today is white damask edged with golden cord. He stands on the first step up to the altar, his face pale but determined, his hands clasped behind his back. Something about the tightness of his knuckles and angle of his fingers makes me think he's trying to keep them from shaking. The music changes to the traditional wedding march, and immediately all the guests rise to their feet.

The doors open once more, a grandiose flourish like the bow of a performer. In the same moment, the sun finds the chapel window and pushes through, alighting on the figure in the doorway.

Marie d'Odette looks like the lonely goddess, incandescent and melancholy, as though she has been seized from the heavens and brought to the mortal earth against her will. She wears a gown of shimmering satin, delicate silver embroidery depicting overlapping feathers along her bodice. Pearls glint in her hair and at her neck, and a white mantle of feathers rests on her shoulders. There are more feathers swooping around her head, arching over her ears in a champion's wreath.

My chest lurches in furious longing. At the altar, Aimé's eyes light in wonder. His throat bobs as he takes in his betrothed, and all I can think is *That should be me*. Then the Dauphin's gaze – and the gaze of everyone present – drifts to the object in Marie's hands.

The Couronne du Roi.

My heart jumps at the sight of the bejewelled golden circlet. The light seems to shy away from it, leaving the piece of jewellery in shadow, a smear of rusty ink against its lambent surroundings. I clench my hands, swallowing back eager hunger. It's here. The only object powerful enough to summon back Morgane. So close, and yet so far from me.

Marie walks down the aisle, dainty as a doe, her steps so light they can barely be heard despite the trapped, breathless silence. Sunlit smoke curls around her in a hazy shroud. As she crosses the great expanse towards the waiting Prince, I cast my eyes about for my father. I spot him near the side of the chapel, standing among the lower-ranked courtiers. His lips are curled upward in a not-quite smile, the look of a wolf scenting prey.

I lean back, biting my lip. What is he planning?

Ahead of me, Marie finally reaches the Dauphin. The musicians break off, and one of them seemingly misses the cue, because he plays a millisecond longer than the rest, eliciting a few amused chuckles from the crowd. Aimé turns red – his hands are definitely shaking as he kisses Marie's cheek. Marie smiles kindly, and raises the Couronne to place it on his head. Queen crowning King. An ancient tradition.

Aimé licks his lips nervously and takes Marie's hands. I notice her running her thumbs over his knuckles, a soothing gesture. My stomach knots in what I refuse to acknowledge as jealousy.

The priestess in white begins to speak, and my attention immediately falters as I realize she has quite the speech to go through. Restless, my hands drift to my pocket, and I find myself fidgeting with the dried petals of the yellow flower, crushing them between my thumb and forefinger. I remember the pages in the Step-Queen's journals, and hope Aimé has at least stopped taking her potions.

I pull my hand from my pocket, a few crumpled petals dusted on my fingertips. I shake them off, and notice a faint scent in the air, barely there. It smells familiar, muskily sweet, but it takes me a moment to place it.

Then I realize: it's nearly the same as that of the substance that flaked off the Step-Queen's dagger. The one that destroyed the owl-face pendant's spell.

Ahead, the officiating priestess is droning out vows, and Marie and Aimé are echoing them in subdued voices. Wrongness creeps up on me. Something squirms in my memories, begging for attention. The Step-Queen's notes in her journal: *lower dosage ineffective, led to disastrous results*. Aimé's scream. The monster appearing right after, with no Aimé in sight. The words *I need it for my nerves*.

Whatever the dagger had been coated in, it had been made from the same yellow flower as Aimé's potions. If a small dose was capable of destroying a spell as intricate as Regnault's, what could a higher dose do, taken daily? Could it suppress someone's magic altogether?

I realize now why the blue petals seemed so familiar. Because I'd seen them before, when I was flipping through *Medicinal Applications of Sorcerous Elixirs*. *Bluefang*, the flower had been called. *A universal antidote*.

Horror suddenly clogs my throat. I know what my

father's plan is. I know what the Step-Queen's potions were for – they were not meant to harm the Dauphin after all.

They were meant to suppress something inside him.

I straighten in alarm. At the altar, Marie and Aimé are done repeating their vows, and the officiant has procured a long dagger from a pillow of velvet. As per tradition, she will cut the palms of both the betrothed, and they will press the weeping wounds together to signify an unbreakable bond – eternal dedication. She snatches Marie's palm roughly and drags the dagger across it. Marie winces as crimson blood wells from the wound, while the priestess moves on to Aimé's hand.

I start forward, adrenaline screaming through my veins, but in the same moment I feel the prickle of heated eyes on my face. I turn to see my father watching me. He shakes his head minutely – a warning. Get in the way, and there will be no coming back from this.

Conflict judders through me, and I hesitate for a heartbeat. Too long. Too late. The priestess runs the dagger meticulously over Aimé's palm.

There is a second of silence while blood gathers at the edge of the wound.

Then the first droplet slips out on to Aimé's flesh, glittering in the brightness of the chapel.

A disbelieving murmur crawls through the crowd. Several people crane their necks, as if they can't quite tell what they're seeing. An old woman gasps, clutching her shawl.

'By the Mothers,' she says, her voice carrying over the din. 'His blood is gold.'

SCENE XXVII

Château. The Chapel.

Aimé snatches his hand away, but it's too late. Metallic blood leaks down his wrist, smears across the lace of his cuffs.

'Sorcier!' someone cries.

Chaos erupts – noblesse start to their feet, shouting and pointing. Marie takes a wobbling step back. Someone calls for guards, whether to protect Aimé or capture him, I can't tell. One of the priestesses tries to pull Marie away, but she resists. In an instant, I'm barrelling back down to the main floor of the chapel, but before I can get near the altar, a cold hand grabs my forearm.

I whirl on my assailant, only to come face to face with Regnault. He shakes his head at me, seeming to almost gorge himself on the chaos, a smug smile stretching across his face. He's waiting for something. As I look into the crowd, I see the Regent glance towards Regnault. The men lock eyes knowingly.

The Regent nods. Then he turns to the guards. 'Get to the Dauphin!'

That's when the severity of the situation truly hits Aimé. His face whitens, his pupils wide and moving erratically as he searches the room, in vain, for an escape. He shrinks in on himself, curling over his bleeding hand. He looks helplessly towards Marie, but Marie is staring at him in open-mouthed shock, clearly reeling. I can sympathize with that – this is the second time she has been betrayed in two days. It never hurts any less.

Aimé's guards start towards him. My brother is at their head, desperately shoving through the crowd, clearly trying to get to his beloved Dauphin before anyone else. But even Damien looks conflicted. I can see *doubt*. I know what he is wondering – the same thing everyone in the chapel most likely is. *Did Aimé know? Has he been lying all this time?*

From the gut-wrenching, undiluted fear in the Dauphin's eyes, the answer is clear.

There is a second when Aimé is swarmed from all sides. A mass of hands reach out for him at once, some aiming to seize him, others to pull him from harm's way. He vanishes behind a throng of people.

Then, a growl fills the room.

The world goes still.

Another growl. The sound scrapes along my bones, rattles my teeth.

For my nerves, Aimé had said.

But it was never about the nerves.

With a snarl, Aimé shoves back the throng of guards. The blow is impossibly powerful, so powerful that it sends several men flying off their feet, crashing to the white marble. Seeing the carnage, the Prince whimpers, turning away. He tugs at his collar agitatedly, pulls the Couronne off his head as though it is constricting him. His chest rises and falls in panting breaths as he struggles against something, something within himself.

Suddenly, his spine stiffens.

The Regent whips around, facing the crowd. 'Out!' he roars. 'Everyone *out!*'

Then Aimé *transforms*.

It happens in the blink of an eye, but that does not make it any less brutal. His body jerks and spasms, sending him crashing on to all fours. His spine arches, vertebrae expanding until they seem about to pop through his thinning skin. His ribcage balloons, his limbs bending at unnatural angles. An agonized scream pulls his mouth open, exposing a wolf's worth of canines, his gums dripping golden blood. The muscles of his face tremble as his features stretch, yanking his lips into a rictus grin. Last come the boar tusks, slicing their way from between his lips in a gush of saliva and torn flesh.

Aimé-Victor Augier is gone. In his place stands the beast.

And between its feet lies the Couronne du Roi.

Beast-Aimé roars. Any noblesse that weren't already running turn on their heels and scramble for the doors, pushing one another heedlessly. Regnault grabs me and pulls me against himself. He brings us both against the chapel wall, out of the way of the human stampede. In front of us, women trip over the hems of their dresses, men lose their shoes. A few guards attempt to get control over the crowd, to no avail. I think I hear Marie's cry of alarm over it all, but I can't see her.

Somewhere to my left, a musket goes off. Golden blood gushes from the beast's shoulder as the shot meets flesh.

The creature roars and charges, only to be stopped by a row of bristling bayonets from the regrouping guardsmen.

'Aimé!' Marie cries, trying to push her way between two guards, to get to the beast. 'Don't hurt him!'

'The Couronne,' Regnault says into my ear, a simple order. I nod curtly. Then I'm moving, dodging my way through the ebbing tide of noblesse. The snarling beast has backed up against the feet of Morgane, momentarily cornered, though I doubt it will last. The Couronne lies between the monster and the guards. I need to get their attention away from it. But that means taking their attention off the bloodthirsty beast they're trying to contain.

It's a risk I have to take.

I skid to a stop in the middle of the aisle, put my fingers to my mouth, and wolf-whistle.

The sound is loud and sudden enough to turn the attention of at least half the guards towards me. They realize their mistake too late – the momentary distraction allows the beast to bat away their muskets, sending the weapons skittering across the floor. Then it ploughs through the guards, grabbing one of them in its jaws as it goes, tossing him aside like a rag doll. His strangled cry is cut off in a gurgle when he hits the ground. Blood splatters the white marble.

Then the beast is charging directly towards me. I pull out Buttons and stand my ground. Fuelled by a moment of ridiculous sentiment, I try to meet its eyes, to see if I can trigger even a flicker of recognition. There is nothing. Its pupils are slit with hatred. The beast snarls, saliva dripping from its torn lips – it reeks of sour magic and fresh viscera.

I wait until the last moment to roll aside. The movement dislodges the mask on my face, sending it clattering to the ground as I come back up on my feet. As I expected, the beast doesn't seem particularly intent on killing me specifically – once I am out of the way, it simply continues its rampage, reaching the chapel's double doors. It slams its way through, crushing an elderly nobleman as it goes.

'After it!' the Regent commands, but most of the guards are already in pursuit. I spot Damien among them, his jaw set in determination. Only a handful of guards remain – I recognize Armand, pushing Marie behind himself. They remain by the altar, both panting, both flecked in blood, though none of it appears to be theirs. A disembodied arm lies amid the diamond flowers, dripping gore, as though it is meant to be part of the arrangement. The Regent stares down at it with his lip curled. Familiar footsteps behind me alert me to Regnault's approach.

But none of that matters to me. Because at my feet, kicked there by the beast's claws during its rampage, gleams the Couronne du Roi.

I bend to pick it up, half expecting it to vanish before my eyes, a figment of my imagination, a deluded mirage. But no. My touch meets smooth, cool gold. I pause – I'd expected some great burst of breathtaking magic to fill me, but I feel nothing at all. Then – as I run the crown through my hands, as I feel the facets of each jewel placed along its circumference, a gentle thrum passes through my limbs. It feels less like a blaze of power and more like the breaths of a slumbering bird. Flighty. Mesmerizing.

'Odile.' My father's voice reaches me as though through a haze. 'Give it here.'

I turn to look at him, not moving from my position. He looms over me, arm extended towards the Couronne, hand open and expectant. He is silhouetted against the window – I can't make out his features beyond the dark hollows of his eyes. His cloak seems to swallow light.

I don't know why, but I flinch away from him, bringing the Couronne to my chest protectively.

'Odile.' The tenderness in Marie's voice reaches for my heart like a lover's hand. I move my attention away from my father, to watch Marie make her careful way down the altar steps, blood smearing over her hem. Her mantle is torn, shedding feathers with every step. 'Don't do it, please.'

'Little owl,' Regnault says, an odd strain entering his voice. He flexes his hand demandingly. 'The crown.'

'Odile,' Marie says again. She stretches out her palm, fingers opening like blossom petals.

My awareness fades to three things. Two hands: one spindly, talon-like and familiar, the other elegant and softly golden. One that I have known since I was five years old, the other that I think about holding more often than I care to admit. And between them, the Couronne. Its faint, rolling purrs sink into my skin, flowing through my flesh like the sluicing of water. I wonder how it would feel to set it upon my head. I wonder if I could wrench free whatever unnatural magics were trapped in it by the Spider King and summon Morgane here and now. I wonder if I've ever really needed anyone at all.

'Remember yourself,' my father murmurs. The sound slithers from between his teeth, twining around me.

'Don't do this,' Marie whispers. 'Give me the crown. We'll solve this together – we'll save Aimé, we'll explain everything to him, we will find a way to bring magic back.'

Regnault chuckles. 'Lies, lies, *lies*.' He steps closer to me. 'You know her words mean nothing. She stood by while you were put in a cage. She used you and then discarded you. If you give her the crown, she will merely put it back on that blonde brat's head – assuming he ever comes out of that bestial form. Nothing will change.'

He's right, that volatile little voice in my mind whispers. *Why would Marie choose the side of the girl who ruined her life? Who cursed her and lied to her? Why, unless she had something to gain?*

Yes, I think. I can't believe a word she says – I can't *afford* to believe a word she says. But Regnault – Regnault is safe. He came back for me. He may have questionable methods, but they're effective. He has promised to teach me magic – he has promised me greatness. And he, at least, has always kept his promises.

I remember Aimé's words from earlier.

A snake holds some affection for its prey, I believe, as it sinks its fangs in slowly and waits for the venom to spread. That doesn't make it any less vile.

Why should I fight to save someone who has never even gave me a chance?

Vile, vindictive, villain.

The words that have become my anthem, my obituary. But did I not want to be the villain of this tale? Was I not proud of that, once upon a time?

Villains are pitiless. Villains are unfeeling. Villains can't be hurt.

And I am so *tired* of being hurt.

I straighten. My breath rattles out of me in a jagged, wearied sound. I tighten my grip on the Couronne; its thrumming seems to intensify, pricking at my fingertips.

I turn. Slow, but certain.

And I place the Couronne du Roi in my father's hands.

SCENE XXVIII

Château. The Chapel.

I expect my father to take the crown from me gingerly, to treat it with the reverence he has always used when speaking of it. Instead, he seizes it from me like I have handed him a firework with the fuse lit, as though he is running out of time, as though if he doesn't take it fast enough, I might change my mind.

I hear Marie's sharp intake of breath. 'Odile,' she whispers, and in her voice is pure, devastated *sadness*.

I can't look her in the eye. *I'm sorry*, I want to scream. *I told you trusting me was a mistake.*

Marie turns her attention from me, looks fiercely to the guards. 'Stop him,' she orders. Her voice is steady despite the tight lines of her face.

One of the guards starts forward, but the Regent puts up a hand. 'No.'

'No?' Marie echoes in disbelief.

The guard freezes, his lips twisted in conflict. He makes me think of Damien – torn between duty and his own internal morals.

'No.' The Regent juts his chin out. 'Monsieur Regnault is working under my orders.'

At that, Regnault chuckles quietly. Marie's eyes widen. I can see the exact moment she realizes the Regent has allied with my father. There is something terrifying about the utter calm that consumes her, the furious evenness of her voice as she says, *Traitor.*

'Believe me, Mademoiselle, I am doing this for the good of the Crown.' The Regent flicks his finger at the guards. 'Seize the would-be Dauphine, please, and take her to her chambers. She is clearly distressed from her betrothed's betrayal. Oh, and –' his mouth tilts up smugly – 'ensure she remains there – the palace is too volatile right now for her delicate sensibilities.'

Both guards hesitate. They can clearly see the lie in the Regent's words, but to disobey him would be treason.

They step forward. I wonder if Marie will fight, but strong as she is, she could not defeat two fully armed guards. She pulls her arms away from the guards and strides for the exit with her head held high, forcing them to follow after her. It's a small reclaiming of power, but it leaves me breathless, my gut clenched painfully in regret.

'She's impressive,' Regnault says quietly. His eyes glitter as he watches Marie be escorted. 'I can see why she turned your head. Now –' he holds up the Couronne, flutters his fingers along the rim with a resonant *tap tap tap* – 'it is time, I believe.'

He raises the crown to his brow.

Immediately, the Regent surges forward and snatches my father's wrist. 'What do you think you're doing?'

I get between them instantly, pointing Buttons at the Regent with a snarl. 'Let him go.'

'It's all right,' Regnault says, putting up a hand. He tilts his head innocently at the Regent. 'Whatever do you mean?'

The Regent keeps his voice low, out of earshot of his guards. 'I kept my side of the bargain. Now keep yours.'

My father gives the man a civil smile, but there's a taunting edge to it. 'I have kept my promise, have I not? I exposed Aimé's true nature. I believe that accomplishes your goals.'

'You promised me the crown.'

'No, I promised you the *throne*. Which you now have. I can't sit upon it myself, after all. I need a royal puppet whose strings I can pull.'

'You *dare* –' The Regent purples. 'I should have known better than to treat with peasant filth!' He releases Regnault's wrist and backs away, pointing. 'Guards! Seize this man! He intends to steal our Prince's crown!'

Three things happen then at once: the remaining three guards rush forward, pointing their muskets at Regnault. I move to defend my father, Buttons raised. And Regnault places the Couronne du Roi on his head.

It seems as though, for a moment, the world hitches – like a caught breath, a missing puzzle piece slotting into place. Regnault's eyes turn black as ink, molten gold gathering at their corners like tears.

He stretches out his hand towards the approaching guards, spell-threads trailing loosely from his fingertips, bunching between his fingers like cobwebs.

Beside the altar, the twin tarasque statues begin to *move*. They leap forth from their pedestals, spitting out the braziers in their jaws, shattering the chains around their throats.

Then they charge.

The thuds of their metal feet echo throughout the chapel. Within an instant, one of the serpentine monsters leaps in front of Regnault and me, while the other one stalks up to the guardsmen, impossibly long fangs bared and dripping golden magic. A horrid, screeching growl rises from its throat, like metal dragged over stone.

'What is this?' The Regent stumbles back, wide-eyed, as the statue herds him up to the altar. The other statue does the same with the guards. One of the musketeers fires at the beast, but the shot bounces off its gilt shell.

'Not the monsters!' the Regent screams at him. 'The sorcier, shoot the sorcier!'

Before I can react, another guard turns and shoots at my father.

I scream, but the shot never lands – before it can strike home, it erupts into a shower of black feathers. Regnault bares his teeth. 'You truly thought it would be that easy?'

The threads around his fingers flare with new light. As if hearing an unspoken command, one of the tarasques lunges for the man with the gun, clamping its fangs around his arm. The man screams. The tarasque shakes its head like a hound, crushing bone, before unlatching its jaws again. The guard crumples to the ground.

'That was a warning,' Regnault says pleasantly, approaching the Regent. He runs his fingers down the older man's throat before moving them to his shoulder, where they rest with casual menace. 'Have you any more concerns about our bargain?'

The Regent swallows audibly. 'N-no.'

'Good. Now, let us put your men to better use. I want them to hunt down that beast of a Dauphin and bring him back. *Alive*. Subdue him by any means necessary, but I need him breathing. The guardsman named Damien is also to be seized and returned to the Château for questioning. Oh, and send away the guests – tell them the Dauphin's *condition* is under control, but it has taken a heavy toll on him. The wedding, therefore, will not be taking place.'

'And what of Marie d'Odette?'

'Kill her.'

My heart slams into the pit of my stomach. '*What?*'

To my surprise, the Regent says the same. 'No, we can't,' he adds, side-eyeing the golden tarasques as if one might maul him for simply speaking. 'We can't afford to offend Auvigny – we need that province's access to the sea. No . . . I have a better solution. Once I become King, I will marry her.'

I nearly gag at the mere thought. 'Papa,' I cut in, careful to keep my voice light, almost coy. 'Might I propose another alternative?'

He turns his eyes on me slowly. His cheeks are stained with golden tear-trails. 'What is it?'

I shutter away any emotion, any remorse, that I may feel at my next words. 'I want her.'

'*Want* her?'

'As my pet. A reward for all I accomplished.'

The Regent makes an indignant sound, but Regnault shushes him. 'I cannot have her running around the Château and sowing discord. I fear she will be more trouble than she's worth. And a distraction to you.'

I shrug. 'Lock her up in the Dauphine's rooms, then, and keep guards on her. The Regent is right – we need the alliance of Auvigny. But I guarantee I can control Marie far better than he can.'

Regnault rubs his chin, considering. 'Very well,' he says finally. 'It will be so. Yes, Monseigneur?' He levels the Regent with a stare, as though daring the man to argue, but the Regent remains stiffly silent, a muscle ticking in his jaw.

'Of course,' he grits out. I give him a winning smile.

Regnault folds his hands behind his back, nodding to the guards. 'You have your instructions, then.'

With an easy gesture, he calls off the tarasque statues. When the beasts amble away, the Regent heaves a relieved breath, while two of the guards rush to their mutilated companion, who has fallen unconscious. They drag him away, throwing Regnault resentful glares.

The Regent gathers whatever scraps remain of his dignity and follows after the guards, smoothing out his coat and carefully avoiding the pools of drying blood on the floor.

Once he is gone, Regnault turns to me.

To my utter shock, he pulls me into an embrace.

'Well done, little owl,' he croons, smoothing down my hair. 'I am proud of you.'

His arms are not warm, like Marie's, and his hold is stiff and too tight, more a cage than a cradle. Still, my heart swells, and I press my forehead into his chest, basking in the rare moment of pride.

Finally, when I feel like I might burst, I pull away. 'How did you know about the Dauphin's curse?'

'The yellow flower you showed me,' Regnault says. 'It's a weed called sorcier's bane – it suppresses magic. Before Morgane's disappearance, it was fed to sorciers who had broken the law. It turned them into red-bloods, prevented them from using sorcery.' One of his tarasques approaches him, and he strokes its head idly. 'I thought the flower had stopped blooming after magic disappeared. It seems Anne de Malezieu managed to coax a few stunted ones into growing.'

'Does this mean Aimé is a sorcier?' I ask. 'Why does he transform into a beast?'

'I do not think he is a sorcier – I do not sense any innate power in him at all. I think, rather, he is cursed. Possibly by Morgane herself.'

'Why would he be cursed?'

Regnault seems to measure his words carefully. 'Perhaps he, or one of his ancestors, offended the Mothers.'

I sense there is something he isn't telling me, but if that is so, then no prying will coax it out of him. Instead, I ask, 'What do you intend to do with Aimé?'

Regnault taps his nails along the tarasque's snout. 'In order for the Regent to be accepted as the new King, Aimé's legitimacy must be called into question. The courtiers and all the city must see the beast Aimé has become.'

'You intend to make a spectacle of him.'

'That is one of my intentions, yes.'

Despite everything, the image of Aimé in chains, put out for ridicule like a carnival attraction, makes me nauseous. I rein in my guilt, force myself to remain practical, ruthless like my father. I made this decision, and I cannot regret it.

'What of the Couronne?' I ask. 'When will you summon Morgane?'

'Once I have established my foothold in the palace.'

I frown. I had always assumed it would be his first line of action after we succeeded in our plan. 'Can you not do it now?'

He clicks his tongue. 'You are always so impatient, Odile. To bring back magic now would be to throw Auréal even further into chaos. Let this affair with the Dauphin pass, let the Regent take his place. The crown grants me enough power to protect us both. I fear it might lose its powers once I perform the . . . summoning.'

I nod, trying to accept his words, though some part of me fidgets with dissatisfaction. My gaze is drawn to the Couronne upon his head, the memory of its power humming through me still fresh in my mind.

'What does it feel like?' I ask, unable to hold back the curiosity. 'Using the Couronne's magic?'

Regnault smiles at me, and there's something manic about the expression, something not quite human.

'It feels like endless power.'

SCENE XXIX

Château. The Queen's Tower.

My father comes to me that night, a bottle of wine in hand.

The Château has hollowed out, guests fleeing after the horrors of the almost-wedding, leaving the palace feeling like a belly with its organs scooped out, a ribcage with no heart to protect.

Regnault joins me in the old Queen's Tower, the place I have decided to make my new lair. I have cleared away the tarps, revealing the glossy ebony furniture. I have called in maids to chase away the dust. I have opened the windows to let wind howl through the room. As long as I don't breathe too deep, look too hard, I can forget this is the place Aimé's mother died.

Besides, something about the view is comforting – the rooms are in the Château's tallest tower, and I can peer down at the palace grounds and feel felonious, feel irreverent, a thief crowing over their newly robbed jewel. I can feel like this was all worth it.

My father and I drink to our victory. I still have no taste for wine, but I guess this one is expensive since it came from Aimé's private collection. I try not to think of Marie alone in her rooms, once again locked in a cage, her future uncertain. I try not to think of Aimé and his strange curse – who has yet to be captured, who was last seen fleeing into the forest by the guards trying to chase him down. I try not to think of my brother, who has not been seen since the Prince's escape. Part of me hopes he's clever enough to stay away from the Château for good.

I don't think about them. I drink, and the more I drink, the more I revel in my success. This is what I wanted, what I worked for all my life. I infiltrated the palace, I stole the Couronne, I avenged the sorciers who came before me. And that is what Regnault reminds me of as he pours himself another glass of wine.

'This palace is ours now,' he says. 'If we bide our time, if we play this game until the end, I will eventually sit on the throne, as Bartrand de Roux should have done.'

'And what of me?' I ask, voice slurring and head spinning. When did I drink so much?

'You –' Regnault moves on from his glass to mine – 'my dear, sweet pet, will be by my side as you have always been. Nothing will change – I will always need you here, my knife in the dark, my shadow. I am certain I will soon find another mission for you.'

I frown. Somehow, that sounds wrong. I had thought that stealing the Couronne would put an end to my missions. Have I not proved myself enough already?

But when I try to articulate that, I can't seem to find the words. My mind feels loose and billowy, a cloud blown away in a breeze. I curl up wearily at Regnault's side.

'Rest,' Regnault says, standing and picking up the wine bottle. He sways a little himself, his eyes drunken-bright.

I notice, distantly, that he is still wearing the Couronne. 'Tomorrow, our reign truly begins.'

He leaves me staring through the window at the scattered stars in the sky, trying in vain to find the shape of a swan's wings within them.

The last thing I feel before falling asleep is a pang of heartbreak.

Over the next few days, Regnault buries his talons in the Château, curls them deep into its thick walls and constricts the castle's very soul. Through the Regent, he sends away any straggling guests, along with Pierre, the Step-Queen's young son. He takes control of the search for Aimé, and ensures the right rumours about the wedding's events are spread: that the poor Dauphin turned out to have been cursed by his own stepmother. He will be sent away to the sea for recovery from this episode, and the Regent, being next in line, will take his place on the throne.

I spend the next few days attempting to embrace my newfound status, eating from porcelain plates, standing at Regnault's side protectively and trying not to think of Marie d'Odette – the last of which I fail at spectacularly. The moment my focus wavers, she is there, the warmth of her hands and fullness of her lips, like a blemish that refuses to vanish. Yes, that's what Marie is, I resolve. A *blemish*.

And yet I still think about visiting her. Sometimes I imagine strolling into her chamber and gloating. Others I think of kneeling at her feet and begging for forgiveness. Others still, I offer her a place at my side, to be my ally and friend again.

But when a guard approaches me and tells me Marie has asked for an audience, I turn him away. Because no matter how I might imagine it, I can't bear the idea of looking Marie in the eye and facing her devastation, her disappointment.

By the next day, half of the palace's guards have deserted.

I am with Regnault and the Regent when the news is broken. The two are having a meeting – I am standing in the corner, trying not to shuffle restlessly. I'd spoken up once, to lobby for keeping on all the palace staff, and received a lukewarm, disinterested nod. I've spent the last half-hour simmering at a lovely medium-temperature fury, so when the young guard-in-training comes to tell us of the guards, I almost hope my father will ask me to stab him, if only so I can unload my frustration *somewhere*.

'What do you mean, *deserted*?' the Regent says in a low tone.

'I-I mean they r-ran away in the night. To the city, I think. At least h-half the garrison is gone. I overheard them yesterday evening. They don't trust you, Monseigneur, because of your alliance with the sorcier. They've lost their faith in the Crown.'

The Regent opens his mouth to speak, but Regnault cuts in.

'You overheard them discussing this yesterday, boy?'

The lad nods, fumbling with the lapels of his coat.

'And you did not think to warn us earlier?'

'I . . . I didn't realize they would go so far, I didn't know –'

'Very convenient,' Regnault says acidly. 'Very convenient. But even if what you say is true –' he traces his finger in the air as he speaks, leaving behind spell-threads – 'you should have known *better*.'

The spell flares to life.

Instantly, the guard's body is swallowed in a golden shell. Where there was flesh, there is now hard metal, sleek and reflective. The Regent shouts in alarm, too late. My breath hitches in surprise. Before us stands a boy-shaped statue, his hands still at his lapels, his eyes wide and frightened and innocent.

Regnault straightens, smoothing out his coat, and I've never seen such fury in his eyes, such unfettered madness. It is almost like an unveiling – as though a restraint has been released, a collar removed. This has always lain beneath my father's skin, I realize. This is merely the first time the mask has slipped.

'Have a servant bring this statue to the barracks,' Regnault commands. 'A warning. Anyone who attempts to desert will end up the same.'

The Regent seems to reel. 'You can't simply – you – that is not how you –' He cuts off when he sees Regnault's hand moving again. But my father is only inspecting his nails.

'These men had no respect for you,' he explains casually. 'They will now, when they realize how ruthless you can be. I guarantee, my dear King-to-be, there will be no more desertions.'

The Regent balls his fists, unclenches them again. The words *King-to-be* work their magic on his ego. He draws himself up with a huff. 'Very well,' he says, and calls for servants.

The servants come. The boy – well, former boy, now golden statue – is carried off. The meeting continues.

I wipe sweat from my palms and remind myself that Regnault knows what he is doing. That he would never do the same to me.

And yet, once evening arrives, I find myself seeking out my father. I know he has taken up residence in the King's apartments, the ones King Honoré occupied before his death. The way there is long and dark. Somewhere along the hall, a window has been cracked open – the frostbitten wind pulsing down the corridor tastes of oncoming snowfall. The flames of the candelabra in my hand flicker. The doors emerge from the gloom – heavy constructs of obsidian wood, carved twin tarasques coiled around them like a frame.

I can hear movement beyond, the quiet footfalls of Regnault moving around the room. I walk up to knock, but something stops me – it feels almost like a palm in the centre of my chest, pushing me back. A burst of wind gusts down the hall, whipping around me, blowing out my candles and carrying in a few flecks of soot-black snow. I could swear there is a voice whispering on the wind, feminine and rasping – *Be silent and watch, Daughter of the Blood.* My skin crawls, my breath stutters. In front of me, one of the doors creaks open a crack.

I peer into the room. Within is a restless dark, lit by a scattering of dying candles, the obscure silhouettes of furniture forming odd, crooked angles. This must be the sitting room. Regnault works at a writing desk, hunched over a heavy book, muttering to himself. The Couronne gleams in his hair.

As I watch, he raises his right hand to his brow to take it off, then freezes, his fingers just inches from the golden ring. 'No,' he says sharply. 'I will not. You are mine, and I will not.' He lowers his hand and barks a laugh, a frightening, erratic sound. 'Morgane, Morgane, *ma chère* Morgane. Your madness and mine have always been one, have they not? We're intertwined. It will take more than the threat of insanity to part us, I think. Yes. I think so indeed.'

He chuckles brightly to himself, lowering his hand back to the book, turning a page.

'Fret not, my dear. You will not have to suffer much longer. Once I have ended that Augier brat's life, you will no longer be bound to that lineage. Your powers will be mine entirely. Then, I will bring your sisters to join you.' He laughs again, as though he has just shared a joke, as though there should be a room laughing along with him.

I back away from the door, the candelabra in my hand long gone cold. More snow blows past me, melting into dark puddles on the marble. My mouth is dry, horror throbbing within me. *That Augier brat*, my father said, and I know he was talking about Aimé, about killing him. But for what?

Morgane . . . He keeps saying her name as though he is speaking to her. Could it really be? Is it possible that the Good Mother we have been trying to summon never left us at all?

Could it be she's been in the palace all along, trapped in a crown?

Back in my rooms, I fumble for Bartrand de Roux's journal, which I have carefully hidden beneath a loose floorboard. I don't know what I'm looking for, but I don't have anywhere else to go for answers, and something, *something* about my father's words rings eerily familiar. I go back to the passages I had read the first time: *We long for freedom. Should it all go as planned, we will gain the power we have always deserved yet never been given. We will have endless power, endless potential. No more limits. No more fear.*

I had assumed Bartrand had been speaking of freeing the sorciers from the Spider King's restraints. But now the words take on a more sinister turn. No more limits, no more fear. Trap an ancient, powerful spirit and keep her powers only to yourself.

I keep searching the journal. Passages that were previously mundane musings begin to sound like ramblings, begin to sound like *plotting*. Another paragraph catches my eye: *Reinforced by ancient bloodlines, the collar should be strong enough to hold even the most powerful of creatures. The problem is, no one has seen it in centuries, since the tarasque first appeared in the southern provinces.*

The collar ... Could he be talking about the Golden-blooded Girl's collar? The one she initially used to control the tarasque?

I growl under my breath, wishing Marie were here. I am certain she could solve this enigma faster than I. I continue searching what remains of the journal, but too many pages are missing, torn out by the wind; I find no more answers in the text itself. But there is something here. A certain familiarity I had not noticed before – in the shape of the script, the turns of phrase. *Endless power, endless potential.* That is what Bartrand de Roux wrote in his secret journal, two hundred years ago.

And yesterday, after the coup, when I asked my father about the crown, isn't that exactly what he said?

A horrible, acid dread crawls up from my stomach. My ribs feel as though they are tightening over my lungs, squeezing the air from me until I cannot find breath. I close the journal, turn it over to stare at the filigree bird on the back.

'It can't be,' I whisper.

But it is. I know it with horrid certainty.

It all makes abrupt, awful sense – the secrecy, the alias, the mask he is never seen without. And how else could he have possibly known so much about the Couronne?

Regnault isn't merely Bartrand de Roux's descendant.

He *is* Bartrand de Roux.

SCENE XXX

The Dauphine's Apartments.
Night deepens.

Thudthudthudthud. I pound desperately on the door to the rooms that have become a prison. I have dismissed the guards that stood on either side, leaving me alone in the snaking corridor. *Thudthudthudthud.* I try again, and again. My breath is short, my pulse erratic. No answer. The silence feels pointed, grimly stubborn. 'Come on,' I mutter, raising my fist for a final attempt. *'Please.'*

Thudthudthudthud –

This time, the door whips open.

And there she stands.

Marie d'Odette d'Auvigny, a silver flame against the dark of night. Her hair tumbles around her shoulders in frizzing waves, her eyes are bleary, and the light of the candelabra highlights the pillow-creases on her cheek.

She's never been more beautiful.

'Marie,' I say breathlessly.

If the Swan Princess is surprised at the sight of me, she gives no indication. Her face has that impassive politeness she wore the first night at the Théâtre.

Shame gutters in the pit of my stomach. 'Marie, please.'

She begins to close the door. I push back before she can, and we grapple momentarily. It's Marie who lets go first, her eyes hard.

'Please, there's something you need to know.'

Still no reply. I release the door, open my palms before me. 'Will you not even speak to me?'

'What do you want me to say?' she replies finally, her voice even.

'Anything.' *Shout at me, be angry with me. Anything but this apathy.*

'They said I am to be your pet,' she says. For the first time, genuine *hurt* creeps into her voice. 'I thought it was a lie, but when I asked to see you, they told me you wouldn't speak to me. I . . . I feel like an absolute fool. I saw the signs, but I disregarded them, because I . . . because I *liked* you. Tell me, was there ever any truth to our friendship?'

Yes, there was, I want to tell her. In a fleeting moment strolling through Verroux's streets, in a quiet dawn when I held her in my arms. Beneath the full moon by the old dock, bulrushes rustling around us.

'They wanted to kill you,' I say. 'It was the only way I could think of to keep you alive. I was . . . I was trying to protect you.' I offer a grin. 'Consider it payback for throwing me to the wolves the moment you stepped back in the palace. Now we're even. I tricked you, and . . .' I trail off as I notice Marie's startled look of confusion.

'What are you talking about?' she asks. 'I have only ever tried to help you.'

'My father said you had been telling people I misled you, that I . . . that I corrupted you.'

Her brows furrow. 'I . . . Perhaps I said something of the sort. But I had a ruse to maintain. I had to keep my standing at the court if I was to free you.'

'And how did marrying Aimé factor into this?' I challenge.

'If I'd broken off the engagement, that would have destroyed not only my chances at success, but my family's reputation. Besides, I could have helped you far better once I had the authority of Dauphine. Surely you, of all people, understand that!'

I blink. She did all this . . . to help me? After everything I did? 'But . . . you're not . . . you're not angry with me? For the necklace?'

'I was, for a moment,' Marie says slowly. 'But the more I thought about it, the more I realized . . . part of me always suspected it was you. I simply did not want to admit it to myself. Those memories of us as girls are some of my most treasured, and I didn't want to lose that. To tarnish it. So I chose to ignore any suspicions I had, in favour of clinging to those last moments of freedom.'

'Marie,' I say, and for the first time in perhaps all my life, my heart aches. 'I –'

'I *am* sorry,' she interrupts. 'About that day in the stables. I should have said it long ago. I didn't want to . . . to bring it up. To reopen old wounds. But . . . I never should have left you there. My mother . . . Well, I told you I was a coward. And it is her I've always feared most of all. It's not that I didn't want to stop her, Odile, I swear it. It's that . . . I couldn't. And I'm so very sorry.'

'I understand,' I say. And I do. Perhaps part of me always did, just as part of Marie always knew it was I who stole the diamonds. But I'd clung to the pain of that moment because I *wanted* to be angry, to justify the actions I had taken after. To feel righteous instead of guilty. 'I'm sorry, too.'

Marie gives me a grateful smile, her eyes rippling with sorrow. I feel the cracks between us like they are a chasm – I don't know how to repair them, I've never had to before, but I can't stand seeing her anguished. There's a strand of hair curling loose and unruly over her face, and on impulse, I reach up to tuck it behind her ear.

When I draw back, her cheeks are pink, her lips parted in surprise. Her reaction fills me with sudden, wicked delight. Feeling impish, I poke the tip of her nose.

Marie blinks, cat-like. Then she turns away abruptly. 'Come inside,' she says, curt and formal, almost comically so. 'And wipe that smug smile off your face.'

I follow Marie back into the Dauphine's chambers. She settles primly on a couch, curling her feet under herself, while I set my candelabra on the vanity and remain standing, full of tense, erratic energy.

Marie leans forward. 'What is it that you wanted to tell me?'

'My father is Bartrand de Roux,' I blurt immediately. 'At least, I believe he is. It should be impossible, I know. But Aimé and I once stumbled across a journal entry that said sorciers could prolong their lives, somehow. And I think . . . I think that's what he did. To live this long.'

I explain my discoveries to her, about Regnault and about the Couronne, and watch as her face grows drawn and troubled. 'If what you say is true . . . then he is perhaps more dangerous than we could imagine.'

'I'm not certain, yet. I hope I'm wrong.' I rub my arms. I know in my gut that I'm not.

'I . . . I fear I have made discoveries of my own,' Marie says. 'After you were arrested, I went back to Madame de Malezieu's study, in hopes of finding something that would clear your name. Did you know she kept a diary?' She lifts something off the low table in front of her – it's an unassuming, leather-bound journal. 'I took my time to read it. It was . . . Odile, we could never have known what we were getting into.'

'What do you mean?'

'Did . . . did Aimé ever tell you how his mother died?'

I shake my head. 'He only told me she died after he was born.'

'That's because no one knows the cause of her death,' she says. 'All that is known is that she died soon after childbirth, supposedly from illness. But it turns out that's not true at all.'

I have a horrible feeling I know what Marie will say next. And she does.

'A beast killed her. Or rather, King Honoré, as a beast. This curse on Aimé? It's generational. And according to Anne, it's awakened by strong emotions. King Honoré kept a controlled grasp on it all his life. Until his son, his heir, was born, when he was so overwhelmed that he transformed and killed his own wife.' She looks down at her hands, pained.

'Anne told me the King married her because she was a sorcier,' I recall.

Marie nods. 'She was a mere herbalist from Verroux. The King gave her the estate of Malezieu so she might have a title, and took her as his wife. In exchange, she made medicines that helped suppress the curse.'

I begin to pace, my mind racing. 'So King Honoré needed the potions, too.'

'He was much better at keeping it secret,' Marie says. 'It took Anne some time to perfect the potions – they had side effects of their own. Erratic behaviour. Paranoia. The night of the King's death, it seems she gave Aimé too small a dose, and it didn't work.'

I pause mid-step, turning to her in realization. 'He fought with King Honoré that night, after the ball. If heightened emotions trigger the change, well . . .'

'Indeed. Anne recounts that she went to comfort Aimé in his rooms, but he was gone – he had run away to the lakeside, where he transformed and disappeared into the forest. King Honoré went after him.'

'And the beast slaughtered him,' I finish. 'But how did Aimé turn back into a human afterwards? Did Anne help him somehow?'

'She writes that the transformation doesn't last long – about an hour or so. He falls into a deep sleep afterwards, which is how Anne found him. She took him discreetly back to his rooms. It was in that time that Damien found the bodies.'

'So he became the scapegoat.' I walk over to the couch and slump down beside Marie. 'Regnault intends to kill Aimé,' I tell her sombrely. 'I don't know why. I could hardly understand his ramblings, but when he was speaking to Morgane – if it truly is Morgane, in the crown – he said that he would bring her sisters to join her, that he . . . *Oh.*' Understanding strikes me like a punch to the gut, leaving me breathless. I reach out to grip Marie's arms. 'Oh, Marie. The mission, the ritual, all of it . . . it was never about bringing back one of the Mothers. It was about imprisoning all of them.'

Her eyes widen in understanding, her fingers tightening around my wrists. 'And he needs to kill Aimé to do it.'

I nod sharply. 'I need to get that crown away from my father. If it truly is Morgane that is trapped within, we need to free her. Perhaps then we will be able to lift Aimé's curse.'

Marie shifts towards me, eyes thoughtful. 'But how do we free her?'

'By destroying the Couronne, I assume.'

I know in my heart it will not be that easy. But I remember the invisible force that pushed the door open earlier, that first spoke to me in the strange not-dream in the cells. *Daughter of the Blood*, it keeps saying. Someone – some*thing* – is helping me. I have to hope it will guide me when the time comes.

'Regnault will not give up the crown willingly,' I say. 'He doesn't take it off at all, which will make stealing it difficult. I need to wait until he is asleep. Tomorrow night,' I decide, stringing together the first threads of a plan. 'That's when I'll do it. I will come to free you afterwards, so be awake and wait for my signal. We will need to run.'

She tugs on one of her curls worriedly. 'Is there nothing I can do to help?'

'No. This is something I must do on my own. Sooner or later, I will have to confront him.'

She lowers her hand, and our eyes catch almost inadvertently. I try to give her a reassuring, confident smile.

Marie looks down at her hands. 'Odile, I – if something goes wrong, shatter a window.'

I raise my eyebrows. 'What? Why?'

'There's . . . It's hard to explain. Perhaps it's better if I don't, yet. I'm not entirely sure of it myself.'

'Taunting me with a mystery, Princess?' I say silkily, leaning towards her, if only to see her blush again. 'Very well, then. I'll take it as a challenge.'

'You're preposterous,' she says, laughing softly.

Then she darts forward and kisses me on the cheek.

She's pulling back before I know it, but she might as well have marked herself permanently on my skin. It's a stardust feeling, prickling and shivering and ephemeral, leaving me light-headed and bursting with warmth.

I must look truly undignified, because Marie giggles. Then she pushes lightly on my shoulder. 'Go to sleep, sorcière,' she says. 'And stay safe. For me.'

SCENE XXXI

Château. Morning.

The greatest challenge awaits me the next morning. How can I act normal, when my world has been turned upside down? Yet when my father joins me for breakfast, I meet his eyes and make idle conversation while searching the corners of his too-wide grin, the sharp tips of his teeth, for a single clue I may have missed. And yet, his mask is pristine. Any madness from last night – any trace of the true Bartrand de Roux – is meticulously buried.

For once, I am glad I am a good actress. Because I too can put on a mask. I can play at obliviousness, feign confidence. I can ignore how badly I still wish to please my father – how I still bask in the smallest compliment, how I look for his approval when I threaten away a courtier who tries to question his position.

The day grows warmer, the dark snow melting to hideous grey stains on the pale courtyard cobbles. Its remnants pool beneath the shutters of windows, track all over the entrance hall on the boots of noblesse. It is especially abundant on the heels of the square-jawed, handsome nobleman who demands an audience with the Regent and his 'pet sorcier'.

I know immediately why he is here. From his features alone, I can guess he is a relative of the young messenger from yesterday. I know this also because as soon as he lays eyes on Regnault, he crosses the room and punches my father in the face.

The retaliating smirk Regnault gives the man oozes enough menace to make me shudder. 'That's not very polite,' he drawls.

'Bring back my son!' the man screams, turning on the Regent. 'Tell this monster to bring him back, or you are asking for war with Marsonne!'

This is the first time I have seen the Regent look truly worried. 'Calm yourself, Monsieur. Your Louis was punished for assisting in desertion.' There is an edge of panic as he turns to Regnault. 'But I agree. I think the boy learned his lesson. It is time to turn him back.'

'I don't know why you keep this monster around,' interrupts the newcomer. 'I'd heard rumours, but I did not believe you would ally yourself with a golden-blood until I saw him standing here. And letting him wear the Couronne! Have you gone mad?'

Regnault's smile tightens. The small shift in expression is enough to make my gut clench.

The Regent, oblivious to the danger, waves his hand placatingly. 'He is assisting me in bringing order back to the Château. It is only a temporary arrangement, I promise. Now –' he clasps his hands together, turning to Regnault – 'if you wouldn't mind turning young Louis back –'

'Turning him back?' Regnault interrupts. 'You think I am a dog, to be ordered around as you please? You think I'll undo my actions like a coward because of some petty threat? No, no, not at *all.*' That maddened edge has returned to his voice, the one I heard last night.

'No, lovely Regent. But if you fear that this gentleman here is going to pose a problem, then let me solve it for you.'

Before either I or the Regent can even scream, Regnault has traced a pattern of spell-threads, and the nobleman before us has turned to gold.

A choked sound escapes me. Regnault glances in my direction, a devious light in his eyes, and I know he is looking for admiration in my face, for me to relish the cruel deed as much as he does. I force myself to smirk. In reality, I want to double over and vomit.

The Regent, however, does not hide his opinions. He spins on his heel, practically spitting. 'What have you done?'

'Gotten rid of your problem,' Regnault says casually, brushing invisible dust from his shoulder. 'Marsonne cannot go to war with us if there is no one to lead it.'

'He is the Duke of Marsonne! How am I supposed to explain this to . . . to *anyone?*'

'Tell them he crossed the wrong man.'

The Regent wipes his mouth. 'This is enough of your madness. So far, I have been honouring our bargain, doing as you say, but if this continues, I will have you arrested and exiled. Your smug little daughter, too.'

Regnault stiffens. A flame lights in his eyes with such fury that I can almost feel the heat from where I stand. *'What did you say?'*

The Regent falters somewhat, and I can tell he knows he has gone too far. His gaze flicks panickily from the gold-encased nobleman to Regnault's twitching fingers.

'I only mean,' he says, lowering his voice, 'that you promised me a throne. But I cannot rule over ruins.'

'You think you are ruling at all?' Regnault barks a laugh. 'If I could claim that throne now, I would. Unfortunately, I need someone of royal blood upon it to ensure some semblance of peace. But worry not. Once my plans are complete, thrones and crowns will be meaningless in the face of my new power.' He pats the man firmly on the back, teeth locked in a vicious smile. 'I would caution you not to question my methods again. And even more so, I would caution you to keep any mention of my daughter out of your filthy mouth.'

With that, he strides off. As he walks past me, he crooks a finger in my direction. 'Come, Odile. Let us stroll in the gardens – *our* gardens – before dinner.'

I trail after him, part of me still stunned, still ecstatic, that he defended me so fervently. A month ago, it might have been enough for me. But now, all I can think of is how I plan to betray him, and what he might do to me if I am caught in the act.

I wait until Regnault has retired for the night before sneaking back down to the Step-Queen's study. The room has been locked, but I doubt anyone has been brave enough to touch its bizarre, sorcery-soaked contents. My assumption is confirmed when I pick the lock and step inside, finding everything exactly as it was the last time I was here – including the traces of my own blood, dried and glimmering on the floor. The sight sends a phantom pang of pain through my ribs, and I rub the still-healing wound as I pull out the satchel I have brought with me.

I take out *Medicinal Applications of Sorcerous Elixirs*, and seek out the recipe I discovered while flipping through it last night – a herbal mixture that makes one drowsy when it is burned. My father is too suspicious to drink anything given to him by another, even me, but this . . . this might work, if I play my cards right.

I find the ingredients I need in the Step-Queen's arsenal. Thankfully, it is not a complicated recipe, and within an hour I am holding a small fistful of brittle leaves. I tuck them into my sleeve and head to Regnault's rooms.

This time, there is no invisible force pushing me to the door, no voice in my mind. I simply knock and enter, to find my father in simple breeches and a loose shirt. Only his mask remains in place. He looks smaller, like this, more human somehow, without his layers of black and gold and feathers.

'Odile,' he greets me. 'How are you feeling?'

The question takes me aback – he's never asked me such a thing before. 'F-fine,' I stammer, wandering over to the crackling fire. I stretch my hands in front of it, glancing at my father over my shoulder as he crosses the room. Once his back is turned, I shake the herbs out of my sleeves and into the hearth. I keep talking, trying not to arouse suspicion. 'Perhaps . . . perhaps I'm a little shaken, I admit.' A lie in a truth. 'Everything is happening so fast.'

'It is what must be done,' Regnault says, turning to face me again. 'You understand why I did it, yes? I must eliminate anyone who threatens our position.'

By turning them into statues? I want to ask, but I keep quiet. Already, I can feel the herbs taking effect as they burn, releasing their fumes – my eyelids grow heavy, and I notice that Regnault's are doing the same.

'I . . .' I yawn. 'I do believe I'm going to retire for the night.' I turn away from the hearth, and after a moment's hesitation, I walk up to him and kiss him on the cheek, like I've seen daughters do to their fathers. 'Goodnight, Papa.'

'Goodnight, little owl,' he says, eyes already closing.

When I return, Regnault is asleep. He did not even make it to his bed – he's sitting on a couch, his head lolling back. A book lies cradled in his lap, pages fluttering softly, as though he still attempted to read before falling asleep. He looks vulnerable in sleep, and seeing him like this nearly makes me question my resolve. This is the man, after all, who coaxed me out of a Verroux gutter, who held my hand and whispered promises of power. He is Bartrand de Roux. He wants to trap the Good Mothers and seize their power for his own. He is slipping into the Couronne's madness.

But he is also my father. If I go through with this, I will never have a father again.

I swallow past a lump in my throat. Reach for Regnault's head, gingerly slip my thumbs under the rim of the Couronne, warm from the heat of his skin. Its magic skitters down my arms – I hold my breath. Begin to lift up the crown –

Regnault reaches up and seizes my arm.

'How dare you.'

Ice fills me, freezing me in place. I stare down at my father's eyes, thunderous and unforgiving, obsidian shards poised to pierce into my soul.

I snatch my hands away. 'Papa, I . . . I thought . . . I might take it off, you were asleep, and it looked uncomfortable . . . I –'

'What a miserable lie,' he snarls, his grip tightening on my skin, his nails digging in. 'I thought I taught you better than that. Did you truly think something as paltry as a sleep charm would work on me?'

He drags me towards him, buries his hand in my hair and pulls me down, so I can feel his hot breath on my cheek. 'I'm almost impressed,' he whispers. 'After all, I taught you this. To steal, to betray. I *made* you. And this is how you repay me.'

Then he shoves me across the room.

My back slams into the wall, then my head, leaving me winded and gasping. Blood trickles from my wrist where his nails broke the skin. I can taste more of it welling on my tongue.

Regnault stalks up to me. I back away from him, but my spine only hits the wall again. My vision blurs; I can't help the pathetic whimper that escapes me. I am more terrified than I was with the Step-Queen, or with the beast.

'Oh, *ma fille*.' Regnault crouches before me. Brushes his fingers tenderly across my cheek, swipes at the blood pooling under my lip. I shudder, but he pays no heed. 'I do not wish to hurt you. But you know I must punish you for your betrayal.'

'My betrayal?' I whisper, spitting up a glob of blood. 'You lied to me my whole life. You were never going to free magic, were you, *Bartrand*? You were only going to claim it all for yourself.'

His eyes widen a fraction, but he masters himself quickly. 'Is this discovery the reason for your little rebellion?' he demands. 'You don't understand, you could never understand. I *do* want to free magic. I want to free it from the control of those old gods, from having to obey their caprices and whims. Once I have trapped all three Mothers, I will be able to turn Auréal into an unstoppable force. We could take the continent, take the world.'

I waver, my head spinning. 'What are you talking about?'

'Let me tell you a story.' He sits back on his heels. 'About a young, ambitious sorcier, advisor to a young, ambitious King. A sorcier who had faith in his craft and in his patron, Morgane. Who turned to her when a blight killed most of the kingdom's crops, begging her for the power to turn stone to gold to help his people out of poverty. Who was refused. "That is too much," said Morgane. "So much change would upset nature's balance." For centuries, she had granted sorciers the power to create paltry trinkets, buttons that could become firearms or necklaces that altered the wearer's appearance. Those, Morgane said, were small magics, temporary, affecting only a few. But to save a kingdom – *her* kingdom, the kingdom she claimed to protect – she couldn't bend the rules for that.' He scoffs.

'The King and I were horrified. We did not feel Morgane deserved her power any more – none of the Good Mothers did. So we hatched a plan to claim their power for our own. For the sake of the kingdom.'

I stare up at Regnault, whose eyes are far away, two hundred years into the past. A throb runs through my head from where I hit it. Blood trickles down my neck. I slump back against the wall, gathering my strength, listening in confusion as my father unveils his secrets.

'I began by creating the Couronne,' he says. 'I stole the Golden-blooded Girl's collar from the monastery where it had been hidden for centuries. I set about altering it, increasing its power, so it could hold even the most powerful creature of magic. To complete the spell and bind Morgane, I needed blood. But not just any blood. There is power, you see, in legacy. And bloodlines are one of the truest legacies there is. King Ludovic and I went together to the old shrine in the centre of the lake, and together we spilled our blood: mine, golden, from the ancient de Roux sorciers. And Ludovic's, royal, older even than mine, old as Auréal itself. Together, we summoned Morgane. We tricked her, and we trapped her.

'When she realized what was happening, she lashed out with her powers, trying to punish us. She cursed me, stealing my magic, tearing my own birthright from my blood. The temple crumbled – I was thrown into the water. I came up on the side of the city, barely alive. I wandered the streets of Verroux for months after, pathetic and half mad. I could not remember how I had gotten there – I did not remember my own name. Years passed before the first trickles of memory returned to me, and more years before I began to be able to use magic again.'

'King Ludovic was cursed, too, wasn't he?' I realize. 'But his curse was different – it turned him into a beast. And he passed it on to King Honoré, who passed it to Aimé.'

Regnault gives me a look midway between resentment and pride. 'You were always too clever, weren't you? Impatient, reckless, but clever when forced to be.' There's that gleam of insanity again, sparking in his eyes and then vanishing. 'In truth, even I did not know of his curse. I had my suspicions, but they were only that. I did not dare return to the court after I regained my memories – by then, Ludovic was a blubbering madman, calling himself the Spider King, blaming everyone but himself for his misery.'

We stare at one another in silent understanding, the brunt of the past and its mistakes coming to rest between us. Then Regnault straightens so he towers over me, a nightmarish figure, all angles and too-long limbs. His eyes are dark hollows – his teeth gleam white and ravenous.

'You see now, surely. You see why I must finish what I started. I made a mistake, reinforcing the Couronne with two bloodlines. I split its loyalty in two. I cannot access its full power. But I can break that bond by killing the last Augier heir at the place the Couronne was forged.'

'But Aimé is not the last of his line,' I try to argue. 'There's Pierre, Anne's son.'

'Only true heirs carry the power. Pierre would have had to be named heir to the Crown by Honoré in order to be a threat. As it stands, the boy is hardly better than a bastard. He is of no consequence.'

My stomach sinks. There is truly nothing standing in his way any more. 'So you intend to capture all three Mothers.'

'Yes.'

'And in doing so, you will claim all magic for yourself.'

He inclines his head. 'The world will be mine to bend. Flowers will bloom and snow will fall whenever I will it. I will be a god.'

'That's impossible, and you know it.' I struggle to my feet, gesturing at his head. 'Listen, Papa. That crown – I think it's affecting you. It drove the Spider King mad. It's starting to do the same to you.'

Regnault's expression darkens, but I press on, desperate. 'Take it off, please. Take it off, maybe you can –'

His laugh is like the gnashing of teeth, like the crushing of bone. 'Your concern is appreciated, Odile, but unnecessary. I'm no Ludovic, magic-less and weak-willed. I can control it.'

'And what about me?' I whisper. 'Where am I, in this grand plan of yours?'

'You?' He looks at me pityingly. 'You needn't be afraid. I will always have use for you.' He takes my face, one hand large enough to encompass my jaw, his nails pressing into my cheeks. 'You are my daughter, Odile, as if you were my own blood. As long as you apologize and swear your loyalty to me, I will forget this little incident. What do you say, little owl?'

There was a time, perhaps, when I would have done anything he wished, because his promises were so much greater than his flaws. But now I can see beyond them. Beyond the affection he doles out in drops, just enough to make me crave more, but never enough to satisfy.

I think of the tarasque, faithfully following the Golden-blooded Girl to the town square. I think of collars. And I think perhaps, perhaps, being alone is better than being chained. Than being led to my own end.

I look up at him, forcing tears into my eyes, feigning contrition. 'I'm sorry, Papa,' I say. Then I stumble forward and hug him tight. In the same motion, I pull out Buttons. Turn him over three times.

And aim the pistol at my father's head.

Regnault senses something is amiss at the last second. He shoves me aside just as the shot goes off. I hear him hiss as the iron ball skims his upper arm – it shatters the balcony window. I crash to the floor once more, the firearm knocked from my grip. I don't bother going after it. I run for the door.

Regnault whirls on me, lips pulled back, eyes wild. His hand shoots out, spell-threads glowing between his fingers, and the floor near the balcony turns to ice just as I pass it. I lose my footing, a scream escaping me as my knees crack brutally against the ground. From the now-open balcony window, winter wind rushes in, howling, shaking the curtains and bedframe.

'I should have known,' Regnault shouts over the wind, approaching me. His hand rises again, fingertips glowing. The ice beneath me melts, rising into the air, gathering instead into a slender, frosted shard aimed straight for my heart. 'Pathetic street rat. What will you be without me?'

I raise my chin. Meet his eyes, chest heaving, licking blood from my split lip.

'Free,' I hiss.

He lets the ice shard fly.

I squeeze my eyes shut in anticipation of pain. In the same moment, something warm and downy wraps around me. My world is suddenly muffled.

Startled, I open my eyes once more, and am greeted by a swathe of white. The breath rushes from me in a gasp as I realize what I'm looking at.

Wings. I am encompassed by wings.

I hear my father snarl. 'You think you can stop this, foolish girl?'

Behind me, my saviour grunts in pain, but the shield does not loosen. Soft hands wrap around my waist. 'You've done well, sorcière,' murmurs a gentle, impossibly familiar voice. 'Now, don't resist.'

Then I'm pulled into the air.

SCENE XXXII

The Lake. Night.

The Château grounds pass below me in a blur, nothing but glints of spindly steel and skeletal trees all coated by black-as-soot snow. I fade in and out, half dazed and half weary, but fighting stubbornly against unconsciousness, dreadfully afraid of letting my guard down again. I don't know what to think of the fact that Marie holds me to her chest, her chin against the crown of my head, and wings – her wings, glorious wings – spread out on either side of us.

Absurdly, I think, *It's a good thing I'm not afraid of heights.*

Then I close my eyes and lose the battle against darkness.

I am drowning.

Water fills my nose, my mouth, bitter and ink-dark, tasting of fish and rust and flesh. I struggle, looking around myself, searching for the surface, but there is no surface in sight. Far below, I can barely make out the serrated outline of ruins – crumpled columns and shattered statues and an altar split neatly in half. A temple.

My lungs burn. I thrash, attempting to kick away from

the temple, but I can't seem to move. I know that, by now, I should have inhaled water, should have drowned. But I can't. I'm trapped in stasis, not drowned but nearly there, my body begging for air.

Little owl.

The voice comes from everywhere at once, sing-song, fluid as the lake's water. It floods into my nostrils and streams between my teeth, pushes all the way into my bursting lungs.

Little owl, little owl, should I let you drown?

Little liar, little thief, who stole your father's crown.

Suddenly, the ruins below me are gone. In their place is a colossal statue.

A woman, her pinned-up hair and smooth skin forged of cracked marble, with half the skin of her face missing, exposing the golden bone of her skull. Tiny black and white fish swim around her, small as ants. Slowly, from the depths, her hand emerges, reaching for me like a great sea beast's maw.

Little owl, little owl, what is it that you seek? Morgane demands.

I shouldn't be able to speak as I drown, but somehow I can. 'I want to destroy the Couronne du Roi.'

Little liar lies again. The Mother's mouth doesn't move, her eyes unblinking. Her hand comes ever closer to me, and I thrash, trying to escape, but to no avail. Her littlest finger is the length of my body – somehow I know that if she traps me, I will be trapped forever.

Panic seizes me. 'But that's what I want! I want to destroy the crown so my father can't use it, so I can free you and bring magic back.'

But why, Morgane demands. Her hand stretches, wider and wider, as though to catch me. *Why do all this?*

'I want to become a sorcier!'

Colder, she sings.

'I want to be powerful!'

Glacial.

I grit my teeth, my eyes pricking. 'I want to feel like I'm worthy.'

Ah. Warmer.

'I'm scared that if I'm not worthy, if . . . if I don't prove myself, I will end up alone again.' The admission pours out of me in a flood. Tears slip from my eyes, mingling with the water around me. They are, I realize hazily, gold.

Morgane's hand recoils from me. *Little owl, little owl, looking for a nest. No one's daughter, no one's prize, whenever shall you rest?*

'What do you want from me?' I sob, furiously brushing the tears from my eyes.

Morgane stares at me, unmoving. *I want to tell you a story.*

'Then *tell* it,' I snarl. 'Or let me drown.'

So eager to self-destruct, Morgane remarks. *But very well. The story goes thus, little owl, little liar: once upon a time, an ambitious King and his doubly ambitious advisor sought to steal magic from its protectors and unleash it lawlessly upon the world. So they took the collar that had once restrained a beast and re-forged it into a crown. They were of two powerful bloodlines – but you have heard this part of the tale. You have heard how they trapped me.*

What you do not know is how they tricked me. In my own shrine, my own home. They came to me eager as young gods themselves, saying they had a great gift: a body for me to inhabit, to walk the mortal plane, to transform not only with my magic but with my hands. With it, I could taste the magic of my sisters. I could create and destroy as only humans can.

My sisters always said I was too curious about humans, too kind to them. They said I should have never given that little saint my gift of golden blood. And perhaps I shouldn't have, for it was turned against me. But I did not know that until I had put on the crown they gifted me, and I only had time to cast a curse of vengeance upon them, condemning them to face their worst fears: the King, to lose the control he so craved; the sorcier, to lose the magic that never seemed to satiate him. She sounds pleased with herself, as though the curses are some clever accomplishment, and I resist the urge to scoff. Then she finishes, mournful: *That is all I could do. Next thing I knew, I was trapped in a deep, drowning darkness, not unlike this one.*

'So how do I free you?' I ask, my head spinning.

Little owl, she says kindly, *little lost one, looking to atone.*

Little owl, little sorcier, always on your own.

'Enough with the rhymes!' I grit out.

Enough with the rhymes? Morgane echoes petulantly. *Very well, if that is what you ask.*

And she begins to sink back into the deep.

'No!' I shout, despair filling me. 'No, wait, I'm sorry, please, you have to help me, *please*.'

The statue's full lips stretch into a stony smile, revealing teeth sharp as needles.

That which gives the most strength can also be the greatest weakness.

'Wait!' I try to shout again, but all that escapes my mouth is a gurgle. I choke, water searing my sinuses, clogging my throat. My body convulses, once, twice, my vision fogs and darkens.

Alone again in the dark, I finally drown.

I jolt upright, coughing violently, and immediately double over. My hands scrabble for my chest as I try and fail to force up lake water, over and over again, though my mouth is dry and there is no lake at all.

'Odile?'

I'm too panicked to identify the voice calling my name. I press my palms to the dusty floor, taking wheezing, desperate gasps. Reality trickles in slowly, leaving me only more disorientated, only more uncertain.

'Odile, what's happening?'

That's when I realize who it is that's standing beside me, hands extended hopelessly, his eyes wide and earnest and oh, I'm going to *kill him.*

'You.' I whirl on Damien, wiping my mouth, my chest hot. 'What are you doing here?' I reach into my pockets for Buttons and come up empty-handed, my panic only amplifying as I realize I'm defenceless. 'Where am I? How did I get here?'

My chest heaves. My vision spins. I don't know who I'm angriest with – Morgane, Damien, myself, or the fact that I have just drowned in my own dreams.

Distantly, I recognize my surroundings – this is the uppermost room of the Théâtre, beneath the cupola. In the middle of the floor is the hole through which the chandelier can be pulled up. It feels almost manipulative that Damien has brought me here of all places, to a spot I remember so fondly.

Damien himself stands stiffly before me. He looks uncharacteristically dirty and dishevelled – his black hair is mussed and uncombed, and he's clearly gone unshaved for at least two days now. He's still wearing his guard's uniform, cape and all, but it is grimy and torn, the edges frayed.

He holds his hands up slowly, as though to surrender. 'I'm not going to hurt you. Mademoiselle d'Auvigny brought you here. She's been helping me keep you safe.'

'Where is she now?' I demand. I remember the haze of my rescue. The feeling of white wings wrapping around me. The feeling of *flying*. 'Where is Marie?'

'She's gone to gather information. She'll be back soon.' Damien makes a placating gesture. 'Please, Odile, I can explain everything.'

'You don't need to,' I snap. 'You explained enough when you betrayed me to the Regent and got me arrested, you absolute assh–'

'I know,' Damien interrupts. 'What I did was stupid. I was wrong. I didn't – I'd spent days fermenting my anger and doubt. All I knew was this: the night after you arrived at the palace with some sort of covert mission, I found the King disembowelled by the lake. Then I was seized and blamed and thrown in a dungeon and told I would be executed. What was I supposed to think? Especially after you came to see me with Aimé, seemingly for no purpose other than to gloat.'

'Gloa– I was trying to help him find the killer, you dunce.'

'I couldn't *tell*. I hadn't seen you in five years. I wasn't sure who you were any more.' He looks away. 'Before I knew it, I was being transferred to the city prison, to a tiny, crowded cell, where I rotted in uncertainty. Until Aimé showed up, saying my name had been cleared, because the Queen was killed by the same sorcier that killed his father and he thinks I might know how to find her, and I –'

'You thought it was me,' I say, dismayed.

He runs a hand across his face. 'You were acting so cryptic!'

'Right, so you thought to yourself, *Oh, my sister is surely transforming into a horrifying beast and going around ripping out people's organs.* A *very* logical conclusion, of course.' I give him a scathing smile. 'But you've always assumed the worst of me, haven't you?'

'Dilou . . .'

'Don't call me that,' I growl. Now that I'm properly awake, I become slowly aware of the aches of my body – the throbbing at the back of my skull, the protests of my wounded knees where they're bent beneath me. I look down to see that they've been bandaged. The previous day returns to me in a blur – Regnault turning the Duke of Marsonne into a statue, my attempt at stealing the Couronne, and the disaster that followed. The reminder only fuels my anguish.

'Don't pretend you've changed your mind about me,' I snarl at Damien. 'You made it clear when you left, five years ago.'

'Mademoiselle . . .' A new voice joins in hesitantly. I whirl to meet the wide, soft eyes of Aimé-Victor Augier, who has been sitting behind me all along, watching everything unfold with nervous worry. His golden hair tumbles loosely around his shoulders, and he's wrapped in a blanket I recognize distinctly as having once belonged to Damien.

He's still wearing his clothes from the wedding, albeit torn and dirtied, but there isn't a claw or tusk in sight.

In normal circumstances, I might have been relieved to see the Dauphin. But I'm still rattled from the nightmare, shaken by my father's brutality, and all I can remember is how he spoke about me to Marie right before the wedding.

I am acutely aware that both Aimé and Damien were responsible for putting me behind bars, and Regnault, the only person I thought I *could* trust, turned out to be the greatest liar of all. I feel like a caged animal, surrounded by hunters on all sides. So I whirl on Aimé-Victor Augier, hackles raised. 'Bold of you to interject, considering everything that's happened,' I say. 'Last time I saw you, you were busy slaughtering innocents, committing all the crimes you locked me up for.'

Aimé pales immediately, and my brother shouts, 'Odile! How could you *say* that?'

'N-no,' Aimé says painfully. 'She's right. And the truth is I . . . I simply didn't know. I had no memory of when I . . . when – Anne hid it from me my whole life. She told me the gaps in my memory were . . . episodes. Because of . . . nerves. And that night, in her study, all I remember was seeing you transform. Next thing I knew, Anne was dead, and everyone was blaming a sorcier. So I thought –'

'Yes, I know what you thought,' I interrupt darkly, something inside me twisting and shattering. 'You made that *perfectly* clear.'

Aimé recoils as if stung. I have to shove my teeth into my lower lip to keep a sob from breaking free.

'Dil– Odile,' my brother tries cautiously, 'you know that isn't fair. You aren't exactly the victim in this situation.

What happened to you was a mistake, but you . . .' *You brought it upon yourself*. He doesn't say the words, but he might as well have screamed them.

I march up to him, ignoring the protests of my injured knees. 'You know very well none of this would have happened if you hadn't abandoned me five years ago. If you hadn't left me, just like our parents did.'

Damien blanches. 'You . . . you *told* me to leave!'

'Yes, because you said you didn't want to be around someone as cruel and vindictive as me!' I shout. Damien looks stricken. Before he can say another word, I turn and rush for the door.

I barrel out of the room. My body screams at me to slow down, to take a breath, but I refuse to rest, refuse to stay here, refuse to look my brother or the Dauphin in the eye. And I know, distantly, that my reaction is extreme. That perhaps I should have considered that my knees are bandaged, that I was covered in a blanket when I woke, that both boys were clearly keeping vigil over me. But there is a fissure between us now that is not easily mended. And if there's anything I've learned, it's that kindness can be a weapon, too.

I make it down the stairs and into the hollow Théâtre entrance hall, my chin ducked and my vision blurring. *Don't cry*. I try to force the tears back. *Don't cry don't cry don't –*

'Odile?'

I was so focused on holding myself together that I didn't notice the familiar figure striding towards me through the grand foyer. When I do look up, it's like a fist has closed around my heart.

Marie d'Odette approaches the stairs, delicate as seafoam and powerful as the pull of tides. She's wearing peculiar clothes – a silver, puffy-sleeved doublet and narrow breeches I recognize as belonging to a dancer's costume.

Poking over her shoulders are the tips of white wings.

She's beautiful as ever, the Swan Princess, and seeing her is like being blessed, like the merciful touch of a deity's hand. The relief that washes over me is so heady that it nearly sends me to my knees.

'Marie,' I whisper.

Then I run down the stairs and launch myself into her arms.

SCENE XXXIII

Théâtre du Roi. Day.

Marie makes a small sound of surprise, swaying a bit as she embraces me. She wraps her arms around me tightly, one hand sliding into my hair, and I duck my face into her shoulder as I try in vain to swallow back tears.

Marie must hear the hitch of my breath. 'Odile, what's wrong?'

I shake my head against her shoulder. *Not yet.*

She hums softly, understanding, and I feel a swell of gratitude. Finally, when I'm no longer in danger of hysterically sobbing, I pull away, sniffing wetly. Marie looks me over without a word, then raises her hands to my face, thumbing away the lingering tears under my eyes. 'What is it? You look like you've seen a ghost.'

I don't know where to begin. I can't pinpoint where my anguish is coming from, only that there is *so much* of it. Morgane's dream, and Damien's accusatory words, and my father . . . my *father*.

'He tried to kill me,' I whisper miserably. 'He raised me, and then he tried to kill me.'

'Oh, Odile.'

'He never cared about me. He promised me power,

promised me magic, but he was going to take it all for himself and leave me with nothing. And the worst of it is, he made me think that, without him, I would be alone. That only *he* could understand me. He drove a rift between me and Damien, and between me and you, and I regret nothing more than giving him that damned crown –' I rub the tears from my eyes, frustrated at myself. 'Mothers, I'm sorry that you have to see this. I don't think I've cried since . . . since I was eleven.' Since I scraped my knees and my father told me to never let anyone see me bleed.

'There is nothing wrong with crying,' Marie says gently. 'And try not to be too angry with Damien. He's been worried sick about you. I don't know him well, but he seems like a good man.'

'He is,' I say, making a face. Because it's true, and I hate that I know it. For all his blustering words, Damien has only ever cared about protecting the few he loves. Myself, and Aimé. The bandages on my knees are testament enough.

'Oh, Marie.' I slump down on the stairs. 'This is all my own fault, isn't it?'

Marie shakes her head. 'No.' She crouches in front of me, gripping my fingers in her own. 'Your father did this. All of this. He manipulated you, he used you.'

'I was his tarasque,' I say bitterly. 'I thought I was the Golden-blooded Girl, but I was just his pet on a leash, doing his bidding. And I would have done it and done it and done it forever, if it weren't for . . . for you.' I smile at her crookedly. 'If you hadn't believed there was more to me.'

'Odile . . .' She runs her thumbs over my knuckles.

'And I'm sorry,' I say quickly – might as well get everything out at once, since my defences are already in ruins – 'I'm so sorry about the necklace.' To my horror, I nearly start crying again, and Marie shakes her head, ever the pillar of calm.

'We can talk about that later,' she says. 'When you've recovered somewhat.' She begins to stand, reaching down for me. Suddenly, she winces, sucking in a breath of pain.

'Marie?' I ask shakily. 'Are *you* all right?'

'It's fine,' she says. 'Just a scratch.'

'A *scratch*?' I repeat, worry suddenly overtaking me.

'I'm fine, Odile.'

I crook an eyebrow. 'Now that I've stopped lying, you've started?'

She sighs, and I know I've won. 'It's just my wing.'

Oh, yes, then there's *that*. 'Just your *wing*,' I echo.

'Your father stabbed it with one of his ice shards when I res– when I found you.'

'Were you going to say you *rescued* me?'

She looks away guiltily.

'No no, go on, I like it.' I gesture for her to continue, grinning. 'My knight in shining armour.'

'That's not what I –' The wings on Marie's back flex in exasperation. I stare, mesmerized, before I notice the wet bloodstains on the feathers near her shoulder blade.

'Oh, Marie, that doesn't . . . Have you not been able to bandage it?'

She doesn't answer, and I get to my feet, walking around her so I can see more clearly. Now that I'm not fighting off tears, I realize the back of her wing, not far from her shoulder, is slick with blood, the feathers plastered together. It would be a difficult spot to reach, certainly. 'You've just been bleeding all over like this? Did you even clean it?'

'I had other concerns.' Judging by the way she refuses to meet my eyes, I wonder if those other concerns were me. Warmth blooms in my chest.

'I know how to take care of wounds,' I tell her. Mothers know, I've patched up my own all my life. 'Let me do it.'

She presses her lips together. 'I'm not all that helpless, Odile, truly. I can take care of myself.'

'Perhaps, but you've just let me sob all over your shirt. This way we can be equally mortified. Come, let's go somewhere less . . . open.'

And so we find ourselves in the dressing rooms for the first time since that fateful night, Marie cross-legged on the floor, me staring at the length of her spine while my heart does jittery backflips. I can see now why she changed into the doublet she's wearing – it's held together with laces at the back, and she has left them loose around her wings.

Her *wings*. A contradiction within themselves, thick and powerful yet lined with fragile, diaphanous feathers. She untucks the injured one carefully from her shoulder, lowers it so it splays on the ground. It reaches across the entire room, the tips of her primaries brushing up against an open chest of assorted props – papier-mâché fruits and masks and the disembodied hoof of a goat.

I've brought a candelabra to our side, and the flame limns each oval covert and shivering piece of down in trembling bronze light. I swallow, hard. Then I force myself to study the vertical gash that splits the feathers near her spine in a brutal groove. It must have happened when she wrapped me in her wings, and it clearly has not been looked after. the edges inflamed and a sticky yellowish pus visible at the deepest point.

'It really was fine,' Marie insists, dropping the wing lower and wincing as I run a damp cloth along the injury. 'I must have aggravated it when I flew back to the palace. I was trying to get more of those yellow flowers for Aimé, but I was caught by a patrolling guard. He tackled me to the ground, and my wings got stuck under me. I managed to get free and fly off, but I had to go in the wrong direction to throw him off my trail, so I couldn't really take care of it until now.'

I clean a few particles of dirt out of the wound, wrinkling my nose. 'Are you going to explain these to me, then?'

'I told you –'

'Not the injury, Princess. The wings.'

'Ah.' She lapses into momentary silence, and I focus on rinsing the cloth in a basin of water before bringing it back to the wing. 'Honestly, I was hoping *you* could explain it. You are the expert in sorcery, after all.'

'Expert is a *significant* over-exaggeration,' I say morosely.

'Oh? But you acted so confident, that first night by the lake.'

I nudge her. 'Hush, you.' She giggles, and I can't help my own smile. 'Tell me how it happened, first. Perhaps that will help me understand.'

'It's all a blur,' she admits. 'The first time I did it, it was when you were running from the beast. After I escaped Anne's guards, I tried to follow you, but I couldn't find you. Suddenly, I heard the glass shatter. I wasn't far from the chapel, but I wasn't close enough, either, so all I could do was run to the nearest window and look out and –' Her voice softens. 'And I saw you fall. It was all instinctual, the first time. I jumped after you, and it just . . . happened. I thought I'd imagined it, afterwards. That in my haze, I'd somehow . . .' She breaks off, laughing weakly. 'I don't know.'

I furrow my brow, running through what little knowledge I do have of magic. 'Regnault told me once that when spells go wrong, they can transform people into something they did not intend. I think . . . hmm.' I reach out towards her with my mind, searching for traces of spell-threads. There is *something*. A small glimmer, barely there, escaping my grip every time I attempt to grasp it. 'I think part of my father's curse was trapped inside you when I tried undoing it. I can still sense a piece of it, but . . . I'm not confident I could fix it. Not without a better understanding of magic. Though of course, if you want me to try –'

'No,' she interrupts. 'No, I want to keep it. Keep *them*.' She gestures to the wings. 'I know it sounds strange, but they give me hope. That I don't have to be swan or girl, that I can take control. I have never dared to do that before now. I've always surrendered myself to fate – first to my mother, then to being a swan. My life has never been *mine* before.'

'It shouldn't have ever had to be that way,' I say abruptly, unable to stifle the rising guilt. 'It's my fault, all of it. If I hadn't stolen the necklace . . .'

'No,' she says, shaking her head. 'It was never really about the necklace at all – my mother merely used my guilt to get me to bend to her will. For years, I had been the only variable she couldn't control, and finally she had the chance. I was only ever a tool to her, and somehow she convinced me that it was all for the good of the family. I never truly realized what she was doing . . . until you told me about your father. About how he treated you.'

I bow my head. One of my hands rests on the edge of her wing, and I inadvertently bury my fingers deeper into their downy surface. 'We were both fooled.'

'Yes, but we can change,' Marie says. 'We can grow past what they made us into. That's what I decided after you came to visit me in the Dauphine's apartments. That I wouldn't be locked away again. That I was going to start making my own decisions, no matter how much it frightened me. When I heard your scream, and the shattering of glass . . . I didn't hesitate. My doors were guarded, but my windows were not, and I simply . . . *knew*. Knew that I could summon my wings again, if I jumped. So I did.'

'And then you saved me,' I say softly.

She hums, clearly unwilling to agree outright. I lean back, studying her wound, which looks much cleaner now than before. 'I'm going to wrap this,' I decide. 'I would also advise not moving this wing too much for some time. Else you'll keep tearing it open.'

Marie laughs under her breath. 'Yes, doctor. And whatever shall I owe you for such tender care?'

The heady warmth of her voice travels from my head to my lower stomach, where it sits, pleasantly curled. I'm glad her back is turned, because my cheeks must be flaming. 'A kiss would be sufficient payment,' I say, unthinking, and immediately wish I could evaporate.

Marie makes a contemplative sound. I realize, with sudden clarity, that she is so close to me, the sides of her doublet pulled apart. She seems to have cut a hole in the shirt beneath, leaving her spine bared. Small feathers trail from her wings on to her shoulder blades like white petals, and it takes all my willpower to keep from touching them.

I shake my head, and lean down to pick up the scraps of linen on the floor. I cut them from one of the cleaner-looking costumes, and I have to hope they'll be enough.

I have to tie two of the strips of linen together to make a bandage long enough to wrap around the wing. I do it carefully, feathers brushing my wrist, the faint heat of Marie's body pressing in against me. 'There,' I say finally, running my hand down the breadth of the wing. It's an almost thoughtless act, but I pause when Marie gasps softly in surprise.

'What is it?' I ask.

She shakes her head. 'They're . . . sensitive.'

Oh.

I grin wolfishly. 'Are they now?' Unable to help myself, I stroke her wing again, letting myself delight in the feeling of the feathers against my palm.

Marie makes a breathy sound of pleasure and abruptly turns around, lifting her injured right wing out of my reach while her left one comes to curl around me. 'I think I owe you a payment for your services, doctor,' she says, her forehead nearly against mine, her exhalation tickling my lips. She smells of spices, of clove and vanilla and fiery, sweet cinnamon.

She's magnificent. Once, I'd wanted to ruin her; now, I want her to sanctify me.

But first, I'm going to put up a fight.

'Alas, I've had to raise my prices,' I say, looking up at her mischievously. 'I fear one kiss will no longer suffice.'

Marie brushes her fingers, tantalizing, along my jaw. I can't help but follow the trajectory of her touch, tilting up my chin. She smirks – *smirks* – all power and control, her lashes lowering as she gazes at my lips.

'Very well, then,' says Marie d'Odette, and brings her mouth to mine.

SCENE XXXIV

Théâtre du Roi. Backstage.

Later, I lie awake at Marie's side, pillowed by the breadth of her outstretched wing, my body no longer fully mine. Because how can it be, if my skin still sparks where she straddled my hips, where my hands glided up her spine? If my wrists still remember how she seized them both, pressed them over my head and kissed me ever deeper. If I can still taste her, every part of her, lingering on my tongue and lips and the back of my teeth.

I am made of echoes, of after-images, and they all belong to *her*.

There is a heartbeat of silence, and I can almost feel the Théâtre hovering protectively over us, slowing time so we may finally breathe. And I do, deep and full for the first time since I can remember, one breath for every one of Marie's soft inhalations. *Thirty-four, thirty-five . . .*

Marie stirs delicately, turning over to me. Her lashes are long and heavy – they rise like a curtain, revealing gleaming dewdrop irises. 'Hello, sorcière,' she says, and pokes the tip of my nose.

An exhausted, ecstatic laugh escapes me. 'How was that for affection?' I tease. The fabric of her chemise has slipped off her shoulder, and I reach over to pull it up, pushing back a silvery-gold curl as I do. We stare at each other, reluctant to leave this intoxicating, impossible dream.

Then, someone bangs on the dressing room door.

'Odile? Mademoiselle d'Auvigny? We have a problem!'

Marie jolts upright at the urgency in Damien's voice. I growl in frustration and follow suit, bending down to pick up my discarded clothing, then stumble as my injured knees make themselves known. Marie catches me before I fall, righting me. Wordlessly, I gesture for her to turn, and help her do up the laces on the back of her doublet around her wings.

'Marie? Odile?' When neither of us answers immediately, Damien adds, 'Are you . . . all right in there?'

'We're all right,' Marie replies politely, at the same time as I shout, 'If you come in, I will decapitate you!'

We both emerge from the dressing room half-undone. Marie looks somewhat abashed, while I meet my brother's eyes defiantly, daring him to make a single comment.

Damien merely runs a hand through his hair and says, 'We're running out of time.'

We gather under the cupola again. I press close to Marie, still feeling the lingering anger from my earlier outburst. I can't look Damien in the face, and he seems to avoid my gaze just as stubbornly.

Once we are assembled, my brother holds up a folded letter. 'An urchin from Verroux left this on the Théâtre's doorstep. It's a tip-off from the guards that deserted the Regent.' He looks over at Aimé pointedly. 'I told you, most of your men are still loyal.'

From the way Aimé looks at his feet, I can tell this is the continuation of a discussion they have had before.

'One of the guards stayed behind to relay information. He has learned that Regnault is doubling his efforts to find us, and that he is going to lead the soldiers on a hunt tonight. The first place they are going to raid is the Théâtre, which means we cannot stay here. According to rumour on the streets, he's making it known that you've run away, Aimé, because you don't want to be sent to the coast to recover, and the Regent is deeply concerned about his nephew.'

'My father's a good liar,' I say quietly.

Damien doesn't look at me. 'He's also blaming the disaster at the wedding on the presence of a raven-haired sorcière. Apparently, Odile, you put the curse on Aimé, and now you are to be brought in to face justice.'

I grip my hands together, suddenly nauseous. Marie reaches over to twine her fingers with mine, and I give her a grateful look.

'You should hand me over,' Aimé says quietly. He looks exhausted, buried in his blanket.

'Regnault wants to kill you,' I point out. 'And if he does that, I shudder to imagine the power it will give him.'

'Then let him kill me,' Aimé says. 'I'm a danger anyway –'

'Aimé . . .' Damien says, and I've never heard him sound so helpless.

'You know it's true!' the Dauphin exclaims. 'We don't have access to the potions any more, which means that every time I feel too afraid, or too angry, or too . . . anything, it might trigger a transformation.'

'Aimé . . .' my brother tries to cut in again.

Aimé ignoes him. 'I don't want to do this any more. I can't, Damien! I don't want to kill any more people!' His voice rises on the last word, and I see my brother's eyes turn guarded, his posture becoming alert, anticipatory.

Aimé sees it, too, and his shoulders slump. 'See? Even you don't trust me.'

'Aimé,' I say cautiously, bringing his attention over to me. 'I mean, Monseigneur, I suppose, since we don't *really* know each other. That all sounds very noble, but I have a better idea than surrendering yourself to my psychopathic, two-hundred-year-old adoptive father.'

'Hold on,' Damien interrupts. '*Two hundred?*'

I wave a hand at him. 'I'll explain in a moment. But I think . . . I think there is a way that we can break this curse that's been laid upon the Augiers.'

I explain everything to them. The journal, the bluefang I'd put in the tea; Regnault's true identity, the horrors and havoc he has wrought inside the Château; his plan to kill the Dauphin and claim the power of all three Mothers, his growing madness; my desperate escape plan, my confrontation with Morgane in my nightmare – then I break off, realizing something that makes my blood run cold.

'Aimé,' I say faintly, already dreading the reply, 'how did you know that Damien would be able to find me?'

Aimé frowns in thought. 'My uncle told me. It was all a blur, I didn't think twice about it, but . . .'

'But the Regent knew,' Marie murmurs, and I know she's already pieced this together.

I look down at my hands, calloused and scraped and nimble, a thief's hands – hands that I used to be so proud of, knowing I'd developed them on Regnault's missions. I have to force every stinging word past my lips. 'He knew, Regnault told him. Regnault told him I was the sorcier he was looking for, and that I was Damien's sister.' I see everything with new, horrifying clarity. 'Regnault orchestrated the whole arrest.'

My throat feels horribly tight, my stomach churning. All this time, I thought it was Aimé and Damien who had betrayed me, but really it was my own father – planting the seeds of doubt, watching them grow. Just as he'd taught me to do. I raise my eyes to the Dauphin's horrified face.

'Before you arrested me, I was going to confess my true identity to you, tell you all about my plans. I was beginning to think that maybe, just maybe, I could do this all without lies, without violence. That we could, all of us, work together to bring magic back.'

Aimé swallows. 'I would have helped you, Madem-Odile. I would have.'

'I know,' I say regretfully. 'Regnault must have sensed that. He must have known I was planning to involve all of you, and that he was losing control of me. So he –' My voice breaks. Marie shifts closer, and the comforting weight of one of her wings drapes along my shoulder. 'I believed him. I've always believed him, always done as he told me. I'm such a *fool*.'

'Dilou –' The hoarseness of my brother's voice draws me up short. I glance up sharply, and I'm startled to see moisture pooling in the brown depths of his eyes. My chest lurches. I've never, in all my eighteen years, seen Damien cry.

'Hey,' I say in annoyance, feeling my own eyes begin to sting. 'Stop that right now. Because if you cry, I might cry, and Aimé is already about to cry, and then we'll be a whole pathetic circle of tears and Marie will have to try to save the world on her own.'

Behind me, Marie tries to muffle a sniff, and I groan.

'Never mind, we're doomed.'

Damien presses his arm to his eyes and turns away, his throat bobbing. In my ear, Marie whispers, 'Affection.'

'He's my brother.' I pretend to gag. 'That's disgusting.' But I'm already getting to my feet, reluctantly trudging over to him. I open my arms, feeling ridiculous.

Damien pulls me against him.

And I realize I don't remember the last time I hugged my brother. Not since we were very young, certainly. Not since I began going on Regnault's missions. He's sturdy and warm and he smells dreadfully unwashed, but he's my brother. He's always been my brother. How could I have forgotten that?

'I know you tried to protect me,' I say into his shoulder, as he rests one large, comforting hand on the back of my head. 'You were right. When you told me you wanted to leave, I *was* selfish – I was only thinking about what I wanted. I didn't consider your happiness, and I should have. Because let me tell you,' I add wickedly, 'noblesse are *fantastic* kissers.'

He shoves me away, groaning. 'Agh – Odile! I didn't need to know that!'

I look over at Marie, with her eyes glittering fondly, and at Aimé, who seems to have livened up at last, a tentative smile on his face. And I realize that this is what Regnault took from me, with his lies and his promises. And now I'm taking it back.

'Very well,' I say, turning to my friends. 'My proposition is this: we get the Couronne du Roi back, and we free Morgane. Once she is free, we ask her to undo Aimé's curse.'

'Can it be done?' Aimé asks shakily. He sounds like he's afraid to hope.

'Possibly,' I say. 'Morgane said this when I asked her how to destroy the Couronne: *That which gives the most strength can also be the greatest weakness.*'

'It's the blood,' Marie says immediately. 'You said the Couronne was strengthened using the blood of both the Spider King and Bartrand de Roux. That's why Regnault wants to kill Aimé, isn't it? So you need Regnault's blood, and Aimé's, to destroy it. And . . .' She trails off and I'm mesmerized by the way her lower lip juts out as she contemplates Morgane's riddle. 'The temple. That's where it must be done. In the place of Morgane's trapping. That's why she showed it to you in the dream. That's where the curse can be destroyed.'

Damien looks puzzled. 'To the temple . . . that drowned in the *lake*.'

'Regnault must know how to get to it. He wants to kill Aimé there: at the place the Couronne was forged.' The glimmerings of a scheme begin to take shape in my mind. 'We'll need his blood. And yours, Aimé. And we need to trick him into showing us the way to the temple.'

Damien crosses his arms. 'This is sounding more impossible by the minute.'

'Only if you lack imagination,' I tell him sweetly. Then I give a grand flourish, puff out my chest, and announce,

'*Mesdames et Messieurs*, I do believe I have a plan. It requires some acting, a considerable amount of acrobatics and, on my part, a brazen betrayal. Are you with me?'

I grin as I'm greeted by a chorus of agreement. I sketch a grand bow.

Then I begin to explain.

We wind through lower Verroux, the streets a blur of yellow windows and narrow, slouching buildings, foul-smelling and filthy and sleepless. Damien leads the way, broad shoulders barely concealed by a cloak, eyes peering out watchfully from beneath his hood. Marie and Aimé are between us, both members of the noblesse wide-eyed and cautious as we leave the protective airiness of the wealthy upper sector and plunge deeper into the city's gullet.

'So this is where you grew up,' Marie says. Her wings are gone – it seems to take her much effort and time, but she is able to make them vanish on command.

'More or less,' I say, putting a hand on the small of her back.

'I wished to tell you earlier,' she says, 'but I've always admired this about you. How you came from the shadows, yet you burn so bright. You always seemed so brave to me, so *bold*. You hold on to things so tightly, while I seem to always let them slip through my fingers.'

'It's called being selfish, Princess,' I tell her. 'You simply break off a piece of the world and keep it all to yourself.'

She hums. 'What if that piece of the world is a person?'

I tilt my head. 'Oh?'

'What if . . .' She he looks away, her cheeks flushing in the lamplight. 'What if it's . . . you?'

My heart stutters, tripping over itself. Warmth fills me, and I feel my own cheeks heat. Marie is adamantly refusing to meet my eyes, and, on an impulse, I reach out, tilting her chin towards me, forcing her to meet my eyes.

'Then I'm yours,' I say quietly.

Her breath hitches. Before either of us can say anything more, we are interrupted by distant shouting, and the sound of a bottle shattering. Aimé flinches.

'I did not know that my father had let Verroux come to such a state,' he says, more to himself than to us. 'There are commissioners in each quarter, why have they not been called to . . .' He trails off. 'Something should have been done.'

He lapses into silence at that, visibly uncomfortable. Since our departure from the Théâtre, anxiety has been radiating from him in waves, and it only grows with every step towards our destination. And the task that I have laid upon him once we arrive.

'It should be here somewhere,' Damien says, taking us carefully around the corner of a butcher's shop, its windows black, entrails slathered on the street alongside it.

'Assuming the letter was telling the truth,' I hiss at him. 'It could very well have been forged.'

'No,' Damien says curtly. 'I know Thomas's handwriting. Ah –' his eyes brighten – 'it's here.' Ahead is a tavern, perched quiet and unassuming on a street corner, horses tied by the building and a drunken man sprawled beneath the eaves.

Damien begins to approach the doors, but Aimé shrinks back. 'I don't think I can do this,' he whispers.

Damien pauses and doubles back, resting a hand on

the Dauphin's upper arm. 'You can. It's just like we talked about. I will speak to the men first, and then you can come in after me. They are *your* guards, Aimé. They defected because they do not think the Regent is the rightful heir to the throne.'

'Yes, but they don't think I should be King, either,' Aimé argues. 'They're simply preparing to leave Verroux. That's what Thomas said in the letter.'

Damien sighs. 'I know. But that's because they believe all the lies they were told about you. You simply need to prove otherwise.' He gives Aimé a reassuring smile. 'It will be all right.' And then he turns and enters the tavern. Marie starts to follow, and Aimé makes a move to go in, too, but I hold him back. 'One moment,' I say, then nod to Marie. 'Go, introduce the Dauphin. I'm going to instruct him in making an entrance.'

Aimé eyes me mistrustfully as she leaves us, and I chuckle. 'Very well, I deserve that. But I only wanted to give you something.'

'Give me something?' he echoes. His voice is distracted – he keeps rubbing his hands together, and even in the darkness I can see their trembling. I reach into the small pouch I have brought and pull out a circlet I found in the dressing rooms.

'See this circlet?' I say. 'This is a relic from three hundred years ago. It was worn by the father of King Ludovic. He lived in harmony with magic, and under his rule the kingdom prospered.' I move quickly, so he doesn't notice that the circlet is made quite roughly, a thing wrought of crude golden spirals barely clinging to a blue-painted rock. I place it on his head, then take a step back.

'There. Now you're ready to command your men.' I give him the most formal curtsy I can manage. '*Votre Majesté.*'

He's staring at me, and I know he is looking for the lie in my words, trying to discover how I am tricking him. 'But what if I turn into the monster again, Odile?' he says tightly. 'What if I do more harm?'

'You won't,' I say firmly. 'I trust you.'

And for once, I'm telling the truth. Aimé exhales shakily, and I can almost hear the distant *click* of a lock being sprung. No, two locks. Two locks for two cages. The turtle dove and the owl.

'Thank you, Odile,' Aimé says, adjusting the circlet resting on his brow. Then he offers me his arm. 'Come, let us go meet my guards.' He crooks a grin at me, and he looks momentarily like the roguish princeling I met my first night at the palace. 'But if I *do* turn into the beast again, I'm eating you first.'

In the end, Aimé proves himself capable, far more capable than even I could have guessed him. He pulls down his hood, uncovering golden ringlets and eyes firm as aquamarines, and before him the palace guards sitting at the bar's tables all straighten. The men's attention goes to the circlet on his head, to the piece of jewellery representing Aimé's status.

Aimé clasps his hands behind his back, and only I can see them shaking as I stand behind him in the shadows. The circlet has no magic, but clearly wearing it – feeling the weight of a crown, even if it is merely a theatre prop – seems to bolster his courage. He speaks like a king, every word landing with considerate, weighty gravitas. He lets his earnestness shine through, and though his voice may waver, the men listen. He explains his curse – he tells them he is trying to break it, and reclaim his throne in the process. Finally, he drops down on one knee before them, pressing his fist to his chest.

'I am not my father,' he says. 'I am not his father. I do not want the Crown as they did. But I want to see snow fall white and flowers bloom, I want to see Verroux and Auréal flourish. I know you are all afraid – you have lost your faith in the Crown, and you do not want to fight a meaningless battle. I too am afraid. Afraid of failure. Afraid of fighting alone. Afraid of this curse of mine. But fear . . . it only means I'm human. It only means I have something to fight for.' He looks around the room, and the rugged faces of his men, as they straighten their spines and their chests swell with renewed faith. 'So I ask your forgiveness, and your faith. To fight alongside me, and see Auréal restored.'

Silence settles over the dimly lit tavern. The men all look to the guard seated in the middle of the room. I recognize Thomas, the large guardsman who once stopped Aimé and me from entering the chapel. He seems to have now assumed the role of leader.

Slowly, he glances down at the tankard in his hand. Then he gets to his feet and raises it high.

All the other men follow suit, forming a ring around Aimé. Marie and Damien join in. Aimé gets to his feet, looking dazed but elated. He smiles as the guardsmen salute his health and his long reign, looking more like a king than ever before. Then, once they have settled down, he begins to explain my plan to them.

While the room's attention is focused elsewhere, I slip unnoticed out of the door and into the dark alley. There, I draw a scrap of paper from my pocket and pull up my hood before setting off. It doesn't take me long before I find a hungry-eyed urchin and trade a coin – pickpocketed from Aimé – for the boy to deliver a message to the Château.

Then I look up towards the smoke-veiled sky, and puff out a tense breath of cold, billowing air.

Tomorrow, I will tell my last lie. It will be my greatest performance, my grand finale, my swansong. After that, I will leave behind this life of treacheries and masks and schemes.

I will bring magic back.

Or I will die trying.

SCENE XXXV

The Lake. Dawn.

I drag Aimé-Victor Augier through the dense woodland, ignoring his feeble struggling and muffled cries for help.

'No one is going to come for you, princeling,' I snarl at him, slackening my grip on his collar as he stumbles over a log. 'They're all fast, *fast* asleep.'

'Please,' he whispers brokenly, and I refuse to look him in the face, to see the tear tracks on his cheeks. 'Please, don't do this. After everything... I trusted you. We all did.'

The last words hit me like a fist in the gut, and I flinch. Aimé notices, and gives a brittle, agonized laugh. 'So there is some humanity still left in you. Please, Odile, you –'

'Shut up!' I snarl, unable to take his snivelling any more. With all my force, I shove him through the treeline.

Aimé crashes to his knees on the uneven, muddy earth of the lakeside, right at the feet of a black-cloaked figure in a feathered mask.

'You delivered on your promise,' Regnault says delightedly.

Aimé drags in a ragged breath as he recognizes the sorcier. He tries desperately to get to his feet, an act made difficult by the rope binding his wrists securely behind his back. I sneer as I watch him struggle. Ahead, a cold wind sends the lake rippling, harsh and accusatory. The fog is thin today, eddying around the decaying dock and blurring the grimy orange dawn smeared overhead. It makes Regnault look all the more menacing, all the more mythological, as he bears down on the Dauphin, the Couronne du Roi gleaming in his hair.

I have to force my eyes away from the crown. 'I hope this makes up for my mistakes,' I say to my father.

Regnault glances at me, his eyes lightless. 'Almost,' he says, then cocks his head at Aimé, birdlike and malevolent. Aimé tries to move away, but only loses his balance and falls on to his back, meeting the mud with a squelch.

'Little tarasque,' Regnault croons at him. 'Fooled into capture, just like the creature you carry on your banners.' He reaches down and seizes Aimé's jaw. 'How I will enjoy watching you bleed out at my feet.'

'Careful,' I caution Regnault, as Aimé begins to tremble. 'Those ropes will not hold if he turns into the beast again.'

Regnault gives me a knowing look, and pulls a dagger from his belt. 'You think I did not come prepared?' he asks, letting me see the sticky yellow substance coating the blade – more of the sorcier's-bane potion, like the one the Step-Queen stabbed me with. With a *snick*, he sheathes it once more. 'I must wonder, how did you manage to capture this one?' He points his chin at Aimé. There's true suspicion in the question, barely veiled. He doesn't fully trust me. 'Was he alone?'

'He was with his guard and intended. I drugged them.' I bare my teeth. 'Still had some of those herbs I tried, and failed, to use on you.'

'Impressive,' he says, but his eyes are flinty, cutting into me and through me. 'I have one more mission for you, to prove your loyalty.'

'And what is that?' I ask, holding his gaze.

'Once we are in the temple, you will be the one to kill the Dauphin.'

Aimé whimpers miserably. 'No. You can't. Odile, please, don't do this.'

I give him a pitying look, before turning back to Regnault. My heart aches, but I say the words without hesitation. 'Whatever you ask of me, Papa.'

Regnault's gaze softens, and I feel truly wretched. He does love me, I realize. It is a twisted love, a self-serving love, perhaps the only way he knows how to give love at all. But it is *love*. And some part of me still craves it, despite everything.

'I am glad you came to your senses, little owl,' Regnault says sincerely. 'Come, it's time.' He looks towards the lake, before reaching down and seizing Aimé by the arm. The Dauphin cries out as Regnault hauls him to his feet, and my heart clenches.

No, I tell myself. *Don't feel bad for him. You're the villain. This one last time.*

I follow Regnault on to the dock, the brittle wood bobbing under our feet, sending frantic ripples across the lake. He stops at the very end and releases Aimé's arm, then extends his hand over the lake. He traces spell-thread after spell-thread, his face set hard in concentration.

I watch in morbid fascination as he spins a thick cobweb of magic.

Finally, he lowers his hand.

For an instant, nothing happens. Aimé turns wide, anxious eyes to me, and I throw him a quick wink, trying to appear confident.

Then the lake shrieks.

It's a sound like claws drawn over stone, like the scrape of a whetstone over a sword. The formerly placid, black waters of Lac des Cygnes begin to bubble and churn, sloshing and rising up in great waves. On the far bank, the flock of swans startles and takes to the air, one by one, fleeing the awakening lake.

At the very end of the dock, the water begins to swirl. It whirls and whirls until there is a narrow, dark tunnel leading from the dock under the water's surface, plunging into the lake's belly. Uneasiness fills me. The tunnel is too steep to walk down, the walls formed of restless, swirling water – we will have to jump in and slide through it. All it would take is one spell from Regnault and those walls would close in again, drowning us all.

So I can't give him the chance.

'Now!' I shout, unsheathing a dagger from my sleeve.

A figure leaps from the trees, white wings spreading with such force that they rattle the treetops. Diving like an arrow, Marie slams into Regnault, sending him toppling. As soon as she does, I run to Aimé and slash his bonds before turning back to Regnault and Marie. Regnault loses his balance, back thudding down on to the dock – the Couronne slips off his head and falls on the planks with a metallic *clang*. He scrabbles for it – Marie is faster. She seizes the crown, and tosses it to Aimé just as a hulking golden shape slams into her, sending them both crashing into the bulrushes that surround the dock.

'Marie!' I scream, as one of the metal tarasques from the chapel pins her under the water.

Regnault scoffs, wiping a trickle of golden blood from his nose. 'Did you really think I would come here alone, without reinforcements?'

'Did you think *we* wouldn't?' I reply, seething.

That's when the first gunshot rings out.

Regnault stumbles, snarling in pain as the shot nicks his arm. I seize the moment to spring forward, knife at the ready. Before he can recover, I run it firmly across his leg, golden blood gushing over the blade. Nausea fills me at the sight, but I don't have time to feel guilty, as another gunshot ricochets from the shell of the tarasque, the sound echoing over the lake. It does little damage, but it's enough to distract the creature, allowing Marie to come up for air, beating her wings desperately against the water.

'Go!' she shouts to Aimé and me.

'Guards, protect Marie!' Aimé commands.

At his cry, the guardsmen step out from the treeline, muskets raised and swords drawn, Damien at their head. The tarasque whirls upon them, uttering a shrill cry – there comes an answering screech from nearby, and the second tarasque charges out, barrelling into the guardsmen.

Chaos breaks out. I want to run to Marie, to protect her, but a hand seizes me from behind. I turn to meet Aimé's eyes. He shakes his head minutely.

'We have to go.'

I know he's right, but it doesn't make it any less difficult to turn my back, to leave behind my brother and my lover and my injured father.

But I have to do this.

Aimé takes one of my hands in his, the other clutching the Couronne to his chest. Together, we jump into Lac des Cygnes.

SCENE XXXVI

Under the Lake.

The way to the temple is long and cold. Aimé and I plunge into darkness in a dizzying spiral, water soaking through the backs of our clothing. The walls ripple around us, the silver bellies of fish flashing in the gloom. What little light there is begins to wane the further we get into the depths.

After what seems like an eternity of tight-throated panic, the tunnel spits us out on to a hard, flat floor of slippery stone. I lose my grip on Aimé's hand, catching myself on my hands and knees. Aimé is less lucky, and he lands on his side with a grunt. He lies there with a martyred expression, his eyes unfocused.

It takes a moment for my head to stop spinning. When it does, I stumble over to the Dauphin and extend my hand to help him up.

'Are you all right?' I say worriedly, referring both to our fall and to my performance earlier. I was not kind to him, but that was precisely what he'd asked of me. *Do what you must to make it convincing*, he'd told me, as I tied his wrists together before we entered the forest.

He seems to understand. 'Quite all right.' He pats me on the arm reassuringly. 'Say, Mademoiselle, have you ever considered a career in acting?'

I give him a shove, rolling my eyes, then turn to survey our surroundings. We are standing at the edge of the drowned temple, a ruin of pale stone tangled in pondweed, surrounded by columns, some crumbled, some still standing upright, as though the structure had simply slipped into Lac des Cygnes' waters. The lake surrounds us. Only a few pale rays of light reach us from the rippling surface far above. And yet somehow, the temple remains dry, water surrounding it but seeming to shy away. The air smells ancient, of must and decomposing reeds and things long drowned.

In the very middle of the temple stands a grand altar. Once upon a time, it might have borne intricate carvings, but all that has been eaten away by time. Still, I can make out the three Mothers depicted on one side, their arms intertwined.

I walk up cautiously, Aimé trailing behind me. Across the altar spans a starburst of fissures, as though it was struck long ago by something heavy.

'Do you think this is where Morgane appeared?' Aimé asks, tracing one of the cracks.

'It seems so,' I say, holding out my hand for the Couronne. Aimé passes it to me, his jaw tight with anticipation.

'Morgane, let this work,' I murmur, reaching to my belt for the dagger with Regnault's blood on it.

My fingers close around empty air.

'No.' My heart drops into my stomach. 'No, no.' I pat my pockets, looking around frantically. Nothing.

'What is it?' Aimé asks worriedly.

'The dagger. The one with Regnault's blood. I must have ...' In that moment, I spot the weapon lying at the very edge of the temple, where the tunnel-mouth ends. I rush towards it, dread filling me. 'Please, Morgane, *please* –'

But before I can reach the dagger, a horrifyingly familiar, black-cloaked figure emerges from the tunnel. He steps out of it casually, nothing like our uncontrolled plummet downward, as if he is merely walking into a sitting room. He is no longer bleeding – his sleeve and trouser leg are crusted over with golden blood.

My pulse begins to pound. I bite my lip, praying at least that the dagger by his feet goes unnoticed, but of course, of course, because the Mothers must *hate* me, his attention falls immediately upon it.

Aimé grabs me before I can lunge forwards. I'm forced to watch helplessly as Regnault crouches by the weapon and picks it up. He turns it over with a languid motion, then sticks it into his belt, his eyes taunting and vicious as he regards me.

'How kind of you, my darling daughter, to bring my sacrifice all the way to his altar.'

SCENE XXXVII

The Temple Under the Lake.

Once, I wanted nothing more than to be exactly like my father. I'd look in a mirror and imagine myself his reflection, his successor, a black cloak on my shoulders and a raven-feathered mask on my face. Now, when I look at him, all I see is a remnant of the past – my past. He may wear a mask, but that is only a distraction, like the flourish of a magician meant to conceal a paltry trick. The real lies are his charisma, his promises, the morsels of praise he doled out in crumbs to me, knowing I was starving.

He kept me busy begging at his feet so I would not turn around and see a feast. So I would not realize it was all a mirage.

But I've had my fill now. I will not cower before him.

At least, that's what I tell myself as I take a shaky step back, as I pull Aimé behind me and curse under my breath. I tell it to myself as Regnault advances upon us, those tunnel-dark eyes trained on the Couronne du Roi. I tell it to myself as I ball my fists, preparing to fight if I must.

I tell it to myself, but I am afraid.

At my back, Aimé presses something into my fingers. 'Take it,' he whispers. I look over to see that he has picked the Couronne back up off the altar. His palm is wrapped around one of the crown's sharp tines, and a rivulet of his blood crawls over its shining surface.

'It won't work,' I whisper urgently. 'I need his blood, too.' I incline my chin at my advancing father, who has madness in his eyes now, his too-wide smile that of a wolf anticipating a meal.

'Oh, don't worry, *ma chérie*,' Aimé says with a wink, before a shudder runs through his body. 'I'll get it for you.'

I shake my head frantically. 'Wait, Aimé, not here –'

But the Dauphin is already *shifting*, his body lengthening and joints cracking. The last thing he manages is an apologetic 'I couldn't hold it in much longer anyway,' before he has fully become the beast, stone skin and curling tusks and bloodshot, crazed eyes.

I barely manage to come to my senses in time to duck aside and crawl behind the altar. Ahead, Regnault freezes, reaching slowly for his own dagger, the one I know to be coated in sorcier's-bane poison.

The beast locks eyes with my father, and it roars, a hollow, deafening sound that fills the drowned temple. Then it charges.

Regnault moves with impossible speed. He ducks out of the beast's reaching claws, rolls nimbly and comes up on his feet. The beast swipes, and Regnault crouches, the blow whistling inches from his head. I nearly call out to Aimé, nearly remind him to avoid the sorcier's dagger, but I know Aimé has no control like this – if I call out, he might very well come for me. So I press my palm over my mouth and watch in horror as Regnault slashes at the beast again and again, lithe and brutal, forcing it to back up until its hind limbs hit one of the standing columns. Finding itself cornered, it rears back, lashing out with both claws, and this time Regnault is not fast enough – the beast pins him to the marble, one of its claws digging into his shoulder, dripping shimmering blood as it pulls the paw back again for another strike.

I pump my fist in the air. Success. I look around, trying to decide the best approach to get to the blood without being caught in –

Suddenly, the beast screams in agony. My head snaps towards the sound, just in time to see Regnault pull his dagger out of the beast's foreleg. Blood spurts from the wound, and the beast falls back, groaning, shaking its head.

'No!' I shout. I tighten my fist around the Couronne. I have to get to them, I have to help before Aimé is turned back, I have to . . .

That's when I look down once more at the temple floor and realize it is chequered. Black and white, just like in my dreams of Morgane. I remember her words to me in the dungeons:

Your time is coming, Daughter of the Blood. Claim your power.

But I have no magic – no power.

And yet . . . what was it that Regnault had said?

There is power in legacy.

Realization seizes me. Grabbing a large, jagged piece of stone, I turn to the altar and slam the Couronne down in the very centre, all the while gripping the rock with all my force until I feel it break my skin, until it presses deeper and deeper and I feel blood burst from my palm. Pain surges up my arm, but I do not care. I wipe my bleeding hand on the Couronne and bring the rock down over it. Once, twice. Not even a dent. A third time. Still nothing. Sweat drips into my eyes, my arm begins to ache, but still I have hardly made a mark. I curse. It isn't breaking. Why isn't it breaking? I raise the rock again, and –

'Odile, wait!' Regnault has gotten to his feet, dagger still drawn, a look of crazed command in his eyes. Behind him, Aimé lies limp, human once more, his clothing in tatters. 'Wait,' Regnault repeats. 'Please, listen to me.'

It is enough to stay my hand. Even now, I listen to him. Even now, he has me chained.

'You know that won't work,' Regnault says, and I can tell from the restrained way he speaks that he is trying to keep his voice from shaking with fury. 'You need my blood to destroy it. It was forged with the power in *my* bloodline, a bloodline you do not carry. Without me, you can do nothing. You . . . you will *be* nothing. You will be alone once more, as you were before I found you.'

'Before you found me,' I say quietly, 'I had my brother. And you tried to make me hate him.'

He scoffs. 'The red-blooded oaf? Please, Odile, he's not worth this. Lower the stone. You and I have far more in common than you ever had with him.'

'Is that why you isolated me?' I demand. 'Why you made sure I had no one but you? You turned me into a tool, into a pet. I depended on you for everything. I never questioned you, not once.'

'I was guiding you!' The words are a violent growl. He presses the mask to his face, runs a hand through his hair. 'I was guiding you,' he repeats again, lowering his voice. 'So that you would have what it takes. So that you could do what was needed to claim the Couronne, to claim the *throne*, as the Golden-blooded Girl should always have done. I did all this for you. I made you, and you know it. So lower the stone, little owl. I will forgive you, and we will rule together. I will forgive you, because I always do, no matter how much you disappoint me.'

I swallow thickly. 'Why?' I whisper, letting my grip on the stone waver. 'After all I've done, why do you still want me back?'

'My dear little owl.' Regnault opens his arms, his smile benevolent. 'I will always want you back. I am your father, after all.'

I let my hand fall to my side, tears gathering in my eyes. 'If you are telling the truth,' I whisper, 'then swear one thing to me. Swear that you will never replace me – that I will always be your heir.'

'Of course,' he says gently. 'Of course you will be.'

Then he freezes. His smile drops as he realizes his mistake.

I grin triumphantly. 'Thank you for confirming,' I say, dropping my pitiful act. 'If I recall correctly, you said something about heirs carrying power?'

His eyes widen in horror. 'Wait –' he cries, but I don't hesitate.

I bring the rock down on the Couronne du Roi.

This time, it's like striking a pane of glass. The crown shatters into a thousand tiny, glittering fragments, a bloom of golden light exploding from within. A voice fills the temple, archaic and momentous and familiar as drowning.

Well done, little owl, little champion, Morgane crows. *I am free at last.*

For a moment, the tiny shards of gold hover around me, suspended, before the light vanishes again, and they all fall to the ground, the sound soft and high, like windchimes.

I whirl, seeking Morgane, but the spirit is nowhere to be seen. Columns stand solemn and imposing around me, the lake's undulating waters stretching out on either side. In the distance, a school of tiny fish picks at pondweeds on the lakebed. Everything is oddly peaceful.

Then Regnault shoves past me, crashing to his knees at the base of the altar. 'No!' he cries, reaching down, attempting to sweep up the shards of the Couronne as though he might reassemble it. 'No, no, no!'

'Papa . . .' I whisper, pained.

Before I can say anything more, the temple begins to shake.

The chequered floor beneath my feet bucks and fissures. I scream as one of the columns behind me topples, water gushing in around it.

'Papa, we have to go!' I scream, grabbing my father's shoulder, but he only slaps my hand away. When he looks up at me, in his eyes is nothing but potent, condemning hatred.

'You did this,' he seethes, spittle flying from his mouth. 'Traitor.'

My heart shatters. Tears prick my eyes, but I know I can't wait a moment longer. I race past Regnault and towards

Aimé, hauling him from the ground. Ahead, Regnault's tunnel has disappeared.

'We're going to have to swim!' I say, and Aimé nods, then pulls me against himself as what little remains of the temple's roof caves in, sending in another gush of water. The floor of the temple begins to flood, water racing across the chequered stone, breaking upon the altar like an ocean wave. Cold water surrounds my boots, my ankles.

'Let's go now!' I take Aimé's hand, ready to jump out of the temple and into the lake surrounding us, when the water overhead begins to churn.

It's like the heavens open up. The oppressive darkness of the lake is pushed apart as though by a pair of invisible hands, revealing a bright azure sky, thin sugar-spun clouds and a white-winged girl flying towards us, haloed by glorious sunlight.

'Marie!' I shout in relief. Marie swoops down to us, and I push Aimé towards her as she reaches out. 'Take him first!' I say, and Marie doesn't argue, heaving the Dauphin up in her arms. She brings her wings down in a powerful stroke, lifting them both away from the flooding temple, and I turn, seeking Regnault.

Conflict roils within me. I know I should leave him behind, but there is a piece of me that still feels obligated to him, for taking me in, for raising me. He's still by the altar, and I run towards him once more.

'Papa! Come, please. I know you're angry, but you'll die if you stay here. Please, we can –'

I break off when I see the dagger in Regnault's hand.

He gets to his feet slowly, raising the weapon, and advances on me. His mask is gone. For the first time in my life, I see Regnault without the ornate, feathered accessory that he has always worn. I had once wondered if he was hiding a scar behind it, some mark of his mysterious past. But behind it there are only signs of age, a wrinkled brow and crow's feet and bruised shadows under eyes oozing desolate, irrational fury.

I stumble back, nearly falling when another tremor shakes the temple, another column falling and shattering against the ground. The water is nearly to my knees now – it sloshes as I back away, Regnault coming ever nearer, one hand reaching for me, the other holding aloft the knife.

Suddenly my heel strikes a piece of detritus, and I lose my balance. Regnault leaps at me, the dagger arcing downward, just as a strong pair of arms seizes me from behind, lifting me from the water and out of the dagger's reach. 'Get away from her!' Marie d'Odette commands.

'No!' shrieks Regnault, but Marie grips me to her chest, one hand under my knees, the other clutching at my shoulders. She grunts with effort, her wings pumping wildly. Behind us, one final tremor runs through the temple. Water cascades in around us with violent, triumphant force as the lake reclaims the structure that has so long lain dormant in its depths. I know Regnault cannot escape in time, and perhaps I should turn back, take one last look at him, but I can't bring myself to do it. I simply bury my face in Marie's collarbone and let her bring me back to safety.

Marie alights on the shore of Lac des Cygnes with difficulty, panting as she places me back on the muddy shore. I try to stand, but my knees crumple beneath me. Before I can hit the sand, another pair of hands catches me, this time thick and calloused.

'You're safe,' Damien whispers, and grips me tightly. I lean against him, grateful – mainly for the warmth, because I am soaked and freezing – then pat him awkwardly on the back.

'I am,' I say, disbelieving, before pulling away. 'Mothers, we did it.' My chest burns – I'm somewhere halfway between laughing and crying. 'The Couronne is destroyed. Morgane . . . Morgane is free. Magic will return.'

'Magic *has* returned.' Aimé walks up beside Damien, and I notice he's wearing the circlet I gave him. His hand is pressed to the shallow wound near his shoulder where Regnault stabbed him, and he pulls it away briefly, showing me his palm. 'Look.'

His hand is smeared in blood. Red blood. A mundane, undeniable crimson, bright as ripe cherries or mid-autumn leaves or rubies polished to a shine.

'The curse is broken,' I breathe, and Aimé nods, grinning with tired relief.

I move my attention to the lakeside, where the guardsmen are busy gathering their dead and hacking at the dented corpses of the golden tarasques. Aimé follows my gaze to the lifeless monsters. 'Apparently they stopped moving right before we arrived.'

I make a contemplative noise. 'Must have lost their magic when the Couronne was broken.'

'And what of Regnault?' Aimé asks carefully. 'Did you leave him behind?'

'I did not want to,' I admit, swallowing tightly. 'I tried to save him. But he . . . preferred to drown.' I rub my face, then chuckle wryly. 'He even tried to stab me as a parting gift. Marie, ever my gallant defender, pulled me away before I could accept.' I turn back to Marie, grinning. 'Frankly, Princess, I'm surprised you're not yet tired of rescuing m–'

I break off.

The Swan Princess is kneeling in the sand, her eyes unfocused, her smile not a smile at all but a wavering, pained grimace.

My stomach drops. 'Marie?'

'It's nothing,' she whispers hoarsely.

Then she crumples to the ground.

From between her shoulder blades, just to the left of her spine, protrudes Regnault's dagger.

SCENE XXXVIII

The Lake.

'No.' Panic surges through me, brittle and horrified and desperate. I run to Marie, falling to my knees at her side. Lake water laps at my ankles – the sun shines with vicious, mocking brightness.

'Marie?' I whisper, hovering my hands over her spine, over her wings, over the dagger sunk hilt-deep into her back. And I know, I *know*, this is not the sort of injury anyone survives. But I still wrack my brain for a solution. I have so many skills, yet, in the face of this, I come up empty-handed, useless.

I'm useless.

'Oh, Marie, no, please –' Numbly, I reach for her face, wanting to lift her away from the wet earth that now sullies her clothes, her cheek. Marie's eyes flutter open, then closed again. Blood trickles from the corner of her mouth, from the dagger wound; it sinks into the beautiful white feathers of her wings, and I try, ineffectively, to wipe it away.

'What happened?' Aimé kneels beside me, and, unfairly, I want to shove him away, to tell him to leave. 'How did this happen?'

'Regnault,' I spit, between chattering teeth. 'He must have thrown it as her as she was carrying me away.'

'Oh,' Aimé manages, his voice cracking, his eyes already pooling with tears. 'Oh, *Marie*.'

Behind me, I can hear Damien shouting for the guardsmen to get to the Château, to fetch a physician, but I know it is too late. It is far, far too late.

It hits me, with violent certainty. 'This was my fault,' I whisper. 'She came to save me, I should have known better, I should have told her not to come back, why didn't I *tell her that* –' I grab Aimé's lapels, shaking him, and he endures it with a pitying look, brushing tears from his eyes.

I shove him away, turn back to Marie, running my fingers along her cheek. 'Why did you have to come back for me?' I whisper. 'Why did you *always* come back for me?'

'Because I love you,' Marie says weakly.

It's just like her, to break such devastating news in the most logical, matter-of-fact manner. But the words might as well be a dagger, because they embed themselves ruthlessly in my heart.

'*What?*' I burst out. 'You fool, why . . . why would you do that?'

Marie laughs weakly, another ribbon of blood dribbling from her lips. 'I'm not certain.' Then she seems to gather her strength, and pushes herself up from the ground, soil sticking to her hair, smeared across her cheek. I grab her before she can fall back down again, pull her against me, carefully avoiding the dagger.

Marie's eyes flutter closed, then open again, their usual beautiful silver clouded over with pain. 'I'm not certain,' she says again, gazing at me. 'Perhaps it's because you are headstrong, and obnoxious, and conniving. Perhaps it's because I like the way you laugh, too loud and sharp and free, like you don't care who hears. Perhaps it's because when I'm with you, I feel like I'm stretching my wings after years of being caged. I don't know the true reason.' She smiles, her chest hitching painfully. 'Isn't that ironic? *This* is the puzzle I can't solve.'

'That's why you have to stay alive,' I plead, frantic. 'We'll solve it together. We'll learn to navigate this *together*.'

'I wish we could,' Marie says, swallowing painfully. Her breathing is dreadfully shallow, her fingers cold when they brush my cheek, trying to collect the tears there. 'But I fear I . . . I haven't the time.'

'Marie, *please* –'

But her eyes are already closed again, her chest barely rising.

'Marie!' I say desperately, shaking her cruelly, trying to bring awareness into her freezing body. But there comes no reply. 'Marie, open your eyes, damn you –'

Through a haze of red-hot anger, I can barely make out Damien crouching beside Aimé, reaching gently for Marie's wrist and seeking out her pulse. Whatever he finds, it makes him draw in a rattling, harsh breath. He meets Aimé's eyes and shakes his head, and I watch as Aimé crumples against my brother, sobbing.

'No!' I snarl, because the pain is unbearable, the pain is no longer one dagger but a thousand, and I am pierced over and over again. 'No, no, she can't be dead, don't lie to me!'

Damien reaches for me, but I slap his arm away.

'Get away from me!' I say, because all I can feel is anger, because this is not how a story should end, because the heroes are not supposed to be the ones who die, because I don't want to be alone again, because because because –

Because I never told her I love her too.

I let loose a terrible growl, all my frustration and panic escaping through my teeth. I pull Marie closer against me, tilt my head up to the sky. 'Morgane!' I scream. 'Morgane, I know you're there!' I flex my fingers, imagining magic pooling between them, and I'm surprised to see them glow briefly gold. *So it is back*, I think numbly, and somehow the thought is cruelly punishing, because magic may be back but Marie is dead, and I don't know any spells that can change that.

'Morgane!' I shout again, my voice carrying across the lake's placid waters. 'I freed you, and now you owe me a debt! Come back and pay it!'

Nothing happens. No answer comes. I drop my eyes, chest heaving. The world suddenly feels like it is tightening, compressing, grasping at me and the body in my arms.

I press my forehead into Marie's pale curls and sob in defeat.

I cry, and the world fades out around me, silent but for the distant call of a water bird, the sloshing of the lake against the dock, the whispering of wind over Marie's limp wings. I cry, my shoulders seizing, my world crumbling. I cry, whispering incoherent pleas against the forehead of the girl I might have loved.

Little owl. My head jerks up at the grating, familiar voice.

Around me, the lakeside is suddenly empty. No sign of Damien, or Aimé, or the guardsmen, or the dead tarasques –

there is only bristling grass and withered weeds, and a woman standing over me, beatific and impossible.

Morgane appears just as she did in the lake, though she has done me the mercy of shrinking to a regular human's height. Her skin is cracked stone, aged and water-worn – there are pondweeds wrapped around her arms and the bones of a fish tangled in her hair. Her peeled face appears even more garish in the daylight, the gold skull beneath dull and scratched. Her eyes, too, are stone, and a ring of golden spines haloes her head, more ominous than divine.

I hear I owe you a debt. The goddess purses her lips, as though the idea leaves a sour taste in her mouth. *What is it that you would ask of me?*

I lower Marie's body against my lap, gently brushing her muddied hair from her face. 'I saved your life, by freeing you from the Couronne. Now save hers.' I rest my hands on Marie's chest, as though I might force it to move again.

Morgane's response comes slow and measured. *That is not within my domain, I'm afraid.*

'Within your domain?' I repeat, disbelieving.

She eyes me exasperatedly, looking surprisingly childish. *I am the goddess of transformation, not creation, nor destruction. I can turn one thing into another, but I cannot create flesh where there is none, cannot make life blossom where it is wilting.*

'Wilting? You mean she's not dead?'

Not quite. Seconds from it, to be certain – her heartbeat is very weak, but it has yet to fully stop. You humans are remarkably hardy creatures.

'But . . . but she's going to die.'

Yes.

I shake my head, refusing to accept her words, refusing to lose this battle. 'If you cannot do it, call your sisters. They owe me a debt as well, for I saved them from your fate, from capture by Regnault.'

Morgane looks away from me. *I cannot.*

'Why?'

She is silent for a moment, a troubled look tightening her regal features. Finally, reluctantly, she says, *Because they do not answer my calls.*

I blink. 'What?'

My sisters are missing, Morgane admits. *When I was captured, they fled far from Auréal, and they do not know yet that I have been freed and that they can safely return. Perhaps, if you find them, they might concede and bring back this –* She gestures to the girl in my arms.

'Marie.'

Marie, she amends flatly. *Find them, win their approval, and they might teach you magic stronger than mine, might give you power unfathomable. Or they might kill you. You never know, with siblings.*

I stare down at my hands, still clutching at Marie's doublet, that silver costume that made her look so ethereal. My mind reels. 'But by the time I find them, Marie will be dead.'

This I can help with, Morgane says, sounding pleased at the notion. *To repay my debt, as you have asked.*

She crouches beside me, and it takes all my willpower not to flinch away. 'What are you going to do?' I demand, covering Marie's body with mine defensively.

Peace, Morgane scolds. *I am going to preserve her. If she allows me to, of course, and if she has the willpower to survive the process.*

'Will it be painful?'

Morgane regards me flatly. *Do you want my help or not, little owl?*

I grit my teeth but sit back reluctantly, lowering Marie to the ground with as much gentleness as I can. I roll her carefully on to her side, so the dagger in her back isn't jostled. I want to touch her one last time, to reassure her, but before I get the chance, Morgane snatches the dagger in Marie's back and pulls.

There comes an explosion of brilliant light, Marie's body vanishing beneath a veil of golden, blinding brightness. The light grows and grows and grows, until I am forced to close my eyes, until I am falling back, pressing my arm protectively against my face, heat searing my skin –

Then, just as quickly as it started, the light vanishes. I lie on my back, blinded and breathless, awareness returning to me slowly, then all at once. Suddenly, I'm hearing Damien's and Aimé's panicked voices by my head.

'By the Mothers, how did this –'

'Is she all right?'

'She's all right, but –'

'How is this possible?'

'Odile, can you hear me?'

Nearby, I can make out the awed murmurs and gasps of the guardsmen. I blink furiously, trying to dispel the black after-images impeding my vision. Someone helps me sit up, and I groan, pressing the heels of my hands to my eyes. 'Damned Mothers.'

'Odile, what happened?' Damien asks, a strangely breathy, awed note to his cadence.

'I spoke to Morgane,' I grit out into my hands. 'Tried to bargain with her.'

'And is . . . is she the one who did this?' Aimé asks, his voice still croaky from crying.

'Did *what?*' I demand. Then I look up, and a broken sound escapes me.

Where Marie had been lying just moments before stands a beautiful, mournful statue.

It's Marie d'Odette, lithe and elegant, her every feature moulded perfectly in pearlescent stone. Her wings are outspread, her full lips parted in a hopeful smile, and one of her hands reaches upward, as though trying to seize the sun from its lofty perch. Her hair unspools around her, wild and free, her bare feet barely touching their marble pedestal, mere seconds from leaving the ground and taking to the sky.

Wordlessly, I walk up to the statue, clutching my hands to my chest, wishing I could grip my heart and force it to stop aching. Tentatively, I reach out, pressing my fingertips to the statue's knee. Half of me still expects to find smooth, warm skin, as I felt last night in the Théâtre's dressing room. But only cold stone greets my touch, sending a chill down my arm. I quickly pull away, biting my lip.

'Odile?' Damien calls behind me. 'How did this happen?'

I don't answer him. I can't. A troubled, numb sort of peace spreads over me as I walk around the statue, as I catch sight of the golden streak that runs along Marie's wing, widest in the spot the dagger had sunk into her flesh.

'Odile?' my brother asks again. I let a breath judder out between my lips. Then I straighten my spine slowly, forcing every vertebra to click into place. Firm. Unwavering. For the first time since I broke the Couronne, I can feel the trickle of magic in my veins, testing the limits of my skin, begging to be used.

I turn back to the onlookers, meeting my brother's uncertain gaze, then Aimé's earnest blue one. I smile at them, strained and sharp-edged but determined.

'She's not dead,' I say. I don't explain further – there is no point telling them what I learned from Morgane about the missing Mothers. The kingdom has enough trouble brewing without mixing in the affairs of sorcery. 'And I'm going to get her back.'

I take one final look over my shoulder. My heart is heavy, full of doubt and grief and regret – I leave all of it at the feet of Marie's statue, along with a promise to return once I have the power to heal her.

Then I turn back to my companions.

'Let us go back to the Château,' I say. 'We have a king to crown.'

SCENE XXXIX

Château. The Stables.

It's going to snow.

I can feel it on the breeze as I step out of the Château stables, gulping my fill of rousing, frostbitten air. My ankles throb from dancing – a small pack bounces heavily against my shoulder. Curls of frost have already begun to paint the iron-rose hedges and ahead, the borders of Lac des Cygnes are limned with rime.

My fingers, clutched around reins, are already aching from the cold. I give the leather straps a gentle tug, and the good-natured gelding ambles behind me, his heavy snorts pluming in the air. He's pure black of coat, and his tack shines with fresh polish, the buckles of his bridle glinting in the midday light. He was a gift from Aimé, one the Dauphin – well, the former Dauphin, now King – had insisted I take on my journey. *He's well trained and of good stock*, Aimé had assured me. *And . . .* He'd looked away, sheepish. *I don't want you to be alone.*

I pat the gelding's neck as I lead him down the narrow path that will take us into the Château courtyard, then around the lake towards the city. From there, I don't know where we'll go – Orlica, perhaps, or Lore. 'I could pay Princess Turnip-hair a visit,' I tell the horse, smirking to myself. For now, I'm following my instincts, tailing rumours of strange apparitions in forgotten places, unusual happenings and newly spawned myths. Anything that might lead me to the two missing Mothers.

At my back, the revelry continues, music surging in cheerful swells from the Château's open windows, eager chatter and laughter carrying across the grounds. I smile, tightening my grip on the reins, and begin to angle the horse towards a small stump with the intention to mount.

'Running away already?'

I turn to see my brother approaching from the Château, rubbing his hands together against the cold. The tips of his nose and ears have gone an endearing red, and his shoulders are hunched beneath his cloak. 'They're telling your story in there, you know.' He gestures to the palace. 'The white swan and the black, but they keep getting the details all wrong. I heard someone say it was Aimé and Marie who jumped into the lake. Another is convinced there was a unicorn involved.'

'A unicorn?' I echo.

'A *purple* unicorn,' my brother says gravely. 'Perhaps you would like to go back inside and dispel these offensive rumours?'

I smile, but it's strained, heavy with all the uncertainties of the future. 'I can't. You know I can't. Besides, if Aimé sees me leaving, he's going to cry.'

Damien huffs a laugh. 'That he will.' Then his smile fades. His eyes have gone horribly, revoltingly, soft, an unbridled look of fondness on his face. 'Must you leave so soon, Dilou?'

'You and Aimé have enough work on your hands without me around causing trouble.' I pull my cloak tighter around myself. Another gift from Aimé, it's a beautiful thing of black wool, decorated with golden cord and obsidian wolf's fur. It looks expensive, and I know I'll have to replace it with something plainer once I'm out of the city. But for now, I wear it proudly, the Augier tarasque gleaming on the clasp at my throat.

'Besides,' I add, 'tensions are still high in the court, even now that the Regent is in prison. You saw how long it took the noblesse to accept Aimé back, even though his curse is broken and his blood is red. They need some time to adjust before they welcome a court sorcier.' I roll my shoulders, turning my eyes to the sky. A strange wistfulness grips me. 'Do you think it will be white?'

'I think so,' Damien says, following my gaze. Ever since we freed Morgane, it's as though colour has returned to Auréal. The fog has vanished from over the lake, the sky has brightened, and a single, true rosebush sprouted recently among the Spider King's iron conjurations, entirely out of season. It bloomed this morning, just in time for Aimé's coronation – sky-blue in colour, the shade favoured by the young King. I'd made sure to declare it an auspicious omen to any noblesse within earshot.

'Odile.' My brother calls my attention back to himself. When I look at him, he rubs the back of his neck sheepishly. 'I'm going to miss you.'

I raise an eyebrow. 'What was that? I think I misheard.'

My brother rolls his eyes, and I grin at him, though my heart clenches strangely. *I'm going to miss him too*, I realize. Filled with a sudden, protective tenderness, I close the distance between us and gently cup the back of his head, pressing our foreheads together.

'I'll come back,' I promise. 'Once I've learned enough magic and found a way to save Marie. After that, I will stay. For good.'

'No more missions?' Damien asks, drawing gently away.

'No more missions,' I reply, and tell myself the prickling of my eyes is from the cold. Flustered, I turn back to the gelding and mount, gathering up the reins. I sweep the wide-brimmed hat off my head to give Damien a dramatic salute.

Then I wheel my horse around, taking one final glance over my shoulder. At the Château, rising into the sky, home to a promising young King. At my brother, standing alone on the stable path, his hand raised in farewell. At Lac des Cygnes, mirror-smooth and reflecting a clear blue sky, the Théâtre watching me mournfully from the far bank. And finally, my eyes land on the beautiful, forlorn statue at the lake's edge, guarding the heart of a girl I have vowed to bring back.

I force myself to look away, ahead. At the path that will lead me far from the world I have always known. My heart pounds with restless anticipation, eager for the next mystery, the next discovery. My cheeks sting from the cold – my hair whips against my face.

As I leave the Château Front-du-Lac behind, it begins to snow.

This time, it falls white.

Epilogue

The sorcière comes when the snow melts.

Cloaked in modest black, she wears little adornment but for the ruby in her ear, glinting in the timid sunlight. She leads a steed the colour of pitch, and beneath the brim of her hat, her eyes are shrewd and wide. You must not look into them, for if you do, you will see impossible things, future and past and diverging paths tangled within those golden depths.

She comes with the first of the Aurélian flowers, those precious snowdrops soft as an infant's palms. She stoops to pick one, prising it gently from the heavy, sodden snow. She tucks it behind her ear and smiles to herself, a smile that is too wide, hiding power in the corners of her mouth and unknowable wisdom under her tongue. Then she picks a second one, and this one she holds carefully, as though it is a gift for a lover.

She comes in the warm hour before the sun takes its bows. Her arrival fills the air with magic-scent, impossible to deny – not just of the sage-sharp Mother of transformation, but the sweet freshness of creation and the heady incense of destruction. Unlike most sorciers, she draws powers not only from Morgane, but from all three sisters. They weigh heavy on her shoulders and press creases into her brow, but her footsteps are light and proud, almost eager. Power comes with a price, but it also comes with promise.

She comes to the edge of Lac des Cygnes, and inspects herself in its waters, letting her steed drink while she attempts to restrain her wild black hair, sweeping it behind her ears. She looks almost mortal, then. Almost vulnerable. But do not let that fool you – she is a trickster, and there is only one who has ever been able to truly tame her.

That is where she heads now. Along the lake's edge, through the tender blooms and the crisp, shimmering crust of snow, her chin raised and mouth tight with determination. There, by the newly rebuilt docks, near the fresh tulips and elegant boats floating among the duckweed, is the Guardian of the Lake. A statue, in white marble veined in gold, of an angelic girl. Her features are long, elegant, bright with hope – her hand reaches and reaches and reaches into the sky. From her back, half outspread, sprout beautiful swan's wings.

The sorcière releases her steed's reins, allowing him to wander off and graze. Then she begins to approach the statue, and she appears to grow nervous – a rarity, for one with such power as hers. Slowly, she extends a shaking hand. Slowly, she lays it on the girl's outstretched wing.

Then she does something truly bizarre. She draws a strange shape in the air, and steps up on to the statue's pedestal. Rivulets of shimmering, golden liquid run down her wrists, dripping off her fingers. This is true magic, you see – not a street performer's disappearing scarf or the distant burst of fireworks, but a sticky, thick fluid, flowing with power. The sorcière brings her dripping hands up to the statue's face, cupping the other girl's cheeks, gentle as the sun telling the moon to rest.

Then she kisses the statue on the mouth.

It is an act of grief and an act of despair and an act of hope. It awakens a flash of golden light, blossoming in the space between the girls' hearts, one of flesh and one of stone.

And then, as though by a miracle, as though by a curse, the marble girl's stone skin begins to melt away. It melts, revealing the graceful column of a throat, the curve of a jaw, the slope of a calf. It melts, revealing the silk of a doublet, the curve of a breast, the intricate feathering of wings. It melts, revealing a spot of blood on the back of the girl's shoulder, the flesh quickly knitting back together until no more than a scar remains.

The marble girl, marble no more, lowers her hand. A heavy breath escapes her, a sound both weary and relieved, the sound of a caged bird finding freedom at last.

There is a shudder of silence, filled with nothing but the beating of two hearts.

Beat, beat.

The girl with the white wings remains rigid in the sorceress's arms.

Then, as the first rays of sunset seep like golden blood into the lake, she kisses back.

FIN.

Acknowledgements

Most authors will warn you about the dreaded book two and the sophomore slump. I would love to say I avoided that curse, but unfortunately, that could not have been less the case. Something about writing a book under contract for the first time, having to deal with tight deadlines and the pressure of replicating the quality of your first book, is truly merciless.

And yet I did it. It was a challenge, but that only means the end result is twice as satisfying. They say diamonds are made under pressure, but I think *A Treachery of Swans* is more of a ruby – opulent and romantic and deeply Gothic. I'm so damn proud of her.

This process was made so much more bearable by my wonderful publishing team at Penguin Random House, who put up with my shenanigans with the patience of saints. First and foremost, thank you to my editor, Carmen McCullough, for seeing the potential in what was a rather dreadful first draft, and helping build it into something worthwhile. Managing editor Shreeta Shah, for enduring countless late edit deliveries and ensuring *ATOS* is in the best shape possible. Editorial director Linas Alsenas, for those vital last-minute edit notes. My publicist, Sarah Doyle, and Stevie Hopwood, marketing genius. Emily Smyth, for designing such a gorgeous, evocative cover, and the talented Holly Ovenden, for illustrating it so beautifully. Adam Webling, Katherine Whelan, Eleanor Updegraff, George Maudsley, Sarah Hall, and every member of the PRH team that played a part in bringing *ATOS* to life.

Thank you to my agent, Victoria Marini, who is always there to answer my questions or to humour my strange book ideas. My UK agent, Catherine Cho, who has been so supportive in bringing my books to the UK. My critique partners, Marisa Salvia and Sarah Underwood, who make life brighter. Bea Fitzgerald, Kat Delacorte, Ellie Thomas, and the rest of the wonderful London bookish community, for every hang-out and writing-date-turned-yapping-session. My family, of course, for giving me a port in every storm. My cat, Neptune – I miss you, buddy. We will meet again.

Because no book exists in a vacuum, thank you to the artists that inspired *ATOS*: Andrew Lloyd Webber, who lit the Gothic theatre-loving flame inside me with *Phantom of the Opera*; Taylor Swift for 'Better Than Revenge', the official Odile anthem; Margaret Owen and Holly Black for writing gremlin girls and reminding me that chaos is, in fact, always an option. And, of course, ATEEZ, whose music is a safe space for the starry-eyed daydreamer inside of me, who told me to 'just keep it up', so I did.

Lastly, but most importantly, thank you to all of you. To the booksellers who championed my debut, and who have anticipated *ATOS* with such enthusiasm – I could have never gotten here without you. To the influencers who have supported my works across social media, and all the readers who take the time out of their day to send me positive messages and comments. Please know that when I write, I write for every single one of you. I hope this book's ending makes up for all the emotional damage I caused with *Where the Dark Stands Still*. Sorry about that, by the way.

Kind of. Not really. But truly, you guys mean the world to me.